An Archway Three-in-One

The Nancy Drew ™ Files

Books in The Nancy Drew™ Series

Sinister Paradise
Trouble in Tahiti
Vanishing Act

Carolyn Keene

AN ARCHWAY PAPERBACK
Published by SIMON & SCHUSTER
New York   London   Toronto   Sydney   Tokyo · Singapore

An Archway paperback
first published in Great Britain
by Simon & Schuster Ltd in 1993
A Paramount Communications Company

Copyright © 1988 by Simon & Schuster Inc

Simon & Schuster Ltd
West Garden Place
Kendal Street
London W2 2AQ

NANCY DREW, AN ARCHWAY PAPERBACK
and colophon are registered trademarks of Simon & Schuster Inc.

THE NANCY DREW FILES is a trademark
of Simon & Schuster Inc.

Simon & Schuster of Australia Pty Ltd
Sydney

A CIP catalogue record for this book is
available from the British Library

ISBN 0-671-85221-3

Printed and bound in Great Britain by
HarperCollins Manufacturing, Glasgow

Sinister Paradise

Chapter

One

"OH, NANCY, CAN you believe this place?" Bess Marvin climbed up the pool ladder, water streaming off her. "I feel as though I've died and gone to heaven!"

Nancy Drew leaned against the diving board. Trade winds stirred her reddish blond hair. "It's a big change from River Heights, Bess, I'll admit that."

"They're probably knee-deep in snow back home." Bess plucked a fluffy towel from the deck chair. "Coming to Hawaii was a *great* idea."

"Too bad it's not a pleasure trip," George Fayne remarked. She stood beside the pool, vigorously toweling her dark hair. "And by the way,

Bess, you pronounce it *Huh-wah-ee,* not *Huh-why-ee.*"

Nancy heard the tapping of high heels on the patio tiles. Turning, she saw their hostess, Alice Faulkner, heading their way. Mrs. Faulkner was a slim, aristocratic woman in her early seventies, with soft white hair and penetrating eyes. Nancy's mother's family had been very friendly with the Faulkners, and Mrs. Faulkner kept in touch periodically after Nancy's mother died.

The day her granddaughter disappeared, Mrs. Faulkner had phoned Nancy in River Heights and asked her to help locate her. Sixteen-year-old Lisa Trumbull had mysteriously disappeared from school on Friday. Mrs. Faulkner feared that the girl had run away.

Mrs. Faulkner's polite smile flashed at Nancy, then at Ned Nickerson, Nancy's boyfriend, who stood beside the pool ladder. "Aren't you two going swimming?"

"I would, only I left my suit back on the *Kahala,*" Ned replied ruefully.

The *Kahala* was their temporary home in Honolulu. It was a fifty-five-foot motor cruiser, the property of Mrs. Faulkner, moored at the Ala Wai yacht basin. Mrs. Faulkner had insisted that they use it.

"Did you manage to get in touch with your daughter?" Nancy asked.

"Yes. She's waiting for you downtown." Mrs.

Faulkner gestured at the broad Victorian-style plantation house. "Nancy—Ned—why don't we let Bess and George enjoy their swim? We can talk up there."

She led them through the miniature rain forest that served as her garden. Tall feather palms cast cool shadows over brilliant displays of pink hibiscus and white gardenia.

Soon the three of them were seated in comfortable wicker chairs on the first-floor verandah. Resting her clasped hands on her knees, Nancy remarked, "Mrs. Faulkner, you said Lisa vanished on Friday."

"That's right. Friday afternoon. Diana phoned me as soon as she heard."

"It's Monday now. Why haven't you gone to the police yet?"

Alice looked around uncomfortably. "If it were up to me, I'd have the National Guard scouring the island. But my ex-son-in-law, Ross Rafferty, has forbidden it. He and Diana are Lisa's guardians." Her lip curled in disdain. "Ross wants the police kept out of it. You see, he's concerned about his reputation. I don't know why. He doesn't have much of one to protect."

"Mrs. Faulkner, you still could have gone to them. What's *your* reason for not contacting the police?"

A troubled look shadowed the old woman's

face. "The publicity would hurt my bank, Windward Fidelity. Windward Bancorp owns the bank. I have controlling interest in Windward Bancorp." Frowning, she leaned back in her chair and seemed to become lost in thought.

Nancy reached out and touched the woman's wrist gently. "Is that the real reason?"

Alice Faulkner shook her head slowly. Beneath Mrs. Faulkner's tough exterior, Nancy could see a tired old woman, worn down by her present problems. "Actually, I'm worried about Lisa, Nancy. I'm afraid I've made enemies in the business and banking community. Powerful enemies! They wouldn't hesitate to strike at me by harming my only grandchild."

How could they harm her if she ran away? Nancy thought. "Why are you so sure Lisa ran away then?"

"Diana never let me see much of my granddaughter." Alice's face filled with regret. "Like a fool, I stayed away. Still, I could see that Lisa wasn't happy. How could she be with all that turmoil in her life?" She shook her head sadly. "Apparently, Lisa had been planning this for quite a while."

"Why do you say that?"

"Because of the way she did it," Alice explained. "Diana was planning an art exhibit on Maui. She asked Lisa to stop at the bank to pick up her travelers' checks. You see, Diana kept extra checks along with her valuables in a safety deposit box at the bank."

Ned whistled in disbelief. "And the bank let her in? Just like that?"

Alice gave him a frosty look. "Young man, Lisa is a *Faulkner!* Windward *is* the family bank. Anyone in our family can enter the bank at any time and for any reason."

"What happened then?" Nancy asked.

"Once inside the safety deposit vault, Lisa grabbed her mother's diamonds and quite a few bearer bonds. Then she strolled out the door —and she hasn't been seen since!"

"And since anyone can cash in a bearer bond," Ned said, nodding, "Lisa will have enough money to do whatever she wants for a long time. How many bonds did she take?"

Alice sighed, her misery lining her troubled face. "Four hundred thousand dollars' worth! Her little surprise withdrawal wasn't discovered until closing time. When Lisa failed to return home, Diana called Ross at the bank. He checked the vault and very nearly had a heart attack! Diana phoned me immediately after that. Ross sent our security people to the airport, hoping to stop Lisa from leaving Hawaii. But Lisa never showed up."

Hawaii was a very difficult place to enter or leave, Nancy knew. Honolulu was the only international airport, and everyone had to pass through customs. Moreover, the North American mainland was more than two thousand miles to the east, beyond the range of most aircraft. Only a major airline could get Lisa to California.

So Lisa still had to be in Hawaii. There was no way the girl could convert those diamonds and bearer bonds to cash over the weekend. The process could take many days.

Nancy shivered suddenly. A teenage girl with four hundred grand in her purse was a walking target for every crook in the city!

Alice glanced at Nancy. "When you get to be my age, dear, the money doesn't seem that important anymore. *Family* is what really counts. I—I'm afraid I haven't been very lucky with mine." Taking a deep breath, she forced herself to go on. "My boys both died young. As for Diana—well, we haven't been close for many years. Since my husband's death, Diana has had very little to do with me. She's carved out a life for herself as an artist. After her divorce from Ross, she lived with Lisa in a condo on Kalakaua Avenue." The woman's haunted gaze traveled from Nancy to Ned. "I've made up my mind. I'm going to get custody of Lisa and start all over again." Tears glistened in her eyes. "I think I'll take Lisa back to Texas. Give her a good stable home for a change." Lower lip quivering, she blinked at Nancy. "Find my granddaughter, Nancy. Please. She's all I have left."

* * *

A short while later Nancy and her friends climbed into their rental car. Nancy settled comfortably behind the steering wheel and turned the key in the ignition. Then, swiveling the stick shift, she executed a perfect three-point turn and steered the tan sedan through the massive wrought-iron gates of the Faulkner estate.

"You know, I could really get used to this climate." Bess rolled down her rear window, letting the air wash over her. "I am going to be as brown as peanut butter when we get back to River Heights."

"I still can't get used to that estate," George said. "Has it been in the family long?"

"Since I hadn't spoken with the Faulkners recently, I did a little background reading on the family," Nancy replied, carefully guiding the car around a sharp turn. "Mrs. Faulkner's husband, C. K. Faulkner, was a self-made man and one of the richest people in the Islands. He left Mrs. Faulkner very well provided for. He bought the house and large pieces of oceanfront real estate all over the Islands."

"How big is this bank she mentioned?" asked Ned.

"Big!" Nancy whistled softly. "According to the magazine article I read, the bank's assets total nine hundred million dollars! Windward Fidelity is the biggest lender to all the countries of the Pacific Rim."

While she talked, Nancy kept her eyes straight

ahead. Tantalus Drive was a rattlesnake of a road, all winding curves and sudden downhill plunges. Luxurious estates, hidden by jungle growth, bordered the narrow road as it wound down into the city.

The car picked up speed as they descended an old lava ridge. The road swerved suddenly, heading straight for a jungle-covered hillside. Then it zigzagged again, carrying their car across a ridgeline that offered panoramic views of the Koolau Mountains and the sapphire-colored Pacific Ocean.

Nancy tightened her grip on the wheel. Tires squealed softly as they rounded a long bend, and Nancy's reddish gold hair whipped into her face. She pressed the brake again. The car slowed once more.

Ned touched her shoulder. "Better slow down, Nancy. We don't want to *fly* into Honolulu."

Nancy frowned as she studied the sheer basalt cliffs. "This road is one surprise after another. What did they do? Pave an old mule trail?"

Ned smiled. "I have confidence in your driving, Nancy."

Nancy had opened her mouth to reply when suddenly she no longer felt any pressure under her right foot. The brake pedal sank to the floor.

The sedan started down a long slope. Nancy felt the car shudder as it picked up speed. Frowning, she stomped on the brake pedal. Once, twice!

The pedal rested uselessly on the floor. Nancy's face turned white.

Ned clutched her shoulder. "Nancy, what's wrong?"

"Brace yourselves, guys!" Nancy watched in horror as the speedometer needle soared past fifty. "This car has just lost its brakes!"

Chapter

Two

Tires squealed in protest as the car fishtailed around a long bend. Nancy could feel it lightly touching the road, a sure sign that it was about to spin out and roll over. The rear wheel skidded ominously toward the edge of the road.

Nancy cut the wheels to the left, then to the right. The car seesawed back and forth across the center line, but its tires held the asphalt. Wide-eyed with terror, Nancy watched the speedometer needle creep higher and higher.

Fifty-five—sixty—*sixty-five!*

Ahead, Tantalus Drive dissolved into a series of sweeping hairpin turns. Nancy's stomach felt as if it were falling down a well. The car was

10

traveling much too fast. Unless she could find a way to slow it down, they would go hurtling right off the side of the mountain!

She tried to pump the brakes again. Nothing! And the first hairpin turn was coming up fast.

Nancy's eyes flew desperately around the front seat. Then they zeroed in on the stick shift. I'll put the engine in another gear, she thought. That ought to cut our speed.

Nancy jammed the stick shift into low gear. Then, gripping the steering wheel even harder, she hollered, "Hang on!"

The sedan took the bend on two wheels, hugging the forested slope. But with the engine in a lower gear, the car began to slow down. The needle fell past sixty. The car felt heavier—more a part of the road.

On the next straightaway, Nancy swung the steering wheel from side to side. The sedan performed a lazy ballet, losing speed with each swerve. Nancy knocked the speed down to forty. But the next hairpin turn boosted it right back up to sixty again!

Nancy wanted to weep. They were still rolling too fast. At this speed, they were certain to jump the road on the next turn.

Suddenly Ned shouted, "Nancy, look!"

There was a grassy area on the right-hand side of the road, just before the bend.

"Nancy! The turnaround! Bank into it!" Ned cried.

Nancy spun the wheel all the way over. The car shuddered as it jumped the embankment. Gritting her teeth, Nancy held the wheel steady.

Screeeeeeech! The car performed a perfect loop, its tires chopping up the grass. Then Nancy yanked on the emergency brake, and the car shrieked to a halt, rocking on its springs. Its blunt nose was pointing back uphill.

Nancy exhaled heavily, resting her forehead on the steering wheel. She peered out the side window—and shuddered violently.

Just inches from the car's tires, the grassy area plunged abruptly into a misty valley. A long sea gull whizzed past, oblivious to the car perched above him.

Trembling in relief, Nancy whispered, "Everybody all right?"

Ned nodded. He stumbled out of the car, and Bess and George followed a moment later. Nancy waited until she was sure her legs would support her. Her knees felt as limp as cooked spaghetti.

Ned was studying the tire gouges in the turf. Looking back uphill, he remarked, "This is *not* a road to lose your brakes on. We're going to need a tow truck. We broke the axle when we spun around."

"Ned, would you stay with the car until the tow truck gets here?" Nancy asked. "I'll call a garage from the marina."

"You mean we've got to *walk* back to Ala Wai?" Bess protested. "Nancy, I don't know if I'm up to it. Not after that!"

"Well, we don't have to walk all the way." Nancy smiled reassuringly. "I noticed a bus stop at the bottom of Tantalus Drive."

"Let's go," George urged, turning her back on the wreck. "The less I see of that car, the better I'll feel."

George led the way downhill. Bess trudged along right behind. "And on top of everything else, it's so hot," she complained. "You're the one who likes hiking cross-country, George."

Nancy brought up the rear. She couldn't stop thinking about the accident. If a car's brakes were going to fail, Tantalus Drive wasn't the place for it to happen. Yet the car was last year's model. Had it been tampered with?

Nancy made up her mind to find out.

Nancy replaced the cordless phone in its bulkhead cradle. "We're all set," she told George. "The tow truck's on its way out. But the guy at the gas station said we have to go to the airport to fill out an accident report for the car rental company. Feel like taking a ride?"

"Love to."

Nancy crossed the *Kahala*'s teakwood cabin and peered into the aft stateroom. "How about you, Bess?"

13

"Not me!" Bess lay on the double bunk, her arm draped across her forehead. "Not after that hike. I thought Oahu was a *little* island!"

"Suit yourself." Nancy began to close the louvered hatch, then thought better of it. "Bess, after we're gone, make sure you lock the hatch, okay?"

Bess blinked in surprise. "Okay. But why?"

Nancy had made up her mind to ask the rental people a few pointed questions about that car. But there was no sense in getting Bess all worked up over what might turn out to be nothing.

"It's a good habit to get into. Don't mind me, I'm just a little jumpy today." Nancy closed the hatch. "We'll be back in a little while."

After taking a quick shower, Nancy retired to her cabin and put on a cream-colored sailing shirt and shorts. Then she and George hailed a cab to take them to the airport.

They found Sunrise Rentals in the main terminal, sandwiched in between the lockers and a fast-food restaurant. The Sunrise clerk was a slender young woman with large glasses who looked very shy. A name tag reading "Meredith" was pinned to her shirt.

She smiled as George and Nancy approached. "Hi! May I help you?"

"We're here to report an accident," Nancy said, slipping off her shoulder bag. "One of your cars. We rented it from another clerk—Janine —first thing this morning."

Meredith immediately reached for an official-looking document. Picking up a pen, she asked for Nancy's name and a description of the accident. Then she turned and studied the pigeonholes behind her. "One moment, please." She reached into a slot, withdrew a piece of paper, and stared at it for a long moment.

Facing the girls again, Meredith lowered her glasses. "That can't be right. We have *no car* rented to a Nancy Drew!"

Chapter

Three

"WHAT!" NANCY EXCLAIMED, surprised. "I was here this morning. Janine made me sign for it. You people rented me that car."

Meredith showed her the front of the paper. "I'm sorry, but your name's not on the master list. You're not in our records."

"Wait a minute!" Nancy rummaged in her shoulder bag. "I've got the rental agreement right here." She put it on the counter. "Janine gave me this when I arrived. While she typed it up, she had me sign your master roster and list everyone in my party. Then she gave me this agreement and the car keys, and I left."

Looking a bit confused, Meredith glanced at

the shelf again. "Hmmmm. Maybe Janine mis-filed it."

Nancy waited patiently while the girl carefully examined the rental agreement. All at once, Meredith's face brightened with understanding. "Ah, now I see." She put down the agreement. "We were booked solid yesterday. I talked to your credit card company—told them we had no cars available. Didn't they get in touch with you?"

Nancy sighed. "If they tried, we were probably already airborne. "But if my request didn't go through, why was this car waiting for me when I arrived?"

"Someone else rented the car for you." Meredith pointed out a block of print. "See? 'Hold for Nancy Drew and party.' Just before we closed yesterday, a woman called and said she wanted to rent a car for you."

"A woman?" George said. "Mrs. Faulkner?"

"She didn't identify herself," Meredith answered. "She said she was from the Malihini Corporation and asked for one of the corporate cars we keep on standby. She even named the car—tan four-door sedan, license number HI-9876."

"Corporate cars?" echoed Nancy. "What do you mean?"

"We keep a number of cars set aside for use by companies here in Honolulu," Meredith explained. "These companies have long-term rental agreements with us. Whenever they need a rental car in a hurry, we send one right over."

"Do you own these cars?" Nancy asked.

"Oh, no. We lease them on a six-month basis from car dealerships here in the Islands," Meredith replied.

Nancy frowned thoughtfully. "This Malihini Corporation—have you done business with them for very long?"

Meredith shook her head. "No. As a matter of fact, they're brand-new clients. I processed their agreement just the other day."

Just then, the airport intercom blared, "Nancy Drew, please report to the courtesy desk. You have a phone call."

Excusing herself, Nancy hurried across the lobby. At the paneled courtesy desk, a clerk handed Nancy a telephone.

"Hi, Nancy." It was Ned, and he sounded weary. "Bess told me you were at the airport. I'm down here at Kamaaina's gas station. We just finished putting that car on the lift."

"Is it in bad shape?"

"It was in bad shape when you rented it, Nancy. The brake drums are as bald as an eagle!" Anger sharpened his voice as he told her what else was wrong with it. "You want me to come down to the airport?"

"Stay where you are, Ned. We'll pick you up in a little while."

"Good enough. See you later."

After handing back the phone, Nancy returned to the Sunrise desk. "Meredith, you said the Malihini Corporation *specifically* requested that car for me?"

"Yes, they did."

Replacing the rental agreement in her bag, Nancy asked, "Where did that particular car come from?"

"We leased it from Smiling Al's Auto Sales in Pearl City." Meredith adjusted her glasses. "He sent it over first thing this morning."

Nancy took a pen from her shoulder bag. "Could you get me Smiling Al's address?"

"Certainly."

Meredith copied the address from the central file and handed it to Nancy. In another instant, Nancy and George were hurrying out to the taxi stand.

"Where are we going now?" George asked.

"First we pick up Ned," Nancy replied, opening the rear door of a cab. *"Then* we're going to see a man about a car. Ned says it was a rolling death trap." Nancy sat down and slammed the door shut. "I want to know *why* it was waiting for us when we arrived at the airport."

Smiling Al's Auto Sales wasn't hard to find. Its three-story cartoon billboard loomed huge above the Punanai Hills.

One of the showroom salesmen conducted them to the manager's office. A short, jowly man

19

with bushy eyebrows and a receding hairline sat behind a sprawling mahogany desk. He had more diplomas on his wall than a doctor.

He looked up with a broad salesman's smile as Nancy and her friends entered. "Hi, I'm Al Lutsen. Smiling Al. What can I do for you?"

"I had a problem with one of your cars, Mr. Lutsen," Nancy said. "The brakes failed!"

"What car?" Al's smile vanished instantly. "When did this happen?"

"About two o'clock this afternoon," Nancy replied. "It was a tan four-door sedan. Remember it?"

"Vaguely." But Al's face gave him away. Nancy could tell that he remembered the car quite well. "What was wrong with it?"

Ned counted off points on his fingers. "One, the brake drums were bald. Two, the axle had rusted out. Three, the muffler fell off while it was on the lift—"

"I didn't sell you that car," Al blustered. "Why are you so interested?"

"You leased it to Sunrise Rentals this morning," Nancy replied. "They rented it to us. We were nearly killed in that clunker. So we're here for some answers, Mr. Lutsen."

Al cleared his throat and began shuffling through some papers. "Well, if you rented it from Sunrise, you'll have to take it up with them. I'm not responsible for cars once they leave the lot. I'm a busy man. Lot of work to do. Goodbye. Please close the door on your way out."

Ned leaned across the desk. "We're not leaving until we get our answers."

"I don't discuss the firm's business with outsiders."

Nancy cocked her head to one side. "Would you like to know where we're going next?" she asked.

Al's eyebrows lifted. "Where?"

"The Department of Transportation!" Nancy rested her fingertips on his desk. "I think they'll be very interested to hear that Smiling Al is putting unsafe cars on the road."

As the three turned to leave, Al jumped out of his chair and beat them to the door. "Whoa-whoa-whoa! Wait a minute! Let's talk about this, eh?" His salesman's smile had magically reappeared.

"How'd you come by that car?" Nancy asked.

Al shrugged. "I picked it up a couple of days ago. Got it from the Malihini Corporation."

Nancy's eyes widened. She glanced at George, who mirrored her look of astonishment. Al bit his lower lip. "Um, I said something?"

An excited note in her voice, Nancy asked, "How did this Malihini Corporation get in touch with you?"

"That's the funny part," Al recalled. "They sent me a telegram. 'Dear Mr. Lutsen.' I thought they were hitting me up for a donation at first. It was a little strange, but what a deal!"

"What do you mean, 'strange'?" Ned interjected.

"Well, the Malihini Corporation offered to sell me that car, but only if I leased it immediately to Sunrise Rentals," Al replied. "I had to scramble to do that. But it was worth it. The Malihini Corporation sold me that car for half the book value!"

Nancy scowled. "Why didn't your mechanics check out the car before you leased it to Sunrise?"

"I—I—I didn't have time for that," Al said lamely. "I had to have that car on the Sunrise lot first thing this morning. That was the deal. Hey, I couldn't pass that up. Half price? No way!" He stared uncomfortably at the trio. "Look, it was legitimate business. If you've got a beef about those brakes, you should talk to Sunrise."

"But it wasn't legitimate," Ned said. "You bought a clunker sight unseen and then dumped it on a rental agency. Pretty sloppy for a sharp businessman like yourself."

Nancy stepped forward. "Tell me more about the Malihini Corporation. Who are they? Have you ever done business with them before?"

"With them? Nahhhh! But I pick up old cars from companies all the time . . ." Meekly he sank into his chair. "Uh, maybe I could make it up to you, eh?"

"Yes, you could," George fumed. "Why don't you test-drive that car?"

"Now, there's no need to get nasty." Al's smile resurrected itself. "I understand your situation. You're in Hawaii, and you don't have a car for sight-seeing. But, listen, I'm always willing to help. Why, I'd be delighted to rent you lovely ladies—and you, sir—a brand-new car right out of the showroom for as long as you're in the Islands."

"No charge!" added Nancy grimly.

Al scratched the back of his head. He showed Nancy a sidelong frown. "Ah—couldn't we negotiate something about mileage?"

An hour later in a new car provided by Smiling Al, Nancy drove her friends back to Honolulu. She steered the car down the Kamehameha Highway, keeping an eye on the rush-hour traffic.

Nancy's thoughts were racing. The Malihini Corporation had originally owned that damaged car. They had sold it to Smiling Al at a price he couldn't resist—but only on the condition that he lease it immediately to Sunrise Rentals. Next, the Malihini Corporation had called Sunrise and arranged to have that particular car waiting for Nancy Drew.

Ned gave her a long look. "You're awfully quiet."

"I'm thinking about that nice little booby trap the Malihini Corporation left for us," Nancy replied as she steered the car down the exit. "Whoever they are, they went to a lot of trouble to cover their tracks. They knew we were going to visit Alice Faulkner. They knew we would be coming down Tantalus Drive on the way home. You can guess the rest."

"You bet," Ned replied. "Our crash would have looked like a simple accident. No one would have traced it all the way back to the Malihini Corporation."

"Nancy, what do you make of all this?" George asked.

"I don't know, George." Sighing, Nancy turned the car into the Ala Wai parking lot. "None of it makes sense. What is this Malihini Corporation? Why did they try to kill us the moment we arrived in Honolulu?" She eased the car into a parking space. "Ned, George—we'd better be very, very careful from now on, okay?"

Ned nodded in agreement. "I'll go along with that."

After grabbing their gear, the trio headed down the floating walkway that connected the individual berths. Sunset painted the sea a vivid bronze. Fat gulls rested on barnacle-encrusted piles and watched the boat owners close up for the night.

The *Kahala* lolled at her berth. Her fiberglass hull made thudding noises as it jostled the pier. George sighed. "Am I glad to be home. Know something? I haven't had a bite to eat all day."

"Why don't you and Bess make sandwiches?" Nancy suggested. "That'll give me a chance to phone Mrs. Faulkner's daughter."

Just then, Bess appeared at the *Kahala*'s fantail, smiling and waving a greeting. All at once a look of horror flashed across her face.

"Nancy! Behind you! *Look out!*"

Nancy turned just in time to see a sailboat's boom swinging toward them. The thick wooden beam was hurtling straight at her face!

Chapter
Four

NANCY GRABBED HER friends and threw herself forward. The sail struck her high on the shoulder, but the boom sailed harmlessly past.

Nancy, Ned, and George hit the walkway together. The impact drove water through the slats, soaking the trio to the skin.

"Oh!" a woman cried out. "Are you kids all right?"

"Nobody was hurt." Getting up, Nancy saw a plump woman standing on the deck of a moored Catalina whose boom was suspended over the walkway.

"Talk about 'low bridge'!" George exclaimed, standing up.

"I'm awfully sorry," the woman said. "I thought that winch was locked. It started unwinding the minute I turned my back. I never meant to—"

"That's okay. No harm done." Nancy smiled reassuringly.

Nancy and her friends pushed the boom back aboard the woman's boat. Then they joined Bess at the *Kahala*. After assuring Bess that they were all right, they boarded the cruiser.

While Ned and George were changing clothes, Nancy used the boat's cordless phone to call Lisa's mother. The phone at the other end rang three times. Then a woman's voice answered. "Hello?"

"Mrs. Rafferty, this is Nancy Drew—"

"Nancy Drew!" the woman interrupted. "Where have you people been? Mother said you were coming hours ago."

"Our rental car broke down. We were delayed reporting the accident. I am sorry," Nancy said apologetically. "Listen, I can be there in half an hour."

"All right. Come right over."

"See you then." Nancy hung up. "Bess, you and George stay here and cover the phone in case Mrs. Faulkner tries to reach us. We'll be back soon."

"Okay." Bess put a couple of sandwiches and two cans of soda in a plastic bag, then handed the bundle to Nancy. "Good luck."

Grinning, Ned opened the hatch. "We may need it."

Diana Rafferty's apartment was two miles east of the marina, in an ultramodern building. Nancy parked in the beach lot opposite it. Then dodging the traffic, she and Ned dashed across the street.

Nancy pressed the doorbell at an upper-floor apartment. The door swung open to reveal a slender, tight-lipped woman with a soft blond ponytail and Alice Faulkner's blue eyes.

Diana blinked in surprise. "Nancy Drew?"

"That's me." Nancy offered a pleasant smile. "And this is my friend Ned Nickerson."

"Excuse me, it's just—" Flustered, Diana opened the door all the way. "Well—you're a *kid.*"

"Eighteen, Mrs. Rafferty," Nancy replied, holding her smile in place. Alice Faulkner's polished manners hadn't rubbed off on her daughter.

"I hope my mother knows what she's doing." Diana led the way into her living room. "Please. Make yourselves comfortable. Oh, I really should mention that I don't like to be called that name. I prefer 'Diana Faulkner.'"

Nancy nodded politely and sat down. Her gaze wandered around the room, taking in the large windows, modern furniture, and tropical plants. Diana's paintings hung in prominent places

28

along the walls, each one emblazoned with her signature. The paintings were all nature studies —flaming volcanoes, ferocious blue seas, stormy landscapes.

"The last time you saw Lisa was Friday morning, wasn't it?" Nancy asked.

"Yes." Diana gave a dramatic sigh. "When she left for school." Her voice quavered. "I—I just don't understand why she did it—why she ran away. I mean, if she had a problem, she could have come to me. Right? I'm her *mother.*"

Toying with an earring, Diana added, "I suppose I ought to be grateful for your help. Do you think you can find her?"

"The more you tell me, the better our chances." Nancy settled back in her chair. "Why did you send Lisa to the bank that day?"

"I needed my travelers' checks. I was planning to be gone a few days. An exhibit of my work." Her lips tightened. "You see, despite the opposition of my mother and my ex-husbands—all four of them!—I've made quite a name for myself as an artist. That's why this business irritates me no end!"

Puzzled, Nancy asked, "What do you mean?"

"I had to miss my opening because of this mess. I'm supposed to be on Maui, not sitting around here trying to figure out what got into Lisa!"

Diana's self-centeredness took Nancy's breath

away. With Lisa missing, how could Diana even think about an art exhibit?

"Why didn't you go to the bank yourself?" Nancy prodded.

"There was a strike at the hotel I was booked into. I had to make other arrangements."

"Did Lisa do this sort of thing for you often?"

"Now and then. I tried to get her to be more helpful around here. She was so sullen at times. As if she held me personally responsible for all the trouble in her life. Trouble! That girl doesn't know the meaning of the word!"

"She does now," Ned observed quietly.

Ignoring his comment, Diana scowled and snapped, "How could Lisa do it? How? If word of this ever gets out, I'll be the laughingstock of Honolulu!"

No wonder poor Lisa ran away! Nancy thought.

"Can you tell me something about Lisa's friends?" she asked, resting her chin on her fist.

"Not much. There was a girl who was always hanging around here—Dawn something. I forget her last name. I met her only once or twice." Diana pushed her dainty glasses up on her nose. "I happen to be a very busy woman. Most people think artists work when they feel the urge. Not so! When I prepare for an exhibit, I have to do ten or twelve canvases." Closing her eyes, she stroked her forehead gingerly. "I—I can't understand it. I just can't! Lisa knew how important that exhibit is. How could she *do* this to me now?"

Stifling a surge of irritation, Nancy stood up and exhaled slowly. "Ms. Faulkner, could I look at Lisa's bedroom?"

"Go ahead. It's upstairs. Second door on the right."

"Thanks. I'll be right back. Ned, maybe you could get directions to Lisa's school from Ms. Faulkner. We'll definitely want to visit there."

Nancy climbed the carpeted stairs and slipped into the darkened room. She flicked on the light, noting the cedarwood bureau and sound system and home computer. On the bed, a teddy bear forlornly awaited his owner's return.

There was a personalized notepad on the ink-stained blotter on Lisa's desk. Picking it up, Nancy tilted the top sheet toward the light. Faint impressions were visible. If she could enhance them, there might be a clue here.

Nancy took a lead pencil and lightly colored across the paper. Only a few impressions came through in the sheen of gray. The upper left corner showed the clearest markings:

Miss Mi
1276 Pr
San Fra

An address, Nancy realized. Miss Mi? Who could that be? Perhaps a friend of Lisa's.

31

Peeling the paper from the pad, Nancy folded it and tucked it into her shoulder bag. Just then, a hanging object drew her gaze. It was a model helicopter, an army Huey, suspended from a nylon thread.

All in all, the rest of Lisa's room seemed pretty normal for a sixteen-year-old girl. But that model helicopter didn't fit. Nancy studied it for a long moment, then shrugged.

Next she picked up a photo cube on the bureau. All six photos were of a lovely girl with brownish blond hair and striking blue eyes. Three of the pictures showed Lisa alone. One pictured her with a cute dark-haired girl —another with a grinning strawberry blonde. The final snapshot showed all three girls at an airport, hamming it up in front of a Huey helicopter.

Looks as though Lisa is interested in flying, Nancy thought, glancing back at the model. I wonder if her mother knows how much?

Nancy felt a twinge of sadness. Since her mother's death, Carson Drew had tried to be both a mother and a father to her. What would my life have been like if Dad had been like Diana Faulkner? she wondered. If he had been too wrapped up in himself to care about me?

Dismissing that depressing thought, Nancy stood at the corner of the window and peered through the venetian blinds. Across the street, black feather palms waved languidly in the night breeze.

And then Nancy saw him.

He was a dark-skinned, broad-shouldered man in a Hawaiian shirt. Moon face and slicked-back hair. Nervously tapping his toe on the sidewalk, he was leaning against a streetlight, arms folded —his gaze never leaving Lisa Trumbull's window.

Who was he? And why was he spying on Lisa's bedroom?

"Ned! Get up here—quick!" she called.

Footsteps sounded on the stairs. Ned burst through the doorway with Diana right behind.

"Somebody on the sidewalk is watching this window," Nancy whispered.

Ned circled the window and came up on Nancy's side. Easing a slat upward, he glanced at the street. Then he looked at Nancy. "You're right."

"Who?" Diana rushed to the window.

Nancy tried to stop her. *"Don't!* He'll see you—"

Too late! Diana's outline broke the shaft of light. Glancing at the street, Nancy saw the moon-faced man flinch. He averted his face at once and turned away, heading for the nightclub district with a hasty stride.

No doubt about it. He was spying on Lisa's bedroom. And now he was getting away!

Chapter

Five

"COME ON, NED!"

Nancy dashed out of the bedroom and down the stairs. She reached the front door in thirty seconds, yanked it open, and rushed onto the outdoor balcony.

She just caught a glimpse of the man's Hawaiian shirt in the park across the street. Then a bus hissed to a stop at the curb. The dark-haired man jumped aboard. With a throaty rumble, the bus lumbered away. She'd lost him!

Ned came up behind her. "Great try, Nancy. We would've had him if we'd been on the first floor."

They turned and headed back into the apartment. Diana was waiting at the door, her face tense. "Who was that man?" she asked.

"We were hoping you could tell us," Nancy replied.

"I haven't any idea. I've never seen anyone hanging around in front of our building. Do you think he had something to do with Lisa's running away?"

"He may have. But I'll tell you one thing, Ms. Faulkner." Nancy tilted her head toward the window. "If that man or anyone had anything to do with Lisa's disappearance, then your daughter may be in a lot of trouble. I'd think long and hard about calling the police. I'd think *really* hard."

Diana swallowed hard. "Wha—what are we going to do?"

"We're going to find Lisa," Nancy said simply. She asked for permission to borrow the photo cube. Diana consented readily, and Ned hurried upstairs to fetch it.

Diana sat down slowly, her head bowed. Tears collected in the lower rims of her eyes. "I—I tried my best." She began to sob. "I did! We just c-could n-never talk to each other. Please try to understand that."

Nancy touched the woman's shoulder as Ned arrived with the photo cube. Without a word, Nancy tilted her chin toward the door. She and Ned left quietly, and she closed the door gingerly behind her.

35

"What do we do now?" asked Ned, escorting her back to the parking lot.

"Go to Lisa's school first thing tomorrow and find out who her friends are. We'll talk to them." Nancy opened her car door. "Maybe they can tell us where she might have gone."

Ned dropped into the passenger seat. "You look pretty grim, Nancy. What is it?"

"I'm feeling pretty grim." Nancy turned the ignition key. "I don't like the way this is shaping up, Ned. Mrs. Faulkner hires me to find her missing granddaughter. A company I never heard of tries to kill us. An unknown man has Lisa's home under surveillance. What's the connection?"

Ned shrugged. "You've got me."

"It's not what we know," Nancy replied, shifting into reverse. "It's what we *don't* know! And in a case like this, what we don't know can get us all killed!"

Promptly at eight the next morning Nancy drove into the parking lot of Roosevelt High School. Bright sunshine dappled the huge lawn and isolated coconut palms of the campus.

Bess stepped out of the car, turning her face toward the sun. "Glorious!" she said. "If I lived in Honolulu, I'd have the worst attendance record in school."

Nancy smiled and pulled on the brake. Earlier that morning Bess and George had volunteered to go undercover at the school, to try to learn more about Lisa. Ned had offered to talk to the custodians.

"First stop for me is the principal's office," Bess announced. "I'll pretend to be a transfer student. Maybe I can get a look at Lisa's file."

"I'm going to the guidance office," George said.

Ned grinned. "It's the boiler room for me."

Nancy stepped out of the car. "Okay, we've all got investigating to do. Let's meet back here at ten-thirty. Good hunting."

The first bell jangled as Nancy was crossing the campus. Kids in jeans and button-down shirts ambled into the cinderblock building, jostling and laughing with one another. Threading her way through the crowd, Nancy headed down the hall.

Although she had Lisa's photo, Nancy was reluctant to show it around. The minute she did, she'd be marked as an outsider. So she drifted from group to group—introducing herself as a transfer student, seeking out the class gossips, dropping a question here and there.

By the time the homeroom bell rang, Nancy had learned a number of things about RHS. Karen Rothenberg was running for junior class president. Super-hunk Troy Shepherd had broken up with Marcia Kirtland. And Lisa Trumbull's best friend was named Dawn Burnham.

A girl pointed out Dawn's homeroom. Nancy

took up a position by the door. Ten minutes later, the electric bell cut loose with an earsplitting clang and kids streamed into the hallway. Nancy spotted Dawn at once.

"Hi, Dawn! Wait up a minute, will you?" Nancy followed behind her.

Dawn halted and turned, an inquiring expression on her face. Nancy answered the unspoken question. "I'm Nancy Drew. I just transferred in."

Dawn smiled uncertainly. "Maybe I've seen you around."

Nancy fell into step beside the girl. "I was wondering if you and Lisa Trumbull could help me."

"Depends." Dawn shrugged, hugging her books close.

"My dad's in the navy. Just got transferred to Pearl," Nancy said smoothly. "When we lived in Florida, I was in a flying club. I want to join one here."

Dawn's eyes lit up. "You're into flying? Fixed or rotary wing?"

"Rotary." Nancy was suddenly glad that Ned had talked her into learning to fly a couple of years ago.

"Oh, boy! Lisa is sure going to want to meet you." Dawn grinned as the two of them hurried along. "Lisa and I belong to a flying club in Wailuha. Lisa's way ahead of me, though. She's got her pilot's license and instrument rating, and she's about ten hours away from getting her rotary-wing ticket. Lisa loves choppers. Last summer, at camp in California, she went up in a Huey, and it was love at first sight."

"She went to flight school in California?"

"No, just summer camp. Picasso sent her to a ranch near Bishop."

"Picasso?"

"Lisa's mom. Di the Artist. Usually, Lisa hated being sent away like that. But this gave her a chance to be with Michele again."

"Michele?" Nancy prodded.

"Yeah. Michele Woodbridge." Dawn's sigh was nostalgic. "Me, Lisa, and Michele used to hang out together in junior high. We were real close, all three of us. Then Michele's parents got a divorce, and she moved to San Francisco with her mom." A sad look came over Dawn's face. "By that point, things were getting pretty nasty for Lisa at home, too. Her mother's latest marriage was breaking up. Lisa told me her mother and that Rafferty guy used to fight like cats and dogs. Flying kitchenware and everything!" Dawn shook her head. "Boy, when I think back, it sure wasn't easy for Lisa. Di used to fight with all of her husbands. When we were little, Lisa practically lived at Michele's house—"

Brrrinnnnng! The late bell jangled mercilessly. Dawn cast a worried look at her classroom. There was time for only one more question.

"San Francisco? You guys must really miss Michele. Do you stay in touch?"

"Lisa does. She writes once a week. Me, I'm no writer. Listen, Nancy, I've got to go. See you at lunch?"

"One of these days. Take care, Dawn."

Doing a brisk about-face, Nancy headed up the corridor. Ned and Bess met her halfway. "Did you learn anything?" Ned asked.

"A little. I think now I understand why Lisa ran away." Nancy turned to Bess. "How'd you make out?"

"Not so well. I got into the central filing system, but all I found was Lisa's locker number —four-forty-seven," Bess replied.

"How'd you manage that?" asked Ned.

"Easy. I told the main secretary I was a transfer student. She asked me for my transcript, and I told her it was back home in North Dakota. When she went into the principal's office to make the call privately, I sneaked a peek."

"North Dakota?" Nancy echoed.

"Yeah, I told her I was Bess Summers from Grand Forks, North Dakota. I figured that would keep her on the phone for a while," Bess added proudly.

Nancy cleared her throat. "Bess, did you stop to think what will happen when she calls Grand Forks and finds out Bess Summers doesn't exist?"

Just then, the overhead intercom blared, "Bess

40

Summers, report to the front office. Bess Summers, report to the office *immediately!*"

"Better go hide in the car," Nancy suggested. "Your cover is blown!"

Ned hurried down the hall. "I'll go look for George."

"Good idea. I'll be along in a few minutes." Nancy took off in the opposite direction. She had something she wanted to try.

Nancy found Lisa's locker in the science section. Kneeling, she put her ear to the steel. Her fingers turned the dial to the left. A musical *ting!* sounded. Taking a deep breath, she reversed the turn ever so slowly. Once, twice around the dial, then—*ting!* She wiped her sweating fingers on her pants leg, then painstakingly moved the dial to the left again. *Ting!*

Nancy stood up and gave the handle a quick tug. The door swung open. Immediately Nancy noticed a colorful bit of paper on the top shelf. She pulled it free. It was an airline brochure, a schedule of flights and departure times. One line was circled in ink.

FLIGHT 227 HNL-SFC 2:30 P.M.

Familiar with airline codes, Nancy knew that HNL-SFC stood for "Honolulu to San Francisco." She grinned excitedly. It was all coming together now. She pulled out the note she had taken from Lisa's bedroom.

Miss Mi
1276 Pr
San Fra

Now it's clear, Nancy thought. *Mi* stands for *Michele*. Michele Woodbridge. And Michele lives in *San Francisco*.

Now Nancy understood how Lisa had pulled it off. Lisa had been angry when she wrote to Michele. Perhaps she had hinted at leaving home for good. Perhaps Michele had offered her a place to stay. Lisa's big problem had been getting the airfare to fly out of Honolulu. And Diana had solved that problem when she had sent Lisa to the bank. Only Lisa had never made it to the airport. She was still out there. . . .

Suddenly a brawny hand closed around Nancy's wrist. She gasped.

"What are you doing here?" a man's voice growled in her ear.

Chapter

Six

Turning, Nancy looked into a rugged face. The man was big and broad-shouldered. He looked like a boxer with more losses than wins. Beside him stood a tall, goateed black man. They were both too old for high school.

"I asked you a question," the first man muttered. His grip tightened on Nancy's wrist.

Nancy's heart thudded against her rib cage as the man backed her up against the locker.

At that moment a teacher stepped out of the biology lab and came forward, her face stern. "Gentlemen, I'll have to ask you to leave. If you don't stop bothering that girl, I'll call the police!"

The white man sighed. He reached into his

43

blazer, produced a wallet, and flipped it open. A silver badge gleamed. "We *are* the police."

"We'll handle things from here on in, ma'am," the black man said, leading Nancy away. He clucked his tongue in reproof. "Breaking into other people's lockers? Young lady, it looks as though you've got some detention time ahead of you."

"Wait a minute!" Nancy said. "I'm not a student here. My name is Nancy Drew. I'm a private investigator from the mainland. I'm trying to find Lisa Trumbull. She's run away."

"A PI, eh?" the white cop remarked. "And I suppose you don't know that all private eyes must register with the local police department before they go to work here in the Islands."

"I'm not a licensed investigator," Nancy explained. "I sort of help people out when they're in trouble."

"I think I've heard of you." The black cop studied Nancy with a new respect. "You cracked that airlines case in Seattle, didn't you?"

"That's right," Nancy said.

"Then it's a pleasure to meet you, Nancy." The first cop offered his hand. "I'm Tim Di-Prizio, detective-sergeant, Honolulu P.D. This is my partner, Detective-Sergeant Martin Giles."

Martin took out his notebook. "What's this about Lisa Trumbull?"

"Aren't you two here to investigate Lisa's

running away? I thought her mother had decided to call you."

"This is the first I've heard of it," Martin said.

Nancy hastily explained how she had been called into the case. When she had finished, she asked, "Why were you guys watching Lisa's locker?"

"Marty and I are on street detail this week," Tim DiPrizio explained. "We patrol the malls —keep an eye out for con artists. This morning, one of our informers told us that something big is going down. There's a girl on the street—Lisa Trumbull—with something very valuable to sell. The word is, she's got diamonds."

"The name didn't ring any bells with us," Martin added. "So we decided to check the high school. We staked out the girl's locker. Figured to ask her a few questions when she showed up."

Nancy was really worried now. Cops never heard anything first. If the word had gotten to them, then every street person in Honolulu must know that Lisa Trumbull was carrying something worth big bucks. Lisa was in more danger than ever before.

"Look, maybe we can help each other," Nancy suggested. "You guys know the street scene. You can tell me where Lisa might try to sell those diamonds. In return, I'll tell you what I know."

"Sounds good to me," Tim said. "Where do you think Lisa's headed?"

"San Francisco. She has a friend there named Michele Woodbridge."

"We'll check it out." Martin turned to his partner. "Hey, Tim, if you were a high schooler looking to unload merchandise, who would you go to?"

Tim snapped his fingers. "Boomer! He's a fence—you know, he buys stolen goods," he replied. "Boomer hangs out at the Ala Moana shopping center. Big, beefy guy in his early twenties." They described him further. "Someone's bound to steer Lisa to him."

Nancy smiled grimly. "I think I'll have a talk with this guy."

"No way," Tim warned. "You'll never get near him. We've sent our best undercover people after him. Boomer has a sixth sense about cops. And he can run like a jackrabbit."

"But I'm not a cop," Nancy replied, heading for the exit. "Thanks for the help, guys. I'll be in touch."

A short while later Nancy, Ned, and Bess stood in the middle of the Ala Moana mall. "Bess, I need your shopping expertise." Nancy steered her friend toward a classy boutique. "Go in there and get me some earrings and bracelets."

"Hey, that's easy!" Bess giggled and hurried into the store.

Nancy and Ned waited beside the tall fountains in the center of the mall.

"I wonder how George is doing at the bank," Nancy remarked.

Ned shrugged. "I hope she's getting more out of Mr. Rafferty than we got out of Lisa's mother."

Bess rejoined them a half hour later, proudly displaying a pair of gold earrings and a trio of shiny bracelets. Nancy examined each one carefully and tucked them in the pockets of her jeans.

"You guys go watch the exits," she suggested. "I'll stay here. Flash me a signal if you see anyone who matches Boomer's description."

Ned and Bess sauntered off to their respective sentry posts. Nancy seated herself on a lava wall and settled down to wait.

Two hours passed. Nancy breathed deeply, forcing herself to stay alert. Sooner or later, their quarry would show.

Nancy's gaze drifted toward Ned. She sat up straight. Ned was vigorously scratching his ear!

Anxiously she gazed through the crowd. And then she saw him. Boomer was taller than she'd expected, with bushy hair. Ultra-dark sunglasses concealed his eyes. He walked like a lion on the prowl.

Nancy strolled up beside him. "Hi, Boomer!" She dug into her pocket, then displayed the earrings in her upturned palm. "What do you think of them?"

Picking up an earring, he studied it carefully. "Expensive."

47

Nancy grinned slyly. "Not when you've got a five-finger discount."

"My favorite kind!" Boomer laughed, then stared at Nancy with mock severity. "You? A shoplifter? Shame on you!"

"Only when I need the money." Nancy pretended to look around nervously. "How much can I get for this stuff?"

Boomer stared at her for a long moment. Finally he tossed the earring into her outstretched palm. Walking past her, he whispered, "Parking garage. Ten minutes."

Nancy breathed deeply, then coughed, as the strong gasoline fumes of the Ala Moana garage filled her lungs. She was perched on her car's front fender. Casting a glance to the right, she saw Ned loitering at the up-ramp. Just knowing he was there made her feel better.

Then Boomer came down the steel stairway from the mall, boot heels hammering the metal. Looking around suspiciously, he went straight to Nancy's car.

"Here's how we work it," Boomer muttered. "You get half now. Then you take your stuff upstairs, go to the public phone, and leave it in the coin return. The rest of your money'll be in there."

"How much?" asked Nancy.

"Thirty bucks."

"In the coin return? Anyone could take it!"

Boomer grinned evilly. "It's being watched. No one will—"

He halted abruptly. Face frozen, he stared at a reflection in the neighboring car's windshield. Nancy heard a footstep behind her.

Glancing over her shoulder, she gasped out loud. Approaching the stairs was the moon-faced man—the same man who had been spying on Lisa Trumbull's apartment!

Boomer seemed to sense Nancy's anxiety. "Be cool. He's not going to bust us."

"You know him?" Nancy blurted.

"Nahhhh, but he's a cop." Boomer leaned casually against the other car. "I can tell. That joker's got *plainclothes* written all over him."

Nancy sneaked a quick glance. The moon-faced man lingered at the bottom of the stairs. Then, pretending not to look at them, he ambled over to the *Star-Bulletin* dispenser and bought a newspaper.

Alarmed, Nancy realized that he was shadowing her!

Nancy's heartbeat seemed to fill her chest. The moon-faced man stood blocking the stairs, pretending to read his paper.

Nancy turned and noticed Boomer's suspicious gaze. He was glowering at her. His expression grew more menacing as he realized he couldn't escape up the stairs.

Suddenly his hand darted inside his leather jacket. "Now I get it! He's with *you!*" A small pistol appeared in his big hand. "You set me up, you little—You're a *cop!*"

Before Nancy could move, Boomer had looped his arm around her neck. He held her in a choke-hold, using her as a shield as his pistol swiveled toward the moon-faced man. "Game's over, cop! Back off, you hear me?"

Nancy felt the cold steel of the gun against her temple.

"Back off, I said, or this is the end of her!"

Chapter
Seven

"THIS IS IT, cop!" Boomer tapped the muzzle against Nancy's head. "Say goodbye to your partner."

Mouth agape, the moon-faced man stared at them. He held out a quaking hand. "N-now wait a minute, buddy! You got it all wrong!"

"You're following me!" Boomer roared, his left arm locked under Nancy's chin. "Lousy, stinking cop!"

Uttering a frightened yelp, the man turned and fled.

Boomer leveled the pistol and took careful aim at the man.

Now! Nancy thought.

Her head whipped back, striking Boomer flush on the chin. He yowled. Feeling his grip loosen, Nancy slipped out from under and gave him a solid judo chop to the ribs. Boomer stumbled. Nancy jumped him, grabbing his wrist with both hands, and hammered his gun hand against the fender. The pistol clattered to the floor. Nancy's foot swept it under a nearby car.

She heard running feet—the anxious shouts of Ned and Bess.

Boomer bolted. "More cops!"

After he ran up to Nancy, Ned hugged her. "You all right?"

"I'm fine." She pointed at Boomer, who was heading for the stairwell. "After him, Ned! We can't let him get away."

Ned and Nancy took off in pursuit. Bess brought up the rear. They charged up the stairway in single file, Ned in the lead. Nancy took the steps two at a time. She was thinking, What was that moon-faced guy doing here? Was he following me? But how does he know who I am? He couldn't have seen me in Lisa's window!

Clang! Boomer pushed a steel trash can over the edge of the stairs. It tumbled toward them!

Ned tried to dodge, but his foot slipped on the step. The can rolled right over him, and he went down hard.

"Ned!" Grabbing Bess, Nancy pushed her against the railing. The can bounced past them, spilling trash all over the stairs.

"I'm okay, Nancy. Go get him!" Ned said.

Nancy raced to the balcony. She spotted Boomer's blue- and orange-flowered shirt just ahead, disappearing into the mall crowd.

Shoving people aside, Boomer bulled his way down the main corridor. Angry shouts exploded all around him. Nancy stayed on his heels, zig-zagging between startled shoppers.

At last the crowd thinned out and disappeared. They were in a little turnoff now, a hallway lined with supply closets. Once in the clear, Nancy put on a sudden burst of speed. She came right up behind Boomer and brought him down with a tackle worthy of a pro football player.

Nancy and Boomer rolled over and over across the polished floor. Breaking free, Nancy jumped to her feet. Boomer got up groggily, saw who it was, and—snarling with rage—threw himself at Nancy.

Nancy's right leg scissored in a flawless judo kick. Her sneaker clobbered Boomer's chin—he went over like an old dead tree.

Boomer lifted his hands in surrender. "Okay, okay—that's enough. I'm busted, man. I want to see my lawyer."

Nancy knelt beside him. "Boomer, I'm not a cop."

"We're just concerned citizens," Ned added, coming up behind them and pinning him to the floor.

"Then how about letting me go?" Boomer tried to sit up.

"After you put a gun to Nancy's head? No way, pal!"

"Boomer, we've got you cold on assault and unlawful possession of a gun." Reaching across the floor, Nancy retrieved her shoulder bag. "Tell you what, though. If you'll answer a few questions for me, I won't mention that you took aim at that black-haired guy."

"All right." Boomer sighed. "Ask your questions."

Nancy took the photo of Lisa Trumbull out of her bag. "Have you ever seen this girl before?"

"Yeah, I've seen her." He tilted the photo slightly. "She came up to me on Waikiki Beach yesterday. Two o'clock or so. She wanted to sell me a diamond. Real quality stuff, too. I offered to set up a meet, but she wouldn't go for it. She said she'd make the arrangements." He lowered his voice. "Look, don't go spreading this around, okay? I don't want people to think I'm a double-dealer." He sat cross-legged on the hallway floor. "The whole scene felt wrong, you know? She didn't seem like the type to be fencing diamonds. I thought maybe it was a cop setup. So I followed her."

"Where did she go?" asked Nancy eagerly.

"A rundown apartment house. The Ka Lae, it's called."

Suddenly a pair of uniformed security men

rushed up to them. "What's the problem here, miss?"

"This man pulled a gun on me in the garage," Nancy explained, brushing her hair back. "Place him under arrest."

The guards hauled Boomer to his feet. He struggled in their grip, yelling, "Hey! Where's my lawyer, man?"

"We'll need to ask you a few questions, miss," one guard called back over his shoulder. "Could you come with us?"

"Be glad to," Nancy answered. But as she and Ned followed, she was worrying about the moon-faced man. Who was he? First he'd been watching Lisa's apartment. Then he'd shown up at the garage. And judging from his reaction to Boomer's threat, Nancy had been his quarry.

A sudden chill touched Nancy's heart. There were too many wild cards in the Lisa Trumbull case. The Malihini Corporation was one. That moon-faced man was the other. Were the two connected? Or were they operating independently?

Either way, Nancy knew, she had to fit those puzzle pieces into their proper places. Otherwise, she and her friends might not get out of this alive!

"Uh-oh! Looks like there's roadwork up ahead," Nancy announced.

They were heading north to Honolulu's financial district. Long, low-roofed bungalows from the 1940s flanked the street on either side, a reminder of the days when Paawa had been a suburb of the city.

"How bad is it?" asked Bess.

Nancy stuck her head out the side window. Up ahead, the line of traffic was snaking around a city water department excavation. Propped up against a sawhorse was a huge sign: WARNING! EXPLOSIVES IN USE! TURN OFF YOUR RADIO!

"Slow going, but we'll get there." Nancy put the car in neutral.

"We should've called George at the bank. Let her know we're coming," Bess observed. "You know how she hates to be kept waiting."

Nancy sighed. "It can't be helped. I'm sure she'll understand."

"What's the next stop after the bank?" asked Ned.

"The Ka Lae apartment house." Nancy frowned in determination. "I want to see how reliable Boomer's information is."

The car ahead of them lurched forward. Nancy shifted into gear. then pressed the gas pedal. As their car rolled forward, she checked the dashboard, making certain that their radio was off.

The flagger waved his red banner back and forth. Beside him stood a mammoth pile of black volcanic sand. Halfway up the pile sat a small battery-powered lantern.

Suddenly the lantern's bulb turned bright red.

Nancy spotted it at the same moment the flagger did. Dropping his banner, he made shoving motions at Nancy's car. "Go back! Go back!"

Whonk-whonk-whonk! A klaxon bleated a deafening tone.

Uttering a cry of alarm, the flagger threw himself on the ground.

Bess blinked in bewilderment. "Nancy, what's going on?"

Nancy shoved the gearshift into reverse just as a fireball erupted from the pit, hurling a shower of debris straight at them!

Chapter

Eight

D UCK!" NANCY YELLED.

Covering her head, she leaned against the steering wheel. Ned braced himself behind the glove compartment. Bess plunged down behind the front seat.

The blast wave bounced the car on its springs. Rock fragments spattered the roof and hood, and the stench of burnt TNT permeated the air.

Coughing, Nancy switched off the engine. "Everybody all right?"

Ned got back into his seat. "I'm fine," he murmured.

"No injuries here," Bess said. "Nancy, what was *that?*"

The flagger came running, with a police officer right behind. The construction crew stood farther away, jabbering in confusion.

"Are you kids okay?" the cop asked. The name tag above his silver badge read "Pukui."

"Nobody hurt," Nancy reported. "Just a little shaken up."

Hands on his gun belt, Officer Pukui asked, "What happened here?"

"A TNT excavation charge went off," the flagger said, gesturing at the smoking trench. "Good thing the work crew was on break." He glanced at Nancy. "Didn't you see the sign? Why didn't you turn off your radio?"

"My radio wasn't on," Nancy replied.

"It must've been. The charge can't go off by itself!"

"Are you certain of that?" asked Officer Pukui.

"Positive!" The flagger lifted the brim of his safety helmet. "The charge was armed with a radio detonator. If someone comes too close with an FM radio, the signal can set it off."

Officer Pukui sat behind the steering wheel and turned the ignition key. The engine purred to life. "She's right. The radio wasn't on," he told the flagger. He turned to Nancy. "Did you leave anything in the trunk? A transistor radio from the beach, maybe?"

"This is a rental car. We haven't even opened the trunk!" Nancy replied.

The cop switched off the ignition. "I'm going

59

to try something." He lifted his walkie-talkie from his gun belt and turned it on. Static crackled harshly. His thumb turned the dial. All at once, a pulsing squeal burst out of the speaker. "Something in this car is broadcasting at seventeen hundred and sixty-eight megahertz. That's what set off the TNT," the officer said grimly.

"Ned, Bess—help me look," ordered Nancy.

"Got it!" Ned announced after a minute of searching the underside of the seats. He withdrew his hand to show them a small electronic device. The unit was the size of a cigarette case. A tiny operating light on its side glowed green.

"May I?" Nancy took the unit and examined it closely. Two inscriptions were stamped into the black vinyl—one in Japanese, the other in English. The English phrase read "Higashi Electronics, Ltd.—Osaka."

"What is it?" asked Bess.

"A radio transceiver—a bug," Officer Pukui said, taking it from Nancy. "Higashi specializes in this miniature stuff. This baby can probably transmit fifty miles."

Fifty miles, Nancy mused. That would cover all of Oahu!

"I sure hope this wasn't someone's idea of a joke," the cop said. "Letting you drive around with a live transceiver under your seat. That explosive charge could have killed you *and* a whole lot of innocent bystanders."

Satisfied that Nancy and her friends were not

at fault, Officer Pukui took their statements and gave them the transceiver. They continued on their way after Nancy had disabled the bug.

As they drove through downtown Honolulu, Ned said, "Nancy, do you think that was done on purpose? Did somebody try to get us blown up?"

Nancy shook her head. "I doubt it. For one thing, they had no way of knowing we would drive by *any* construction site, let alone that one. No, somebody decided to eavesdrop on us."

"When do you think it was planted?" asked Bess.

"Probably last night. Anybody could have walked by our car in the Ala Wai lot, opened the door, and stuck that thing under the seat."

Ned cast her a curious sidelong look. "Do you think it might have been someone from the Malihini Corporation?"

"Could be. Or it could just as easily have been the moon-faced man. Or somebody else." Nancy let out a deep sigh. "All we really know is, someone is awfully interested in what we talk about! Let's go pick up George."

Her face was grim. Someone was hunting them—that was certain. Some faceless, ruthless enemy was tracking them back and forth across the island.

And Nancy hadn't the slightest idea where that enemy would strike next.

* * *

The Windward Fidelity Bank was a sleek, clean-lined monolith that dominated the business district. After Nancy had parked the car, the three of them dashed across the boulevard and strolled into the airy lobby of the bank.

The tellers' windows were packed with customers, so Nancy tried the loan section. A good-looking young man with chestnut hair was leaning over a calculator at the main desk.

Nancy cleared her throat. "Excuse me."

He looked up and smiled. "Hi! What can I do for you?"

"I'm Nancy Drew." She gestured at her friends. "Bess Marvin—Ned Nickerson. We'd like to see Mr. Rafferty, please."

"Oh, of course! You're with George. She's upstairs with the Old Man right now." Rounding the desk, he extended a welcoming hand. "I'm Jack Showalter, junior accountant."

"Have you worked here long?" asked Nancy.

"Since June. I just graduated from business school." Jack picked up his telephone. "Let me call the Old Man for you."

Jack buzzed Mr. Rafferty's secretary and told her that Nancy had arrived. Then, looking puzzled, he hung up.

"What is it?" Nancy asked.

"Odd. She said he'd be down in person," Jack replied. "Mr. Rafferty *never* does that!"

Bess pointed at the elevator. The green light

descended the row of numbers. "Here he comes."

The elevator doors slid open. Nancy found herself staring at an irate middle-aged man in a navy blue pin-striped suit. Ross Rafferty was a slim, vain-looking man, with pudgy jowls and thick auburn hair combed into an unlikely pompadour.

Then Nancy noticed the men in the elevator with him. Big, competent-looking bank guards. They had their guns out.

"That's them!" Ross Rafferty pointed at Nancy. "Place those kids under arrest!"

Chapter

Nine

Under arrest?" echoed Bess.

The bank guards surrounded them.

"Bring the other one," Ross Rafferty ordered.

A tough-looking guard ushered George out of the elevator. Her eyes blazed furiously as she looked at the banker. "Mr. Rafferty, your hospitality leaves something to be desired."

Facing him, Nancy said, "Mr. Rafferty, my friends and I were hired to find your stepdaughter."

"I know who you are." Mr. Rafferty flexed his shoulders arrogantly. "You private eyes are all alike. This is nothing but a cheap shakedown."

Nancy blinked in disbelief.

"I know how you people operate," Rafferty continued. "You've conned poor Alice into thinking you can help. You'll feed her little bits of information—just enough to keep her anxious. Then you'll milk this—this situation—for years!"

Anger colored Nancy's face. "That is untrue —and unfair, Mr. Rafferty!"

"Save your breath!" Rafferty looked highly pleased with himself. "I've got you all now, and I'm going to turn you over to the police!"

Nancy managed to stay calm. "Mr. Rafferty, I intend to find Lisa—with or without your cooperation. Frankly, I'd rather work with you than have to tell Mrs. Faulkner you wouldn't cooperate." She pointed at Jack Showalter's phone. "So why don't you give her a call and tell her what you think?"

She could see that she had called his bluff. As the leading shareholder in Windward Bancorp, Alice had the power to fire him instantly. Which meant Rafferty didn't dare defy her!

"We'll see about that!" he said huffily.

Nancy watched as he picked up the telephone and dialed the Faulkner estate. "Hello, Alice? Ross Rafferty here. I've captured that girl who was conning you. With your permission, I'll turn this Nancy Drew over to the—"

Ross Rafferty wilted like a balloon with the air leaking out. "But—but—but—!" He sounded like an old motorboat.

"Yes, Alice. Of course, Alice. Good day!" Ross hung up quickly. He pressed a crumpled handkerchief to his lips, then turned to face Nancy and her friends. "Ahem! Perhaps I was a little brusque before."

He dismissed the bank guards, then told Jack Showalter, "I'd like you to serve as the bank's liaison in this matter." Turning to Nancy, he said, "Since we have to work together on this, I suppose we should make the best of it." He spread his hands in mock invitation. "How can I help?"

"I'd like to look at the safety deposit vault, if you don't mind." Nancy circled the table. "And I'd like to ask you a few questions."

Ross Rafferty led them all downstairs. The vault was as large as a barn, with a huge circular door. Inside, a tall Japanese man was examining some papers. He had iron-gray hair, a bristling mustache, and mournful eyes that reminded Nancy of a basset hound's.

"Nancy, this is Mitsuo Kaimonsaki, the president of the bank." Ross caught Nancy's questioning glance and explained, "I'm chief executive officer of the company that owns the bank. Mitsuo here is in charge of the day-to-day operations of the bank itself."

Mr. Kaimonsaki cocked a slim eyebrow. "This is related to the matter of Mrs. Faulkner's granddaughter?"

"Yes," Nancy replied. "Mr. Kaimonsaki, did

you suspect anything Friday when you let Lisa into this vault?"

"Not at all," he answered. "Lisa ran errands for her mother on several occasions."

That fit with what Diana had told Nancy. "Tell me, who had access to Ms. Faulkner's safety deposit box?"

Rafferty seemed to bristle at the phrase "Ms. Faulkner." Nancy guessed that the divorce hadn't been his idea.

"The immediate family," Kaimonsaki replied. "Alice, Diana, and Lisa. Bank employees need authorization to enter the vault—a pass signed by the three highest officers of the bank. The officers, of course, have routine access to the safety deposit boxes."

"Who are they?" asked Nancy.

"Myself, Mr. Rafferty, and Amy Sorenson, the bank's vice-president."

Nancy nodded in understanding. "Could I talk to Ms. Sorenson?"

"Perhaps later. She'll be back soon." Kaimonsaki looked apologetic.

Ross Rafferty fingered his tie. "Mitsuo, why don't you show Nancy's friends around the bank? She and I have to talk."

As soon as the others had gone, Rafferty said, "Nancy, I'm afraid I may have given you the wrong impression a little while ago." He smiled feebly. "We've all been under such a strain these past few days. Some of us more than others."

Nancy said nothing. Rafferty rushed to fill the conversational gap. "I—I don't know what Diana may have told you, but, well—I'm quite fond of Lisa, even if she isn't my natural daughter. I want Lisa home safe and sound. The same as you and Alice."

Nancy wasn't convinced. "Mr. Rafferty," she asked, "why didn't you want to cooperate with me?"

"I was afraid your involvement in this matter would upset an already delicate situation. The bank has certain—difficulties. I'm not at liberty to discuss them. Forgive me. Of course, I'm willing to give you all the help I can."

Sure you are! Nancy thought tartly. She was remembering what Dawn Burnham had told her about Lisa's home life. Ross Rafferty would never win a Father of the Year award!

Nancy wondered if Ross's "difficulties" had something to do with his stepdaughter's disappearance. Was Ross Rafferty a man with a closet full of nasty secrets?

Would one of those secrets get poor Lisa killed?

The Ka Lae was an old hotel, a 1920s tourist mecca that had fallen upon hard times. Still, its whitewashed facade, Moorish arches, and lush garden made it stand out in its rundown neighborhood.

George reached for her door handle. "Let's wrap this up."

"Not so fast, George," Nancy said softly. "I think maybe we'd better try a soft probe first. You know, the more I learn about this case, the less I'm certain of. Someone's trying to keep us away from Lisa. Why?" She glanced at each of her friends. "Both Alice and Ross mentioned business difficulties. How do they fit into Lisa's disappearance?"

"I thought Lisa ran away," George commented.

"So did I, at first. Now I'm not so sure." Nancy studied the front entrance. "Lisa couldn't afford airfare to get to San Francisco, right? Then how can she afford to stay *here?*"

"You're right, Nan," added Bess. "She didn't sell anything to Boomer."

"Bess, I need you and George for a diversion," Nancy said, opening her car door. "Get the desk clerk out of the lobby for a few minutes, okay?"

"You bet!" Bess said enthusiastically. "The Undercover Cousins strike again."

Nancy and Ned waited until the cousins had entered the lobby, then strolled up the front walk. Ned lingered at the right side of the entryway. Nancy peeked around the door jamb. She heard a TV set somewhere in the lobby.

"Kilauea volcano erupted today, spewing tons of lava into the air. Geologists say this is the biggest eruption in ten years. . . ."

Nancy tuned out the broadcast, straining to hear the girls' conversation with the desk clerk.

"What can I do for you, ladies?"

"My cousin and I are looking for an apartment," George said.

"Well, you girls are in luck. I've got three vacancies. Let me shut this thing off, and I'll show you around."

"Observers report volcanic blasts sixty feet high . . ."

Click! The TV died. "This way. Hey, what do you girls think of our volcano, eh?" asked the clerk.

Bess chuckled nervously. "I'm glad I don't live next door to it!"

Their footsteps receded into the distance. Nancy peered around the corner. The lobby was completely deserted. "They've gone. Let's go!"

Dashing quietly across the lobby, Nancy reached the desk and turned the guest register around. A name jumped out at her. *L. Faulkner!*

Nancy lifted the master key from its wall peg. "It's got to be Lisa," she whispered. "She's using her mother's maiden name."

Minutes later Nancy and Ned arrived at Room 232. Nancy eased the key into the lock and pushed the door open. "Lisa?"

Nancy switched on the overhead light, then gasped.

The apartment was completely deserted!

Nancy and Ned walked through the living

room, looking around in confusion. Not a stick of furniture in sight. The place had been picked clean!

Kneeling, Nancy ran her fingertips along the floor. "The floor's just been waxed. Somebody cleaned out this place very thoroughly. Let's have a look around."

They split up. Ned took the bedroom. Nancy checked the kitchen. Every wall and floor had been washed. They couldn't even find a stray fingerprint.

Frustrated, Nancy headed for the living room again. Lisa couldn't have cleaned this apartment all by herself. Indeed, why would she even bother?

Nancy suddenly remembered the transceiver in their car. She distinctly recalled having mentioned the Ka Lae by name. Now it was clear. Someone had tipped off Lisa and warned her to leave.

Another—more ominous—thought entered Nancy's mind. Suppose Lisa Trumbull had been *forced* to leave?

Nancy's gaze was drawn to the window. Gauzy drapes hung there, suspended by rings from an old-fashioned brass rod. The last two rings on the right were dangling—they'd slipped off the rod.

Rising on tiptoe, Nancy removed the entire rod. The brass was lightweight, probably hollow. An ornate bulb capped each end.

Somebody had taken this off the window,

Nancy realized. When they'd tried to put it back, there was nothing to use as a stepladder. They'd had to stretch, the way she did. Those last two rings had slipped off, and they hadn't bothered to replace them.

The bulb came off in Nancy's hand. Excitement set her nerves tingling. The curtain rod *was* hollow! And Nancy's probing fingers could feel something inside!

Tilting the curtain rod, Nancy withdrew a tube of heavy bond paper. As she did so, a smaller tube of onionskin paper slipped out and danced down to the floor. Puzzled, she picked it up. Then, tucking the onionskin under her arm, she hastily unfurled the bond document.

The corporate logo of Windward Fidelity Bank was the first thing that caught her eye. Just beneath, in bold type, was the message "You will pay to the bearer upon submission of this bond note the sum of fifty thousand dollars."

Chapter

Ten

NANCY'S BREATHING QUICKENED. This was one of the bonds Lisa ran off with!

"Ned!" she called in a stage whisper. "Come here—quick!"

Looking the bond over, Ned gasped, "Wow! But why didn't Lisa take this bond with her?"

"I'd say Lisa moved out of here in a hurry," Nancy replied. "She grabbed the curtain rod and shook out the papers. Only these two got stuck inside. . . ."

Ned pointed at the onionskin tube. "What's that?"

"Let's find out!" Nancy hurriedly unrolled it. The paper was a shipping manifest. Nancy's eyes skimmed the list of items. "Pieces of radio equipment," she said. Then the paper quivered in her grasp as she saw the name of the buyer.

Malihini Corporation
P.O. Box 4237661
Honolulu, HI

"Looks as if our two cases are coming together, Ned. There's our link between Lisa Trumbull and the Malihini Corporation."

"And our link with the transceiver we found in our car." Ned's thumb tapped the shipper's name. "Higashi Electronics."

Nancy checked the items. "You're right. There's the transceiver the Malihini Corporation ordered. So they're the ones who did it." She rolled up the two papers again. "First they tried to stop us from searching for Lisa. Then they tried to spy on us."

"I don't get it." Ned replaced the curtain rod. "How did a Malihini Corporation shipping manifest wind up inside a Windward bearer bond?"

"It has to be one of two things," Nancy replied. "Either Lisa found this manifest somewhere else and included it with her papers, or the manifest itself was tucked inside the bearer bond."

"For what reason?" asked Ned.

"Your guess is as good as mine. Let's go talk to the desk clerk."

74

Nancy and Ned left the building via the fire escape. They waited in the garden, watching Bess and George walk back to the car. Then they strode through the front entrance.

"Afternoon." The clerk smiled. "What can I do for you?"

As they crossed the lobby, Nancy took out her photo of Lisa. She put it on the counter. "We're private detectives. We're looking for this girl. Have you seen her?"

"Miss Faulkner? Sure!" He glanced at the photo, then handed it back to Nancy. "You just missed her. She checked out about an hour ago."

Nancy replaced the photo in her bag. "How'd she pay for the room?"

"Credit card. But it wasn't her credit card. It was charged to a company account—the Malihini Corporation."

Them again! "Any idea why Miss Faulkner left?" Nancy prodded.

"I guess it was because of that phone call," the clerk replied. "Came about four o'clock. I handle the switchboard and put it through. Next thing I know, the girl's bolting out of here. Didn't even sign out! Then the movers showed up . . ."

"Movers?" echoed Nancy and Ned in unison.

"Yeah, the same bunch that brought that furniture a few days ago. They had orders to clean out the place. Kahuku Moving Van Company."

"Thank you." Nancy stepped away from the

counter. "Listen, if you hear from Miss Faulkner again, please contact the Honolulu police."

"Why? What's the problem?" The clerk looked wary.

"She's a runaway," Ned answered.

"Okay, I'll call them."

His bland tone told Nancy that he wouldn't even try. A place like the Ka Lae wanted no trouble with the police.

Silently she followed Ned out to the car.

Outside, the Hawaiian night was cool and still. A golden glimmer rested on the mountains, the last remnant of sunset. Nancy quickly told Bess and George what had happened inside. Then, flushed with inspiration, she led her friends down the street to a corner convenience store.

"I've got an idea," Nancy murmured, checking the shopworn Yellow Pages at the pay phone. After popping her coins in, she punched in the numbers.

The phone at the other end rang twice. A woman answered. "Good evening. Kahuku Moving Van Company."

"Hi, I'm Lisa Faulkner," Nancy said, winking at her friends. "You people moved my furniture this afternoon. But you left my couch behind. Could you send your men over to pick it up, please?"

"I'm sorry, Ms. Faulkner, but you'll have to clear that with the people who rented the van."

Nancy experienced a tingle of foreboding.

"Uh, no problem." She waited several seconds, then added, "Oh, dear! I seem to have lost their number. Could you?"

"Sorry, Ms. Faulkner, but we have no phone number for them. Just their post office box." The woman sounded sympathetic. "Why don't you call the operator and tell her you need the number for the Malihini Corporation?"

"I'll do that. Thanks." Nancy hung up.

When Nancy had related the gist of the conversation, Ned said, "This is crazy! Why would a bunch of business people help a teenager run away from home?"

Bess looked around nervously. "I don't know about you guys, but I'm scared. Who are these Malihini guys? They set us up—planting stuff in our car! I don't like being a target!"

"Neither do I," Nancy said, rounding the front of her car. "I think it's high time we had a talk with Alice Faulkner."

"About what?" asked Ned.

"The business difficulties she and Ross mentioned," Nancy replied. "Every time we go after Lisa, we run smack into the Malihini Corporation. How come? There's a business angle to this case that just won't go away." She lifted the door latch. "And it's time we found out what it is."

The plantation house gleamed in the moonlight. Palm trees rustled in the soft breeze. As Nancy and her friends approached the house, a woman's silhouette appeared in the bright rectangle of the doorway.

Alice Faulkner leaned forward expectantly. "Nancy! Have you found her?"

Nancy felt miserable. Breaking this news was a hard thing to do. "I'm sorry, Mrs. Faulkner. Somebody tipped Lisa off that we were coming. It's just a temporary setback, though."

Alice's proud shoulders drooped, but she managed to conceal the extent of her disappointment. "Please come in. I do hope you'll stay for dinner. I could use some pleasant company for a change." With a weary smile, she led them to the dining room. "Ross and his associates are here. Trying to comfort me, or so they say. Personally, I'd rather have them out looking for Lisa."

Nancy stepped into the dining room, where vast sliding-glass doors offered a panoramic view of the palm-studded garden. Ross Rafferty stared into the night, shoulders tense. Mitsuo Kaimonsaki stood by the liquor cabinet. He was pouring brandy for a woman who was standing next to Rafferty.

The woman was nearly as tall as Mitsuo in her stiletto heels. An aquamarine cocktail dress molded her superb figure. Her beautiful face was framed by a tumble of stylishly coiffed blond hair.

Alice went right over to her. "Amy, I don't believe you've met Nancy Drew. This is Amy Sorenson, the bank's vice-president."

Flashing a warm smile, Amy nodded. "How do you do, Nancy."

"My friends—" Nancy gestured at her companions. "Ned Nickerson—Bess Marvin—George Fayne."

Amy's green eyes blinked in disbelief. Nancy sensed Amy's sudden coolness.

"*You're* George?" The woman's tone dripped disapproval.

"I have been all my life." George lifted her chin. "Do you have a problem with that?"

Looking a little embarrassed, Amy smoothed the skirt of her dress. "Er—no, it's just a bit unusual, that's all."

Holding a chair for Alice, Mitsuo remarked, "Why don't we start dinner? The food smells delicious."

Nancy and her friends enjoyed the old-fashioned Polynesian dinner: roast suckling pig with baked taro, cooked spinach, and *poe,* a starchy pudding made of papaya, mangoes, and bananas.

Midway through dessert, Nancy asked, "Mrs. Faulkner, what do you know about the Malihini Corporation?"

Clink! Ross dropped his fork, his eyes round with shock. Amy cleared her throat and lowered her eyes. Mitsuo stared quizzically at Nancy.

Alice looked troubled. "Nancy, where did you hear that name?"

Snorting in disgust, Ross threw his napkin on

the table. "Go ahead, Alice. Tell her! Then we can take out an ad in the *Star-Bulletin* and tell the whole world!"

"Mind your manners and hush!" Alice said sharply. "This is my home, and Nancy is my guest. I want to know where she heard about the Malihini Corporation." Alice looked at Nancy purposefully. "Well?"

So Nancy told her. When she had finished, Alice leaned back in her chair. "It fits. It fits so well." She closed her eyes in misery. "It's what I feared all along. They're using Lisa to strike at me."

"Who are 'they'?" Nancy asked.

"The Malihini Corporation first appeared in Honolulu a year ago," Alice explained. "They bought real estate all over the Islands. In time, they became Hawaii's biggest developer. But nobody seems to know who they are."

"Why are they after you, Mrs. Faulkner?"

Alice made a steeple of her fingers. "Our bank has been putting money into the Konalani project. It's a planned community on Oahu's north shore. We have a lot of money riding on the outcome of that project."

Ross thumped the table with his fist. "And they're trying to sandbag us! You see, Nancy, our bank has been having a serious problem with cash in recent years. The Konalani project will save us. But if our investors ever learn that the project is in danger of collapse, they'll sell their shares of Windward Bancorp stock!"

"You lost me," Bess murmured.

Amy smiled indulgently. "It's simple economics, dear. Windward Bancorp is the company that owns the bank. They have stockholders, just like any other company. If the stockholders dump their shares, someone else can buy them all up and take control of Windward Bancorp."

So that was why Ross Rafferty didn't want to go to the police, Nancy thought. The merest hint of Faulkner family trouble might trigger a panic among Windward stockholders. But how could he be so callous? There was no way the bank's well-being measured up against the life and safety of a human being!

Nancy's brow furrowed. "And you have no idea who's on the board of this corporation?"

"None whatsoever." Amy shook her head. "Believe me, we've tried to find out. No luck! Not even Lester could learn anything."

"Who's Lester?" asked Ned.

"Lester Jarman, my late husband's business partner," Alice explained. "He and Charlie founded Windward Fidelity Bank thirty years ago. Lester's retired now. He's still sharp as a tack, though. Next to me, he's the biggest stockholder in Windward Bancorp."

Nancy tapped her lower lip thoughtfully. So the Malihini Corporation was trying to steal the bank away from the Faulkner family. That made sense. But how was helping Lisa run away from home supposed to accomplish that?

Nancy shivered. To save Lisa Trumbull, Nancy would have to trail a pack of killers through the strange and treacherous world of high finance!

Chapter

Eleven

THE NEXT MORNING Nancy and Ned visited the main station of the Honolulu Police Department. A grizzled desk sergeant directed them down the hall to the office of the Criminal Investigation Division.

"Hi, Nancy!" Tim DiPrizio called out. He was in shirtsleeves, his feet propped on the desk. Martin Giles sat across the aisle, painstakingly typing with two fingers. "What brings you kids downtown?"

"We need some information, Tim." Nancy quickly explained how the Malihini Corporation had foiled them. When she had finished, Tim remarked, "Malihini Corporation, eh? Never heard of them."

"I'm not surprised," Nancy added. "They keep a really low profile. I was hoping you guys could dig up some tax information on them."

"Be happy to." Tim glanced at his partner. "You're the team intellectual, Marty. Where do you go for corporate tax records?"

"The state Department of Accounting and General Services," Martin answered, pulling on his suit jacket. "My friend Darlene works over there. Let me go talk to her. You folks sit tight. I'll be back."

Martin was as good as his word. He returned to the detectives' office an hour later and handed Nancy a slim manila folder. He wasn't smiling.

"That's a copy of the state tax file," Martin told her. "There isn't a whole lot on this Malihini Corporation. This just says they're an overseas investments firm. They don't even have an office here, just that post office box. According to Darlene, the Malihini Corporation was chartered in the Cayman Islands. They're very careful not to break any laws. They always pay their city, state, and county tax assessments. They always pay by mail, too, using checks drawn on the Bank of Nova Scotia."

Tim sat on the edge of his desk. "What's the bottom line, partner?"

Martin sighed. "These Malihini dudes are under a cloak of total secrecy. There's no way to get a handle on them. Compared to the Malihini Corporation, the mob is a bunch of blabbermouths."

Disappointed, Nancy handed back the file. "Thanks, guys."

Martin stroked his goatee thoughtfully. "Know what's bothering me?"

"What?" asked Tim, standing up.

The black officer's gaze shifted curiously to Nancy. "You tried to find these Malihini guys. No luck! I tried the state tax people. Nothing! So how did Lisa Trumbull find them?"

"Maybe they came to her," Ned offered.

"I think you're right, Ned." Nancy's voice turned somber. "No one tries to kill people in a rigged car accident unless they've got something to hide."

"You think the girl's in trouble?" asked Tim.

"I think she got in over her head," Nancy answered honestly.

As Nancy and Ned walked out the door, Martin said, "You kids be careful, all right? If you need any help, give us a call. I don't like the sound of all this."

Nancy slogged unhappily through the thick sand of Waikiki Beach. Two hours had passed since their visit to the police station. Since then, Nancy and her friends had split up, pursuing a number of different leads. Nancy and Bess were at the beach, interviewing lifeguards and surfers.

So far, it hadn't been a productive effort. Nancy had shown Lisa's photo up and down Waikiki, but no one remembered the girl. She looked too much like all the other teenagers wandering around.

Suddenly Nancy heard Bess's excited voice. "Nancy! Come quick! I found someone!"

Nancy trudged back up the sandy slope. Bess waited anxiously beside a tall surfer who was diligently waxing his board. "I figured you ought to talk to him, Nan. His name's Lance, and he's seen Lisa!"

Lance straightened up. With his well-muscled physique and skin the color of old hickory, he reminded Nancy of an ad for suntan lotion.

Lifting the photo, she asked, "Do you recognize this girl?"

"Yeah, I've seen her." Lance studied the photo carefully. "This morning. Just after sunrise. I was riding my board about a mile out. Pretty good surf here when it's high tide. Not as good as Kuilei or the Banzai Pipeline, but it's a wild ride coming in."

Nancy took back the photo. "Lisa was surfing?"

"Awww, no. She was with a big guy. They were walking on the beach. Like they were looking for something, you know? Then the big guy started yelling. The girl got scared and tried to run, but he grabbed her wrist. Then this car pulled up. A brown-haired woman got out and held the girl.

Meanwhile, that big guy went crazy! He was dumping out litter baskets—kicking the trash around. I figured the girl needed help, so I started in on my board."

"Then what?" asked Nancy, listening intently.

"The brown-haired woman got him calmed down. All three of them got in the car and took off." Lance's face showed regret. "They were gone by the time I got to shore."

After thanking Lance for his help, Nancy and Bess headed back to Kalakaua Avenue again. Nancy's thoughts were racing. What if the people with Lisa had been part of the Malihini Corporation? If so, they must have counted Lisa's money the previous night and come up fifty thousand short. They would have made Lisa retrace her steps, hoping to find the missing bearer bond —the one Nancy had found at the Ka Lae apartment house.

She explained all this to Bess, who asked, "Why would the big guy get so upset, Nan? It's Diana Faulkner's money."

"Bearer bonds can be cashed by anybody," Nancy replied. "The Malihini Corporation was planning to double-cross Lisa all along. I'll bet they promised Lisa they'd help her get to San Francisco to live with Michele." Nancy's stomach felt hollow. "Only I don't think Lisa realizes just how vicious the Malihini Corporation really is. She doesn't know how they've tried to hurt her grandmother. She probably thinks they're on her side, never realizing that they could turn on her at any time."

"At least Lisa's still alive," Bess added.

"As of this morning." Nancy flashed a worried look at her friend. "But you heard what Lance said. They're no longer treating Lisa like a guest. Sounds as if she's their prisoner now."

As they passed a dress shop, Nancy turned her gaze toward the window. She ignored the fashions on display, concentrating instead on the mirrored reflection of the street. It was an old detective trick, a way to check to see if she was being followed.

Ice water seemed to fill Nancy's veins. A familiar face had appeared in the crowd behind her. A moon-shaped face topped by slick black hair!

The International Market Place was just ahead. Nancy steered Bess toward the entrance. "We're being followed," she whispered, shepherding Bess into the mall. "I want you to go to a gift shop and pretend to be shopping. Make yourself noticeable. I want his eye on you."

"What will you be doing, Nancy?"

"I hope to set him up."

Nancy left Bess's side the minute she entered the gift shop. Nancy took cover behind a concrete pillar. Bess put on a nice show, playing the part of an airhead tourist. The man's face appeared in the window. Nancy flattened herself behind the pillar. His gaze on Bess, he moved farther along.

As soon as he was out of her line of sight, Nancy crossed the lobby and entered a phone booth. The phone at the other end rang sharply. George's voice answered. "Hello?"

"George, it's me." Nancy exhaled in relief. "Listen, our friend is back—the one with the moon face." Not pausing for an instant, she told George the plan. "I'm going to lead him back to the boat. You hide out on the pier while Bess and I go aboard. When the man leaves, I want you to follow him."

"All *right!* It's about time I got in on the action."

"Don't take chances, George. Okay?"

"Okay. Be careful, Nan!"

Nancy hung up. As she emerged from the phone booth, she saw Bess in the Market Place lobby wearing a floppy straw hat.

Her smile forced, Bess shifted her eyes to the left. "He's outside."

"I've set him up, Bess, but I'll need your help to pull it off. It's acting time again. Do a lot of talking while we walk. Tell me about Hawaii."

As they strolled back onto the sidewalk, Bess began a rambling monologue about beaches, gift stores, and palm trees. This left Nancy free to check the window reflections and make sure their enemy was still on the trail.

He was! The moon-faced man sauntered along, completely unaware that Nancy had identified him. Bess was doing a great job. Between her giggly chatter and Nancy's leisurely pace, the man probably thought they were out on a shopping trip.

When they reached Ala Wai, Nancy boarded the *Kahala* and pretended to check a mooring line. Bess went straight below. Peering out of the corner of her eye, Nancy saw the moon-faced man loitering at the dockmaster's shed.

Nancy went below. Hot, stifling air filled the cabin. She cranked open the hatch. A blast of cool sea air streamed past her face, filling the main salon.

Bess stood in her stateroom doorway. The giggling tourist was gone. "Nancy, is he still out there?"

Leaning against the bulkhead, Nancy eased the blind away from the porthole. Her gaze swept the parking lot. It was empty!

"Bess, I don't see him—!"

Thump! Nancy's gaze zipped upward. Something had hit the roof of the cruiser's main cabin.

The noise sounded like footsteps. And they were heading straight for the open hatch!

Chapter

Twelve

THUMP-BUMP-BUMP! Nancy looked around desperately for a weapon. He was almost to the hatchway!

Something flashed through the opening. Gasping, Nancy raised her fist. The object struck the deck with a hollow thump, bounced toward her—and came to rest between her sneakers.

Nancy grinned. It was a white rubber ball covered with blue stars.

Bess groaned in relief and slumped against the wall.

A childish voice yowled. "Maaaaa! I *lost* it!"

"Jason, I told you not to play around other people's boats!"

Nancy returned to the porthole. She saw a tired-looking woman drag a sniffling toddler back to another cabin cruiser.

Across the lot, the door at the rear of the dockmaster's shed suddenly swung open. The moon-faced man appeared, wiping his hands on a paper towel. He crumpled it into a ball, lobbed it into the trash can, and moved toward the *Kahala.*

At that moment a brunette in a swimsuit approached from the other direction.

"George!" Bess gasped, standing at Nancy's elbow.

"I told her not to take chances," Nancy said in a worried voice.

As George approached the man, Nancy fretted. It was too late to warn her friend away now. . . .

"Excuse me. Are you looking for somebody?" George asked, her hands on her hips.

The man produced a battered wallet. "Yeah, you might say that." He flipped it open, revealing a laminated card. "I'm a private eye. I'm looking for Nancy Drew. You live around here?"

"Yes, I live here." Deadpan, George gestured at a big motor sailer at the end of the pier. "Lived here two years. Never heard of a Nancy Drew."

"Maybe you've seen her around, then." He put away his ID. "Tall girl. Reddish blond hair. Lives aboard that boat there."

"The *Kahala?*" George feigned a look of confusion. "That's Mrs. Faulkner's boat. Are you sure you're at the right marina?"

Nonplussed, the man pressed on. "Maybe you've seen Nancy's friends around. A blond girl. Couple of guys named Ned and George."

Nancy sucked in her breath sharply.

Mischief gleamed in George's eyes. "Hmmmm, maybe I have seen George around. What a hunk! He plays football for Oklahoma State." She grinned. "Want me to pass on any messages?"

"Ah, thanks—but no." Looking very worried, the man retreated across the parking lot. "I got to get back to work. See you!"

George watched him dash across the street and climb into the driver's seat of an older-model car. Tires squealed as he pulled away from the curb. George smiled and made a circle with her thumb and forefinger.

Nancy and Bess hurried out to greet her.

"If you want to find him, his license number is HWI zero-two-eight," George said, beaming.

"Nice work, George." Nancy hugged her friend. Then the three of them headed back to the boat.

Bess and George decided to return little Jason's rubber ball. While they were gone, Nancy, on impulse, flagged a cab and headed uptown. She had a few things she wanted to clear up before she looked for the moon-faced man. She had to learn more about the Malihini Corpora-

93

tion. Why did they operate out of a post office box? Why had they incorporated in the Cayman Islands? Once she was able to answer those questions, she hoped she'd be able to figure out what they wanted with Lisa Trumbull.

And Nancy had a good idea who to ask. . . .

Jack Showalter was on the phone when Nancy arrived. Flashing a welcoming smile, he gestured at the guest chair beside his desk.

"Yes, well, those interest payments are due, Mr. Gavalu." Jack made an apologetic motion with his free hand. "I understand. Yes. Nice talking to you, sir. Goodbye!" Hanging up, he let out a low groan. "What a day!"

"Who were you talking to?" Nancy asked curiously.

Jack flushed self-consciously. "The deputy finance minister of Kiribati. But he's not the high-priority item around here these days. Lisa Trumbull is. How are you making out?"

"Jack, have you ever heard of the Malihini Corporation?"

"Who hasn't? They're knocking the legs out from under this bank."

"Have you ever run into them?"

"Just once. I put together a nice little loan package a few months ago. I even got old man Rafferty to approve it. Then the Malihini Corporation came out of nowhere, stole my clients, and blew me out of the water!" Scowling at the memory, he added, "Why are you so interested in them?"

"I did some checking with the Honolulu police. They said the Malihini Corporation was set up in the Cayman Islands," Nancy said quietly. "You're the banker, Jack. Is there anything significant in that?"

Features thoughtful, Jack leaned back in his chair. "Caymans, eh? You know, those islands have the tightest bank secrecy in the world. Tighter than Switzerland! Some people use the Cayman Islands as a tax dodge. In my trade, we call it 'chasing the hot dollar.' What people do is go to the Caymans and set up their own private corporation. Then they open a bank account in the corporation's name, using a bank with a branch office here in the States."

"Like the Bank of Nova Scotia?" Nancy asked.

"Exactly!" Jack warmed to his topic. "It's a cute way to cheat the government. You make money in the corporation's name, squirrel it away in the Caymans, and, if you ever need any, draw it out through the branch bank. Let's suppose you made a million dollars, Nancy, and reported only ten grand to the IRS. How is the government going to prove you're a liar? It can't get into your Cayman bank to see how much you *really* made. That's what I mean—it's the perfect tax dodge."

Nancy mulled it over. "Jack, suppose you wanted to run your Cayman corporation out of a post office box. Could it be done?"

"Sure! All you have to do is set up either a telephone or a computer link with your Cayman bank. The bank will issue checks the minute you ask for them. Why, with computer equipment, you could run your corporation from the seawall at Sunset Beach!"

Nancy frowned thoughtfully. At first she'd assumed that the Malihini Corporation was based in the Cayman Islands. Now she wasn't so sure. The Malihini Corporation might be a front for someone in Honolulu. Someone very close to the Faulkners and to Windward Fidelity Bank.

Reaching across the desk, Nancy took Jack's telephone and tapped out the number of the Honolulu police's CID. Seconds later, Tim Di-Prizio's baritone voice answered. "Criminal Investigation Division."

"Tim, hi! It's Nancy Drew. Listen, I've got a lead. A license number. HWI-zero-two-eight. Can you run a make for me?"

"Just a sec." After a couple of moments, Nancy heard a police Teletype rattling noisily. When Tim returned, "We bombed out. That car's rented to a Waikiki agency."

"What about the person who rented it from the agency?" she asked.

Tim sounded frustrated. "The Department of Transportation lists only the owner—the Makaha agency. To get the name of the driver, we'd have to subpoena the agency's records. We can't do that without a court order."

"Oh, well. Thanks, Tim. Bye!"

As she hung up, she noticed Jack's sympathetic expression. He said quietly, "You know, maybe I can help."

Jack picked up the phone and asked to be put through to Mr. Carstairs, the president of the Makaha agency. Then he switched on the speaker.

"Mr. Carstairs, this is Jack Showalter at the Windward Fidelity Bank. We have a little problem here, and I wonder if you could help us."

"Why, of course, Jack!"

"One of our stockholders had his credit card stolen," Jack said smoothly, giving Nancy a sly wink. "The thief apparently used it to rent a car at your agency. Our stockholder was billed for it."

Carstairs apologized profusely and asked Jack for the license number. Jack gave it to him. The phone was silent for several moments. Then Carstairs returned, sounding a bit confused. "Jack, that can't be right. We rented that car just yesterday to the Apex Detective Agency. The bill was sent to the Malihini Corporation. Are you certain about that number?"

Jack grunted. "Let me get back to you on that. Thanks a lot." Hanging up, he took a deep breath and expelled it in a long whoosh. "How was I?"

"Superb!" Nancy left her chair. "If you ever give up banking, Jack, you'd make a great detective. See you later."

"Take care!" he called after her.

Shortly before dusk, Nancy stepped down from the bus in Palama, a rundown neighborhood on the west side of Honolulu. She went to the address of the Apex Detective Agency that she had gotten from the Yellow Pages. The agency was located in a tumbledown office building on Vineyard Boulevard. She rode the dilapidated elevator to the third floor, her thoughts racing.

The Malihini Corporation must have hired the Apex people to search for Lisa, she mused. That's why I saw that moon-faced man staking out Lisa's apartment. Later, after Malihini had made contact with Lisa, they'd told Apex to follow me.

Well, two could play the surveillance game. Nancy intended to make certain that the detective agency was actually in that building. Then she would call in her friends.

The third-floor hallway smelled as if it had just been painted. Nancy sidestepped a full trash barrel as she left the elevator. Her footsteps sounded loud as they echoed in the empty hallway. The other side of paradise, she thought as she looked around the shabby surroundings.

At the end of the corridor Nancy found a frosted-glass door. The name read APEX DETEC-

TIVE AGENCY, with WALLY CERRADO—PRES. in smaller type.

Turning, Nancy returned to the elevator. Apex was here, all right. Now she and her friends would arrange a surprise for the moon-faced man.

She pressed the elevator button. Winches whined in the basement as the car climbed up.

Suddenly Nancy heard a footstep behind her. A broad hand shot out of the darkness, clasping itself around Nancy's mouth. The pungent odor of chloroform filled her nostrils. She kicked and struggled, but it was like grappling with a mountain.

Darkness rimmed Nancy's field of vision. Her knees began to buckle. Then everything went black.

Chapter

Thirteen

Nancy's mind groped its way out of the dark. She was vaguely conscious of motion and of sounds fading in and out. The distant cry of a frigate bird. The *thrumming* of tires on asphalt. The muted *ka-thump* of a car's automatic transmission shifting to a lower gear.

Slowly her eyes opened. She was lying on the back seat of a luxury car. The driver's head loomed above her, round and bald. She started to sit up, then felt a nylon cord wound tight around her wrists.

Looking out into the twilight, Nancy just caught a glimpse of a darker peak through the side window. We're heading into the mountains, she thought. I never should have gone to Apex by myself. Now the Malihini Corporation has me, too!

Minutes later the car slowed to a crawl, then stopped. Nancy heard the driver's door open and then close.

The rear door swung open. A shadowy hulk reached in. Nancy tensed, preparing to struggle, but the man lifted her as tenderly as he might a baby.

Outside, she got a good look at him. He was built like a pro wrestler, but his face had an innocent expression that didn't match his dangerous-looking bulk.

As the man strolled into the garden of a palatial estate, Nancy twisted and struggled. But she couldn't shake his iron grip at all. At last they came to a patio aglow with light from hidden lamps. Three people were sitting in white wrought-iron furniture, sipping tall drinks. Nancy recognized two of them.

Mitsuo Kaimonsaki and Amy Sorenson!

The third was a wizened, shrew-eyed old man whose Hawaiian shirt seemed one size too large for him.

Nancy's captor spoke. "I brung her like you wanted, boss."

"You did well, Oscar boy. Now, set her down," the old man said in a whispery voice. "Hello

101

there, Nancy. I'm Lester Jarman. I believe you already know my guests."

Jarman! Nancy remembered at once. C. K. Faulkner's old business partner, the retired co-founder of Windward Fidelity Bank.

"Oscar, untie Ms. Drew." Lester flashed a contrite smile. "I apologize for the melodramatic way you were brought here to Waikaloa, Nancy. But I think you can appreciate the need for secrecy."

Nancy rubbed her sore wrists. "Did anyone ever tell you that kidnapping is a crime, Mr. Jarman?"

"Seems I might have read that someplace." He sipped nonchalantly from his drink. "You know, you've got my people all stirred up, Nancy."

Folding her arms, Nancy replied, "Why don't you drop the act? It's obvious that you three set up the Malihini Corporation."

Lester Jarman winced. "I knew she'd say that." He turned to Amy. "Well, this was your idea. Would you care to set Ms. Drew straight?"

Nancy blinked in surprise. So these people weren't the Malihini Corporation! Then why had they kidnapped her and brought her here to Lester Jarman's estate?

"Allow me." Mitsuo put his empty glass on the table. "Nancy, some of us feel that you've been a little too . . . indiscreet in your investigation."

"Don't sugarcoat it like that, Mitsuo," Amy

interrupted. She glared at Nancy. "Look, you're upsetting far too many people these days!"

"You mean, like those in the Malihini Corporation?"

"That's exactly what I mean." Amy stood up suddenly. "I want Lisa back as much as anybody. However, I am *not* willing to see the bank destroyed in the process! Ross and Alice told you that our bank is highly vulnerable. The last thing we need right now is you blaring the name 'Malihini Corporation' all over the police teletypes!"

Nancy's eyebrows lifted at that. "And how do you know that I've been to the police, Ms. Sorenson?"

Amy Sorenson flushed slightly. "A pair of detectives came to see me this afternoon. DiPrizio and Giles. They were not very polite."

Mitsuo Kaimonsaki said calmly, "I can assure you, we're not criminals. And never meant to hurt you." His hands fluttered slightly. "We only wanted to have a private chat with you. Please! Can't we keep the police out of this?"

Lester Jarman cleared his throat. His subordinates turned to face him, obedient and expectant.

"Mitsuo, why don't you go in and fix yourself another drink? You too, Amy. I'd like to talk to Ms. Drew alone."

Mr. Kaimonsaki rose immediately and headed

for the luxurious mansion, but Amy Sorenson loitered on the patio. "I wish you'd let me stay, Lester. I'm sure I could convince this girl—"

"Now, Amy, don't you fret. I can handle things."

Beep-beep-beep-beep! All eyes were drawn to the poolside table. The harsh sound was coming from Miss Sorenson's brushed leather handbag. Nancy glanced at the woman just in time to see an alarmed expression cross her lovely face.

No one moved. Lester said querulously, "Will you shut that beeper off?"

"Of course." Rushing to the table, Amy Sorenson grabbed the handbag. The sound died, and she set off for the house, swinging the bag casually.

"I hate those fool things," Lester muttered, shifting his position in the deck chair. He tilted his head toward the house. "Don't you mind them, Nancy. They're just worried about the Malihini Corporation."

"Mrs. Faulkner has better reason to worry," Nancy said, taking a seat. "They've got her granddaughter."

"So I hear."

"You don't sound too concerned about it, Mr. Jarman."

Reaching for his drink again, Jarman said, "Don't get me wrong. I like Alice. I do. I just never could understand her maudlin preoccupation with her family. Kids!" He snorted and took a sip. "Blamed nuisance. Worse than beepers. At least you can shut beepers off.

"Let's deal," Jarman murmured, a fiery gleam in his eyes. "You want something. I want something. You want Alice's granddaughter. I want the Malihini Corporation. I want them real bad, Nancy. *Nobody* tries to steal my bank away from me!" He licked his thin lips wolfishly. "You tell me what you've found out, and I'll tell you what you want to know. Deal?"

Nancy nodded. Then, keeping her voice low, she described her talk with Jack Showalter. When she was through, Lester Jarman chuckled and slapped his skinny thigh. "Cayman Islands, eh? Very clever! I thought Malihini was bribing our employees. But it sure looks as if there's a rotten apple in the corporate barrel, doesn't it?"

"Who could it be?" asked Nancy.

"Someone who knows the kind of bind we're in," he explained. "It all goes back a few years, Nancy. Ross Rafferty came over here from the mainland. Everybody said he was some kind of financial hotshot. He started lending money right and left to all those little countries in the Pacific. Then the world debt crisis caught up with them. The Pacific countries couldn't make their interest payments. We had no money coming in."

"That's what Ross meant by a cash problem," Nancy commented.

The old man nodded. "That's a fancy way of saying old Ross gambled on those Third World loans and came up empty. So Alice and me, we took control of the bank away from Ross and put all our remaining money into the Konalani project. When it's finished, it'll pay off big. We'll have enough to cover our bad loans and have a tidy profit, to boot."

"Then the Malihini Corporation mysteriously appeared," added Nancy. "And they began sniping at your project."

"That's right. What a coincidence, eh?" The old man tilted the brim of his Panama hat. "Ross is right, though. Whoever's behind Malihini wants our stockholders to dump their shares. Then they'll move in, buy them all up, and force me and Alice out."

"They?" echoed Nancy. "How many people could it be?"

"It's hard to tell. Ten—twenty—why, it could even be *one* person." He shrugged his thin shoulders. "Somebody who'd gone to the Caymans and chartered himself or herself as the Malihini Corporation."

Nancy stood slowly. "One thing still doesn't fit, Mr. Jarman. How did Lisa Trumbull get involved with the Malihini Corporation?"

"Good question, Nancy. Wish I knew. And now—"

Suddenly the bushes parted and Oscar appeared on the garden path.

Mr. Jarman finished his drink. "I expect you'll

want to be getting back to town, Nancy. Oscar will drive you." His lips crinkled in a wry smile. "I must say I've enjoyed our chat." As Nancy started down the path, Lester's voice brought her up short. "But watch yourself, Nancy. There are *sharks* in the water. It could be *anybody* behind the Malihini Corporation." His eerie laughter raised gooseflesh on Nancy's arms. "Why, it might even be me!"

Nancy said nothing during the long ride back to Honolulu. She was too busy thinking. Lester Jarman was right. Somebody at the bank was running the Malihini Corporation from behind the scenes. But who?

One by one, the suspects paraded through Nancy's mind.

Ross Rafferty? He was proud and ambitious. It must have really hurt his pride when Alice and Lester took control of the bank away from him. Not to mention Diana's divorce. Perhaps the Malihini Corporation was his bid to grab control of the bank and avenge himself on the Faulkner family all at the same time.

Then there was Mitsuo Kaimonsaki. What did he have to hide? She couldn't forget that it was Mitsuo who had originally let Lisa into the vault.

Amy Sorenson? As vice-president, Amy knew what kind of trouble the bank was in. She had the financial background necessary to set up a dummy corporation in the Cayman Islands. And then there were those instances of odd behavior from time to time. That episode with the beeper, for example. Nancy frowned suddenly, remembering her first meeting with the woman. Why had Amy reacted so strangely when she'd introduced her to George?

Lester Jarman? Nancy shuddered as she recalled his eerie laugh. The Malihini Corporation had plenty of money to spend. Lester was the wealthiest of the suspects. And the most ruthless, too!

Nancy's mind drifted back through the case.

Alice Faulkner? Probably not. Alice might have wanted custody of Lisa, but she would never endanger her granddaughter's life. She wouldn't leave Lisa in the hands of the criminals Lance had seen at the beach. Alice loved her granddaughter too much to ever consider that.

Diana Faulkner? This might be an elaborate scheme on Diana's part to keep custody of Lisa. Nancy hoped that wasn't the case. She didn't want to rescue Lisa Trumbull—only to send Lisa's mother to prison!

Oscar steered the limo into the Ala Wai lot. He got out and opened the door for Nancy. She didn't thank him. He muttered, "Evenin'!" and then got behind the wheel and drove away.

Nancy heard running footsteps behind her. "There you are!" Ned called.

She saw Ned rushing toward her, his arms

outstretched. Then she slipped into the comforting circle of his embrace.

"It's okay, Ned," she said in a small voice. "I'm all right."

Morning sunshine glimmered on the storefront windows of Vineyard Boulevard. Nancy leaned against a mailbox. In her pale yellow knit top and white jeans, she looked like a high school student.

Ned ambled across the street, grinned at her, and looked at his wristwatch. "Almost time. Any sign of Tim and Martin?"

"Not yet." Nancy glanced up the street. "Are Bess and George all set?"

"George is all ready, upstairs," Ned replied. "She signaled me from the hallway window. Our friend is in his office."

"And Bess is watching the alley, just in case he tries to leave that way." Shading her eyes, Nancy peered down the boulevard. "Oh, here they come."

A large sedan rolled up to the curb. Martin got out first. "Hi, Nancy. Is he upstairs?"

"Uh-huh. Are you all set?"

Tim got out of the car. "We'll go in first. Give us five minutes alone with him, then come on up. Having you walk in should really spook him."

Nancy nodded. "Okay, guys. Good luck."

Ned and Nancy waited breathlessly at the

front door. Long minutes passed. Ned kept glancing at his watch. Nancy breathed deeply.

Any minute now . . .

Suddenly Nancy heard a sharp, terrified scream. It was coming from the rear of the building—coming from Bess!

Chapter

Fourteen

"THIS WAY! HURRY!" Nancy pointed to a narrow alleyway beside the building. She and Ned raced down it. Just ahead, they saw Bess grappling with the moon-faced man.

The man looked up and saw them coming. Shoving Bess aside, he ran to the high chain-link fence, jumped up, and frantically tried to pull himself up to it.

There was an aluminum trash can at the corner of the building. Grabbing the lid, Nancy cocked her arm and let fly. The lid sailed across the yard, hitting the man on the back of the head. Yowling, he tumbled to the ground.

Ned grabbed the man's shirtfront and hauled

him to his feet. Huffing and puffing, the man launched a shaky right at Ned's chin, but Ned ducked it easily and put him away with a solid right cross.

"Police! Hold it!" Tim's voice bellowed.

The detectives pounded down the fire escape. Tim held his .357 Magnum service revolver in one hand and his badge in the other. Martin vaulted the rail and dropped into the alley.

Grabbing the moon-faced man by the shoulders, Martin spun him around and pushed him up against the fence. "Spread 'em."

"Hey! What is this?" the man complained. "I haven't done anything wrong. Those kids assaulted me. Arrest *them!*"

"Yeah, you're a regular choirboy, aren't you?" Martin frisked him thoroughly. "Turn! Keep your hands up!"

The man obeyed meekly.

"Are you Wally Cerrado, president of the Apex Detective Agency?" Tim asked.

"That's me." Wally licked his lips in apprehension. "Look, I didn't mean these kids any harm. I was only doing my job."

"Why did you run away when you saw us coming?" Martin asked.

Wally grimaced in embarrassment. "Well, I owe a few bucks around town. I thought you guys were here to collect."

Nancy asked, "How did the Malihini Corporation hire you?"

"I—I don't have to answer that. You're not a cop."

"No, but if I were you, Wally, I'd talk to the young lady," Tim advised. "You picked the wrong client when you took on the Malihini Corporation."

"What do you mean?" Wally mumbled.

"Remember Lisa Trumbull? The girl they hired you to find? Well, they're holding her prisoner," Tim replied. "You fingered the girl for Malihini. So I guess that makes you an accessory, doesn't it?"

"I never came anywhere near Lisa Trumbull!" Wally's desperate gaze traveled from the cops to Nancy. "Come on, you guys. Give me a break!"

"Give *us* one," Nancy urged. "Tell us everything you know about the Malihini Corporation."

Wally thought it over for a long moment. Then he shook his head sadly. "I should've known it was too good to be legit. Okay, I'll play ball. Come on up to my office."

Minutes later they were all gathered around Wally's desk. He pulled his Malihini folder out of an old file cabinet and laid it on his well-used blotter. "This is everything I've got."

As Martin thumbed through the folder, Tim pulled out his notebook and began taking the private eye's statement.

"How did the Malihini Corporation hire you?" asked Nancy.

"They sent me a letter. Express courier, plus a retainer—a check for ten thousand dollars. They told me that Lisa had run away from home. They were sure she was still here in Honolulu, and they wanted me to find her. So I staked out the girl's condo. Asked a few questions around town. But she never turned up."

"Why did you start following me?" asked Nancy.

"They told me to."

"How?"

"I got another express letter from the Malihini Corporation. Haven't had time to cash the check."

"May I see them, please?" Nancy asked.

The check was for twenty thousand dollars, issued by the Bank of Nova Scotia in the Cayman Islands. Wally looked on in dismay as Tim put it into his plastic evidence bag.

Nancy's gaze skimmed the letter. It was on quality bond paper with the legend THE MALIHINI CORPORATION across the top.

Dear Mr. Cerrado,

We are highly satisfied with your work on the Lisa Trumbull case. Now, however, we have need of your services in a more pressing matter. We wish you to place four people under surveillance, two men and two women. They are: Nancy Drew, Ned Nickerson, Bess Marvin, and George Fayne.

We want no action taken against these people at the present time. We will be contacting you in the near future to arrange a time and place for the transfer of your information.

The Malihini Corporation

"I did like they wanted," Wally said as Nancy handed the cops the letter. "I managed to find you three." His face turned rueful. "But I never got a line on that George Fayne guy."

Running footsteps sounded in the corridor. A worried-looking George appeared in the doorway. "Nancy! I've been looking all over for you guys!"

Wally's mouth fell open. "Hey—it's the boat girl!"

"Wally—" Nancy tried not to giggle. "Say hello to George Fayne!"

A short while later Nancy drove her friends to the bank. As they cruised along, Ned said, "You're looking thoughtful, Nancy."

"Curious, isn't it?" Nancy glanced at him. "The Malihini Corporation hired Wally to search for Lisa. Then, after we arrived in Hawaii, they told him to forget Lisa and concentrate on us. Let's look at that sequence of events again, okay?" Nancy tapped her thumb on the steering wheel. "Diana sends Lisa to the bank. Lisa is unhappy and grabs this opportunity to run away.

115

She cleans out her mother's safety deposit box. Later that afternoon, Ross Rafferty checks the vault and discovers the theft. Ross tells Diana what happened. Diana calls her mother." She lifted a forefinger. "Now—very soon after all this, Wally Cerrado gets that letter from the Malihini Corporation. They tell him Lisa is a runaway and give him ten thousand dollars to find her. What do you get from all that?"

"Wait a minute!" Ned frowned thoughtfully. "How did the Malihini Corporation find out about Lisa so fast?

George slapped the front seat. "Of course! The Malihini Corporation is run by one of Windward's top people. I'll bet they were all in Ross's office when he phoned Diana."

"Second point." Nancy lifted her thumb. "How come the Malihini Corporation never bothered with Lisa before? One day, she's a nobody to them. The next, they're ready to spend ten grand to find her. Why?"

Ned laughed aloud. "I get it! Lisa cleaned out the safety deposit box."

"Right." Nancy nodded slowly. "It was only *after* Lisa cleaned out the box that the Malihini Corporation went after her. Therefore, Lisa must have taken something of theirs out of the box."

"But how did something of Malihini's get into Diana Faulkner's safety deposit box?" asked George.

"A member of the Malihini Corporation put it there," Nancy said grimly. "Remember that shipping manifest I found? It was concealed inside one of Diana's bonds. The culprit must have done that with all of Malihini's papers." She eased the car into a parking space. "The way I figure it, Lisa grabbed the Malihini documents by accident when she emptied her mother's box. She found them later. She's probably a bright girl and realized who was behind the Malihini Corporation. So she decided to contact that person and deal those documents."

"And that explains why Wally was hired so quickly," Ned added as Nancy switched off the engine. "The culprit checked Diana's box, realized the Malihini papers were gone, and set Wally on Lisa's trail."

"Right!" Nancy opened her door. "And once they had Lisa safely stashed away at the Ka Lae, they sent Wally after us."

As Nancy and her friends entered the lobby, they ran into Jack Showalter. His tense face relaxed when he spotted them. "There you are! Mr. Rafferty sent me down to intercept you." He led them to the elevator. "Mrs. Faulkner and her daughter are upstairs. It's—well, it's pretty bad, Nancy."

A ripple of dread ran through her. Are we too late? Nancy wondered. Is Lisa dead?

Arriving at the executive suite, Nancy saw

Alice and Diana by the conference table. Diana was weeping like a child.

Between her anguished sobs, Diana gasped. "This is all my fault! I failed her, Mother. Lisa wouldn't have run away if I'd made her happy."

"Don't blame yourself, Di. You did your best." Alice's eyes filled with tears.

Nancy hurried across the room. "Mrs. Faulkner, what has happened?"

Taking a golden bracelet from the table, Mrs. Faulkner gave it to Nancy. "This is Lisa's. I gave it to her last Christmas."

Suddenly Nancy noticed Ross Rafferty, Mitsuo Kaimonsaki, and Amy Sorenson. They stood off by themselves, looking glum and miserable.

Alice handed Nancy a letter. "Ross got this in the mail with it." Her voice broke. "They—they wanted to prove that they really have her."

Nancy's stomach turned to ice as she read the terse, cruel message.

Rafferty—
We've got Lisa. Here's her bracelet. If you call the police, she's dead. Here are our terms: You, Jarman, Kaimonsaki, Sorenson, and the Faulkners will sell your shares in Windward Bancorp to us at a price we will name. Or else you'll never see Lisa again!
                              The Malihini Corporation

Chapter

Fifteen

Coming up behind Nancy, Ross said, "We can't be certain that the Malihini Corporation has Lisa. This could be a bluff."

"Lisa loved that bracelet!" Alice snapped, whirling to face him. "She never would have given it up."

Ross didn't meet her eyes. "We can't sell those shares. We mustn't! It'll be the end of the bank!"

"The bank can go hang!" Alice declared, her eyes flashing. "If I have to sell to save my granddaughter, I'll do it!"

Ross looked as if he'd just been shot. "You —you can't do this to me!"

119

"You did it to yourself, you moron!" Mitsuo exploded, clenching his fists. "You and your grandiose schemes! Lending money to all those small countries. I warned you against it! You've ruined me, Rafferty!"

Ross's face turned lobster red. "I'll remember this disloyalty. I'll get you, Kaimonsaki!"

"Ross!" Amy shouted. "Don't you see? We *have* to sell! The girl's life is at stake!"

As the shouting continued, Nancy and Ned ushered the Faulkner woman out. Taking Diana's arm, Nancy steered her toward the water cooler.

Diana gratefully accepted a cup of water. Gone was the self-centered artist Nancy had met earlier. In her place stood a tense, frightened woman deeply worried about her daughter.

Diana looked at Nancy with haunted eyes. "My agent tells me that one of my paintings may bring two hundred thousand at auction." She sobbed. "Right now I feel like burning it! Why did I let my work come between me and Lisa? She's the most important thing in my life. Why did I have to lose her?"

Nancy squeezed the woman's hands comfortingly. "You haven't lost her yet, Diana. There may still be a way to save her. Will you answer one question?"

Sniffling, Diana nodded.

"What did you keep in your safety deposit box?"

Diana shrugged. "My passport, my jewelry, this and that. I'm afraid I didn't keep track. I left the money matters to my advisors."

"Who were they?" Nancy asked.

"Father left me a substantial portfolio. Mitsuo Kaimonsaki took care of it at first. He's been with the bank since I was a girl. When I married Ross, he took over my affairs." Diana blew her nose softly. "Since we were divorced, Amy Sorenson has been serving as my financial advisor."

Nancy gave her a quick hug. "Thanks, Diana!"

On her way downstairs Nancy mulled over what she had learned. Whoever was running the Malihini Corporation had used Diana's safety deposit box because that person knew she rarely went to it and knew *that* because that person had been her financial advisor.

Nancy stopped in Jack Showalter's office, but he wasn't there. Sitting at his desk, she opened her shoulder bag and spread the clues out in a semicircle—the Higashi transceiver, the bearer bond, the shipping manifest. Nancy looked over the manifest. "Telephone speakers, tape recorder, electronic beeper," she murmured to herself.

Electronic beeper! Amy Sorenson carried one in her purse!

Nancy frowned. She was just beginning to figure this out. Amy had thought George was a *guy.* . . .

Nancy picked up the bearer bond. Too bad Lisa didn't write a message on this, she thought.

She might have told us where she's being held —Nancy paused suddenly.

But the bad guys don't know she didn't leave a message, do they?

She grinned, folding the thick paper once more. An idea was beginning to take shape. It was risky—but if it worked, it would lead her straight to Lisa.

Picking up Jack's phone, Nancy said, "Operator, put me through to the Honolulu police, please."

An hour later Nancy stood on the foredeck of the *Kahala*. A familiar voice hollered a greeting. Turning, she saw Tim and Martin walking down the wharf. Tim carried a brown-paper package under his arm.

"Welcome aboard, guys. That was quick."

"We took off right after you called," Tim said, climbing on board. "This is a dangerous plan, Nancy. Be careful."

"I will." Nancy led them below. "Did you bring all that wiretap stuff?"

"That, and a court order." Tim patted his parcel. "Let's go to work."

They set up shop in the main stateroom. Tim unwrapped the package to reveal a tangle of wires, two plastic components, and a tape recorder. After checking the components, he hooked up the tape recorder to the boat's cordless telephone. Meanwhile, Martin looped the smaller wires over Nancy's head. She concealed them under her collar.

Ned picked up a small plastic component. "What is this thing?"

"A miniaturized tape recorder," Martin explained as Nancy clipped it inside the waistband of her slacks. "The other one's a transponder—it emits a constant radio signal. Helps us keep track of you at all times." He stood up. "There! You're wired, Nancy."

With the others at her heels, Nancy headed for the cordless phone. She tapped out the number of the Faulkner estate.

"Hello?" Alice sounded subdued.

"Mrs. Faulkner, it's Nancy Drew. Listen, you mustn't do what that note says. You mustn't sell those shares."

"But, Nancy, if it's the only way to save Lisa—"

"If you do it, they'll kill Lisa!" Nancy interrupted. "Once they have your shares, they won't need Lisa anymore. Don't you see?"

The older woman sobbed quietly. "What —what can I do, then?"

"Don't do anything for the next ten hours," Nancy pleaded. "Just please—please give me ten more hours to bring Lisa home."

"All right." Alice sighed deeply. "What you have in mind—will it save Lisa?"

"It's our only chance, Mrs. Faulkner. Now, one other favor. Take the phone off the hook.

Don't talk to anyone from the bank. No one! Not even the top brass." She licked her lips nervously. "*Especially* the top brass! Okay? I'll be back with Lisa in a few hours."

As soon as Mrs. Faulkner hung up, Nancy dialed the number of Lester Jarman's estate. Moments later, Lester's whispery voice came on the line.

"Nancy Drew! To what do I owe this pleasure?"

"Mr. Jarman, I am very close to nailing the Malihini Corporation. I thought you might be interested."

"I'm always interested in the Malihini Corporation." Nancy could see him at the other end of the line, leaning forward, eager to close another secret deal. "What have you got to trade, Nancy?"

"I picked up this little item a while ago." Nancy pulled the bearer bond out of her shoulder bag. "I called Mrs. Faulkner to ask her about it, but she's not home. It looks like a deed or something. There's a picture of your bank, and it says, 'Pay to the bearer fifty thousand dollars.'"

"A bearer bond!" Lester exclaimed. "It must be one of the bonds Lisa took from our vault. Where did you find it?"

"A surfer gave it to me." Nancy said, lying. She did not have to fake the excitement in her voice. "There's something on the back. Looks like handwriting."

"What does it say?" Lester gasped.

"That's just it. I can't read it. There's been some water damage."

"Water damage?"

"No matter," Nancy added. "We'll soon find out if it's Lisa's handwriting."

Confused, Lester replied, "How? You said you couldn't read it."

"I can't read it, Mr. Jarman, but the Honolulu police can. They can put it under ultraviolet light. Who knows? Maybe Lisa tried to tell us where she is." Nancy winked at her friends. "I'm going to the police station in a little while. Would you call Mrs. Faulkner and ask her to meet me there?"

"Nancy, this is splendid!" the old man cackled. "You did the right thing in calling me. Indeed you did." His voice turned thick. "I suppose you'll want some money for your trouble."

Nancy scowled. Perhaps Lester Jarman had never broken any laws, but he was a crook at heart!

"I'll get back to you," Nancy said sweetly, then hung up.

Martin was doubled over with laughter. "Nancy, that was one of the best con jobs I've heard. You had him all the way!"

But Bess looked bewildered. "Nancy, I don't understand. Why did you call Mr. Jarman?"

"I need Lester Jarman to spread a rumor for

me," Nancy explained. "Jarman won't keep it to himself. He'll call Alice first. But she's not home. He'll get frustrated. He *has* to check it out! So he'll call the bank. I'm betting he talks to one of them—Rafferty, Kaimonsaki, or Sorenson. They'll want to know why he's calling. Jarman will have to tell them about that bearer bond with the handwriting on it."

Ned's eyes flickered in understanding. "I get it now. The culprit knows Lisa was at the beach!"

"Exactly!" Nancy nodded. "And their imagination will do the rest. They can't be certain that Lisa didn't leave a bearer bond with a surfer."

"How does that help us?" asked Bess.

"Jarman will tell them I'm taking it to the police," Nancy replied, leaning against the helm. "Don't you get it? The Malihini Corporation has to stop me *before* I can get there. They have to come after me right now!"

George grimaced worriedly. "Nancy, you set yourself up as a target!"

Nancy shook her head. "They won't come here, George. They'll try to separate me from you. Then they'll make their move."

"All we can do now is sit and wait." Martin pulled a pack of worn cards out of his pocket. "Anyone for gin rummy?"

They started a game of cards around the galley table, but no one could concentrate. Finally Bess threw her hand in. "Nancy! This is killing me! What if you're wrong?"

"I'm not, Bess." Nancy rotated her shoulders, trying to ease the tension. "They have to grab that bearer bond before I get it to the police. The way I figure it, somebody will call and suggest that I bring it to the bank first. But it'll be a setup. Once I leave the boat, they'll grab me."

"But we'll be able to follow using the transponder," Tim added.

As Bess mulled it over, understanding blossomed on her face. Her gaze flitted to the cordless phone. She swallowed hard. "Then—then the person who calls is the *killer!*"

Nancy smiled wryly. "Not necessarily a killer, Bess. The culprit could always—"

Suddenly the phone cut loose with a loud ring. Nancy picked it up. "Hello?"

"Hello, Nancy." The voice was smooth and calm. "Amy Sorenson here. I thought we might have a little chat."

Chapter

Sixteen

WHAT CAN I do for you, Ms. Sorenson?" Nancy asked pleasantly.

"I've had some rather startling news. Are you alone?"

"Yes, I am."

"Good." Amy sounded relieved. "Lester Jarman told me about that bearer bond. I don't mean to tell you your business, Nancy, but I really think you should bring it here to the bank. It should be under lock and key."

"I agree, Ms. Sorenson. In fact, I was just about to call the police."

"Good idea. There's a safe in my office. Why don't you bring your evidence here and lock it up? Then no one can touch it until the police arrive."

Nancy feigned reluctance. "Well, I don't know . . ."

"Look, I'll send my limo right over. You call the police and ask them to meet you here."

"Sounds good to me, Ms. Sorenson. Where shall I meet you?"

"Oh, I won't be coming. Just look for my car—a beige limousine. My chauffeur, Ramon, will meet you right in front of the marina. Please be careful, Nancy."

"I will. Thanks." She hung up.

Martin ran a quick check on the minirecorder. It worked perfectly. Nancy clipped the transponder to a barrette and put it in her hair.

Ned and the cops followed her onto the deck. Tim said, "We'll be standing by, Nancy. If anyone makes a move to grab you, we'll bust them. Understand?"

Nancy nodded vigorously.

Ned's hand closed around her wrist. "Nancy . . ."

She turned to face him. "I have to do this, Ned."

"I know." Ned's lips brushed her forehead. "Lisa's out there, and she desperately needs help. Still—" All at once, he crushed Nancy to him. "I love you. Always have. Always will. Come back to me."

"I will. I promise."

Minutes later Nancy stood at the marina entrance, watching the traffic roll down the boulevard. Every sound seemed unnaturally loud. The rustle of palm fronds. The *chop-slosh* of waves against the beach.

Got to keep alert, Nancy thought. They'll try to grab me soon. This is the perfect time to do it—when I'm all alone.

Long, tense minutes passed. Then a beige Lincoln took the corner into the parking lot. Nancy caught a glimpse of the driver, a broad-shouldered man in a chauffeur's cap.

He rolled down the passenger window. "Ms. Drew, I'm Ramon Montanaro, Ms. Sorenson's driver. Hop in."

As Nancy opened the rear door, she noticed a pair of nylon-clad legs. Amy Sorenson's navy blue linen suit made her nearly invisible in the gloom of the back seat.

As she sat down, Nancy smoothed the back of her skirt. Her fingertips brushed the minirecorder, switching it on.

The driver did a three-point turn, pumped the gas pedal, and sent the limo speeding back onto the boulevard.

All smiles, Amy remarked, "Mind if I have a look at that bond? I can tell right off if it belonged to Diana."

After taking it out of her shoulder bag, Nancy handed it over. Eyes agleam, Amy studied the document, then flipped it over. Astonishment washed over her face. "What is this? There's no message on this thing!"

Beep-beep-beep-beep! Amy froze at the harsh sound. Nancy looked down at the woman's leather purse. "Aren't you going to answer it?"

Amy's mouth tightened. She said nothing.

"This reminds me of last night at Mr. Jarman's," Nancy observed. "You didn't want me to see your beeper then, either. Go ahead and answer it, Ms. Sorenson. I already know it's a Higashi."

Amy clutched the purse to her chest.

"The beeper's listed on the shipping manifest —the one you hid inside that bearer bond," Nancy added. "There's no need to pretend anymore. *You're* the Malihini Corporation."

With an ironic sigh, Amy reached into her purse, withdrew the beeper, and flicked it off. "I'll bet it's Ross. I knew he'd panic when he found his limo missing. I told him I was on my way to the Faulkner estate."

Nancy frowned. "It's all over, Ms. Sorenson. Tell me where Lisa is."

"Indulge *my* curiosity first." Amy tossed her hair insolently. "How did you know it was me?"

"The pieces were all there," Nancy explained. "It was just a matter of putting them all together. You're Diana's financial advisor. You knew she rarely went into the vault, so you kept all your Malihini stuff in her safety deposit box. Then Lisa cleaned it out. You panicked. Using your

131

Malihini Corporation front, you hired Wally Cerrado to find her." She took a quick breath. "After reading those documents, Lisa realized that you were the brains behind the Malihini Corporation. She came to you and offered to sell the documents."

Amy said nothing.

"You arranged for Lisa to stay at the Ka Lae. Then you heard that Mrs. Faulkner had hired me. So you set up that booby-trapped car scheme," Nancy continued. "When that failed, you sent Wally after me. But that's where you made your big mistake, Ms. Sorenson."

Confused, Amy stared at her.

"When I got to Honolulu, I had to sign for the car at Sunrise Rentals. I listed everyone in my party—myself, Ned Nickerson, Bess Marvin, and *George Fayne*. Sunrise sent a copy of that to the Malihini Corporation. When you read the names, you, quite naturally, thought George was a guy. Later, you passed on that bit of misinformation to Wally Cerrado when you sent him to spy on me. Wally was pretty surprised when I introduced him to George." She glanced sharply at the woman. "But not as surprised as *you* were! I wondered why you reacted that way at Mrs. Faulkner's. You were really shocked to find out that George Fayne is a girl," Nancy added. "After that, it was a process of elimination. The Malihini Corporation had to be either you, Ross, or Mitsuo. I knew it couldn't have been Ross or

Mitsuo. They had met George the day we visited the bank. That left you."

"Very astute, Nancy." Amy's face seemed hewn from ice. "Now what?"

Nancy looked her in the eye. "Just tell me where Lisa is."

"Not a chance!"

"Have it your way, then." Nancy tapped the chauffeur's shoulder. "Forget the bank, Ramon. Take us back to the marina. There're a couple of detectives there who'd like to talk to Ms. Sorenson."

Thump! The rear doors locked automatically. Nancy grabbed the door lever. It wouldn't budge!

"His name is Lew, and he works for me," Amy said, flashing a wicked smile. She took a small automatic pistol from the driver and leveled it at Nancy. "So you want to find Lisa, eh? I think we can arrange that."

The driver gave a sinister chuckle. He steered the limo down the off-ramp, heading for the airport.

Ten minutes later the car pulled up at a ramshackle hangar. Unfazed by the takeoff roar of the jetliners, Amy and Lew marched Nancy into the building. Turning on the light, Amy called, "Company for you, Lisa!"

Footsteps sounded behind Nancy. Turning, she saw a brown-haired woman in boat clothes and a teenage girl with brownish blond hair and striking blue eyes. Lisa Trumbull looked quite a bit different from her photos—rumpled, tired, and very, very frightened.

Amy smiled wickedly. "Has she been behaving herself, Marilee?"

"She knows better than to give *me* any problems," answered the other woman.

Lew locked the outside door. Nancy's gaze circled the room at lightning speed. Secondhand furniture. Heavy-duty wire barred both windows. *No way out!*

"Why don't you girls get acquainted?" Amy suggested mockingly. "I'll be back." Her two henchmen followed at her heels.

Lisa Trumbull eyed Nancy timidly. "Who are you?"

"Nancy Drew. I'm a friend. Are you all right, Lisa?"

"How—how do you know my name?"

"I'm a detective. Your grandmother hired me to find you."

Lisa's chin lifted warily. "How do I know you're not working for *her?*"

"You don't. You'll just have to take my word for it." Nancy drew the wire over her head, then wrapped it around the plastic case. She grinned at Lisa. "This is a miniature tape recorder, property of the Honolulu police. Now I've got to trust you. If you still think I'm Amy's spy, tell her about it. She doesn't know I was wearing it. Do you want to take that chance?"

Shaking her head, Lisa whispered, "No! I trust you."

"Good!" Nancy looked around desperately. "Where can I hide this thing?"

Lisa lifted the cushion of the beat-up sofa. "Here! Nobody will—"

Nancy heard the sound of high heels approaching. Hurriedly she tucked the minirecorder under the cushion, then smoothed it with her palms.

Amy strolled into the room. Aiming her pistol at them, she snapped, "On your feet, you two!" She glanced at Marilee. "Search and handcuff them."

The woman pinioned Lisa's arms behind her back, then snapped on a pair of shiny handcuffs. Marilee's hands drifted down Nancy's back. "She's clean!" Nancy shivered. Close call! If she'd still been wearing the minirecorder . . .

Amy gave the pistol to her henchman. "You know what to do with them, Lew."

Lisa spat, "You won't get away with this, Amy Sorenson!"

"I've already gotten away with it!" Amy flashed a tigerish smile. "You two are just loose ends that need tying up, that's all."

Marilee unlocked and opened the door. Lew shoved Nancy rudely. "Step lively there, Drew!" he muttered. "You're going sight-seeing— courtesy of the Malihini Corporation."

At that moment, an ominous noise overshadowed the background hubbub of the airport —the sound of a helicopter's rotor blades. A Huey helicopter touched down, and the side hatch slid open.

As Nancy climbed aboard, Lisa cried out, "Watch out for the doughnut ring!"

Quickly Nancy stepped over the thick circular cable on the floor. Then Lisa climbed aboard, followed by Marilee. The pilot turned in his seat, saw the girls, and frowned in bewilderment. "Hey! What is this? The boss told me cargo, not passengers!"

Lew put his pistol to the pilot's head. "Want to be a dead hero?"

Gasping, shuddering, the pilot shook his head.

"Smart guy." Keeping the gun on him, Lew climbed into the cockpit and buckled himself into the copilot's seat. "Get us airborne—fast!"

"I have to tell the tower our destination." The pilot flicked overhead switches. Turbines whined. The cabin began to shake.

"The Big Island." Lew pulled his seat belt tight. "I'll give you more details when we get there."

With a roar of power the Huey lifted off, rising slowly into the night sky. Nancy's ears popped. Peering out the side window, she watched the lights of Honolulu fall away. She knew the police hadn't had time to get to them. Amy had had them whisked away so quickly.

Sobbing, Lisa shook her head. "I—I've made such a mess of things. . . ."

Nancy tried to cheer her up. "You kept me from getting hurt a moment ago. How'd you know that ring was there?"

"This is an old army chopper. They used them in Vietnam. Soldiers used to clip their rappel ropes onto that ring and then slide down to the ground." Tears trickled down Lisa's face. "Nancy, I—I'm sorry . . ."

"Don't be." Nancy gave her a sympathetic look. "You didn't invent the Malihini Corporation. Amy did! She used you, Lisa."

"I realize that now." Lisa's voice was taut with anger and remorse. "I—I never meant any harm. Honest!"

"You can't give up hope, Lisa," Nancy said softly. "We'll get out of this, you'll see. I'm not the only one looking for you. My friends, your grandmother, your mother—"

"My *mother?*" Lisa echoed.

"You bet. Your mother loves you very much. You know what she told me? She said she'd burn one of her paintings if that's what it took to bring you home."

"My mother said that?" Lisa replied incredulously.

Nancy encouraged the girl to talk about herself. She knew that would keep Lisa from getting panicky. While she listened, Nancy's agile fingers explored the wall behind her, seeking an object she could use as a makeshift lock pick. In a few minutes her thumb discovered a loose electrical brace—a tiny metallic pin used to hold the wiring in place.

Wiggling the pin into the handcuffs' keyhole, Nancy began working at it painstakingly. Easy does it! She closed her eyes. Any lock can be beaten, she told herself. All it takes is patience.

Over an hour passed. Marilee was no longer watching them. She slumped in her seat, sighing and dozing. Nancy managed to wheedle her pin past a tumbler in the handcuff lock.

All at once, a new sound intruded on the helicopter's droning—a low-throated rumble, like the thunder of a distant storm. The noise grew steadily louder. Curious, Nancy glanced out the side window.

Moonlit hills rolled away beneath the chopper's skids. Ahead, flashes of scarlet lit up the horizon. Then the rumble transformed itself into the earsplitting sound of gas explosions.

Nancy stared down in horrified fascination. Fiery sparks circled a cone-shaped peak. Plumes of red-hot lava shot into the night sky, and billowing clouds of steam drifted toward them.

"Kilauea . . . the volcano!" Lisa cried.

Lew left the copilot's seat. "Bring her right over it," he ordered. "Then hold her steady."

With a flick of his wrist, he disengaged the safety lock and pulled the hatch open. Stinking vapor flooded the cabin. "Come over here,

Drew." He flashed Nancy a grin of sheer evil. "I want you to get a real good look at Kilauea!"

Nancy fought down a surge of terror as she felt the lock's second tumbler give way. Her heart began to pound. One more tumbler to go!

Suddenly the helicopter swayed from side to side. Yelling, Lew grabbed a static line with his free hand. Its snap-link went flopping out the hatch. Aiming his pistol at the pilot, he snapped, "I told you to keep it *steady!*"

"I can't!" The pilot held the control column with both hands. "Too much steam! The up-drafts are too strong!"

Lew turned his gun toward Nancy. "Let's get it over with."

Nancy took a careful step forward. The pin began to slide in her sweaty grip. She felt faint. If she lost it now . . . !

Taking a deep breath, Nancy gave it one last solid push.

Click! She felt the handcuffs loosen on her wrists. Her right hand wriggled free.

Lew made a grab for her. "Come on, Drew! Don't take all night!"

Nancy let his hand close around her collar. Then, cocking her fist, she stumbled against him and planted a hammer-blow on his thigh.

Roaring, Lew collapsed on top of her.

Nancy chopped his Adam's apple. Lew gasped, tackled Nancy, and threw her to the floor. Nancy's knee bashed his stomach. Lew rolled away, his breath exploding out of him. His pistol swung toward Nancy. She threw herself on his arm, grabbed his wrist, slammed it repeatedly against the bench. His trigger finger tightened—

Blam! A bullet smashed the window beside Lisa.

Blam! A crater appeared on the back of the pilot's seat. His hands flew upward. "Aaaaaaaaagh!" he screamed.

In desperation, Nancy lashed out with a straight-legged kick. Her heel clobbered Lew's jaw, and he bellowed with rage. He rolled toward her, bringing his fist around in a vicious left hook. The punch caught Nancy on the chin. Next thing she knew, she was spread-eagled on the floor.

The pilot stood shakily, arching his back in agony. A bright red stain blossomed on his coveralls.

Still stunned, Nancy watched helplessly as Lew staggered to his feet. With a snarl of rage, he lifted his pistol high. He was about to crush Nancy's skull with a single blow!

That same second the wounded pilot slumped over the controls. The Huey's nose dipped suddenly. The floor tilted crazily to the right.

The momentum of Lew's upward swing threw him off-balance. He backpedaled awkwardly, like a cartoon character, heading for the open hatch.

Nancy saw him framed in the hatchway for a

split second. Then he was gone. His shrill death scream faded into the rumble of the volcano.

The chopper floor continued to tilt. Nancy realized that she, too, was sliding down the incline. The open hatch rushed to greet her.

The doughnut ring! she thought frantically.

Nancy lunged at the steel cable. She missed it.

With a wild yell, Nancy felt herself hurtling into space. The cabin's rim rode up her legs, over her stomach—all the way to her armpits. Lisa's terrified scream echoed in her ears.

Then Nancy was falling through thin air —right toward the volcano!

Chapter

Seventeen

Nancy had a sudden horrifying glimpse of Kilauea's fiery vent. Geysers of lava blossomed out of the crater.

All at once, the helicopter's skid swung into view. Nancy's clawing hand grabbed it. She dangled there for an impossibly long moment —buffeted by blasts of steam, watching the dark sky and the erupting volcano change places with each other. Then she doubled her grip.

Without a pilot, the Huey began to fly round and round in crazy circles. Nancy felt as if she were on a nightmarish merry-go-round. No way out this time! she thought, gritting her teeth against the blasts of steam. If the volcano doesn't kill me, the helicopter crash will!

She thought of Lisa, handcuffed and helpless—

Lisa! Lisa was a pilot! She could fly the helicopter and save them!

All Nancy had to do was get back inside.

But each turn of the chopper sent her swinging off to the side like a circus trapeze artist. Get back in? It was all she could do to hold on!

Just then something tapped her wrist. Looking up, Nancy saw a line dancing back and forth.

Nancy rode out the next freewheeling swing. Then, as her body slowed, she hooked her leg over the skid. Acrid smoke smothered the helicopter, and she felt faint. Her drenched hands began to slip. Uttering a breathless gasp, she shimmied down the skid and caught the line as it whipped past.

Nancy tugged on the line to make sure it was secure just as a glowing piece of jellied lava, as big as a basketball, splattered the chopper's belly. Nancy grabbed the line with both hands, her body spinning round and round like a yo-yo at the end of its string.

Wheezing and coughing, Nancy pulled herself toward the hatchway. Her grasping hands inched their way up the thick rope.

Now she'd climbed up past the skid. Her foot lashed out and caught it. That provided some support. Her head peeped over the rim of the hatch. Where was that doughnut ring? As she lunged into the cabin, her right hand closed around it. Thank you, U.S. Army! she thought.

"Nancy!" Lisa shrieked, bracing herself against the cabin wall. "The pilot's unconscious! Get me loose! I can fly this thing!"

The bucking helicopter was about to shake Nancy loose again. Summoning her last reserves of strength, she tightened her grip on the ring and pulled herself all the way into the chopper.

A jet of boiling lava sailed past the open hatch. Rising to her knees, Nancy slammed it shut. Then she crawled over to Marilee's jump seat.

Marilee was screaming hysterically. Nancy shook the woman's shoulders. "The key! Give me the key!"

"My necklace . . ." Marilee wailed.

The key dangled at the end of a tiny chain. Ripping it loose, Nancy stumbled across the seesawing cabin toward Lisa.

Lisa's handcuffs clanged as they struck the floor. On hands and knees, she and Nancy scrambled into the cockpit.

Lisa dropped into the copilot's seat. Her right hand seized the control column. Her gaze took in every flight instrument at a glance. All at once, the Huey stopped its mad whirling. Nancy helped the wounded pilot out of his chair.

"Nancy!" Wide-eyed, Lisa pointed at two U-shaped handles rising from the console beside her seat. These were the thrust levers, which controlled the power output of the chopper's twin engines. "Push those—*quick!* We're losing airspeed! If we ˜stall, we'll drop right into the volcano!"

Now Kilauea's throaty roar smothered all sound. A titanic fire fountain gushed out of the crater. Hot lava spattered the Huey. The Plexiglas windscreen began to bubble and melt.

Grabbing the thrust levers, Nancy threw her weight against them. The helicopter turbines answered the volcano with a roar of their own. Lisa turned the control column to the left. The Huey veered away from the volcano, cutting a path through the swirl of steam and smoke. Nancy held her breath, listening to Kilauea's angry bellow.

Suddenly the steam outside the cockpit gave way to a star-studded sky.

With a sigh of thanksgiving, Nancy slumped to the cockpit floor.

When—if—we get back home, she told herself, I'm going to learn to fly a chopper. An airplane pilot's license isn't enough anymore.

Then she remembered the wounded pilot. Grabbing the microphone, Nancy chanted, "Mayday! Mayday! We have an in-flight emergency. Wounded man aboard."

"Tell them I'm heading for Hilo airport," added Lisa.

Nancy did so, then requested paramedics and

an ambulance. She tossed the microphone aside and grabbed the cockpit's first-aid kit. Pressing a gauze bandage to the pilot's bullet wound, she cast a final glance at Kilauea, now a fiery smudge on the horizon. The volcano thundered in farewell.

The next morning Nancy and Ned waited in the copying room at Windward Fidelity Bank. Peering through the little window, Nancy surveyed the vacant conference room. She smiled to herself, remembering the tearful reunion at the Hilo police station the previous night—how Lisa had rushed, sobbing, into the arms of her mother and grandmother. The expressions on the faces of the Faulkner women had made it all worthwhile.

"Think Jack will be able to lure them all in here?" Ned whispered.

"Sure," Nancy replied. "No one knows the Faulkners are still on the Big Island. They haven't heard from Alice since yesterday. They'll be here."

Muffled voices sounded in the distance, and the suite door opened. Ross, Mitsuo, and Amy walked in, trailed by Jack Showalter.

"What's this all about, Showalter?" Ross asked irritably. "And where is Alice? Not even Lester can find her."

"What did Mrs. Faulkner tell you, Jack?" asked Mitsuo.

Jack's face looked glum. "She's made up her mind. She's not selling those shares."

"That woman is a fool!" Amy cried. "She's doomed her own granddaughter!"

Then Nancy burst into the conference room. "Wrong! Her granddaughter's just fine, Ms. Sorenson. She's down in Hilo, safe and sound. Not inside the Kilauea volcano as *you* intended!"

Amy's eyes widened in disbelief. She whitened and swayed on her high heels. At that moment, Tim and Martin came through the other door. Tim set a tape recorder on the table. Martin flashed his badge, adding, "Honolulu P.D. Have a seat, gentlemen. We'd like you to hear something."

"What's the meaning of this?" Ross asked huffily.

"Ms. Sorenson is an embezzler," Nancy said. "She chartered herself as the Malihini Corporation, tapped into your bank's money, and used it against you."

Amy tossed her hair defiantly. "Preposterous!"

Tim took an onionskin paper out of his breast pocket and showed it to Mitsuo. "This is a shipping manifest made out to the Malihini Corporation. Look at the signature on the bottom. Whose handwriting is that?"

Mouth agape, Mitsuo stared at it. "It—it's Amy's!"

Martin asked, "Sir, will you swear to that in a court of law?"

"Let me see." Ross snatched the paper away. His face turned white. "Amy! What is this?"

"It's nothing." Amy sneered, glaring at Nancy. "There are no laws against incorporating yourself in the Cayman Islands."

Ross stared at her, aghast. "You betrayed us! You stole our money and used it to mess up the Konalani project. *You* tried to make the bank fail!"

"Prove it!" Amy spat. "There's no charge against me. I'm leaving!"

"Not so fast." Nancy slapped an envelope into her hand. "This is a warrant for your arrest."

Outraged, Amy flipped it open. "On what charge?"

"Attempted murder, kidnapping, and extortion," Nancy replied, folding her arms. "You're not going anywhere."

Her green eyes glittering, Amy ripped the document into little pieces. "It's your word against mine, Drew. No court will ever convict me."

"We'll see about that." Nancy reached across the table and flicked on the tape recorder. Amy flinched as her own voice filled the conference room.

"Mind if I have a look at that bond? I can tell right off if it belonged to Diana."

Amy stood transfixed, a look of mingled alarm and horror crossing her face. Nancy let it play until Lisa's voice came on, then switched it off.

"It's true you can't convict with just a tape," Nancy told the woman, "but when the tape is admitted with eyewitness testimony from Lisa and Marilee—well . . ."

Tim began the litany of arrest. "You have the right to remain silent . . ."

Nancy stepped aside to let them pass. A sullen, handcuffed Amy marched between the two detectives. The astounded bankers followed them out. Then, with a sigh of relief, Nancy squeezed Ned's hand and started downstairs.

The evening tide rolled into Ala Wai. Lounging in her deck chair, Nancy could feel the *Kahala* straining against her moorings. She grinned at Ned, who was setting their supper tray on the transom.

"Did Bess and George say what time they'd be back?" Nancy asked.

Ned handed her a hamburger. "Not really. You know how Bess is when she goes shopping." His eyes gleamed. "I won't complain if they're late."

Just then Alice Faulkner's voice called out. "Ahoy the *Kahala!*"

Peering over the rail, Nancy saw her on the walkway. Ned quickly put the supper tray aside, and he and Nancy hustled down to meet her.

"I came to say goodbye," Alice told them smilingly. "Diana, Lisa, and I are going on a round-the-world cruise." Her smile deepened. "Sort of a get-to-know-you cruise, I guess. We're going to try to be a family again. A *real* family."

"How are things at the bank?" Nancy asked.

Alice sighed softly. "Better. We took a little beating in the stock market when the news broke. But it wasn't as bad as it could have been." Then she took Nancy's hands. "I can't thank you enough, my dear. Because of you, I have my granddaughter—and my daughter—back again." Her gaze went from Nancy to Ned. "What are your plans now?"

"We'll be flying out in a few days," Ned replied. "Heading back to River Heights."

There was a merry twinkle in Alice's eyes. "Well, since you'll be here in the Islands for a bit, why don't you take the *Kahala* out on the open sea?"

Nancy blinked in surprise. "Mrs. Faulkner, that's awfully generous of you, but we couldn't—"

"I insist." Alice pressed an ignition key into Nancy's hand. "Go on. You earned it. Consider it a bonus for a job well done. You might consider sailing to Maui," Alice added, a fond smile on her lips. "My late husband and I loved that trip."

Then she walked back to the parking lot, her step as light and lively as a young girl's.

Nancy and Ned stood alone on the wharf. A

breeze stirred Ned's hair. He smiled, sliding his hands around Nancy's waist.

"I wonder what Maui looks like in the moonlight," he whispered.

Nancy lifted her face, waiting to receive his kiss.

"Let's find out, Ned."

Trouble in Tahiti

Chapter

One

NANCY DREW PEERED into the tennis court through the chain-link fence, feeling the warmth of Tahiti's tropical sun on her face. Even though this was strictly a working vacation, she couldn't help but look forward to returning to wintry River Heights with a golden tan.

On the court two women volleyed back and forth. One, a pretty girl of nineteen with long, raven black hair, walloped the ball over the net with a sharp backhand.

Her opponent, a stunningly beautiful blond woman, rushed forward but was a split second too late. The ball bounced twice on the clay.

The black-haired girl grinned. "That's the game, Krissy."

Pouting, the blonde shouldered her racket. "Just wait till tomorrow, Bree Gordon."

Nancy intercepted the black-haired girl at the gate. "Bree? I'm Nancy Drew."

"Hi!" Bree shook Nancy's hand. "You made it. Did you have a nice flight to Papeete?"

Nancy noticed how easily the difficult Tahitian word rolled off the girl's lips: *Pah-pee-ay-tee.*

"A nice long flight." Nancy shook her head ruefully. "Eight hours from L.A.!"

Bree nodded knowingly, then gestured at her companion. "Let me introduce you. This is my father's fiancée, Kristin Stromm. Krissy, this is Nancy Drew."

As Nancy shook the blond woman's hand, she thought with an inward smile how jealous her star-struck friend Bess Marvin would be. Kristin Stromm was one of the most popular actresses in Hollywood.

"Pleased to meet you." Kristin's speech betrayed the soft tones of her native Sweden. "Bree darling, I have to run. The masseur's expecting me in ten minutes."

Bree arched her brows. "Okay. If I see Dad, I'll tell him you're in the body shop."

Nancy noticed the mask of annoyance that suddenly descended upon the older woman's face.

Kristin frowned. "Must you always have the last word?"

"Hey, lighten up, Krissy. It was only a joke."

"I don't think it was very amusing." Kristin

2

pushed open the chain-link gate. "Perhaps I ought to have a word with your father."

"Be my guest." Bree flashed a sassy smile. *"Haere maru."*

After the older woman strode away, Nancy said politely, "Uh, perhaps I came at an awkward time."

Bree's expression was apologetic. "Sorry. I didn't mean to drag you into anything. It's just that sometimes things get a little tense between me and my future stepmother." She frowned, watching Kristin enter the lobby of the luxurious Hotel Taravao. "I wish I knew what Dad sees in her."

Nancy tactfully tried to change the subject. "Bree, what was that you said a moment ago?"

"Haere maru. It's Tahitian for 'take it easy.'" Bree led Nancy through the hotel's garden, alive with exotic flowers in bright colors. "The language is practically second nature to me. I used to live here every summer when I was younger. And, of course, Tayo taught me a lot."

"Who's Tayo?" Nancy inquired.

"Tayo Kapali." Bree's face clouded. "He's the reason I asked you to come."

"What *exactly* is the problem? Let's go over it once. Okay?"

Bree nodded. "At first I thought it was a joke. But when it happened three times . . ." After taking a deep breath, Bree went on. "Somebody keeps sending weird letters to my dorm."

3

"Could you describe the letters?" Nancy asked, prompting her.

"They're crazy!" Bree's pretty face tightened angrily. "Always the same little remark. 'You'd be surprised if you knew what I know about your mother's death.'"

Nancy experienced a shiver of disgust. What a cruel thing to write. No wonder Bree was so upset.

"Anyway, the person's dead wrong," Bree added. "There was nothing suspicious about my mother's death. If anything, it was the most publicized boating accident in the history of the Pacific."

Nancy's mind drifted back twenty-four hours to the time of the two phone calls she had received—one from an old client, Alice Faulkner, who was Bree's godmother, the other from Bree herself. Mrs. Faulkner had given her a few of the details, but Nancy hadn't needed much prompting to recall the accident that had claimed one of Hollywood's biggest stars. "Was that five years ago?"

"Yeah." Bree pushed open the hotel's glass doors. "My parents owned a boat back then. The *Southwind,* a custom-built motor sailer. She went down in a tropical storm with my mother aboard. There was a crewman aboard, too, a guy named Pierre Panchaud." Bree swallowed hard. Unhappy memories brought tears to her brown eyes.

"How did it happen?" Nancy asked softly.

"The *Southwind* lost her anchor during the storm and drifted into the main shipping channel. A tramp freighter rammed her. M-Mother died in the wreck." Bree hastily wiped at her eye. "The local maritime board investigation declared it a simple, unavoidable accident." She took a deep breath. "Gosh, look at me. You'd think I'd be over it by now."

"You never really get over a tragedy like that, Bree." Nancy touched the girl's shoulder sympathetically. "I know. I lost my mother when I was three."

"I'm sorry," Bree murmured.

Nancy changed the subject as Bree led her past a bank of public elevators to a smaller one marked Private. "Let's concentrate on this letter writer. Tell me, where were the anonymous letters mailed from?"

"That's what's *really* strange. They all came from Tahiti." Bree halted at the door to the elevator and slipped a key out of her pocket. After unlocking the door, she continued. "I haven't been here in four years. All my old friends are grown up and gone. Nobody even knew I was going to UCLA."

"Where does Tayo come into it?" Nancy asked, searching for any connection.

"Tayo used to be the *Southwind*'s chief mate. He taught me to scuba dive." The girls stepped inside, and Bree pushed the only button. "Tayo knows practically everybody on the island. I

figured he could help me track down the weirdo."
A worried look crossed her face. "But I can't find
Tayo *anywhere*. He didn't return my calls, and no
one I asked had seen him. When I went to his
house, it was all boarded up, as if he'd left a long
time ago. I started to investigate myself, but I got
a creepy feeling, as if somebody was watching
me. I got scared."

The elevator doors opened suddenly, exposing
a plush penthouse suite. Tropical plants hung
from metal flowerpots. Stylish teak furniture
filled the room. Huge windows offered panoramic views of Papeete's sky-blue harbor and the
jungly neighboring island of Moorea.

"Bree, could I have a look at one of those
letters?" Nancy asked.

"Sure. This way." Bree beckoned with her
hand.

Nancy followed her into a spacious bedroom.
A four-poster bed, covered with a lightweight
quilt, dominated the peach-colored room. An
empty plastic shoe tree stood beside the highly
polished dresser.

Bree opened the dresser's top drawer and
pulled out three air mail envelopes.

"Here. Except for Auntie Alice, I haven't told
anyone about them." Bree handed them to Nancy, then seated herself on the bed. "I didn't want
to upset Dad and Krissy, especially with their
wedding coming up."

Nancy flipped through them, noting the Tahiti

postmarks and French stamps. Then she withdrew one of the letters and unfolded it.

The paper was lined notebook stuff, available in any stationery store. It was the rigid lettering that perked Nancy's interest. She frowned thoughtfully.

"What is it?" asked Bree.

"Whoever wrote these took the trouble to disguise their handwriting. The letters are formed with a pen and ruler. There's no way a handwriting expert could even tell who wrote them," Nancy said, her mind racing.

Bree's face fell. "Then they're no help."

"Actually, they're a big help." Nancy's dimpled smile came quick to reassure Bree. "They tell me that the writer is someone you know. He or she was afraid you'd recognize the handwriting. That explains the ruler."

Turning to return the letters to Bree, Nancy spied a sudden movement underneath the bedspread. She froze. Something narrow was gliding along, moving steadily toward Bree.

Nancy thrust out her hand. "Don't move!"

The girl blinked. "What?"

"Keep still," Nancy whispered, rounding the edge of the bed. Her hand gripped the coverlet. "When I throw this back, hop off the bed—fast!"

Puzzled, Bree nodded.

Nancy whispered, "One—two—"

"Three!" Heart thumping, Nancy ripped the coverlet away. A hiss filled the air.

A gleaming black snake lay on the mattress. Bree gasped and leaped off the bed.

Baring its fangs, the snake rose on its coils, ready to strike.

And Nancy was standing right in front of it!

Chapter

Two

H*ISSSSS!* F**ANGS DRIPPING VENOM**, the snake weaved from side to side.

Nancy swallowed hard. Slowly she moved her head to the left. The snake's wedge-shaped head darted in that direction. Seeing her chance, Nancy lashed out with her other hand and seized the deadly serpent right behind its head.

A deft flick of her wrist sent it hurtling into the corner. The snake rolled on the rug, stunned. Nancy grabbed the shoe tree and used the prongs to pin the snake to the carpet.

"Call hotel security, Bree."

Thick plastic hooks kept the snake trapped as it wriggled helplessly, wrapping itself into a coil.

Nancy knew she was safe, but she'd be more pleased to be on the safe side of glass observing the slippery reptile in a zoo.

Bree rushed to the telephone, grabbed the receiver, and tapped the *O* button. "This is Bree Gordon in the penthouse. There's a snake loose up here! Help us!"

Nancy kept up the pressure on the shoe tree. The snake's beady eyes gleamed; its flailing tail just missed her arm.

Suddenly Nancy heard a woman's voice behind her.

"Bree?"

Turning her head, Nancy saw an attractive chestnut-haired woman in a crisp lilac linen suit standing in the doorway. "What's going on here?"

The newcomer's gaze traveled from Bree to Nancy to the snake. Then her face went white, her eyes rolled upward, and she slid to the carpet like a dress off a hanger.

Bree hung up the phone. "Oh, Manda!"

"I hope you can take care of her." Nancy glanced at the writhing snake. "I'm a little occupied at the moment."

Bree knelt beside the unconscious woman. Two minutes later the hotel manager and two khaki-clad security guards bustled into the suite. Nancy was grateful when one of them took over the snake-guarding duty from her. The other slipped a snare's noose around the snake's neck and toted it away.

Nancy helped Bree and the manager move Manda onto the bed. The manager patted her wrist repeatedly, uttering apologies in high-speed French.

Nancy soaked a facecloth in the bathroom. "Is she a friend of yours, Bree?"

"Not quite. Manda's practically family."

Bree explained that Amanda Withers was her father's executive secretary. She had worked for film director Brian Gordon since Bree was in junior high school.

Returning to the bedroom, Nancy delicately placed the facecloth on Manda's brow. The woman moaned softly. Her eyes fluttered open.

"Bree?" Her face fearful, Manda sat up and embraced the girl. "Bree, are you all right? That snake—"

"I'm fine, Manda." Bree tried to disengage herself from Manda's frantic hug.

"Are you certain?" Seated on the edge of the bed, Manda squeezed Bree's arms and shoulders as an anxious mother would examine a bruised child.

Nancy thought Bree looked terribly embarrassed by Manda's performance.

"Look, I'm *fine,*" Bree said, standing abruptly. "Why don't you go with the manager? The house doctor can have a look at you."

"Please, madame, this way." The manager put out his arm to guide Manda to the elevator.

After their departure Bree shook her head wryly. "Manda Mother Hen." A crooked smile wrinkled her mouth. "Honestly, that woman thinks I'm still eleven years old."

Nancy said nothing, but she had already arrived at the same obvious conclusion. Manda was trying very hard to be Bree's substitute mother—perhaps a bit too hard.

Bree rubbed her arms briskly. "Ugh! When I think about that snake! . . ."

"Bree, I think somebody just tried to kill you," Nancy said, keeping her voice low. "Snakes don't ride elevators and hide under bedspreads. Somebody must have put it there!"

"But *why?*"

"It's possible that the letter writer knows you're after him," Nancy added.

"How can that be? I didn't come up with a single clue. I couldn't even find Tayo."

"Maybe your search made him nervous," Nancy said thoughtfully. "Tell me what you've done so far."

"Well . . ." Bree chewed her thumbnail. "I came across something while I was trying to find Tayo. A friend of mine saw Tayo's boat two years ago. Only it didn't belong to Tayo anymore. I was planning to check the records to see who owns it."

"If you don't mind, I'd like to pursue that line of inquiry myself." Inspiration made Nancy's eyes glimmer. "What was the name of Tayo's boat?"

"The *Rapanui.*" She watched Nancy head for the elevator. "Where are you going?"

Pressing the button, Nancy said, "Bree, I need you to talk to the concierge to see if you can casually find out who came up to the suite today. All right?"

Bree nodded. "No problem," she said.

"Good. Now, can you tell me where they keep the town's official records?"

"Government center, I guess. The gendarmerie is right downtown, just off the Boulevard Pomare."

"Thanks! I'll be back."

After picking up her rental-car keys at the front desk, Nancy went to her own suite and changed her travel clothes for a white tank top and a pair of mint green shorts. Boat clothes, she decided, would keep her cool and comfortable in Tahiti's sweltering climate.

Nancy made certain that her maroon Renault had a road map and a first-aid kit in the glove compartment. Then, after a hasty survey of the map, she drove downtown.

The government center was right on Papeete's sparkling waterfront. Sea birds shrieked at passing yachts. Gentle waves rolled ashore on a beach of black volcanic sand. Nancy was grateful for the refreshing offshore breeze.

The French tricolor rippled from the flagpole. Nancy remembered that Tahiti and her neighboring islands were part of French Polynesia, a self-governing island territory of France.

A wizened old man with a gap-toothed grin

13

directed Nancy to the maritime office. She hoped her years of French at River Heights High would be enough to make herself understood.

Fortunately, the clerk had no trouble understanding Nancy.

"I'm afraid there is no longer an active safety permit for the *Rapanui,*" he said, showing Nancy an official document. "The boat was sold for scrap two years ago."

"Was it sold by Tayo Kapali?" she asked.

"No, mademoiselle, that is not the name on the bill of sale."

That's odd, Nancy mused. Why hadn't Tayo sold the boat?

"Could you tell me who bought the boat, monsieur?"

"It was purchased by Ruau's scrap yard. Just down the beach."

"Thank you." Flashing him a grateful smile, Nancy picked up her shoulder bag and strode away, eager to pursue her first lead.

Leaving her Renault in the parking lot, Nancy joined the flow of pedestrians heading for the beach. Her gaze encompassed all the strikingly different people walking the sands: tourists in sunglasses and straw hats, Frenchmen in knit shirts and faded jeans, breathtakingly lovely Tahitian girls in cool-looking sundresses.

Ruau's scrap yard was just beyond the main boat basin, a field of wooden hulls upended on top of trestles. An old-fashioned steam crane

14

crouched beside the wharves, a plume of smoke drifting from its stack, its engine grumbling ceaselessly.

A workman pointed out the owner, Arii Ruau. Nancy saw a rawboned Tahitian in his early forties, with a tough, shrewd expression.

"Monsieur Ruau, do you remember a boat named the *Rapanui?*" Nancy inquired after she had introduced herself.

"Why, yes, I bought it two years ago." Ruau made an impatient motion with his right hand. "I wanted to refit it, but the bottom was too far gone. So I scrapped the *Rapanui.* A pity, eh?"

"Do you know a man named Tayo Kapali?"

Ruau frowned, then shook his head. "No, the name is not familiar."

"Tayo used to own the *Rapanui* four years ago," Nancy added.

"That's possible." Ruau shrugged. "Boats change hands quite often here in Tahiti. I bought it from Temeharo."

"Who's he?" she asked, trying not to sound too curious.

"A fisherman. He lives on the south side of the island. I can tell you where to find him."

"I'd appreciate that."

Nancy listened attentively as the owner gave her directions to Temeharo's village. As he was talking, she heard the crane's engine suddenly pick up speed.

Nancy was about to ask him to raise his voice

when something caught her eye. She spied a long, thin shadow moving ominously toward them over the sand.

In a flash she realized what it was—the crane's upright boom.

Nancy's gaze lifted, and her suspicion was confirmed. The long steel-girdered boom had drifted into position above their heads. With a metallic creak, it came to a halt.

The rust-dappled scoop, brimming with scrap, swung lazily back and forth.

The scoop's steel hinges groaned suddenly. The noise prickled the hairs on the back of Nancy's neck.

The scoop's jaws were opening!

Nancy's eyes blinked wide.

Its hinges screaming, the scoop opened and let loose its load of jagged steel scrap.

Chapter

Three

"Look out!" Nancy screamed.

Grabbing Ruau's shoulders, she shoved him backward. They hit the sand together. Still holding on, Nancy rolled with him beneath an overturned whaleboat.

Steel fragments bombarded the sand. A handful of shrapnel hammered the boat above their heads. When the noise had stopped, Nancy lay still for a moment, shaken by the close call. If it hadn't been for the whaleboat's hull . . . Nancy shook her head slowly. After a minute she peeked out. The empty scoop spun at the end of its cable. Steel scrap littered the sand.

The workers came running. One helped Nancy to her feet.

Ashen faced, Ruau tottered upright. Brushing off the sand, he yelled, "Imbeciles! You almost killed me! Who was running that crane?"

A confused babble of voices broke out as the workers pointed accusatory fingers at one another. Ruau waded into the crowd and began berating them all. Nancy glanced quickly at the crane itself. The cab was empty. Farther down the beach, a cabin cruiser lolled in its berth.

Nancy cautiously climbed the crane's caterpillar treads. A quick check of the cab confirmed her hunch. The scoop hadn't been opened accidentally. Its jaws were locked with a hydraulic valve that had to be turned by hand.

After jumping down from the cab, Nancy carefully checked the ground on the opposite side. Two deep footprints marked the turf. Kneeling, she examined the treads' pattern more closely.

Diamond-shaped indentations filled each print. Nancy frowned in recognition. Boat shoes! That tread gave sailors better traction on a wet deck.

Hmmm, she thought. Someone climbed into that cab, swung the boom toward us, and opened the scoop. Then he jumped to the ground, leaving those two deep prints, and hightailed it out of here.

"Mademoiselle, what are you doing?" Ruau appeared at the crane, flanked by excited workmen.

Nancy's eyes quickly scanned everyone's feet.

No boat shoes. They were all wearing construction boots.

"You saved my life." Ruau squeezed Nancy's hand thankfully. "If not for you, these idiots—"

"Don't blame your men. They're not responsible," Nancy interrupted. She hurriedly explained her deduction.

Concern tightened Ruau's features. "Maybe we'd better call the police."

"First let's check out that boat," Nancy suggested, pointing at the nearby cabin cruiser. "Maybe someone on it saw something."

As they strode toward the dock, the boat's engines roared to life. White water burbled around the stern. The cruiser pulled away casually, heading for the open sea. Shading her eyes against the sun's glare, Nancy caught a glimpse of its gilt-edged name: *Sous le Vent*.

Nancy smiled ruefully. "So much for that idea."

She watched the cruiser fade into the distance. Of course, it could merely be a coincidence that the boat's skipper had chosen that moment to depart. Her smile faded. Then again, whoever had tried to kill them could be on board, making an escape.

After saying goodbye to Ruau and his men, Nancy walked to the dockmaster's shed. The dockmaster was a sharp-nosed elderly Frenchman in a tattered tan beret and a flowered shirt. An unlit cigarette dangled from his lips.

Sudden inspiration caused Nancy to take a less

direct tack with the older man. She wondered if being too open in her quest for information could be dangerous.

"Excuse me," Nancy said, flashing her sweetest smile. "The boat that just pulled out of here—is it for sale?"

The dockmaster squinted out to sea. "Eh? The *Sous le Vent?* No, no, not for sale."

"Do you know who owns it?" asked Nancy. "Maybe I'll make him an offer, anyway."

"That's Chaumette's boat." Somehow he managed to talk around his cigarette. "Henri Chaumette."

Nancy thought. Chaumette. That name didn't ring any bells, but she filed it away for future reference.

After thanking the dockmaster, Nancy headed back to the gendarmerie. As she strolled along, she mulled over her first eventful day.

Were the two murder attempts connected? Whoever had planted that snake in Bree's bed could have seen Nancy with Bree. If that person had overheard their conversation about the anonymous letters, then he or she knew Nancy was a private investigator.

Suppose the would-be killer then followed Nancy to the gendarmerie and the scrap yard. Ruau's idling crane had offered the perfect opportunity to set up a phony accident.

Nancy's frown deepened as her thoughts returned to the *Sous le Vent.* Was it used to make an escape? Could Henri Chaumette be after her?

And, if so, what was his connection to Bree Gordon, or to Tayo Kapali?

Nancy began to wonder about the former chief mate. How did Tayo lose his boat two years ago? Most important, why had he dropped completely out of sight?

A cool sea breeze raised gooseflesh on Nancy's bare arms. The mystery, it seemed, went far deeper than a handful of hate-mail letters!

The next morning Nancy and Bree drove south to find the fisherman who'd sold Tayo's boat. Nancy steered the Renault down the Taapuna Highway, past the elegant mansions and lush ironwood groves of Tahiti's western shore. Beyond the sprawling estates the blue Pacific exploded into spray on the narrow rampart of a coral reef.

"What did you find out from the concierge yesterday?" Nancy asked her companion.

Bree frowned. "Nothing much. He said he didn't see anyone unusual go near our elevator yesterday. Just Dad, Krissy, and Manda—all family, more or less. But he wasn't watching the entire time. I got him to admit that he was back in his office, arguing with a crazy customer for about half an hour. So anyone could have gotten hold of a key and gone up during that time."

Right—or it could have been one of the "family," Nancy added mentally. But there was no point in voicing that possibility to Bree. It would only upset her.

"Did your friend Tayo ever mention an Henri Chaumette?" Nancy asked.

Shaking her head, Bree replied, "Not to me."

"What about your mother? Did she ever mention that name?"

"She might have. I honestly don't remember." Bree made a rueful face. "Mother knew just about everybody on the island. I think she wanted to be queen of Tahiti." She sighed nostalgically. "Mother was from Peru. She got her start in Rio, as a showgirl in one of the big nightclubs. By the time she was twenty-one, she was doing TV and movies. She hit it big in a low-budget comedy called *Coralita*. It established Mother as *the* biggest star in South America."

Nancy wasn't much of a Hollywood fan. But because Bess was, she did know a little about Lucinda Prado's career.

"Then she came to Hollywood and did *Shivaree* and *The Tall Timber,* right?" Nancy remarked.

"Yeah. Dad directed *Tall Timber*. That's how they met." Bree smiled impishly. "They got married the minute the film wrapped."

"How did you all wind up in Tahiti?"

"When I was a kid, Dad and Mother formed their own production company and did *Typhoon* down here," Bree explained. "That made tons of money, so they did a couple of sequels. Mother just fell in love with the island. Tahiti became our permanent vacation home."

Coconut palms flashed by on either side of the road. Nancy could understand just how Bree's mother felt. She glanced at her companion. "Sounds like an exciting life."

"Well—up to a point, yes." Bree turned serious. "Toward the end, though, Mother was fed up with the film industry. She was forty, and they were still casting her in Coralita parts. She wanted to prove that she was a serious actress. And I think maybe she was a little jealous of Dad's success."

Nancy caught an undertone of sadness in the girl's voice. "It got a little tense at home, huh?"

"A bit!" Bree said candidly. "When you've got two creative, opinionated people married to each other, you're bound to have friction. And Mother had a temper!" She exhaled deeply. "I got pretty good at disappearing at the first sign of tension."

Nancy thought it was time to change the subject. "We're heading inland again. How do we get back to the shore?"

"Oh!" Bree sat up attentively. "There's a dirt road just ahead. It goes right along the bay. The village is down there."

They found what they were looking for within five minutes. Temeharo's fish market was right on the beach, a long corrugated tin shed with a thatched roof. Fresh tuna and halibut rested on smoking blocks of dry ice.

Temeharo was a fiftyish man in a khaki shirt and oil-stained trousers. He flashed a gleaming smile of welcome, and Nancy was instantly taken by his open, friendly manner. "Come in! How may I help you?"

"My name's Nancy Drew." Nancy shook hands with him. "And this is Bree Gordon. We're looking for a friend and thought you might be able to help. I understand you sold a boat two years ago—the *Rapanui*."

"Yes, I sold her in Papeete."

"Did you buy it from Tayo Kapali?" asked Nancy.

His eyes gleamed in recognition. "No, not from Tayo himself."

"But you know of Tayo," Nancy added quickly.

The fisherman brightened. "Of course. He came from this village."

Mystified, Nancy asked, "Who did you buy the boat from?"

"The bank." Temeharo saw Nancy's confused look. "Tayo still owed money on her," the fisherman explained. "The bank foreclosed after his death."

Nancy blinked in amazement at this unexpected development.

"After his—"

"Yes, mademoiselle. Tayo is dead. He was killed four years ago."

Chapter

Four

N O!" BREE CRIED, rushing forward. "That's not true. I talked to Tayo four years ago. He was alive."

Temeharo offered her a look of sympathy. "I'm sorry, but I saw his body with my own eyes. Tayo was killed in a shark attack." Nancy grimaced but pushed the gruesome thought from her mind.

"When did it happen?" she asked, placing a comforting arm around Bree's shoulder.

"October, I think," the fisherman replied.

Turning to Bree, Nancy added softly, "When did you last see Tayo?"

"A-August." Bree began to sob. "I—I had no idea . . . he . . . Tayo's *dead!*"

Nancy walked Bree back to the car. She opened a fresh package of tissues from the glove compartment and offered one to Bree. Temeharo came over to see if she was all right.

Nancy led him away from the car. Bree deserved a little privacy for her grief. And she still had a few questions for Temeharo.

"What's this about a shark attack?" Nancy asked.

Temeharo's smile was one of admiration. "Tayo was the best diver on the island. That was why everyone was so shocked when it happened to him." He glanced out to sea. "Tayo went diving off the *Rapanui* one afternoon. A few people claim they saw another boat out there too. Who knows? Suddenly, the people tell me, the water started to foam. Shark fins were everywhere. A couple of men in a canoe drove off the sharks with rifle fire. They brought Tayo in." He made a sudden sickish face. "Or rather what was left of him. Tayo must have cut himself on the coral down there. Sharks go crazy at the smell of blood, you know."

Nancy thought immediately of the two recent murder attempts. "Did the police consider foul play?"

Temeharo shook his head. "There was no way to tell. Those sharks didn't leave much for the coroner."

Nancy stared in dismay. The trail seemed to have come to an end. Without Tayo, unraveling the mystery of the anonymous letters would be much harder.

Nancy brightened a little at her next thought. If I can't talk to Tayo, I'll talk to someone who knew Tayo very well.

"Did Tayo have any relatives?" Nancy asked.

"Just one," Temeharo replied. "His sister, Opane. She lives up there on Orohena." The sweep of his hand took in most of a lofty mountain rising behind the village. "Just ask around. People will tell you how to find her."

"Thanks." Giving him a grateful smile, Nancy headed back to the car.

Bree's sobbing had subsided to sniffles. Dabbing at her eyes, she stared out the windshield as they drove back to Papeete.

Nancy tried to draw the girl out. She wanted to know more about Bree's friendship with Tayo. She was beginning to wonder if Tayo's death could be linked in any way to the recent close calls in the porthouse and at the scrap yard.

"What brought you back to Tahiti four years ago?" Nancy asked.

"Dad had a few legal matters to tie up." Bree crumpled the tissue in her fist. "I didn't really want to come—Mother's death was still fresh in my mind. I spent most of the time with Tayo. It was a rotten trip all around. Even Tayo seemed sort of—well, distant."

Nancy cast her a quick glance. "Distant? What do you mean?"

27

"Tayo had something on his mind," Bree recalled. "He didn't want to talk about it. He said he had to check something out first. He made me promise to look him up the next time I was in Tahiti."

"And then he died," Nancy concluded for her. "Bree, did Tayo ever mention his sister?"

Bree's brown eyes widened in surprise. "Tayo had a sister? I didn't know that."

"Mr. Temeharo says Tayo has a sister living up on Mount Orohena." Nancy steered the car around a long shoreside bend. "Shall we go tomorrow?"

"Sure!" Bree's smile reappeared.

Two hours later as the girls sauntered through the hotel lobby, the desk clerk lifted a white envelope and called out, "Message for you, Mademoiselle Gordon."

Bree ripped the envelope open and withdrew a folded note. She scanned it quickly, then smiled wryly.

"We're both invited to dinner at Krissy's place tonight. And we're not to come in jeans. What do you say, Nancy?"

Grinning, Nancy brushed her reddish blond hair back over her shoulder. Her blue eyes sparkled. "Sounds good to me. I've got an outfit for a special occasion."

Kristin's estate, Faretaha, dominated a small plateau overlooking the windswept sands of a private beach. The house was enormous, with the high windows and lacy woodwork of the French colonial period. Tall, graceful coconut palms shaded a tropical garden ablaze with white gardenias and orange hibiscus.

As Nancy paused before the door, turning to admire the purple streaks the sunset had painted in the sky, the romantic setting made her feel wistful for a moment. Into her mind flashed an image of Ned Nickerson, and she suddenly missed her boyfriend. If only he could have come with her!

Her reverie was short-lived however. Just then the door opened and a Tahitian servant conducted Nancy and Bree into the drawing room. Two men sat in comfortable wicker chairs. One was tall and tanned, his thinning brown hair flecked with gray. Horn-rimmed glasses and an aquiline nose gave him a professorial look. The other man was shorter, pasty faced, beady eyed, about fifty pounds heavier, and was wearing a wrinkled summerweight suit.

Bree hugged the man with the glasses. "Hi, Dad!"

"All through gallivanting, eh?" Brian Gordon stood up and took Nancy's hand. "You must be Ms. Drew."

"It's a pleasure, Mr. Gordon." Nancy was surprised to find his handshake frail and tentative. Although he put on an amiable front, Nancy sensed that he was intensely private, perhaps a bit frightened of other people. "I saw *Canaveral* back home. I liked it very much," she offered.

The director looked pleased. "Thank you. Personally, I think it's my best."

The man in the wrinkled suit uttered a morose grunt. "It lost money."

Bree gestured toward him. "Nancy, this is Rupert Holmberg, a producer."

Standing, Rupert made a frame of his pudgy hands. "Bree, you're breaking my heart. Look at you. Lucinda all over again. Let me get you a film. Come and talk to me."

"Thanks, but no thanks, Rupert." Bree waved him aside, smiling indulgently. "I want to be a marine biologist, not an actress."

Brian flashed Nancy a look of paternal approval. "A girl with sense."

Then Nancy heard the tapping of high heels behind her. Turning, she saw Kristin Stromm glide through the doorway. The actress was wearing a shirred jade-colored cocktail dress—an original straight from Paris, Nancy guessed.

Smiling coldly at Bree, Kristin drawled, "I'm so glad you could come, dear. You and your friend—ah—"

"Nancy Drew," Bree added sweetly.

Nancy felt the air of tension between Bree and her future stepmother. She wondered why Kristin had bothered with such a petty routine. From the look in the actress's pale blue eyes, it was obvious that Kristin remembered Nancy's name. It was also clear that she wasn't exactly pleased with Nancy's appearance. A long-skirted, peach-colored evening dress highlighted Nancy's shining hair and hugged her trim figure.

A servant approached to announce dinner. Nancy enjoyed the French Polynesian delicacies—fresh fish marinated in coconut milk with smoked breadfruit and *fafa,* cooked Tahitian spinach, on the side.

While they ate, Nancy studied Bree's father. She had a few questions for the taciturn director. Nancy was determined to explore the connection between the letters Bree had received and what Tayo might have known about Lucinda's death.

She worked into it gradually, questioning Brian about his three *Typhoon* movies first. Then she mentioned the boat. "I guess you had the *Southwind* for quite a while, Mr. Gordon."

"Seven years." Brian sipped his coffee.

"Did you enjoy sailing?"

"Once in a while. Lucinda was crazy about it, though."

"I gather your wife was a very experienced sailor," Nancy commented.

"Oh, yes." Brian aimed a conspiratorial smile at his daughter. "Bree and I logged a lot of nautical miles under Captain Prado."

"It seems a bit strange—" Nancy began.

"What seems strange?" Brian adjusted his glasses.

"With your wife so experienced, I'm surprised

31

that freighter was able to run the *Southwind* down."

Brian's good mood vanished abruptly. Fixing Nancy with a frosty stare, he snapped, "I'd rather not talk about that, if you don't mind. My wife's death was a very great tragedy in my life. It's not something I discuss with strangers."

"I'm sorry," Nancy replied apologetically.

"No need to be sorry." Nancy noticed the sudden angry set of his lips. "Just drop it, okay?"

Taken aback by his snappish response, Nancy did not reply. But his overreaction intrigued her. Even if he was still sensitive about the mishap after five years, his reaction should have been sadness, not anger.

An awkward silence hung over the dinner table. Kristin smiled weakly, toying with an earring, and attempted to fill it.

"Darling," she said pleasantly, "I'm wondering if you've gotten those script rewrites yet for our new film."

Plucking an olive off the tray, Rupert popped it in his mouth. "Hey! Now we're talking. *South of the Equator*'s a potential gold mine. Brian, let me line up a few banks and a big-name cast."

Brian looked weary. "Rupert, please! I don't like to talk business at the table."

"Why not? I talk business morning, noon, and night," Rupert offered enthusiastically. "If I were like you, I'd still be selling cars in Cincinnati."

Nancy watched Brian's hands roll over into

fists. His voice was tense. "Rupert, give it a rest, huh?"

Kristin slid her fingertips along Brian's sleeve. "Darling, let's be sociable—"

Looking exasperated, Bree's father drew his arm away. "For pete's sake, Krissy—"

Kristin made a petulant face. "Brian, if your daughter's friend irritated you, that's no reason to snap at *me.*"

Nancy was startled by the spoiled resentment now darkening the actress's face. Kristin's clenched teeth looked ready to snip barbed wire.

"Cover your ears, Bree," she snapped. "Your father and I are about to have a spat."

Too late, Brian tried to make amends. He reached for Kristin's hand. "Now, honey—"

"Excuse me!" Kristin crumpled her napkin and threw it on the table. "I have a splitting headache. I'm going to bed. You may let yourselves out."

Head high, Kristin marched out of the room, slamming the louvered doors behind her. Making a weary sound, Brian left the table and wandered out to the patio. Rupert followed.

Bree looked acutely embarrassed. "And so ends another fun day in the life of the Gordon family. I'm really sorry, Nancy." She lifted her coffee cup in an ironic salute. "And to think people actually wonder why I don't want to get into the movies."

Nancy said nothing but felt a twinge of sympathy for Bree. The Gordon family was far from happy. Nancy couldn't help wondering about the underlying source of the tension.

Early the next morning Nancy and Bree set out again, this time to visit Tayo's sister. They left the car at the edge of a field of wind-tossed sugarcane, then hiked the narrow trail up the south slope of Orohena.

Nancy's cropped striped T-shirt and loose white knit shorts made for comfortable hiking. Ignoring the hum of insects near her ears, she stepped over huge feathery ferns and ducked beneath sodden, thorn-tipped vines.

The jungle thinned out, revealing a village of old-fashioned bamboo bungalows with thatched roofs. A cockatoo heckled them noisily. Shy piglets fled squealing at their approach.

Bree's mastery of Tahitian got them directions to Opane's house. Tayo's sister was in the yard, tilling her garden. She was a heavyset woman in her forties, wearing a brick red wraparound dress called a *pareo*. A huge white gardenia blossom nestled in her ink-black hair.

Opane's French was good. "What can I do for you?"

"If you don't mind," Nancy replied, "we'd like to ask you a few questions about your brother."

She glanced at them suspiciously. "You knew Tayo?"

"He worked aboard my family's yacht, the *Southwind*," Bree answered.

Opane blinked. "You're the movie woman!"

"No, I'm her daughter. Bree Gordon."

"Bree . . ." Opane's lips twitched. Then she smiled all over. Tugging at Bree's arm, she led the girls into her house. "He *said* you would come and you did!"

Nancy's eyes widened in surprise. "Let me get this straight. *Tayo* said Bree would come?"

"Yes. Years ago." She ushered them into the kitchen. "I have something for you, Bree."

Opane rummaged in the overhead cupboard. Then, with a triumphant grin, she withdrew a dusty cardboard box tied with string.

"Tayo was here just before he died," Opane explained, reaching for a paring knife. "He told me to keep this safe and give it to Bree."

Nancy bit the corner of her lower lip. Her hunch that Tayo had known he was in trouble seemed about to be proven correct.

Opane handed Bree the knife. The girl hesitated before the box, holding the blade awkwardly. "What is it?"

Opane lifted heavy shoulders in a shrug. "Don't ask me. Tayo was adamant. No one but Bree Gordon was to open it." Her hands shepherded Bree forward. "Go ahead, *chérie.*"

Bree's blade descended toward the string.

An eerie shiver rippled through Nancy. For four long years that box had been sitting on Opane's shelf, awaiting Bree.

A present from a dead man!

Chapter

Five

SNIP! THE KEEN EDGE cut the string.

Lifting the cardboard lid, Bree uttered a startled gasp.

Two objects lay at the bottom of the box. A barnacled steel anchor with a T-frame and sharp parallel flukes, and a slender, weed-encrusted chain.

Impaled on the fluke was a note in bold handwriting.

Nancy looked at Bree. "May I?"

Bree nodded, reaching into the box for the anchor. Bewilderment flooded her face.

Nancy hastily read the note.

Bree,

If you're reading this, then it's because I'm dead and could not show you the chain myself.

This is the *Southwind*'s anchor chain. Guard it well, Bree, for it is proof that your mother was murdered. I never believed the maritime board when they said the chain broke.

So last year I began diving at the *Southwind*'s old anchorage. I tried to avoid arousing suspicion, but it appears that I wasn't careful enough. Someone ransacked my boat yesterday. I think they were looking for this chain. I know it will be safe with Opane until you can use it to find the one who killed your mother.

I think maybe your mother's murderer is coming after me. If so, he's going to learn that old Tayo doesn't die so easy!

Take care of yourself, child.

Love,
Tayo

Nancy was conscious of a presence at her shoulder. Turning, she looked into Bree's stricken face. The black-haired girl shook her head in disbelief.

"It *can't* be true." Bree's eyes filled with tears. "Mother was *murdered!* It's not possible— I— oh, no!"

Bree broke down completely. Murmuring

words of comfort, Nancy and Opane helped her to the bedroom.

While Bree wept into a pillow, Nancy excused herself and returned to the kitchen. She ran the slender chain through her fingers. She was holding the first solid clue of the case. Now she just had to read it carefully.

Dried seaweed clung to the chain links. Nancy hefted the anchor. One end of the chain was firmly bolted to the anchor's shank. Bone-dry kelp filled the keyhole. Obviously, no one had tampered with that end since the day the anchor had first tasted salt water.

The other end told a different story. The final link had been cleanly severed. Nancy turned the sheared end toward the window and caught her breath. Sunshine gleamed on two long, straight gashes.

Somebody had used a hacksaw on this chain. Tayo was right. The *Southwind* didn't slip her anchor that night. She was deliberately cast adrift.

Opane entered the kitchen, her bare feet *slap-slapping* the bamboo floor. Her round face was solemn.

"I'll make us some tea," she said, moving to the woodstove.

Nancy replaced the anchor in the box. "Opane, when did Tayo give you this?"

The woman's face tensed thoughtfully. "It was the end of September. Four years ago." Tilting a bucket, she filled her brass teapot. "Tayo kept looking over his shoulder. He said, 'Opane, if anybody comes around asking for me, you haven't seen me for years. Understand?' Then he made me promise to give that box to Bree.' "

Nancy nodded. Tayo suspected that the killer was on to him. So he decided to hide his evidence in the safest place he could think of. He knew Opane would follow his instructions to the letter.

"One thing I don't understand," Nancy said, accepting a cup of tea. "Why did Tayo hide the evidence? Why didn't he take it to the police?"

Opane dumped sugar into her steaming cup, giving Nancy an embarrassed look. "He had good reason not to. Tayo was a wild one as a boy. When he was sixteen, he hijacked a rich man's boat to impress his girlfriend. He got caught and did three months at that prison camp in the Tuamotus. I think Tayo was afraid the police would blame *him* for the wreck."

Nodding, Nancy sipped her tea. She understood Tayo's fears. The police might not believe the story of a poor pearl diver with a previous record. No wonder Tayo had wanted Bree to present the evidence.

This also explained Tayo's strange preoccupation the last time Bree was in Tahiti. At that time, he was still trying to find proof of sabotage. He had found the chain at the end of September and had died a week or so later.

Nancy's skin prickled. Had Tayo Kapali been murdered?

It was more than possible. If so, the murderer

might still be loose on Tahiti—and someone like that would stop at nothing to ensure that the *Southwind* case remained closed!

On their way home Nancy and Bree stopped for a late lunch at Vaipahi waterfall. Tiny bright-colored birds fled, squawking noisily, as the two girls spread their picnic blanket on the lush grass.

"What do they call them?" Nancy asked, watching the tiny birds soar past the tumbling cascade.

"Huh?" Bree blinked, opening their picnic lunch. "Oh—those are vini birds. Scared little things. They take off at the first sight of people." With an apologetic look, she handed Nancy a sandwich. "Sorry. I'm not very good company today."

Nancy placed a sympathetic hand on the girl's shoulder. "Bree, are you going to be all right?"

"I-I— Oh, Nancy, I don't know if I can handle it." Bree sobbed, wiping away tears. "It's like Mother dying all over again."

Nancy offered her a soft drink. "Look, you don't have to talk about it if you don't want to."

"I *do* want to talk about it." Bree's eyes looked remote. "Mother was murdered. It's— Nancy, if I don't make sense of this, it's going to drive me crazy."

"Why don't you just start at the beginning?" Nancy advised soothingly. "Where were you when it happened?"

"At Faretaha. Krissy had invited us all to

spend the weekend, even Manda. She had a big party that Saturday night. Plenty of film people. I guess she wanted to show off the place. She'd just bought it with all the money she'd earned from *Horizon of Desire.*" Bree steeled herself to go on. "I didn't stay at the party long. Just long enough to be polite."

Nancy nodded encouragement to continue and bit into her sandwich.

"I woke up in the middle of the night. The shutters were slamming," Bree continued. "I called for Manda. There was no answer. So I went downstairs. It was around two-fifteen—I remember looking at the clock. Everyone was gone. I figured Krissy must have moved the party downtown or something. The storm was getting pretty fierce. So I closed the shutters and headed back to bed."

"When did you hear about your mother?" Nancy asked, brushing crumbs from her lap.

"The next morning," Bree replied. "I was having breakfast on the terrace with Dad and Manda when a police car pulled into the drive. A lieutenant broke the news. I'll never forget the look on my father's face. He went white at first. Then he got this weird expression, as if he didn't know whether to be angry or sad. Manda just sat there, stunned."

Nancy could see that Bree was reliving that awful moment all over again.

"There was so much I didn't understand," Bree murmured, pressing her fingers to her temples. "Why had Mother gone back to the boat? I asked Dad, but he wouldn't talk about it. Every time I mentioned it, Dad put on that steely-eyed expression of his and changed the subject. So I eventually got the story out of Manda." Bree's voice began to break. "It's not pretty, Nancy. My parents had a big fight at the party. A typical Gordon battle. Loud and nasty. Mother slapped him, announced that she was sleeping aboard the *Southwind,* and stormed out."

"Bree, you said your mother *announced* her departure for the marina," Nancy observed.

The girl nodded.

"And she wasn't expected back that night," Nancy added.

"No, we were supposed to stay at Faretaha all weekend," Bree replied. "Nancy, what are you getting at?"

"Just this. No one knew beforehand that your mother would be aboard the *Southwind.* So, the murderer could not have cut the chain before the party. He or she must have been at Kristin's and heard your mother announce that she was leaving. Then the killer followed her back to the yacht."

Before Bree could reply, a screech filled the air. Nancy's gaze darted to the jungle. A flock of vini birds erupted from the treeline, cartwheeling into the sky.

Bree's words echoed in Nancy's brain. "Scared little things. They take off at the first sight of people."

Nancy's gaze dropped into the jungle and its thick moist vines, bamboo thickets, and moss-covered trees.

There's somebody in there! she thought. Somebody who spooked the birds.

Bree eyed her strangely. "Nancy, what is it?"

Just then, Nancy spied a glimmer of sunlight on a metal object. Her gaze zeroed in. A wickedly barbed spearpoint emerged from the foliage.

Shoom! The spear hurtled out of the jungle, speeding straight toward Bree!

Chapter

Six

"Look out!" Nancy cried.

She threw herself against Bree's chest. Both girls went sprawling. A whizzing sound cut the air. Stinging pain kissed Nancy's right shoulder.

Thunk! The spear buried itself in a palm trunk, quivering like a tuning fork.

"This way, Bree—*fast!*"

Nancy hauled the girl to her feet and shoved her into a thicket of tall ferns. Together they dropped behind an ancient lava flow.

Bree gasped. "You're hurt!"

Nancy glanced at her shoulder. The spear point had torn the sleeve of her T-shirt, its razor-edged fluke cleaving her skin. The shallow cut turned crimson. Nancy shuddered. Three inches lower, and that spear would have gone through the middle of her back!

"Just a scratch—I'll be okay," Nancy whispered, turning a fern aside. "Stay under cover, Bree. We don't want to give him a target."

Nancy scrutinized the wall of jungle carefully, but all was still. "No sign of anyone. But don't show your face just yet. He could be reloading."

For long, anxious moments, Nancy and Bree crouched behind the lava bed, waiting for the sniper to make his move. Then finally Nancy heard the start-up roar of a car engine. She ran to the edge of the clearing. Snapping noises behind the jungle's green façade announced the sniper's escape.

Nancy clamped her hand over her wound. "He's getting away!" Determined, she dashed across the clearing and plunged into the foliage.

She caught a glimpse of a small blue car fishtailing down a muddy pathway. The vehicle burst through a wall of greenery and, tires squealing, zoomed onto the main road.

Nancy scowled. The high ferns had hidden the license plate.

Bree came up behind her. "Nancy, you'd better treat that cut," she advised, pointing at the bloody sleeve. "Wounds get infected fast here in the tropics."

"I've got a first-aid kit in my car. Come on."

After bandaging Nancy's cut, the two girls returned to the picnic spot. Nancy went straight to the coconut palm and studied the spear.

"That's a—" Bree began to explain.

"A spear gun shaft. I know," Nancy replied, thinking back to her San Diego adventure, *Sisters in Crime*. "I have a friend who's a diver."

"I'm a diver myself," said Bree. "If you're going to commit murder, a spear gun's the perfect weapon. It's silent, and the carbon dioxide charge can drive a spearhead right through an oak board."

"That's for sure!" Nancy held out her hand. "Would you hand me one of the napkins?"

"What for?"

"I don't want to smudge any fingerprints that may be on the shaft," Nancy explained. "Then we'll see what other clues we can find."

A search of the surrounding jungle unearthed the sniper's hidden position. Pushing aside a thorn-laden branch, Nancy spotted a cluster of broken vines. Drawing closer, she spied the ferns mashed underfoot and the forest debris kicked up by the sniper's hasty retreat.

"Our friend took off like a deer," Nancy remarked, following the footprints deeper into the jungle. "Looks as if he or she didn't want you to catch a glimpse of— Whoa!"

Nancy halted on the muddy trail. Clearly outlined in the ooze was a diamond-shaped tread—a footprint identical to the one she had seen in Ruau's scrap yard.

Kneeling beside it, Nancy studied the print. The toes had dug in deep, but the arch and heel had skidded off to the right. She looked ahead.

The line of hasty footprints ended at a deep automobile tire mark.

It looks as if the sniper skidded on the mud while running to his car, she mused.

"Did you find anything?" asked Bree.

"Boat shoes." Nancy rose to her feet again. "I saw prints just like them at Ruau's, right after someone tried to drop a load of scrap on me. I'm pretty sure it's the same person." She sighed. It wasn't even sundown yet and she felt more than a little tired. "Let's get back to Papeete."

As they drove back to the city, Bree said, "It feels strange, you know? Except for you, I'm the only one who knows Mother was murdered. And I don't *dare* tell my father."

"Why not?" Nancy inquired.

"It's obvious, isn't it? The killer was at the party that night." Bree's eyes narrowed and she set her jaw. "She left right after Mother and followed her back to the boat."

"She?" Nancy echoed, glancing at her companion. "Bree, are you saying Kristin—"

"I don't know!" Thumping the dashboard, Bree groaned in misery. "Oh, what a *mess!*"

"Tell me why you think it might have been Kristin Stromm," Nancy suggested.

Leaning back in the passenger seat, Bree closed her eyes. "It was years ago—back in Hollywood. Krissy had just come over from Stockholm. Mother was a big star then. And— Well, to tell the truth, she wasn't exactly nice to newcomers. Krissy flubbed a take. Mother made a big thing of

47

it. Krissy said something catty. Next thing you know, it's World War Three on the soundstage." She looked somberly at Nancy. "It got even worse. Mother called her 'the Swedish Meatball' in a TV interview. Krissy lost a couple of big parts afterward. She was convinced Mother was deliberately trying to ruin her career."

Nancy took in this information impassively, but a question had been forming in her mind and now was the time to ask. "How do *you* feel about Kristin Stromm, Bree?"

"Well . . . it's hard to say. I don't dislike her—except when she treats me like a little kid. But we're not exactly buddy-buddy. Frankly, I think Krissy's—well, *shallow."* Bree looked highly uncomfortable. "I try to be nice to her. I tell myself, time and again, that I've got to accept it. I know Dad loves her. Still . . ." She bit her lower lip. "Oh, sometimes I wish Dad had found somebody else."

Nancy's mind was clicking away. Bree's answer satisfied her. If Bree had been trying to pin the blame on Kristin unfairly, she would have told Nancy that everything was wonderful.

No, Bree obviously had mixed feelings about her future stepmother. She didn't feel that Kristin was right for her father. And Bree felt guilty about that.

Nancy felt sorry for the girl whose life had seen such upheaval. She wondered if Brian Gordon was aware of his daughter's emotional turmoil.

Her thoughts turned back to the case. So

Lucinda Prado's fiery temper had caused her to make an enemy of Kristin Stromm. But had Kristin hated Lucinda enough to kill her?

Nancy nosed the Renault into the stream of rush-hour traffic in the city. The car crept along the Boulevard Pomare, serenaded by loud car horns.

With a sigh of relief, Nancy pulled into the Hotel Taravao's parking lot. "A traffic jam in Tahiti!" She got out of the car and grinned. "Even in paradise!"

Opening the car's trunk, she removed the spear gun shaft and the box containing Tayo's evidence. She wrapped the spear in a beach towel so it wouldn't attract attention. "One more question, Bree, before I get this evidence locked up. Did you tell anyone where we were going this morning?"

"Yes. I had breakfast with Dad and Krissy. She came over early this morning to see Dad and make up for their fight last night. I told them I was going to Orohena."

Nancy shut the trunk lid. "Were they the only people you told?"

"Yes. Oops, no, wait a minute!" Bree tapped her temple, as if to jog her memory. "Rupert stopped by just about then. He always comes by the hotel and mooches breakfast if he can. Oh, yes, and Manda had some vouchers for Dad to sign. She was there, too."

"Thanks, Bree."

Nancy watched as Bree pushed through the

glass doors into the lobby. In the last forty-eight hours the girl had learned of her mother's murder and the probable murder of an old friend. She was holding up pretty well under the strain, Nancy mused as she headed for the lobby.

A curly-haired Tahitian manned the front desk.

"May I help you, mademoiselle?"

"I'd like to store these overnight in the security vault." Nancy pushed the box and spear across the polished desktop.

The clerk had Nancy fill out a claim check. As Nancy watched him carry the items into the manager's office, she felt a small prick of guilt at not sharing all her suspicions with Bree. Obviously, someone had followed them from Opane's village to the waterfall. But how had he known that they would be at the village in the first place?

There were two possibilities, Nancy decided. Either their pursuer had been out on the highway, watching for Nancy's maroon Renault, or else he or she had overheard Bree telling her father about the trip.

When the clerk returned, Nancy thanked him. Then she realized he might be of more help. "Have you worked here long?" she asked politely.

"Ten years, mademoiselle."

"I guess you know the Gordons pretty well."

Teeth gleamed as he smiled. "Very well, indeed. I remember when Mademoiselle Bree was this high." His palm fluttered beside his waist.

Thinking fast, Nancy said, "We had a lovely drive today. It's a shame Ms. Stromm couldn't come with us."

The clerk blinked in surprise. "She didn't? Mademoiselle, she ran out of here right after you did."

Excitement made Nancy's pulse pound. "Really?"

"Yes." The clerk nodded. "Come to think of it, Madame Withers went out then, too."

Nancy blinked in surprise. "Oh," was all she said.

"Yes. Madame Withers asked me to phone a cab. After that I saw that other fellow—"

"Monsieur Holmberg," Nancy guessed.

"Yes, that's him. I saw him waiting rather impatiently at the bus stop just in front—here," he said, pointing.

"What about Bree's father?" Nancy asked.

"The monsieur I did not see leave," the clerk said matter-of-factly. "He phoned the desk to tell me he didn't want to be disturbed. Strange . . ."

"What's strange?" Nancy asked quickly.

"The cleaning woman said she saw Monsieur Gordon from the sundeck. He was walking down the beach toward the center of town."

"Have any of them returned?"

"I could not say, mademoiselle."

Nancy knew she had taken the interrogation as far as she could without making him suspicious. Thanking him for his help, she picked up her claims receipt and strolled away.

Nancy's mouth was a straight line as she thought, and her blue eyes were troubled. She didn't like the way the facts were adding up. Bree had told all four of them that she was driving down south to visit Opane. Within minutes of Bree's departure, all four had abruptly left the hotel.

Then someone had tried to kill Bree at Vaipahi waterfall. Coincidence?

Nancy couldn't help remembering that the same four people had disappeared from Faretaha the night Lucinda Prado had been murdered.

Kristin Stromm—Rupert Holmberg—Amanda Withers. Was one of them a murderer?

A queasy surge chilled Nancy as she focused on the fourth suspect—Bree's own father!

Chapter

Seven

THE NEXT AFTERNOON Nancy brought her evidence to the gendarmerie. A policeman escorted her to the detective bureau.

Captain Tuana Mutoi, the chief of detectives, was a tall, good-looking man in his early thirties, with curly, jet black hair, deep-set eyes, and a firm chin. Nancy was struck by how dashing he looked in his khaki uniform and white cap.

Mutoi listened politely as Nancy told her story. His eyes dispassionately studied the spear and the severed anchor chain.

"That's where we stand right now," Nancy concluded, smoothing her cotton skirt. "The way I see it, whoever killed Lucinda Prado and Tayo

Kapali is still here on the island. He or she got nervous when Bree started looking for Tayo. That's when the murder attempts began."

"Are you asking for protection for yourself and Mademoiselle Gordon?" Captain Mutoi asked, folding his hands on the blotter.

"Not exactly," Nancy replied. "I was hoping we could work together on this. Maybe smoke him out."

The captain smiled indulgently. "Mademoiselle Drew, I think you'd better leave police work to the professionals."

Nancy had heard words like those enough times before to know that she shouldn't let her frustration show. Instead she gave him an engaging smile and replied evenly, "Captain, I have helped police departments in the States on many occasions—"

"I'm sure you have," he interrupted smoothly, putting the anchor chain back in its box. "And I thank you for bringing this matter to my attention." Skepticism laced his words as he reached for the spear gun shaft. "I'll have the lab dust this for fingerprints."

Nancy's heart sank. From his tone of voice, she could tell that any such test would have an extremely low priority.

Captain Mutoi leaned back in his chair. "Is there anything else we can do for you?"

Nancy chose her words carefully. "Maybe there is. Would you mind if I had a look at the original *Southwind* accident report?"

"What for?"

"Bree's told me so much about it," Nancy added, hoping her alibi sounded plausible. "I'm curious."

"I can't see any harm in that." Leaning forward the captain wrote Nancy a permission slip. "There! You'll find the archives upstairs. Oh, and if you come across anything else like this"—he tapped his pen on the spear-gun shaft—"by all means, let me have a look."

After thanking Captain Mutoi, Nancy went upstairs. The archives clerk handed her a thick volume and pointed out an empty desk at the far end of the room.

Nancy spent the next few hours reading the report of the inquest. She covered everything, from Tahiti's weather that day to a description of the collision to Lucinda Prado's autopsy. On her notepad, Nancy jotted down the names of witnesses who had appeared at the inquest.

When she was finished, Nancy returned the book and went downstairs to the maritime office. Most of the witnesses had been boat owners anchored near the *Southwind.* It was a long shot, but Nancy wanted to see if any of them were still in Tahiti.

She was in luck. Of the eight boat owners who originally gave testimony, two were still listed as residents by the maritime office. Nancy hurriedly copied their current addresses. Then, after thanking the clerk, she strolled out of the office.

As she walked past the detective bureau, she

heard a pair of masculine voices, one of them Captain Mutoi's. Their words caught her attention, and she halted for a moment to listen.

"What have you got on the smugglers, Lucien?"

"My informers tell me there's a new shipment of computer parts in town, sir. Very expensive goods, I hear. Prototypes of Japan's newest hardware—system cards, mostly, with multimegabyte memory capacity. The word is that they're soon to be shipped to South America."

Frustration deepened the captain's voice. "Who, Lucien? Who's behind this?"

"No one knows, sir. They're well organized—and well hidden!"

"Put everyone on it. Double-check every ship leaving Papeete," Captain Mutoi ordered. "This gang has been plundering Japanese computer factories for years. The Japanese police traced them here to Tahiti. Both Japan and our government want us to put them out of business—for good!"

Looks as if Bree and I are on our own, Nancy thought, striding into the parking lot. The Tahitian police have their hands full with those computer smugglers.

Minutes later Nancy was strolling along Charterboat Row, the section of waterfront devoted to sports fishing. Sleek cabin cruisers bobbed in the gentle swell, sunlight flashing on their chrome fittings.

She spied the name *Galilee* on the stern of a

sturdy Gulfstar 36. A wiry, brown-skinned man in a Greek skipper's cap stood on her foredeck, expertly winding a line around a cleat.

Cupping her hands to her mouth, Nancy cried, "Ahoy, the *Galilee!*"

"*Bonjour,* there." The man's U.S. accent fractured the French words.

Nancy switched to English. "Hi, I'm looking for Josh Tuttle."

"You found him."

"My name's Nancy Drew. I'm a friend of Bree Gordon's. I'd like to ask you a few questions about the *Southwind.* Do you mind?"

"Not at all." He walked around the deck and put down the gangway for Nancy. "Welcome aboard! How is young Bree, by the way?"

"Pretty good. She's going to UCLA these days." Nancy followed him into the boat's screened cabin. He gestured to a settee, and she took a seat. "Did you know the Gordons very well?"

Tuttle grinned. "Well enough. There are no secrets in boat basins. I liked them. No moviestar airs on that Lucinda. When she was out here on vacation, she was plain old Mrs. Gordon, and that's the way she liked it."

"How did Brian Gordon strike you?" Nancy asked."

"Money-hungry—" Tuttle broke off quickly and narrowed his eyes. "You ask a lot of questions, Ms. Drew. How come?"

"Some disturbing questions have come up

about the wreck of the *Southwind*. Bree asked me to check them out." Nancy settled back in the cushions. "Would you mind telling me about the accident?"

"Sure! I'm used to it by now. Why, I'm practically the boat basin's official *Southwind* historian." Now Tuttle seemed to enjoy peering into the past. "I'd just gotten back from a day trip. Found a snug anchorage near the lee shore and put down a pair of anchors."

"It seems I've found an expert sailor," Nancy commented.

"Been at it twenty years." Tuttle grinned self-consciously, then took a quick breath. "Anyway, the night Lucinda died, there was a big storm. It kicked up quite a chop. I could feel the surge tugging at *Galilee*'s hull.

"At about two A.M. I heard a motor and thought, 'What fool's out on a night like this?' I went topside, just in time to see Lucinda go by in a dinghy headed for *Southwind*. Thought she'd capsize in the swell, but she just rode the current all the way and climbed on board *Southwind*. Quite a sailor, that woman!

"Anyway, I went below, then I remembered that I'd left my deck lights on. So I went topside again. And *Southwind* was gone now! All I saw was one moored boat and the channel buoy. It sure was rough water out there! The buoy's bell was ringing, and its little green light was swinging back and forth. I doused my deck lights and hit the sack."

"When did you hear about the wreck?"

"Next morning. It was all over Papeete."

Nancy mulled over his story. Tuttle had seen Lucinda board the *Southwind* at 2:00 A.M. When he went topside again at 2:30, the vessel was gone. That matched the times in the official report.

Standing, Nancy gave him a grateful smile. "Thanks for taking time to talk to me, Mr. Tuttle."

"Any friend of Bree's is a friend of mine." He slid the screen door open for Nancy. "You tell her I said hi."

"I will," Nancy promised, halting at the gangway. "Oh, one more thing—you wouldn't know where I might be able to find Pierre Panchaud, would you? I didn't see his name on file at the maritime office."

Genuine surprise washed over his face. "That's strange! Talk around town is that Pierre's got his own boat."

"I didn't see it listed," Nancy replied.

"Maybe you're right." Tuttle shrugged. "I haven't seen Pierre working *these* waters, and I'm out every day. Try the Café Chat Noir ashore. I hear Pierre hangs out down there."

"Café Chat Noir." Nancy committed the name to memory. "Where do I find it?"

"Rue des Écoles." He tilted his head eastward. "But you be careful down there, Ms. Drew. That is one rough neighborhood!"

* * *

The Café Chat Noir stood on a narrow side street, flanked by a couple of taverns. Its checkerboard awning had seen better days. The silhouette of a huge black cat, outlined in neon, perched on top of a weather-beaten cinema marquee.

Clutching her shoulder bag, Nancy walked inside, out of the early-evening dusk. An old-fashioned ceiling fan twirled lazily. An empty stage, its curtains down, marked the far end of the restaurant.

Nancy was suddenly aware of a presence at her side. She turned at once.

The maître d' eyed her coolly. He reminded Nancy of the fat man in the old movie *The Maltese Falcon*.

"A table, mademoiselle?"

"Actually," Nancy said, "I'm looking for a man named Panchaud. Pierre Panchaud. Have you seen him around?"

His lips tightened. "Now and then."

"Do you know where I might find him?"

The maître d' turned his palms upward in a gesture of ignorance.

"How about Pierre's friends?" Nancy persisted.

"You might talk to them." Looking a bit smug, he pointed to a pair of rough-looking French sailors seated at a table near the stage. "New boys in town, but Pierre finds them friendly enough."

"Thank you." Nancy manufactured a bright smile, then headed across the room.

The men stood as Nancy approached their

table. One was thin-faced and swarthy, with buck teeth. The other was taller, built like a linebacker, wearing a striped shirt and a black beret.

"Excuse me," Nancy said. "Could you tell me where to find Pierre Panchaud?"

Thin Face sneered at her. "Get lost!"

Nancy tried her most winning smile. "Look, I just want to ask him a few questions about—"

Black Beret grabbed a tall wine bottle from the table. In one quick move he smashed it against the chair. Brandishing the bottleneck like a knife, he aimed the razor-sharp fragment at Nancy's face!

Chapter

Eight

THE JAGGED BOTTLE EDGE rushed toward her. Heart hammering, Nancy threw herself sideways to avoid the thrust, and at the same moment grabbed the Frenchman's wrist and turned it aside. Then, stepping in close, she smashed her right elbow into the thug's bicep.

Black Beret shrieked in pain. His nerveless fingers dropped the broken bottle. It shattered on the floor.

Thin Face rushed her. "You little—!"

Bracing herself against the table, Nancy launched a scissor kick at the newcomer. Her sole struck the sailor flush on the jaw, knocking him sprawling.

Suddenly a deafening electric bell rang out. Nancy looked up just in time to see the maître d' lift his hand from a countertop button.

A voice hollered, "It's a raid!" A rear door burst open. Dozens of panicky, well-dressed people rushed into the room. Brushing her hair out of her face, Nancy stared in confusion.

Then she caught a glimpse of a stunning blonde in a shimmery emerald evening gown, eyes wide with alarm, sprinting away on her stiletto heels.

Nancy blinked in recognition. Kristin Stromm! What was she doing there?

Nancy heard footsteps running behind her. Turning, she saw her two erstwhile opponents scramble for the front door. Although she was tempted to give chase, she decided to let them go. She was more interested in what Kristin was doing here.

A quick peek through the open doorway provided the answer. A roulette wheel crowned one long table. The others were covered with green felt and white dice.

The maître d' waddled past Nancy and closed the door. "Now that you've chased all my customers away, would you kindly leave?"

Nancy folded her arms. "Gambling's illegal in French Polynesia, isn't it?"

The maître d' tossed her a defiant look. "You didn't actually *see* anyone gambling, did you?"

No, thought Nancy, but I saw you hit the alarm

button. And I doubt Kristin Stromm comes here for the cuisine.

"Goodbye, mademoiselle." His pudgy finger pointed at the front door. "If you really are looking for Pierre Panchaud, I understand he owns a dive shop on the Rue des Halles."

"Why didn't you tell me that before?" Nancy asked, thoroughly annoyed.

The maître d' shrugged indifferently. "I didn't know you were an agent of the Deuxième Bureau before."

Nancy understood at once, and she couldn't suppress a grin. The Deuxième Bureau was the French FBI. Seeing her karate performance, the maître d' must have thought she was an undercover cop and had hit the alarm button.

Smoothing her skirt, Nancy walked out of the café. She couldn't shake the image of the fleeing actress. So Kristin liked to gamble. Nancy wondered what to make of that fact—and if Bree or Brian Gordon knew about it.

Nancy pursed her lips thoughtfully. It was certainly interesting, that Kristin should frequent the favorite café of Pierre Panchaud, the *Southwind*'s sole survivor.

She would look up Pierre as soon as she finished interviewing the other *Southwind* witnesses. She had a few questions for that man.

Later that evening Nancy stepped out of her hotel bathroom, vigorously toweling her damp hair. She was looking forward to relaxing, reading a magazine, and reviewing her notes on the perplexing case. Just then the telephone jangled. Dropping the towel, she tied the belt of her terry-cloth robe and hurried over to the night table.

Picking up the receiver, she heard a male voice say thickly, "Eez thees ze most bee-ootiful girl in Tahiti?"

Nancy was stumped for a moment. Then she caught on. "Ned, that was awful!" she said, laughing.

"Nancy! I can't fool you, can I?" Ned's laughter joined hers on the line. "How are you?"

"Fine!" The sound of her boyfriend's voice was sending a happy tingle through Nancy's nerves. "How are you doing?"

"Tearing my hair out over a term paper. It's half the grade for the course. But I'd rather hear about your case." His curiosity was noticeable even over the wires.

"It's taken a strange turn, Ned."

Nancy quickly filled him in on the events of the past few days. When she was finished, he let out a low whistle.

"A five-year-old murder! You sure know how to pick them, Nancy. You really think it was one of Lucinda Prado's inner circle?"

"It sure looks that way. Lucinda and her family left the *Southwind* on Friday night. Kristin's big party was Saturday night. I read the witnesses' statements. Nobody at the anchorage expected Lucinda back until Monday."

"So the only people who knew she was aboard the yacht were the people at Kristin's party," Ned added. "Who's your number-one suspect?"

"It's too soon to guess, Ned," she replied, holding the phone in her lap. "I still wonder why the house was empty when Bree woke up. And where was Manda? She was an overnight guest there too. Where was Bree's father?"

"Good questions!" Ned's voice sounded troubled. "Listen, if you need me, say so. I can hop a plane and be in Tahiti in twenty-four hours."

"Thanks, Ned, I appreciate that. But I can handle myself. I'll be fine."

"I hope so. You're my precious, irreplaceable Nancy Drew. I do worry about you. Especially when there are nut cases running around with broken bottles!"

A warm feeling rushed through Nancy. With a smile, she murmured, "I'll be extra careful on this one, Ned." She blew a kiss into the phone. "I love you, Nickerson!"

"Love you, too, Drew. Take care!"

Slowly, regretfully, Nancy replaced the receiver. She wondered if she had made a mistake in turning down Ned's offer of help. There was a killer out there, a shrewd enemy who seemed to want only one thing: Nancy Drew and Bree Gordon—dead!

* * *

The following morning Nancy met Bree in the Taravao's broad lobby. They had made plans to visit another witness, Alistair Pendleton, an Englishman who had seen Lucinda on the night of the accident. Bree looked tired and drawn. She put her hands in the pockets of her short denim skirt, her dark eyes mournful. Nancy decided she would try to keep Bree's mind off her mother as much as possible.

As they walked out to the car, Nancy asked, "Bree, has Kristin ever mentioned a café called the Chat Noir?"

"Not that I know of." Bree's eyebrows arched with curiosity. "Why do you ask?"

Nancy opened her car door. "I saw her there last night, gambling in the back room."

Bree made a pinched face. "Oh, brother! Dad will be furious. After the last time, Krissy swore she'd never do it again."

Nancy pushed open the passenger door from the inside. "What happened the last time?"

"Dad and Krissy went to Vegas last year," Bree explained. "Krissy went a little crazy at the tables. Dad covered her losses. They were still arguing when they got home."

Nancy needed no further information to imagine the battle.

"If you don't mind a personal question," she began, "did your parents ever fight about money?"

Bree was silent, obviously reliving the past.

67

"Money was never an issue that I knew of. Not like Mother wanting to quit the film industry. She was determined to retire to Tahiti—and soon. It made for some rousing battles, believe me."

Sensing the girl's distress, Nancy fell silent. She remembered Tuttle's comment. He'd thought that Brian was very interested in money, probably his wife's. However, now, according to Bree, that wasn't the case at all. Nancy herself had gotten the impression that money wasn't all that important to Brian.

Which left only one other motive for him to kill his wife—Kristin Stromm.

With his marriage in trouble, had Brian been attracted to the beautiful Swedish actress? Nancy left the speculation dangling for the moment.

As they drove through Pendleton's neighborhood of Pamatai, Nancy admired the fine old bungalows built on a ridge overlooking a sparkling turquoise bay.

Alistair Pendleton answered the doorbell, finally embracing Bree when his failing eyesight confirmed who she was—the daughter of his old friend. He invited the girls inside. Bree offered to prepare some lemonade in the kitchen while Nancy and Pendleton retired to the drawing room.

"Oh, I'll never forget that night." Leaning back in a plush chair, Pendleton lit his meerschaum pipe. "I was staying on my boat then, and the rough sea kept me awake. Precisely at two A.M. I heard a motor. Looking out the porthole, I saw Lucinda go past in a dinghy. I watched her until she climbed aboard the *Southwind,* just to make certain she was safe, you understand." He took a long pull on his pipe. "Shortly thereafter, I became a bit queasy."

"So you went topside," Nancy prodded.

"Quite." Brows tensing, he chewed the pipe-stem. "The bell buoy was bobbing like a cork in a millrace, green light swinging. I saw the Moorea ferry on her way in, the waves smashing her bow. Oh, yes, and there was that woman."

"What woman?" Nancy asked, her eyes narrowing with interest.

"On the beach. Dark-haired, wearing a trench coat. She was walking up and down. Quite anxious, if you ask me. I assume she was looking for a boat, you know. But I didn't see any, and neither did she." He tapped the pipe against a small ashtray. "She didn't linger. Once or twice, she seemed to look at the *Southwind,* as if trying to come to a decision. Then she drew up her collar and hurried away. Odd, eh?"

"I'll say." Nancy filed away this bit of news. "When did you notice that the *Southwind* was missing?" she inquired.

"At two-thirty, I believe. Yes. I looked out the porthole again. *Southwind* was gone. Lucinda was a smashing sailor, but not even she would have gone out in that storm."

"Had you been surprised to see Lucinda back aboard the yacht?" Nancy asked.

A frown on his lips, Pendleton glanced quickly at the kitchen. Turning to Nancy again, he deliberately lowered his voice.

"I do hope you'll keep this to yourself, Nancy. Bree's a lovely girl, and I know it would only upset her." He lit his pipe again. "I wasn't at all surprised to see Lucinda. She and Brian had had the most dreadful quarrel on deck that afternoon." His face puckered in distaste. "I do wish couples wouldn't fight in public."

That was one story Nancy fully intended to keep to herself. "Mr. Pendleton, would you say the Gordons' marriage had just about had it?"

"Not really," Pendleton replied, after a moment's reflection. "For all his arrogance, Brian's a bit weak. He leaned on Lucinda. She was very proud, fiery, yet old-fashioned in her ideas about marriage. Oh, she talked divorce a lot. But that's all it was—just talk."

Nancy thought of Kristin Stromm. "Would Lucinda have divorced Brian if there was another woman in the picture?"

Pendleton frowned. "Divorce, no. Have a public row, yes."

"She was that jealous, huh?"

"Quite! Poor Brian would have had to scramble up the nearest palm tree."

"Thanks for your help, Mr. Pendleton," Nancy said, smiling in spite of her growing uneasiness about Bree's father.

Bree came in with two glasses and then, catching Nancy's eye, wandered out to the garden.

Nancy pressed on. "Tell me, is there anyone else in Tahiti I could talk to about Lucinda Prado?"

"Well, you could try Rupert Holmberg." The Englishman set aside his pipe. "He was always hanging about the *Southwind,* trying to get Lucinda to sign for one of his comedy films. In fact, he bought his own boat several years ago. Carbon copy of the *Southwind.* Rupert was very much impressed with Lucinda's yacht."

"How do you know that?" Nancy set down her glass. "Are you a friend of Rupert's?"

"Actually, it's more of a business relationship. He's not my sort of chap at all." Pendleton stood up. "Before my retirement I was employed by an insurance firm. Once in a great while I still write a policy. Two months before Lucinda's death Rupert asked me to write a three-million-dollar policy on her."

Nancy stiffened as the significance of the fact sank in. Pendleton caught the look on her face. "I thought the deal a bit dicey myself, but Rupert assured me that it was done all the time in Hollywood," he offered.

"Do you recall the precise terms of the policy?"

"Oh, yes. The coverage was not on Lucinda or her life expectancy, you understand. It was on something called forfeiture of assurance."

"What's that?" Nancy asked.

"Well, apparently Rupert and Lucinda had been discussing her participation in his new comedy film. Although no contract had been signed, Rupert felt that he had Lucinda's 'assurance' that she would star in it. In order to protect that 'assurance,' Rupert took out the policy. In the event that catastrophic illness or death prevented Lucinda from doing the film, Rupert would be able to collect compensatory payment."

To Nancy it sounded like a perfect scheme to swindle the insurance company. "And you're telling me a company *accepted* that policy?"

Looking highly uncomfortable, Pendleton replied, "Well, Rupert did pay cash, you know. A sixty-thousand-dollar premium. The bidding company thought it a marvelous investment. Lucinda was a healthy, vigorous woman of forty-two—they thought they would never have to pay it."

"Big surprise for them," Nancy added. "Do you have any idea why Rupert wanted that policy?"

"He refused to say, but there were rumors of severe money troubles," Pendleton reminisced. "Without Lucinda as the star of his next comedy film, he was certain to end in bankruptcy." He shook his head in amazement. "Protecting that 'assurance' was a most prudent move, as things turned out. That three million bailed Rupert out of financial trouble."

At that moment Bree came back in from the garden. "Am I missing something?"

"Nothing much. Mr. Pendleton has been a big help." Nancy exchanged a look of understanding with the Englishman as he opened the front door. "Thanks again."

"You're quite welcome, Nancy. Take care of yourself, Bree."

As they headed back to the Renault, Nancy pondered these new developments. What did Rupert have in mind when he took out that policy?

Bree had told her that Lucinda was determined to quit the film business. Rupert had desperately needed a Lucinda Prado movie to bail himself out of trouble. He would have gone broke but for that timely insurance policy.

Nancy turned grim. That policy put a whole new light on things. If Rupert had known of Lucinda's decision to retire, then he would have had the strongest motive for killing her—a three-million-dollar motive!

After a shoreside lunch Nancy and Bree visited the Rue des Halles, Tahiti's bustling open-air market. As they strolled along the sun-baked pavement, Nancy had to remind herself to ignore the colorful merchandise that spilled from the jumble of tiny shops. Her one aim now was finding the diving store that belonged to Pierre Panchaud.

A bell jangled as Nancy pushed the door open. A muscular, dark-haired man in his late twenties stood behind the counter, examining a pair of scuba tanks. He had a lean face, with a cleft chin and a pair of piercing hazel eyes.

Those eyes narrowed as the girls approached the counter. "Bree Gordon."

"Hi, Pierre. It's been awhile, I guess." Bree's smile was polite.

Setting aside the scuba gear, he asked, "What brings you downtown, mademoiselle?"

"We wanted to talk to you about the *Southwind,*" Bree said hopefully.

"I did all my talking to the maritime board. The *Southwind*'s ancient history." Pierre's expression turned decidedly unfriendly. "I've put the sea behind me."

Nancy spoke up. "That's not what I've heard."

"And who are you?" he asked dryly.

"My name's Nancy Drew. I'm a friend of Bree's."

"Then I don't need to answer *your* questions." His tone had turned frosty.

Keeping her voice polite, Nancy met his hostile gaze evenly. "Have you something to hide?"

"Nothing at all." Pierre drew himself erect. "I will tell you what you want to know about the *Southwind.*"

"How long had you known Bree's mother before she died?" Nancy inquired.

"Not long. I was in Japan five years ago, I needed a ride home to Tahiti and heard the *Southwind* was fitting out. So I signed on and sailed with her to Tahiti."

"Tell us about the storm."

"There's not much to tell. I had the all-night watch," Pierre said matter-of-factly. "The family

74

had already gone ashore in the dinghy. I took it back out to the boat and relieved Tayo. Then he went ashore in it. Around two A.M., Lucinda climbed up the stern ladder and startled me. I hadn't expected her back until Monday. She told me she was sleeping aboard, then went to her stateroom. That's the last I saw of her." His tone deepened. He seemed to be reliving the accident.

"The storm surge worsened. I went below to check out the pumps. On my way back I stopped in the galley for a bite to eat. The *Southwind* was really rolling with the swell. I could hear the buoy's bell ringing outside. I looked through one of the portholes and saw the buoy's green light and the big Moorea ferry passing astern."

He paused for a moment as Nancy waited expectantly. So far his story sounded no different from the other accounts she'd heard. He took a breath. "When the freighter rammed us, I ran up the companionway, yelling 'Abandon ship!' That boat went down like a brick! I barely had time to grab a life preserver and jump into the sea."

Nancy turned to Bree, concerned that the girl might be finding this hard to take, but her lips were set in a determined line. "Do you know Kristin Stromm?" Nancy pursued.

"By sight. She came aboard the *Southwind* once or twice. And I've seen her movies."

"Have you ever seen her at the Café Chat Noir?" asked Nancy, flashing him a speculative glance.

Pierre froze. His expression suddenly became

angry. "You're mistaken," he said stiffly. "I don't go there."

Nancy recalled what Josh Tuttle and the café's maître d' had told her. "People say they've seen you in there."

All at once, Pierre balled his fist. His enraged blow rattled the counter.

"I don't like being called a liar!" Furious, Pierre shook his fist at Nancy. "Do yourself a favor. Get out of here! If you mess with me, you're *really* going to get hurt!"

Chapter

Nine

Nancy was startled by the hostile gesture, but she stood her ground. "Is that a threat, Pierre?"

"Take it any way you like." He pointed firmly at the front door. "Just get out of here!"

Nancy knew she would get nothing more from Pierre. "Let's go, Bree." Taking her arm, Nancy led the girl out into the crowded street.

Bree trembled with suppressed anger. "He's a bum, Nancy. He always was." She stalked away angrily.

Nancy glanced back at the dive shop. Pierre Panchaud was no friend of the Gordons. As a diver he was certainly familiar with spear guns. But had he killed Lucinda? And, if so, what could his motive possibly have been?

"Where to next?" asked Bree as they headed back to the car.

"I thought we might have a look at the spot where the *Southwind* was anchored," Nancy replied. "Tayo found that chain. Perhaps there's another clue down there."

"Good idea." Bree nodded in agreement. "We can rent some scuba gear back at the hotel."

As they drove back to the Taravao, Nancy mulled over Pierre's story. The man was certainly unpleasant enough, but Nancy found it hard to think of him as a murderer. Pierre had never even met Lucinda before that summer.

The other suspects had genuinely compelling reasons to kill her. Kristin had hated Bree's mother. She had considered Lucinda her biggest screen rival.

Nancy reflected again on the obvious fact that Rupert stood to gain much-needed money. And for Brian, Lucinda's death had been the ticket out of a stormy marriage.

Nancy shook her head as she considered her most recent encounter. Pierre's story meshed perfectly with the reminiscences of the other *Southwind* witnesses. All reported the same things—the ferry passing astern, the green light on the buoy, the ringing bell.

Nancy frowned thoughtfully. So Pierre must have been belowdecks that night, just as he had said. The man's alibi seemed ironclad.

But why did Pierre lie about the Café Chat Noir? And why had those two Frenchmen attacked her after she had casually mentioned Pierre's name?

Nancy had to wonder if the two men were involved in Lucinda's murder. If so, how? They were definitely linked to Pierre Panchaud.

Nancy felt more than a little bewildered by so many possibilities and so little proof. But she was not about to give up. Things were just getting interesting.

After changing Nancy entered the Gordon penthouse suite. She found Amanda Withers on the sofa, prim as ever in a tailored apricot linen suit. She shuffled business papers, her steel-rimmed glasses low on her sharp nose. Nancy paused expectantly in the doorway.

Manda removed her glasses. "Hello, Nancy. Are you looking for Bree?"

"Yes. We're meeting here." Nancy took a chair across from the secretary. "She's renting some scuba tanks so we can have a look at the *Southwind*'s old anchorage."

"That again." With a sigh, Manda set her papers on the coffee table. "Sometimes I don't think we'll ever hear the end of it."

"I guess you've seen a lot working for the family all these years," Nancy commented.

"Indeed I have." Giving Nancy a conspiratorial smile, Manda leaned forward. "I could tell you stories. Of course, it's not my place to gossip. But if you knew the truth about *her . . . !"*

"Her?" Nancy echoed.

"Kristin Stromm." Manda spat out the name as if it were poison. "You know, the night Lucinda drowned, Kristin was nowhere to be found. She left her own party right after Brian and Lucinda quarreled. I wonder where she went. Don't you?"

I could ask the same question of you, Manda, thought Nancy. She ignored the secretary's insinuations, though, and changed the subject. "You don't sound very happy with your job."

"Oh! Don't get me wrong. I adore working for the family. Bree's a darling." Manda's gaze softened. "And Brian, he's such a wonderful man. Absolutely brilliant. A true cinema genius."

"How did you get along with Lucinda?" Nancy asked carefully.

"Fairly well, I suppose." Manda wrinkled her nose in distaste. "She was *such* a demanding woman. She bullied poor Brian unmercifully. Had the vilest temper I've ever seen. I'd have given my notice in a minute, if not for Brian." She tugged self-consciously at her skirt.

"Her death was quite a shock to him. He was so lonely. If only he could have met the right woman—someone kind, thoughtful, even-tempered, intellectual, loving . . ."

Nancy struggled not to smile. She could guess who fit *that* description.

"Well, he does have Kristin," Nancy observed.

"It's a travesty," Manda snapped, tight-lipped with emotion. "Brian and that— *Ohhh!*" Eyes narrowing furiously, she added, "Kristin Stromm is a shallow, man-hungry fortune hunter! She's been chasing Brian for years. The night of the party Lucinda had to drag him away from her. If you ask me, that woman is completely unfit to be his wife!"

"Well, it's his choice," Nancy replied evenly.

Manda stood quickly, an angry blush coloring her heart-shaped face. "How can you be so complacent about it? Bree's your *friend*. Don't you care that her father's marrying that—that tramp?"

The passion in the secretary's voice startled Nancy. Clearly, hidden fires blazed within Amanda Withers.

Just as quickly a cool mask descended on her features. "If you'll excuse me, I have some business to attend to." Performing a quick about-face, Manda marched out of the living room, head high, heels punishing the hardwood floor.

Nancy watched her go, reflecting on the new factor that had been added to the equation. She felt bad for upsetting Manda, but the woman was clearly not very rational on the subject of the Gordon family.

It took no special skill to see that Manda was head-over-heels in love with Brian Gordon. Beneath her prim exterior seethed a savage jealousy. She now hated Kristin Stromm as ardently as she had once hated Lucinda Prado.

Nancy suddenly remembered something. Bree had told her that when she awakened at Faretaha, she had called for Manda. There had been no answer.

Questions flitted through Nancy's mind. Why did Manda leave the estate that night? Where did she go?

Suspicion provided some ugly answers. Manda was practically part of the Gordon family. She knew that Lucinda would never divorce her husband. What if she had taken advantage of the Gordons' quarrel that night?

Manda might have followed her employer back to the yacht. Indeed, she'd lived aboard the *Southwind* too. She knew all about the anchor chain.

How simple it would have been to cut the chain while Lucinda slept, to watch as the *Southwind* drifted toward certain destruction.

Manda's motive would have been simplicity itself. With Lucinda dead, Brian would have been free to marry her!

"Have you ever tried this before?" asked Bree, sliding a flipper onto her foot.

"Once or twice." Nancy smiled. "You may have to refresh me."

The girls were standing in the cockpit of a sleek twenty-foot runabout. Beside the boat, a red-and-white dive flag bobbed on its Styrofoam buoy.

Bree went through a run-down as she boosted a

tank rig onto Nancy's shoulders. "You'll be okay. Just remember to keep an eye on that air gauge."

Nancy buckled the support straps. "What about sharks?"

Bree tightened her weight belt. "Oh, forget all those movies. You rarely see sharks in the boat basin. Besides, they aren't *that* dangerous. They only go crazy if they smell blood. You leave them alone, they'll leave you alone."

Nancy studied the sun-dappled water. "Are you sure?"

"Positive." Bree grinned. "Sharks have their own body language. If you see a shark swimming in a tight circle, with his fins pointed straight down, that means he's angry and will attack."

Gooseflesh rippled along Nancy's bare arms. With a weak smile, she mounted the gunwale. "Thank you, Bree, for knowledge I never want to use!"

After putting the regulator in her mouth, Nancy backflipped into the sea.

Warm waters closed around her. Air bubbles drifted through her floating hair. Waving her arms languidly, Nancy looked around, startled and delighted by the beauty of the lagoon.

A school of bright red clownfish zigzagged through the turquoise water. Anemone strands soared upward from the coral reef, swaying in the mild current. A large sea turtle coasted along the bottom, making a wide detour around the girls.

Bree, in her lemon yellow maillot, performed a graceful jackknife turn and headed for the bottom. Nancy, in her emerald swimsuit, followed close behind.

Soon Bree and Nancy were cruising along the seabed, kicking in tandem, their air bubbles streaming to the surface. This is great, Nancy thought. I could stay down here forever—if I didn't have a mystery to solve!

Halting at a broad, level spot, Bree pantomimed a shipwreck. Nancy nodded in understanding. This was where the *Southwind* had anchored.

Together they searched the area. Nancy's fingertips probed the loose black sand.

She thought of Tayo. How many times had he swooped down to this very spot, searching for the clue he knew must be there?

Just then a shadow blotted out the sun. Looking up, Nancy saw a hull drifting overhead. Her brows knit in concern. Motorboats were forbidden to enter any area with a dive flag. What was the matter with that guy?

Keeping her eyes on the boat, Nancy swam closer to Bree.

A figure appeared at the transom. The hull rocked under its weight. Rippling water distorted the image. Nancy couldn't tell if it was male or female.

The figure lifted a slender object to its shoulder.

Nancy reacted instantly. Rolling in the water, she shoved Bree away with her flippered feet.

Whizzz! A spear gun shaft zipped past Bree, burying itself in the sand.

Nancy looked up. The shadowy figure was hurriedly reloading.

Nancy looked frantically around, seeking cover but finding none. For the killer, it would be like shooting fish in a barrel.

Nancy and Bree were trapped!

Chapter

Ten

NANCY WATCHED HELPLESSLY as the sniper lifted the spear gun again.

Suddenly Bree tapped her shoulder. Whirling, Nancy saw the black-haired girl gripping her own weight belt. Her free hand tugged at Nancy's.

The emergency release!

Nancy pressed the tab with her palm. Instantly the weight belt slid past her thighs. Nancy left the bottom like an air bubble, Bree at her side, speeding to the surface. Remembering what Bree had told her about the possibility of bursting her lungs, Nancy was careful to exhale gradually, matching her breathing to the decreasing water pressure.

Their swift ascent startled the sniper. His

second shot went wild. Bree guided Nancy directly beneath the boat. Barnacled wood met Nancy's outstretched palms.

Relief washed through Nancy's body. The perfect hiding place! So long as they stayed directly beneath the boat, there was no way the sniper could get at them.

Suddenly the boat's twin propeller began twirling. Its hull lumbered forward. Nancy pushed herself out of harm's way. The cruiser surged past, heading out to sea.

As Nancy surfaced in its wake, she caught a glimpse of the gilt-edged name on the stern. Her blood seemed to freeze all at once. *Sous le Vent.*

It was the boat from the scrap yard—the one that had departed right after the murder attempt.

New questions flooded her mind. Was Henri Chaumette, the boat's owner, the one behind that stunt with the crane? She thought about those boat-shoe prints near the waterfall. Was he also the man behind the spear gun? And if so, why? Who was Henri Chaumette?

Nancy treaded water, watching the boat speed away. There was nothing she could do to pursue it. As she headed back to their boat, a sudden realization made Nancy quicken her strokes. She had to return to the hotel. If the enemy was willing to risk another daylight attack, Nancy had to be on the right track!

An hour later Nancy steered the Renault through the broad gates of Faretahà. Bree sat moodily in the passenger seat. Both girls had exchanged their maillots and scuba gear for tank tops and walking shorts.

Setting the brake, Nancy suggested, "Why don't you wait here? I think I can get more out of Kristin if I face her alone."

Bree gritted her teeth but said nothing. Nancy slammed the car door and bent to look through the window at Bree, a smile playing on her lips.

Bree was too upset to respond in kind though. "Can you blame me for being angry?" She fell silent again.

Nancy exhaled deeply. "I know how you feel, Bree. That's why you're going to sit here until you cool off. Kristin may be innocent, you know."

Still fuming, Bree looked away. "I doubt it!"

"Cool off—please?" Nancy added in a conciliatory tone. "I'll be right back."

Bree nodded curtly, her mouth taut. Nancy wasn't at all sure Bree meant to stay put, but there was nothing she could do about it right then. Shouldering her bag, she strode purposefully up the walk.

She found Kristin standing in the parlor, sipping a late-afternoon drink. The actress was wearing a sleeveless silk top and white silk harem-style trousers. Her lush blond hair curled loosely over shoulders. She glanced suspiciously at Nancy. "What do you want?"

"I'm looking for Bree," Nancy replied, using

the cover story she'd prepared. "I couldn't find her at the hotel, so I thought she might be here."

Kristin smiled sourly. "I'm afraid the spoiled Miss Gordon spends as little time in my company as possible."

Kristin's shoulder dipped awkwardly as she started across the room, and Nancy realized that the actress was limping! Her gaze moved to Kristin's slender ankle, where a pressure bandage was just visible under the trouser cuff.

"How did you hurt your ankle, Ms. Stromm?" she asked, her mind racing. The spear-gun sniper had skidded in the mud while running away, according to those footprints Nancy had found. He or she could easily have twisted an ankle.

Kristin seemed shaken by the question. A nervous smile molded her mouth. "I—I pulled a tendon playing tennis with Bree." Her fingers trembled as she fiddled with her pendant earring. "Surely you remember. You were there."

Right, thought Nancy. *And* I was here at dinner the next night, when there was absolutely nothing wrong with your ankle! She made a mental note to find out whether Kristin owned a pair of boating shoes.

Right now, though, there was another angle to explore. Nancy closed the door behind her and took a step forward. "I don't mean to be rude, but I can't help noticing that you and Bree don't get along very well," she said as tactfully as she could.

"That's not *my* fault!" Kristin's hand brushed the silk cowl of her blouse. "Heaven knows I've tried to be civil to her. She resents me because I'm engaged to her father." A petulant expression marred her lovely face. "I wish she'd get over it! It's not as if I'd cast a net over Brian, you know. We fell in love with each other. Now, tell me, is that a crime?" Her blue eyes flashed fire. "You know what Bree's problem is? She's spoiled rotten. And she's just like her mother—stubborn, mean—"

And that's the real reason you dislike Bree, Nancy realized. Every time you look at her, you see Lucinda.

Keeping that thought to herself, Nancy offered a sympathetic smile. "You didn't like Bree's mother much?" she probed.

"Lucinda Prado was a conceited, conniving witch!" Kristin burst out. "She was jealous of me, you know. She tried to ruin my career!"

At that moment the door banged open, and Bree stormed into the room. "I heard that!" she cried. "Don't listen to her, Nancy. My mother had more talent in her little finger than Krissy'll *ever* have. The only thing Krissy's any good at is stealing other people's husbands!"

Nancy was horrified. Bree was about to blow everything! She held out a placating hand. "Bree—" she began. But Kristin cut her off.

"And just what is that supposed to mean, dear?" she purred. Her voice had a dangerous note.

"You should know!" Bree flung back. "Everybody saw you draping yourself all over my dad the night Mother died. Everybody saw them fighting—over you. And everybody knows where you went later. In fact, if it hadn't been for you, my mother would be alive today!" Glaring at Kristin, Bree turned and left, slamming the door behind her.

Nancy winced. Oh, Bree, she thought. Now you've made yourself a real enemy. And you've ruined my chances of getting any leads here!

"Bree's just being silly, of course," Kristin put in before Nancy could say anything. She waved a careless hand. "I had—I had an appointment to keep that night."

"An appointment at the Café Chat Noir?" Nancy asked in a casual voice. She watched Kristin intently to see how she would react.

Her words had a dramatic effect. Kristin looked as if she'd just been slapped in the face. "Who's been spreading those lies about me?" she screamed. "If Manda—I'll kill that woman!"

"It wasn't Manda," Nancy replied. "I saw you there myself."

Kristin's pale blue eyes widened in alarm. "Who sent you to spy on me?" she shrieked. "Was it Rupert?"

Rupert! Nancy was taken by surprise. Where did the producer fit in to all this? What was his connection to Kristin Stromm?

A door slammed behind them. Turning, Nancy

saw Brian Gordon in the entryway. His face seemed chiseled from stone.

"Darling!" Kristin rushed into his arms. "Don't believe a word she says. It's all lies!"

"Calm down, Kristin." Gently but firmly Brian moved his fiancée to one side. Then he bore down on Nancy. "I hear you've been snooping around, Ms. Drew."

Nancy took a deep breath. She could tell this wasn't going to be easy. "I—"

"I thought I made it clear to you that my wife's death was not open for discussion," Brian interrupted. His eyebrows tightened angrily behind his horn-rimmed glasses. "And yet I hear you've been working behind my back. Manda told me how you questioned her, and I can guess what kind of things you've been asking Kristin." His forefinger stabbed once at Nancy. "What's the story, Ms. Drew? Who are you? A reporter searching for an exclusive? Is that why you befriended my daughter? Or maybe you plan to write a book on the 'inside story' of the *Southwind* disaster?"

Nancy could feel her own temper rising, and she had to struggle to keep it in check. In a level voice, she responded, "Wrong on all counts, Mr. Gordon. I'm—"

"Save it!" Brian thrust his fist at the doorway. "I want you out of this house—now. And if you're still on this island at this time tomorrow, I promise you, you'll be the sorriest girl in the whole South Pacific!"

Chapter

Eleven

D AD!" BREE'S VOICE rang out.

Peering around Brian, Nancy spied Bree in the doorway. Obviously she had heard Brian shouting and come back to see what was happening.

Brian frowned at his daughter. "This friend of yours has been stirring up a lot of trouble, Bree."

"I asked her to, Dad." Features grim, Bree entered the parlor. "Nancy's a detective. I invited her here."

Brian looked astounded. "What?"

"Someone was sending hate mail to my dorm. They hinted that there was something suspicious about Mother's death," Bree explained. "Whoever they were, they were *right*. Mother was murdered!"

Brian's face paled. "That's not possible."

Nancy grimaced slightly. Bree's tipping off her father—and Kristin—to the real reason for her presence probably would make her job harder. But there was nothing to do.

"I'm afraid Bree's right, Mr. Gordon," Nancy said. "The two of us went looking for Tayo Kapali. Instead we found a package Tayo had hidden for Bree. In it was proof of your wife's murder. Someone cut the *Southwind*'s anchor chain. Tayo found the chain, but he was killed before he could do anything about it."

Brian's gaze traveled from his daughter to Nancy. In his eyes Nancy could see shock and pain warring with something else. Was this the look of a man who had murdered his wife? Nancy just couldn't tell.

After a second Brian regained his composure. "Why come to Kristin?"

"She was at the party that night, that's all, Mr. Gordon." Nancy knew she couldn't push her suspicions too hard at this point. She turned to the Swedish actress. "Ms. Stromm, won't you tell us the truth about where you went after you left your party?"

"No! I can't!" Kristin shook her head stubbornly.

"Why not?" Bree snapped.

"She's not the police." Kristin's desperate gaze avoided Nancy. "I don't have to tell her anything."

Brian hovered protectively beside his fiancée. "Believe me, Ms. Drew, Kristin had nothing to do with Lucinda's death. You're barking up the wrong tree."

Nancy's lips tightened. She was tempted to ask Brian Gordon where *he* had gone that night. But, for Bree's sake, she held her tongue.

Bree was under no such self-restraint. "Dad! What are you doing? *Make* Krissy tell the truth!"

Kristin clutched his arm. "Brian! Don't let these girls badger me like this! Do something!"

"Dad! Don't you care what happened to Mother?" Anguish sounded in Bree's voice.

Nancy read the sheer helplessness in Brian's eyes. Bree's father seemed paralyzed by indecision, his gaze darting everywhere at once.

Frustrated by her father's silence, Bree turned on Kristin. "You killed my mother!"

Brian grabbed his daughter's wrist and pulled her around to face him. In a low voice he said, "Bree, please listen. Kristin didn't kill your mother. You've got to believe me."

Bursting into tears, Bree pulled her wrist loose. "Well, I guess we know whose side *you're* on, don't we?"

She fled outside, weeping uncontrollably. Nancy stood there, torn between going to comfort the girl and questioning her suspects. Then she made up her mind. She could quiz Brian and Kristin anytime. Right now, though, Bree needed a friend.

Heartsick, Nancy left the house. Things certainly looked bleak. Lucinda had been Kristin's chief rival and worst enemy. And now it appeared that their rivalry had extended to Lucinda's husband, as well. Kristin might have killed Bree's mother so she could marry Brian.

Then again, it could just as easily be the other way around. Brian might have killed his wife so he could be with Kristin. Nancy sincerely hoped that wasn't the case. How would poor Bree ever be able to live with it?

Nancy found the girl on the windswept beach. Bree was sitting on a driftwood log, hunched over, sobbing into her upraised hands. Kneeling down, Nancy opened her shoulder bag and withdrew a tissue.

"He knows, Nancy." Eyes shiny with tears, Bree blew her nose. "My father. He knows Kristin killed Mother. He's covering up for her."

"Thank you, Sherlock. This is the wildest leap of illogic I've ever heard," Nancy scolded gently, handing her a fresh tissue.

"Kristin left the house, and—"

"That's all we know," Nancy interrupted quietly. Bree was too emotional right then to see that she had no real proof for what she was saying. "Let's find out where she went before we start accusing her of murder."

Bree dabbed at her eyes. "Innocent people have nothing to hide. Why don't they level with us?"

Nancy had no answer to that one. Squeezing Bree's shoulder, she stood up. "Want me to drive you back to Papeete?"

Bree shook her head, frowning. "I—I just want to be by myself for a while—if you don't mind."

"All right. I'll be back at the car."

Nancy walked slowly across the spacious lawn. A hot breeze ruffled her hair, blowing reddish gold strands into her face. She brushed them away, lost in thought.

Things certainly looked bad for Kristin and Brian. Yet Nancy was reluctant to point a finger just yet. There were still too many loose ends in this case.

Rupert Holmberg, for instance. Three million dollars was an excellent motive, but how was he linked to Kristin? Why did Kristin accuse Nancy of being Rupert's spy after she mentioned the Chat Noir?

Speaking of the café, what about Pierre Panchaud? Why did he lie about not going there? Was it because he didn't want anyone to think he gambled? That didn't seem very likely. But then what was he hiding?

Then there was Manda Withers, who certainly acted like someone with something to hide. Nancy wondered if Manda had known of Kristin's feelings for Brian. Manda might have killed Lucinda, hoping to pin the blame on Kristin.

Finally there were the letters. Who wrote

them? And why hadn't he come right out and said what he had to say?

No, there were still too many unanswered questions. Plenty of digging remained to be done.

Perspiration moistened Nancy's hairline. Her mouth tasted like beach sand. Thinking in the tropic sunshine was thirsty work.

Fortunately, there was a tiny village half a mile down the road, just beyond Faretaha's coconut groves. She remembered seeing an open-air store there.

A few minutes later Nancy stepped under the store's awning. The owner and his wife occupied a dining table, listening to a battered transistor radio. Nancy greeted them in simple French, handed over a few francs, and helped herself to a soda from the ice chest.

Sipping the frosty liquid, Nancy wandered outside and leaned against the rusting steel railing at the edge of the village's busy waterfront.

Fifty feet away lay the main boatyard. Workmen toiled with sandblasters and chisels. Chainsaws sang. Squawking sea gulls patrolled the boatyard.

Nancy's gaze skimmed the racing sloops and workaday cruisers. All at once she spied a familiar-looking superstructure amid the jumble of boats. Her sharp gaze zeroed in. A small cabin cruiser lay tucked away in a narrow canal. And its name was *Sous le Vent!*

Nancy tossed her soda bottle in a nearby trash

bin. No doubt about it. She'd know that cruiser anywhere.

Its owner had chosen a good hideaway, all but invisible from the main highway. From a distance the *Sous le Vent* looked like one of the vessels in the boatyard.

Leaving the railing, Nancy circled the dockside area. She decided to act as if she were out for a casual walk.

Nancy moved quietly. Reaching the end of a lumber pile, she peered around the corner and saw the cruiser sitting in placid water. Opaque curtains shielded its windows. The hull's creaking was the only sound.

Crouched low, Nancy dashed over to a pile of oil barrels. She peeked around the side. The *Sous le Vent* looked deserted.

She listened carefully. A taut rope hummed. Wavelets splashed against the hull.

Nancy approached the canal's edge, then paused as she gauged the distance between dock and boat. A running leap put Nancy on deck. She immediately flattened against the cabin, waiting to see if anyone emerged.

Nothing. No one.

Nancy made her way aft, then halted before the cabin's door. Her heart was pounding as her hand rotated the aluminum doorknob. After a quarter turn it stopped. Locked!

She studied the lock and was in luck. Checking to see if she was being watched, Nancy took out her wallet and removed her plastic library card.

She eased the card into the gap. The plastic slid beneath the latch. She thrust her hand upward. Click! The cabin door swung open.

The vinyl curtains cast an eerie green light. A wave of heat washed over her. The breezeway's glass door was shut. Nancy guessed that the boat had been closed up much of the day.

An open cardboard box occupied the settee. Japanese lettering covered the side. Sifting through the mass of Styrofoam chips, Nancy's fingers made contact with a Teflon-coated object.

She pulled it out and held it up to the light. Tiny wires littered the surface like a golden spiderweb.

Nancy gasped. This must be a system card, the advanced computer device she had overheard the police talking about. What was it doing aboard the *Sous le Vent?*

Outside, a mooring line groaned in protest. Nancy felt the floor shift ever so slightly beneath her feet.

Someone had just boarded the boat!

Stuffing the system card in her purse, Nancy silently made her way aft. She flattened herself against the bulkhead, keeping her gaze on the door.

Soft footsteps sounded. She stared at the doorknob. It began to turn.

Suddenly a cool breeze broke Nancy's concentration. She frowned in confusion. Wasn't the cabin sealed?

Too late, she heard the hushed sound of the breezeway door sliding open.

Behind me!

Nancy's head swiveled, but she was a split second too slow. Something came whistling out of the shadows.

Nancy's consciousness rode a roller coaster of dazzling fireworks. Then it plunged into blackness.

Chapter

Twelve

At first Nancy was aware of distant sounds. The tinkle of cutlery. The rattle of dishware. The scraping of chairs on a wooden floor.

Then the smells began to register. The oily stink of drying paint. The pungent odor of French cuisine.

Nancy groaned. Her eyes fluttered open.

She was suddenly aware of a thundering headache. She moaned again.

Through bleary eyes, Nancy studied her surroundings. She was slumped in a straight-back chair. Ropes confined her wrists. Gray fuse boxes hung from one wall. Thick metallic cables crossed the room from a sturdy engine to an opening on the opposite wall. Freshly painted stage scenery occupied the far wall.

Nancy tried to reconcile the room's backstage appearance with the restaurant noises beyond. Then she spied a stairwell leading down to a gambling casino.

Of course! Nancy thought. The Chat Noir has a stage. I must be in one of the back rooms.

Nancy grimaced at the intensity of her headache. Sitting up, she felt hemp tighten and bite into her ankles and chest.

Just then, footsteps sounded on the stairwell. Two men marched into the room, toting boxes with Japanese calligraphy. Nancy's eyes flickered in recognition. Her two friends from the Chat Noir—Thin Face and Black Beret.

Ripping open a box, Thin Face remarked, "This is the last of them, eh?"

"Yes. There'll be another shipment next month." Black Beret glanced at his watch. "We'd better hurry though. That ship leaves for Valparaiso with the tide change." An evil smile twisted his mouth as he glanced at Nancy. "Well, well, look who's back with us again."

"Little Miss Deuxième Bureau." Thin Face cruelly tweaked Nancy's chin. She recoiled from his touch. "I still say we should have dumped her in the canal."

Black Beret scooped a handful of system cards out of his box. "She'll be feeding the fish soon enough. You heard what the boss said. She dies —but not around the boat."

103

Nancy rotated her wrists, trying to work some slack into her bonds. "Would your boss's name, by any chance, be Henri Chaumette?"

Black Beret blinked in astonishment.

Thin Face laughed out loud. "Hey, Chaumette!" he cackled. "She knows your *brother.*"

"Shut up, Brumaire! You talk too much." The big man loomed over Nancy. "You think you're clever, don't you? Sneaking aboard our boat in search of evidence. How'd you find out about the *Sous le Vent,* eh?"

"I kept seeing it around." Nancy relaxed in her chair. It was no use—the knots were too tight. "Was that you with the spear gun? Or was it Henri?"

Brumaire's thin face snarled in disgust. "That fool! I told you we should've let the boat stay where it was!"

"Shut up, idiot! When are you going to learn? Don't chat around cops." Chaumette tossed him a computer part. "Here, make yourself useful. I'll see that this one won't cause any more trouble." He picked up a roll of thick, silver gaffer's tape and cut a strip. He said nothing but smiled as he placed it over Nancy's mouth.

Nancy now watched helplessly as the two men brought in a crate of ripe breadfruit. With painstaking care, they pushed a system card through each fruit's pulpy skin.

I must have stumbled onto the smugglers Captain Mutoi was looking for, Nancy realized. She tilted her head back. It was so hard to think with a headache.

Here was another piece of the puzzle. But it made no sense. The *Sous le Vent* was the killer's boat. Twice it had been used in murder attempts against her and Bree. Yet the smugglers acted as if it were theirs.

The Café Chat Noir was the key, she knew. That's where she had first encountered the smugglers. Pierre Panchaud was a regular customer. Kristin Stromm did her gambling there. And, judging from Kristin's outburst, Rupert Holmberg had something to do with the café as well.

But Nancy just couldn't see a link between Lucinda Prado's murder and the computer smugglers.

"There!" Brumaire hoisted a breadfruit crate onto his shoulder. "Let's get this stuff down to the docks."

"Right!" Chaumette sneered at Nancy. "Then we can take care of this little snooper."

The two trudged down the stairwell. The door slammed, cutting off Nancy's view of the casino.

I've got to free myself, she thought desperately. Chaumette and Brumaire won't be gone for long!

An electric guitar twanged. Heavy footsteps trod the stage beyond the wall. Nancy heard a baritone voice. "The last show of the night, boys. Let's make it good."

Behind her the engine clattered to life. The cables began to vibrate. Nancy had an idea!

The band onstage was about to raise the curtains. When they did so, the cables would start to move. Nancy noticed that the cables' metallic texture was as rough as sandpaper.

Nancy's fingers curled around the edge of her chair. Her sneaker soles pressed the floor. The tape on her mouth muffled the grunts of her effort as she jockeyed her chair back, one inch at a time, closer to the cable.

The engine picked up speed.

Ropes bit into her ankles. Ignoring the pain, Nancy shoved the chair back again and again. Gears engaged. The cables began to move. The humming reached a crescendo. Gasping, Nancy threw herself backward. The chair tottered on its hind legs, then came to rest against the cable.

A buzzsaw sound reached Nancy's ears. The ropes around her chest went slack. Leaning forward, she lifted her bound wrists. The thrumming cable ate into the ropes. Hemp began to fray.

Just then the cable quivered to a halt. Nancy exhaled deeply. The curtain must have reached the top.

Gathering all her strength, Nancy strained against her frayed bonds. One by one the weakened strands parted.

After untying her ankles and pulling the tape painfully from her mouth, Nancy hobbled over to the stairwell. Painful pins and needles prickled her legs.

As soon as her circulation was back, Nancy

picked her way down the stairs. She tried the door, the only entrance to that backstage room. Relief washed through her. The smugglers hadn't bothered to lock it.

Nancy swiftly made her way through the casino. White sheets covered the dice tables and roulette wheel. Rock music serenaded her all the way to the door.

Opening it a crack, Nancy peered into the main dining area. A busboy cleared an abandoned table. Otherwise, the place seemed empty.

Dropping to her hands and knees, Nancy crawled into the dining room. Crouching, she moved gradually toward the front door from table to table, hiding whenever the busboy walked by.

All at once Nancy heard masculine laughter. She peered over the top of the neighboring table.

Rupert Holmberg and the maître d' stood together in the foyer. Chuckling to himself, Rupert counted out several large-denomination francs and placed them in the maître d's outstretched hand.

All smiles, the maître d' crooned, "It's always a pleasure doing business with you, Monsieur Holmberg."

"You've always been a very great help to me, Marcel," the producer replied. "See what else you can dig up, eh?"

Nancy studied them intently. Could Rupert be the mysterious boss the smugglers had mentioned?

Putting on his Panama hat, Rupert sauntered out of the café. Marcel carefully counted his loot, then tucked the wad into his back pocket.

Minutes later Chaumette and Brumaire appeared. The maître d' flashed them an impatient look. "It's about time you two got back."

"Don't be nervous, Marcel." Chaumette showed him a smirk. "We weren't going to leave the girl with you."

Sweating apprehensively, Marcel mopped his brow with a handkerchief. "You shouldn't have brought her here at all."

"Don't worry!" Brumaire slapped the maître d's back heartily. "She's coming with us to South America. Well—halfway, at least." He snickered. "Sharks have to eat too."

Nancy held her breath as the smugglers drifted toward her table, laughing at their private joke. She ducked behind the white tablecloth.

Suddenly the kitchen doors swung open behind her. The busboy hurried in, exclaiming, "Dishes are all done, Marcel. Can I go?" Halting, he stared in bewilderment at Nancy. "Hey! What are you doing?"

Blood freezing, Nancy peeped over the tabletop. The two smugglers were staring right at her!

"She got loose!" Brumaire whipped out a switchblade. "Get her!"

Chapter

Thirteen

NANCY BOLTED INTO ACTION. Zipping around the neighboring table, she dashed into the casino. Angry footfalls echoed behind her. She slammed the door shut.

Her gaze found the deadbolt. She thrust it home just as a heavy weight crashed into the door, rocking it on its hinges. There were two more crashes but the stout door held.

Nancy stepped away. The locked door had bought her a few minutes' reprieve, but that was all. They'd soon find something to break it down with.

Her spirits sank. She was trapped. The only other door led to the stairs up to the backstage room where she'd been tied up.

Refusing to give up, Nancy pulled the sheets from the gaming tables. There had to be something she could use as a weapon. Ivory dice mocked her.

Nothing!

The door vibrated under the impact of each savage assault. Nancy clenched her fists, thinking furiously.

Her gaze kept returning to that backstage room. If she could only trick them into going up there, she might be able to get the upper hand.

Nancy's hand closed around a pair of dice. She ducked under the roulette table.

Crash! The casino door splintered open.

"Search the room!" Chaumette bellowed. "She's got to be hiding here somewhere."

Nancy knew her cue. Turning, she flung the dice through the open door. Ivory cubes clattered noisily on the stairs.

"She's in there!" Brumaire cried.

Nancy watched as the two smugglers stormed the stairway. Then, scrambling to her feet, she rushed across the room, slammed the stairway door, and dropped the sidebar, locking it.

Realizing they had been tricked, the smugglers bellowed in rage. Angry fists hammered the door.

Hasty footsteps caught Nancy's attention. Looking to the left, she spied the maître d' trying to sneak out.

Coming up behind him, Nancy tapped him on the shoulder. "Not so fast, Marcel! I know a police captain who'd like to talk to you."

Marcel flinched at her touch, his pudgy face turning pale. Nancy could see that he vividly remembered her karate demonstration.

"Don't hit me!" he pleaded.

"Behave yourself and I won't," Nancy replied, trying hard not to grin. "Now let's go make a phone call."

Ten minutes later the late-night street outside the café was full of police cars. Nancy watched in satisfaction as the khaki-clad officers marched the smugglers out to a waiting van.

Just then, a familiar male voice sounded behind her. "I seem to have underestimated you, Mademoiselle Drew. I've been looking for you." Captain Mutoi's expression was aloof but friendly. "Bree Gordon called me late this afternoon. When you didn't return to Faretaha, she became quite concerned. The young lady and I had an interesting conversation." He glanced at the van. "How did you catch those two?"

"Actually, they caught me aboard their boat, the *Sous le Vent,*" Nancy explained. "The café is their home base. They had a batch of Japanese computer parts in there earlier. Now they've loaded them onto a ship bound for South America." Nancy felt a small rush of pride as the officer gave her a look that said he was impressed.

Captain Mutoi ordered two men to the waterfront to search the ship. Then he walked Nancy out of the café.

"After I talked to Mademoiselle Gordon, I had the lab take a look at that anchor chain. They tell

111

me it was cut," he said matter-of-factly. "I hope you'll accept my apology—for doubting you, that is." A wry smile unfolded on his handsome face.

"That's quite all right. I understand."

Captain Mutoi's smile turned thoughtful. "Now that you've helped me with my big case, perhaps I can return the favor. How are you making out on the Prado murder?"

Nancy quickly brought him up-to-date. When she was finished, he commented, "Who did you say the *Sous le Vent* belonged to?"

"Henri Chaumette, the smuggler's brother."

"Brumaire was making a joke," Captain Mutoi replied. "I know those two. Chaumette has no brother. The name Henri must be an alias."

A frown creased Nancy's brow. An alias? That put a different light on things.

The connections were still there. The killer owned the *Sous le Vent* under an assumed name. The two smugglers used the boat, as well. All three were tied to the Chat Noir.

And so were Kristin, Pierre, and Rupert. Fatigue washed over Nancy like a tidal wave. She was too tired to puzzle it out now. Stifling a yawn with her palm, she murmured, "I'm afraid I'm ready to drop."

Captain Mutoi gestured at a waiting police cruiser. "I'll drive you back to the Taravao. In the morning we'll see if we can't get to the bottom of this mystery."

* * *

The following day Nancy, Bree, and Captain Mutoi drove out to Faretaha. On the way Bree explained that her father had chosen to stay there overnight rather than return to Papeete.

Nancy said nothing. She could see how this case was affecting Bree. The girl's eyes were red rimmed, and her face was a mask of sheer misery. Suspicion had opened an ugly breach between father and daughter.

On arrival they walked up the front lane together. Then Captain Mutoi's fist sounded a brisk tattoo on the oak door.

Manda Withers answered the door. She had obviously accompanied her employer. Surprise flickered in her brown eyes. Brian Gordon appeared behind her, looking older than his years. Behind him, Kristin sat on the sofa, watching apprehensively.

Brian cast Nancy a somber glance. "So you've brought the police. I figured you would."

Captain Mutoi held out his right hand. "I shall have to ask you and Mademoiselle Stromm to surrender your passports, monsieur."

Brian reached into his inside pocket. Sighing, he handed the document over. "For what it's worth, I didn't kill my wife."

Kristin swallowed hard. "Brian, please don't tell them. Think—think of the humiliation."

"Sorry, Krissy." Drawing his shoulders back, he gave Bree a long look. "But if my daughter's going to hate me, she might as well hate me for the right reason."

113

Nancy realized that Bree might be hurt by the answer. Still, the question had to be asked.

"Mr. Gordon, where were you the night your wife was killed?"

He took a long moment to answer. "I was with Kristin."

Bree let out an anguished gasp.

"It's not what you think." Brian's shoulders seemed to sink under a heavy weight.

Lifting his head, Brian sighed once more. "Kristin came up to me at the party. She asked me to help her. Lucinda saw the two of us talking and lost her temper. I told Lucinda she was being rude. Next thing you know, we're going at it hammer and tongs again. Then she stormed out." He rubbed the back of his neck gingerly. "The party broke up after that. I had a cigarette in the garden. Then I ran across Kristin. She was crying. I sat her down on a bench—asked her what was wrong."

Nancy glanced at the actress. Tears were welling up in Kristin's eyes.

"Krissy has always liked to gamble," Brian added. "Five years ago, however, she got in way over her head. She thought she was going to lose Faretaha. Then Rupert Holmberg entered the picture."

Rupert! Excitement prickled along Nancy's neck. "Go on."

"Rupert found out about Krissy's debts," Brian explained. "He paid them himself. Then he offered her a special business arrangement. He

114

would cancel her debts if she signed an exclusive, three-year contract with him."

"What were the terms of the contract?" asked Nancy.

"He wanted Krissy to do five movies for him, working at union scale—the lowest wage possible," he explained. "Krissy's career was just starting to take off back then. *Horizon of Desire* had just made a bundle. Rupert would have owned Krissy outright."

Nancy made a guess. "So you two went to see Rupert."

"I couldn't just stand there and see Krissy's career destroyed," Brian said, lifting his chin in pride. "So I confronted Rupert, tried to pressure him."

Captain Mutoi scribbled in his notebook. "And then what happened?"

"Rupert and I argued for a couple of hours. I threatened to blow the whistle on him. He said he'd turn Krissy's debts over to people who wouldn't be as considerate as he was. We finally hammered out a deal. I promised to direct one of his future films, and Lucinda would star in it. We signed a memorandum of agreement to that effect."

Nancy nodded in understanding. Now she could see why Brian had been so reluctant to discuss his wife's death.

"You must believe me." Brian stared directly at his daughter. "I loved your mother very much. Kristin was only an acquaintance then. I was a long time getting over Lucinda's death. I didn't know I was going to fall in love with Kristin. It just happened."

Eyes downcast, Bree turned her face away.

"One thing puzzles me," Nancy observed. "If Rupert is such a sleaze, why are you still friends with him?"

Brian bristled at that. "I'm not *friends* with him, Nancy. I put up with him, that's all. Technically speaking, I still owe him a movie."

Captain Mutoi cleared his throat. "Monsieur, would you happen to have a copy of this memorandum of agreement?"

"It's with my other papers." Brian led them all to the library. Kristin hobbled along behind them. "I had Manda bring them out here this morning. Figured I'd get a little work done while I was here."

But as they entered the library, a stunning sight met their collective gaze.

Manda was standing beside the fireplace, a manila folder in her left hand. Her right gripped a silver cigarette lighter. Its wick burst into flame.

"Manda!" shouted Brian, too late.

Manda's quaking hand shoved the lighter against the folder. All at once a sheet of fire rippled up its side!

Chapter

Fourteen

RUSHING FORWARD, Nancy knocked the blazing folder out of Manda's grasp. It fluttered to the carpet. Nancy stamped out the flames.

Stooping, she flipped open the charred folder. The letter was brown around the edges but still readable. The Holmberg Cinema Productions logo ran across the top of the page.

Nancy's gaze skimmed the typescript.

This document certifies and attests that Brian Gordon shall direct, and Lucinda Prado shall star in, a film project for Holmberg Cinema Productions within the next seven years. In return for the services listed heretofore, Rupert Holmberg will destroy all instruments of debt in his possession relating to Kristin Stromm. The undersigned readily and without reservation agree to consent to the provisions listed above.

Brian and Rupert's signatures punctuated the text. Nancy checked the date. Brian hadn't lied. This memorandum had been drawn up the night of the *Southwind*'s fatal collision.

Captain Mutoi studied it over Nancy's shoulder, then gave Brian an ironic smile. "You are most fortunate, monsieur. It's still clearly readable."

"You idiot!" Brian grabbed his secretary's shoulders. "What are you trying to do?"

Manda burst into tears. "I—I thought I could help you by destroying the evidence."

"That evidence is the only thing that can clear me!" Deeply shaken, Brian pointed at the door. "Out, Manda! You're fired!"

"It *may* clear you, Monsieur Gordon—*if* this man Holmberg backs up your story." The captain ushered Bree and her father outside. "Why don't you all wait in the hall? Mademoiselle Drew and I will speak to this woman alone."

Nancy held the door for Kristin. "If you don't mind another question—how did you sprain your ankle?" she asked quietly.

Embarrassment painted Kristin's face a deep crimson. "I twisted it running away from the café the other night. I—I didn't want to be arrested in the police raid."

Why hadn't she guessed? Nancy smiled to herself as she closed the door and rejoined the captain.

Manda sat on the armrest of a couch, looking like a little girl on her way to the principal's office. Grim-faced Captain Mutoi made a good stand-in for the principal.

"How could he do it?" Manda sobbed. "How could he fire me that way?"

"Mademoiselle, believe me, that is the *least* of your problems," Captain Mutoi said sternly. "You were caught in the act of destroying evidence in a murder case. For that alone you could spend the next year in our prison."

Wailing in misery, Manda buried her face in her hands.

Nancy cast a sympathetic look at the weeping woman. "What about extenuating circumstances, Captain?"

Captain Mutoi offered her a quizzical look. "You know the reason for her behavior?"

Nancy nodded slowly. "Manda's in love with Bree's father. She has been for years. That's why she tried to burn Rupert's memo. And that's why she sent those unsigned letters to Bree."

Guilt turned the secretary's face pale. "H-How did you know *that?*"

"It wasn't too hard to figure out, Ms. Withers," Nancy replied. "Especially knowing how you feel about Brian. Those letters all had Tahiti postmarks. You knew Bree would recognize your handwriting, so you used a ruler to disguise it."

"I seem to have missed something," Captain Mutoi remarked dryly.

After explaining about the letters, Nancy added, "Ms. Withers thought Kristin was all wrong for Brian. So she mailed those letters to Bree, hinting at some nasty secret about her mother's death. She figured that if she could turn Bree against Kristin, Bree would persuade her father to call off the wedding."

"I-I'm sorry." Manda sobbed. "I c-couldn't stand it, seeing Brian with Kristin—"

"And people in love do crazy things sometimes," Nancy concluded softly, kneeling before the couch. She smiled in sympathy. "I think you'd better tell us everything."

Captain Mutoi stepped closer. "Unrequited love can be a powerful motive for murder." He looked down at Manda. "Did you kill Lucinda Prado?"

All color fled Manda's face. "No! I swear it!"

"Ms. Withers," Nancy said gently. "You were missing from Kristin's estate that night." At Manda's shocked gaze, she explained, "Bree woke up in the middle of the night. She went looking for you, but the house was deserted."

Wiping away tears, Manda murmured, "You're right. After the others left, I went looking for Brian. I saw him in the garden—with *Kristin!*" Her fists clenched angrily. "I was so furious. If he wanted comforting, why didn't he come to *me?*

"I drove back to Papeete, intending to make

him pay. I planned to row out to the *Southwind* and tell Lucinda." She looked thoroughly chastened.

"I walked up and down the beach, looking for a dinghy. There weren't any. My nerve began to fail me. What would happen if I told? Lucinda had such a temper, you see. I was afraid she might hurt him physically! I—I only wanted to make life a little bit miserable for Brian. I didn't want him hurt! So I changed my mind and left." Her voice began to break. "That's why I tried to burn those files. I couldn't bear the thought of Brian being hurt. I *love* him."

Nancy thought back to her interviews with the *Southwind* witnesses. So Manda was the mystery woman Alistair Pendleton had seen that night.

Nancy shook her head. She had thought she was on the brink of unraveling the mystery, but this new revelation raised more questions than it answered. According to Manda and Pendleton, there were no small boats left ashore after Lucinda departed for her yacht. If that were true, then how did the killer get out to the *Southwind?*

"Manda, what time did you get to the beach?" asked Nancy.

"Two o'clock, I think."

Nancy's brows knit thoughtfully. "You're certain that you didn't see any dinghies ashore?"

"None. The beach was deserted." Pursing her lips painfully, Manda aimed a timid glance at the captain. "Will I have to go to prison?"

"That depends." Captain Mutoi squared his shoulders. "We shall see what the judge says, eh?"

Nancy and the captain left Manda in the library alone. After saying goodbye to the Gordons and Kristin, they headed back to the car.

"I think this eliminates Manda as a suspect," Nancy said as they walked along. "Mr. Pendleton saw her leave the beach *before* the *Southwind* was cast adrift."

"Which leaves us with Gordon, Holmberg, and the Stromm woman," Captain Mutoi put in, nodding.

"Not to mention Pierre Panchaud," Nancy said, smiling wearily. "Don't forget. He was on board the *Southwind* all along."

"Ah! But Panchaud has no motive. And he was belowdecks the entire time, remember? He had to be on deck to cut the anchor chain."

Nancy grimaced. Captain Mutoi was right. Pierre had a tight alibi.

"I think, Nancy, we should pay a little visit to Monsieur Holmberg."

Once they reached the car, Captain Mutoi radioed the gendarmerie, requesting the location of Rupert's boat. Four minutes later the dispatcher's voice crackled through the receiver. At last report Rupert's boat, the *Sea Nymph*, was moored in Arue.

To Nancy's surprise, Arue turned out to be the very same village where she had seen the *Sous le Vent*. After parking along the waterfront, Nancy and the captain checked the canal. The smugglers' boat was gone!

Next, Nancy and Captain Mutoi sought out the dockmaster. The young Tahitian pointed out Rupert's boat to them.

A white forty-foot trisail motor schooner with blue trim, the *Sea Nymph* was moored at the main pier. Sunshine gleamed on the boat's brightwork. Her first sight of the elegant vessel surprised Nancy. The *Sea Nymph* didn't seem to fit Rupert's personality at all. And then she remembered that it was an identical copy of the *Southwind,* a craft Rupert had very much admired.

They found Rupert in flashy sunglasses and swim trunks, enjoying a drink as he sprawled on a chaise lounge. Unused scuba gear rested beside the vessel's cabin.

"Look who's here—Nancy Drew." Rupert took a quick sip of his drink, then flashed a welcoming grin. "Who's your friend?"

"Captain Mutoi. He's with the police." Nancy gestured at her companion. "Do you have a minute to talk?"

"Sure." Rupert removed his sunglasses and smiled at his visitors, but Nancy sensed there was nothing friendly in the expression. "I hope this isn't going to take too long. I feel like a swim."

Nancy cast a look at the inviting blue-green water, then turned back to the producer. "I guess Tahiti's been pretty good to you, Mr. Holmberg."

He leaned back, his smile wider than ever. "Truer words were never spoken, Nancy. Hot sun. Sparkling sea. Friendly people." A contented sigh passed his lips. "Heaven!" Opening his eyes again, he glanced at Captain Mutoi. "I'm getting an idea. I think I'll make a Foreign Legion movie. Yeah! What do you say, Nancy? You and your cop friend want to be extras in a remake of *Under Two Flags?*"

Nancy shook her head. "No thanks. I'd rather talk about *your* friend—the maître d' at the Café Chat Noir."

Rupert's smile vanished. His heavy body sat up slowly.

"Me? In the Chat Noir?" Rupert let his hand drift over the side of the lounge chair. "Now, where did you ever get a dumb idea like that?"

"I guess it comes from being at the café myself last night and seeing you pay off Marcel," Nancy replied evenly.

Rupert turned the pale gray of a clamshell.

Nancy confronted him. "Mr. Holmberg, why did you pay him off?"

The producer's hand closed around a spear gun. With a snarl, he swiveled toward them. In an eyeblink the spearhead's razor-sharp tip was pointing at Nancy's throat.

Chapter

Fifteen

"Back off!" Rupert barked, jabbing with the spear gun.

Nancy obeyed at once, her breath caught in her throat. Her shoulder blades brushed an upright object. Reaching behind her, she ran her fingertips along its fiberglass length. A fishing pole!

"Looks as if I've worn out my welcome in Tahiti." Rupert's shifty gaze flitted from Nancy to Captain Mutoi. "No matter. Once you two are tied up, I can be on my way."

Suddenly Captain Mutoi lunged at him. Rupert pointed the spear gun at the officer. "Stay back!"

Nancy saw her chance. Grabbing the fishing pole by its heavy end, she caught Rupert sharply on the wrist with the metal reel. Rupert howled. The spear gun clattered to the deck.

Captain Mutoi pinned the yelping producer to the deck. Then, after slipping a pair of handcuffs off his belt, he locked Rupert's wrists behind his back.

"What are you doing?" Rupert hollered. "Hey, I'm a big man in Hollywood!"

"You may have worn out your welcome in Tahiti." Captain Mutoi hauled the producer upright. "But we'd just love to have you at our jungle prison camp in the Tuamotus."

"P-prison?" Sweat trickled down Rupert's face. "Come on, you guys, where's your sense of humor? It was a joke. Honest!" He gazed imploringly at Nancy. "I only wanted to shake you up a little. It was a gag! Ha-ha—ha-ha-ha— See, I'm laughing."

"I'm sure you'll have all the guards in stitches." Captain Mutoi sat him back on the lounge chair. "The young lady asked you a question a moment ago, monsieur."

Listless, Rupert mumbled, "I forget."

"Why did you pay off Marcel?" Nancy prodded.

"I was buying information." Rupert caught their puzzled expressions and explained. "I knew there was a little action going on at the Chat Noir. I figured to spread some money around— find out things."

"What kind of things?"

"Actors are always getting into scrapes," Rupert explained. "It pays to know what kind of trouble they've had. I like to have that kind of insurance when I negotiate contracts with film people."

"Insurance? It sounds more like blackmail to me," Nancy observed. "Why did you put the squeeze on Kristin?"

"I was stuck with a couple of bomb-o movies five years ago," Rupert said, avoiding their stern gaze. "The banks were after my— Ah, you get the idea. Krissy'd just hit it big in *Horizon of Desire*. When I heard about her gambling debts, I made her an offer." Exasperation made him look like a naughty little boy. "Then that do-gooder Gordon stuck his nose in. I hated to lose Krissy, but he made me a good counteroffer. A movie with him directing and Lucinda in the lead was sure to make money."

"But Lucinda planned to retire. She was through with films," Nancy added. "That put you in a real bind, didn't it?"

Rupert realized the significance of Nancy's words. Looking at her askance, he replied, "What are you trying to say?"

"You had a motive, monsieur," put in Captain Mutoi gravely. "A three-million-dollar profit."

"Give me a break!" Rupert wailed, squirming uncomfortably in his seat. "I took a loss on that deal like you wouldn't believe. Three million? That was *peanuts* compared to the dough I would've made if Lucinda had lived. That woman was box-office dynamite!"

"Brian mentioned a memorandum of agreement," Nancy added. "Could we have a look at your copy?"

Huffing and puffing, Rupert rose awkwardly to his feet. "It's below with the rest of my files."

Captain Mutoi kept a firm grip on his shoulder as Rupert led them to the right-hand side of the boat. They descended the teakwood ladder single file, Nancy in the lead.

Minutes later in the master stateroom, Rupert jutted his chin at the file cabinet. Nancy spent several minutes rummaging through the manila folders. Finally one marked Gordon caught her eye.

She flipped it open and looked down at an identical copy of Brian's memorandum.

Nancy turned to the producer. "So Brian and Kristin were with you most of the night."

"Yeah. That's right. They showed up at my beach house about two o'clock or so."

"Where is your beach house?" asked Nancy.

"The other side of the island. Fifteen, twenty miles past Papeete." Rupert shot them a hopeful look. "I helped you out, right? So you're going to let me go, right?"

"Wrong!" Captain Mutoi steered the hand-cuffed man up the companionway. "You're under arrest, Monsieur Holmberg. That means you're coming with me."

"What!" Rupert balked every step of the way. "Hey, do you know who you're talking to?"

"I'm talking to a man who just confessed to blackmail. Step lively there." Captain Mutoi glanced at Nancy. "Would you care for a lift back to Papeete, mademoiselle?"

Nancy shook her head. Her work here was done. "Thanks, but no. I'll walk back to Faretaha. I want to see how Bree's doing."

"Suit yourself." The captain seized the prisoner's upper arm. *"Au revoir."*

Standing before the galley, Nancy listened to Rupert's desperate pleading. She had to smile in spite of herself.

"C-Captain, you don't really want to take me to jail. Listen, a good-looking guy like you has a great future in the movies. I'm not kidding! You want to be a star? I can make you a star. Come on, talk to me!"

The decisive slam of a car door interrupted the producer's sales pitch. Nancy shook her head, perplexity overcoming the humor of the final scene.

Exhaling wearily, she leaned against the bulkhead. What a case. It was proving to be one of her most difficult. Every single one of the suspects had an alibi.

Brian and Kristin were with Rupert at his beach house, miles away from the *Southwind.* Manda, the mystery woman on the beach, had been seen leaving before the murder. Pierre was on board the *Southwind,* but he had never gone topside.

129

In fact, Nancy remembered, Pierre Panchaud was in the galley when the *Southwind* was rammed.

Nancy peered through the *Sea Nymph*'s galley hatch. The shining countertops, polished table, and swivel seats seemed to jeer at her. It was as if the galley itself were trying to tell her something.

Frowning impatiently, Nancy drummed the bulkhead with her fingertips. This was crazy! One of the suspects had to be guilty. She had seen the hacksawed anchor chain with her own eyes.

If only it were possible to reconstruct the scene of the crime, Nancy mused. But, of course, the idea was ridiculous. The *Southwind*'s wreckage lay strewn all over the ocean floor.

All at once, Nancy snapped her fingers. What was she thinking of? Of *course* it was possible! Rupert's *Sea Nymph* was an identical copy of the doomed *Southwind*.

As Nancy faced the galley hatchway, Pierre's story ran through her mind.

"I could hear the buoy's bell ringing outside. I looked through one of the portholes and saw the buoy's green light and the big Moorea ferry passing astern . . ."

Suddenly Nancy's eyes went wide. There were no portholes at all in the galley! The hatch would have been closed in a major storm like that. Pierre *couldn't* have seen anything!

A grim smile touched her lips. "Nice try, Pierre!"

Four minutes later Nancy was rushing into

Arue's village store. She went straight to the pay phone, popped in a few coins, and began dialing.

The phone at the other end rang three times. Kristin's voice came on the line. "Hello?"

"Kristin, this is Nancy Drew. Would you please put Bree on? This is very important."

"Oh, she just left. She should be there any minute."

A bolt of fear lanced Nancy's heart. "Bree's coming to see me?"

"Yes. Bree walked out of here five minutes ago. She left with that fellow—I forget his name—the one who used to work on their boat. He told me you sent him to fetch Bree."

"What? I did no such thing!" Nancy replied. "Please do exactly as I say, Kristin. The second I hang up, call the police. Tell them Bree's with Pierre Panchaud. He's the killer!"

Nancy hung up. Heart pounding with apprehension, she rushed into the street. She should have known what Pierre was up to the moment she and Captain Mutoi had found the *Sous le Vent* gone.

I was a little slow on the uptake on this one, Nancy thought. Pierre told me the clue himself, but I didn't realize the significance of it. When he joined the *Southwind*'s crew five years ago, Pierre was in Japan. He was setting up his smuggling ring. The *Sous le Vent* is his boat. He registered it under the alias "Henri Chaumette."

Pierre must have heard about his partners' arrest and put the boat to sea. It was only twelve

131

miles to Moorea, the nearest island. He could have anchored there in safety.

Nancy forced herself to remain calm. If Pierre and Bree had left the estate on foot, then the *Sous le Vent* had to be around here somewhere. Pierre was too smart to stray too far from his only means of escape.

Crossing the street, Nancy jogged along the rusting seaside railing, searching the boatyard for the *Sous le Vent*. Finally, her keen gaze spied a small wharf, half-hidden behind a grove of palm trees. Pierre's boat lay at anchor there, hull creaking as it strained against the mooring lines.

Nancy sneaked aboard, intent on disabling the engine. Then she could call the police. Once again she slipped the cabin latch. There was no response from within. Taking a deep breath, she made her way below.

No sooner had Nancy closed the hatch than she heard muffled voices. The boat shifted in the water as people climbed aboard. Nancy flattened herself against the cabin bulkhead, listening.

"I'm glad you decided to help us, Pierre."

"Ah, you can thank Nancy Drew for that, Bree. After she told me about Tayo's murder, I knew I had to come forward."

Nancy eased the door open a crack. Bree was on the starboard side, looking out to sea. Pierre stood several steps behind her. He opened a box of fishing tackle, studying its interior pensively. Then, as if changing his mind, he set it down on a fisherman's chair and went to free the mooring lines.

Nancy fretted silently. At first she had planned to sabotage Pierre's engine. But she didn't dare leave Bree now!

"I hope Nancy gets here soon," Bree said, letting the breeze ruffle her long black hair.

Pierre stood erect. He held a length of nylon rope in his hands. He snapped it once, testing its strength. Then he slowly wound it round his hands.

"So do I, mademoiselle. So do I."

Nancy's blue eyes flickered in alarm.

Pierre quietly came up right behind Bree. Then he lifted the strangle cord with deadly, ominous precision.

Chapter

Sixteen

Nancy burst out of hiding. "Don't try it, Pierre!"

Astounded, Pierre stepped back. Nancy took advantage of his momentary confusion, pulling an equally startled Bree away from him.

Bree stumbled against her. "Nancy, what are you—?"

"He killed your mother." Nancy pointed at the rope in his hands. "He was just about to strangle you."

Pierre dropped the rope. "You're crazy!"

Nancy aimed her forefinger at him. "Everybody had an alibi. Yours is the best one of all. In fact, it's too good, Pierre."

Pierre's hand drifted toward a box of fishing

tackle. He must have a weapon in there! Nancy realized. She darted forward, then stopped short as Pierre's hand emerged, holding a small snub-nosed automatic pistol. "Too late," he said with a sneer.

Nancy took a deep breath to calm herself. Her only hope now was to try to deflect his attention by talking, stalling him until she could think of a way to get at the weapon.

Careful to make no suspicious movements, she slowly lowered her hands to her sides. "Let's go over your story. You said you saw the green light on the bell buoy and the ferry passing astern. The *Southwind* witnesses told me the same thing. Your stories all meshed. But that's impossible!"

Pierre's trigger finger twitched, and Nancy fought to keep all signs of alarm from her face.

"There's one thing wrong with your story, Pierre," Nancy added quickly. "You can't see any of that from inside the *Southwind*. There are no portholes in the galley. The reason you saw all that is because you were on deck with Lucinda Prado. And you were on deck because you killed her!"

"Why on earth would he want to kill my mother?" asked Bree.

"Pierre was a smuggler," Nancy explained, glancing at Bree. "That's why he signed aboard the *Southwind* in Japan five years ago. He was looking for a way to ship stolen computer parts into Papeete. He knew Lucinda Prado was a big star. The customs people were unlikely to search her yacht that thoroughly. So he stashed his goods aboard and returned to Tahiti with you people."

Pierre glanced murderously at Nancy, but she plunged ahead—anything to keep him occupied. "The night of the storm, Pierre had the whole boat to himself," Nancy went on. "That's when he took those computer parts out of hiding. He probably planned to move them ashore in the morning. But then your mother returned unexpectedly, Bree. She caught Pierre with the goods. She went topside, intending to take the dinghy back to shore and report him to the police. Pierre followed her on deck, came up behind her, and killed her!"

A ghastly expression crossed Pierre's face. Nancy could see that the murder had happened just as she had guessed.

She took advantage of his astonishment to race on. "Pierre had to move fast. He had no way of knowing whether or not your father was right behind," Nancy added. "Pierre realized that the anchor winch would make too much noise. So he took a hacksaw and cut the anchor chain. The *Southwind* went out with the tide. Pierre steered her right into the path of that freighter. Then he took a life preserver and went over the side."

Pierre's eyes were desperate. "I didn't mean to—"

"Tell us another one," Nancy urged, seeing that her account of the events had made him forget the deadly weapon he held. "Just like you didn't mean to put that snake in Bree's bed, right? Or drop that load of scrap on me." Looking down, she noticed that Pierre was wearing boat shoes. "You left some nice clear footprints there and at Vaipahi, when you took that shot at us."

Pierre shuffled, as if trying to escape Nancy's accusatory stare.

"And let's not forget Tayo," Nancy pressed. "You found out he was diving at the *Southwind*'s old anchorage. You're a scuba diver. You checked yourself and found the anchor gone. So the next time Tayo went diving, you cruised by in the *Sous le Vent* and shot him with your spear gun. The sharks did the rest."

"You're a smart little snooper, Nancy Drew," Pierre spat. "If I'd known you were that smart, I'd have aimed that spear gun at you instead of her."

He raised the gun's muzzle with an icy chuckle. "Maybe I'll have better luck with this, eh?" He tilted his head at the cabin. "Inside, both of you. Now!"

Nancy had lost her first wager, but she would never give up hope. As she followed Bree through the hatchway she said as bravely as she could, "You can't get away. The police know just as much as I do."

"I've got nothing to lose, if you're telling the truth." Pierre shoved Nancy onto the settee. "They've already got me for two murders. Two more won't make any difference."

Keeping the girls covered, Pierre started up the boat's engines. His free hand spun the steering wheel to starboard.

"I believe you two are about to have a little accident." Pierre pushed the thrust levers forward. The engine roared.

"Like the one you prepared for Tayo?" cried Bree angrily.

"Something like that." Pierre's grin was cold. "I thought I had it all worked out. I forgot about the anchor, though. Tayo didn't—too bad for him! I thought I was home free." He scowled at Bree. "Then you came back to Tahiti. There'll be no slip-ups *this* time!"

Glancing over her shoulder, Nancy looked through the porthole. Arue's waterfront receded steadily, obscured by rolling whitecaps.

Bree began to sob.

Nancy took her hand and squeezed it. "Don't. We're not beaten yet."

"I—I was thinking of my father," Bree whispered tearfully. "I was so *wrong!* I was so unfair to him and Kristin. And now I'll never get the chance to apologize."

"We'll see about that," Nancy whispered. "Just keep your eyes and ears open, Bree. And be ready to follow my lead."

Ten minutes later Pierre cut power to the engines. The boat rolled in the trough of the waves. Crossing the cabin, he jerked his gun muzzle at a pile of scuba gear. "Carry that out on deck! Quick!"

Nancy made certain that she grabbed the air tanks. A desperate plan was beginning to take shape in her mind. It was a very long shot, she knew, but it was all she had.

Pierre ordered Bree to suit up. She obeyed, donning the gear like the expert she was. Her fearful eyes stayed riveted to the gun. Then he told Nancy to put on a pair of flippers. Nancy did as she was told, then slipped one of the air tanks into Bree's harness.

As she hooked up the regulator, Nancy asked coolly, "How do you plan to work it this time?"

Pierre smiled thinly. "Bree went diving and got into trouble. You put on those flippers and jumped in to save her. You both drowned."

Nancy picked up the second compressed air tank. Suddenly she turned to face Pierre, the nozzle of the air tank aimed at his face.

His smile vanished as a jet of compressed air exploded in his eyes.

"Bree! Over the side! Quick!" Nancy called. She kept her thumb on the valve, blinding Pierre with a stinging blast of air. There was a bang as his gun fired wildly into the air.

Dropping the tank, Nancy followed her friend. She reached the gunwale in two seconds and launched herself into the sea like an Olympic diving champion. Long overhead strokes carried her away from the boat.

Just ahead, Bree treaded water, waving frantically. "Nancy, dive! I'll meet you below!"

A rain of bullets kicked up miniature fountains

on either side of Nancy. Taking a deep breath, she plunged into an oncoming wave.

Soup-warm water enveloped her. Kicking from the waist, Nancy propelled herself into the depths. Bree swam toward her, a silhouette in a universe of turquoise light. Slipping the bubbling air regulator from her mouth, she offered it to Nancy.

Grateful, Nancy took a lifesaving breath. Buddy-breathing off the same tank, they could stay under for almost an hour.

They passed the regulator back and forth. Bree pulled insistently on Nancy's forearm, tugging her out to sea.

Minutes later Nancy heard a burbling splashdown behind them. Turning, she saw Pierre beneath the boat's hull, scuba rig on his back, spear gun in his hands. Spying the girls, he moved quickly, a line of bubbles trailing behind him.

Nancy swam deeper and faster, Bree at her side. Water pressure squeezed her eyeballs. Nancy took a long breath from Bree's mouthpiece, then kicked with a powerful, rhythmic stroke.

Ahead, the seabed dipped into a black sand hollow, overgrown with kelp. In the center lay an old Liberty ship left after World War II. The wreck lay on its side, a jagged torpedo crater in her rusting hull. Bree headed straight for it.

Just then, a spear rushed overhead.

Missed us! Nancy thought, but her relief was short-lived. They weren't the target at all!

Pierre's spear struck a yellowfin. The fish writhed in agony. Blood stained the water a dark crimson.

An ominous shadow crossed the sand in front of Nancy.

She looked up. Her stomach felt as if it were full of icicles. The true purpose of Pierre's long-range shot became frighteningly clear.

A school of gray reef sharks cruised near the surface. The scent of blood reached them. One by one, they broke formation and zoomed into the depths.

Terror paralyzed Nancy's every nerve. She watched helplessly as the blood-crazed sharks speeded toward them. Jagged teeth gleamed as they closed in for the kill!

Chapter

Seventeen

Bree's hand tugging at Nancy shattered her momentary paralysis. Taking a quick breath from the mouthpiece, she joined Bree in a frantic descent to the bottom.

Nancy swam desperately, not daring to look back. Fatigue launched painful spasms down her arms and legs. At any moment she expected to feel the slash of a shark's teeth.

A narrow pilothouse window loomed ahead.

Suddenly Bree's hand jerked out of Nancy's grip. Turning, she saw Bree thrashing about. Her eyes bulged in horror. There was a shark at Bree's foot.

The shark had sunk its teeth into Bree's flipper. It shook its head back and forth, chewing the tough rubber the way a puppy tears at a rolled-up newspaper. Bree kicked it savagely in the gills with her free foot. The shark veered away, a semicircular chunk of rubber in its mouth.

But others were closing in fast.

Nancy pushed Bree through the open window, then dived through it head-first herself. A huge shark zoomed past the window frame, missing Nancy by mere seconds.

Nancy and Bree ducked into the ship's inside corridor. Bree pulled the hatch shut. After giving Nancy another breath of air, she led the way down the topsy-turvy corridor.

Nancy trailed her into a small stateroom. Bree ascended abruptly and Nancy followed.

To her astonishment, Nancy's head broke water. The air had a saline reek, but it was breathable. The chill stung her face.

"Where are we?" Nancy gasped.

Bree removed her mouthpiece. "In an air pocket. When she was torpedoed and sank, air got trapped in a few of the staterooms. Tayo showed me this place."

"How deep are we?" Nancy asked.

Bree's face tensed thoughtfully. "Fifty feet, I think. So if I remember my dive tables correctly, we can stay down here for forty minutes without getting the bends."

"Pierre will be here long before then," Nancy said, teeth chattering. "But maybe we can take him by surprise."

"What do you mean?"

143

"Pierre expects us to stay together. If we split, I might be able to sneak up on him," Nancy explained. "Bree, are you willing to play decoy?"

"What do you want me to do?"

"Show me how to get to the torpedo hole from here," Nancy suggested. "Then you go aft and make a break for the surface. I'll try to jump him—"

"Without an air tank?" cried Bree.

"It's our only chance!" Nancy shook her head stubbornly. "Please, Bree, you've got to make a break for it. Don't worry about me. I've been in tough spots before."

Maybe never quite *this* tough, she admitted to herself.

"What are you going to do for air?" Bree asked. "You'll never make it back here on just one breath."

"Give me your knife," Nancy pleaded, extending her open palm. "I'll cut Pierre's air hose when I come up behind him and steal my air from him."

Bree looked at Nancy for a long moment. "I hope you know what you're doing." Then, lifting her leg out of the water, she withdrew her knife from its ankle sheath. Nancy quickly averted her gaze from Bree's savagely torn flipper. No point in adding to her worries now!

After Bree had ducked beneath the surface, Nancy clutched a salt-caked lampstand and forced herself to relax. Long, slow breaths soothed her quivering muscles. With only one chance at this, she had to do it right.

Filling her lungs to the brim, Nancy submerged again.

Her eyes adjusted quickly to the dark blue water. Swimming with a rhythmic breaststroke, she left the stateroom and started down the corridor. Tiny bubbles escaped her taut lips.

All at once Nancy stopped short. Waving her arms to keep her balance, she stayed motionless in the water. Something was moving up ahead. Something *huge!*

Nancy watched in horror as an enormous shark emerged from the shadows. It was too big to be a reef shark—then Nancy glimpsed its pale underbelly. A great white!

The huge predator, ten feet from nose to tail, drifted down the corridor. Its movements told her it hadn't yet sensed her presence.

Nancy looked desperately in all directions, but solid walls hemmed her in. She was trapped. And the great white shark was headed straight her way.

Suddenly Nancy's gaze zeroed in on an empty tool locker. She drifted toward it slowly and deliberately, taking care not to stir up the water.

Slipping inside, she flattened against the locker's back wall, willing her shaking body to keep still.

As nearsighted as a bat, the giant shark swam by. His heavy body jolted the locker. A fin grazed Nancy's legs.

Keep going! Nancy wanted to scream. Keep going!

Her lungs began to burn. Her oxygen was running out fast. Heart beating madly, she watched as the shark's long length glided past.

The shark disappeared into the corridor's gloom. Relief invigorated Nancy's weary limbs. Plunging out of the locker, she rocketed down the corridor, trying to ignore the fire in her lungs.

Seconds slipped by. Nancy swam as fast as her limbs would carry her. Pierre's air tank was her only salvation now.

Nancy was choking. Red mist encircled her field of vision. Her lungs throbbed agonizingly. Only a few seconds of air remained.

The torpedo hole sent a shaft of turquoise light into the ship. Nancy swam straight for it. She popped out of the hull like a runaway cork, looking everywhere at once.

Pierre floated several feet away, his back to Nancy, taking aim with his spear gun. Fifty yards away, Bree was soaring to the surface.

Swimming up behind him, Nancy grabbed Pierre around the head. Bubbles exploded from where her knife severed his air hose. Nancy snatched the writhing hose and helped herself to a life-giving swallow.

Dropping his spear gun, Pierre tried to push her away. Nancy ripped his face mask off. Pierre's outflung fist knocked Nancy's knife away. They wrestled ferociously, then Pierre brought his strength to bear. Thick-muscled arms hurled Nancy away.

Nancy drifted backward, hitting the hull. She watched helplessly as Pierre stooped for his spear gun.

All of a sudden a grayish white torpedo zoomed out of the jagged hole. Nancy blinked in alarm. *The shark!*

The great fish struck Pierre heavily. Limp, he drifted to the seabed, unconscious.

Nancy swam over and grabbed the spear gun. The threat of attack was still horrifyingly real. She tried not to think of the shark's razor-sharp teeth as she took aim, her forefinger tight on the trigger.

Her shot grazed the great fish's side. For a terrifying moment, it continued to come toward her, its savage eyes unblinking. Then suddenly it veered away, speeding toward the open sea. The other sharks, scenting fresh blood, followed in a long string.

Nancy had no time for celebration. Her lungs were throbbing again. Tossing aside the spear gun, she swam over to Pierre and took another breath from his bubbling air hose.

Then, sipping air from his tank, Nancy hauled the unconscious man to the surface.

The water shifted color, from turquoise to sapphire to pastel blue. With a gasp of thanksgiving, Nancy broke the surface. Fresh air had never tasted so sweet!

The rumble of boat engines caught Nancy's

ear. The *Sous le Vent* coasted to a stop nearby. Bree appeared at the gunwale. Relief lit up her face.

"Nancy! You're all right!"

"More or less!" Nancy spit out a mouthful of seawater. "Give me a hand with Pierre, huh?"

Together they hauled him on deck. Nancy gave him artificial respiration. After several moments he coughed up seawater. Then, with a soft moan, he began to breathe normally.

Nancy rolled him over and bound his wrists with a short length of nylon cord.

"I swam to the boat as soon as I reached the surface," Bree said, covering Nancy's shoulders with a dry towel. "But when I got here, I saw shark fins. I thought—"

"Please don't," Nancy interrupted. She drew a deep breath. "We'd better call the police."

"There's a ship-to-shore radio up forward, just above the helm," Bree offered.

"Thanks!" Dizzy with fatigue, her lungs still aching, Nancy pulled herself to her feet.

Two days later Nancy stood in the lush garden of Faretaha. Guests crowded around the bonfire as the chef roasted a pig. Nearby a trio of Tahitian women performed the *tamure,* the island's famous hip-shaking folk dance.

Then Nancy noticed one unsmiling face in the crowd. Bree Gordon stood alone on the terrace, looking sadly out to sea.

Setting her glass of fruit punch aside, Nancy approached her. "Mind if I join you?"

Bree gave her a small smile. "Go ahead. You're welcome anytime." She seated herself on the low lava-rock wall. "I hear you were at the gendarmerie today."

Nancy nodded. "Captain Mutoi took my testimony. It's a busy courthouse. Rupert pleaded guilty to blackmail and extortion and got three years. Pierre goes to trial next month. The captain says he'll probably get life." She sat beside Bree. "I'm glad you and your father decided not to prosecute Manda."

Taking a deep breath, Bree replied, "Well, Dad and I had a long talk about that—among other things."

"And?"

"Dad was a lot more understanding than I thought he'd be," Bree said quietly. "And he's not a bit upset with me at all."

"Then why do you look so sad?"

"It's Kristin." Misery filled Bree's brown eyes. "I finally had a chance to apologize to her. She listened to me politely, gave me this cold look, and then walked away. I blew it, Nancy. She's never going to forgive me."

Nancy smiled in sympathy. "You know the old saying. Try, try again."

"Come on!" Bree glanced at her sharply. "Do you really think Krissy and I can ever be friends after *this*?"

149

"I don't know," Nancy replied. "Do you want to be friends with her?"

"I think I do." Bree's voice was thick with emotion. "I've seen how much she means to Dad. And she's not nearly as bad as I thought she was." She smiled sourly. "Know something? I think maybe I *wanted* Krissy to be guilty, so I could have an excuse to hate her." Looking away, she murmured, "I guess I wasn't that reconciled to their marriage, was I?"

"I guess not." Nancy put her arm over the girl's shoulders. "But you mustn't cut yourself off from them, Bree. That's the worst thing you could do. Kristin's going to be a part of your family. She needs your love and support just as much as your father does. You've got to be there to welcome her."

Bree's uncertain gaze traveled from Nancy to Kristin.

"I don't think she's going to be very pleased to see me."

"Maybe not at first," Nancy replied. "But give her time." She looked into Bree's eyes. "You two may never be as close as you and your mother were. But I think you can be friends. You just have to work at it."

"It's not possible."

"There you go again, jumping to conclusions!" Nancy replied, showing a small smile. "Don't close the case before you've even tried to solve it. Give it your best shot!"

The black-haired girl burst into laughter.

"When the advice comes from a real detective, it would be dumb not to listen, right?" Bree squeezed Nancy's hand thankfully. "Excuse me. I've got to go talk to my future stepmother."

Satisfied, Nancy looked away. Bree and Kristin could patch things up, she had no doubt.

Soft breezes stirred her hair. Leaning against the wall, she watched the full moon paint a silvery sword on the placid surface of the sea.

A masculine voice sounded behind her. "Mademoiselle Drew? You have a phone call."

"Thank you." Nancy followed the servant through the open French windows into the spacious parlor.

Picking up the receiver, she said, "This is Nancy Drew."

"Hi, Nancy!" Bess Marvin's voice exclaimed joyously. "I just couldn't wait to hear all about Tahiti!"

Grinning, Nancy began, "Well, there was this shark—"

"Nancy!" Bess complained. "I don't want to hear fish stories. I want to hear about the *guys!*"

Vanishing Act

Chapter

One

Nancy, GET IN HERE right away! The show's about to start!"

Nancy Drew glanced at her watch. "I'm ten minutes early, Bess," she called out through the open window of her car, smiling. Nancy slid out of her Mustang and started toward her friend. Bess Marvin was standing in the doorway to her house, almost dancing with impatience.

"Come *on*, come *on!*" she said as Nancy sauntered up the path. "George is already here. Do you want a soda or something? No, never mind. I'll get you one when there's a commercial. I don't want to miss even a *second* of this show."

1

"Well, you're certainly not going to," George Fayne commented dryly as Nancy followed Bess into the living room. George was Bess's first cousin, and she and Bess were Nancy's two best friends. "You have time to get fifty sodas if you want. I'm glad you're here, Nancy. It's too much for one person to deal with Bess when she's like this."

"I'm glad to be here, too," Nancy said. "I've been feeling lonely with Ned away."

Ned Nickerson, Nancy's boyfriend, had returned to Emerson College earlier that day after a long weekend at home. Nancy was delighted when Bess had asked her over. Now she wouldn't have to spend the whole evening missing Ned.

Bess wasn't listening to anything they were saying. "I just hope you programmed this thing right, George," she fretted, gesturing at the VCR. "This is one tape I *have* to have in my collection."

"Bess, no one can see if you keep standing in front of the TV," said George. "Just sit down and relax. It's all going to be fine. You'll have your permanent record of Jesse Slade to put in your hope chest. Not that it'll do you any good—unless he suddenly returns one day."

Bess sighed. "I still can't believe he's gone. My biggest idol—the greatest rock star in the world—gone. How could anyone have disappeared like that? Especially anyone so famous?"

"I wasn't as big a fan of his as you were, but I

do understand. It seems unreal to me, too," George said. "I can't believe three years have passed since he disappeared."

Three years. Nancy thought. It *did* seem impossible. Three years before, Jesse Slade had been on the way to becoming the biggest rock star in the country. He'd been only nineteen then, but he had already cut two albums—composing all the music, writing all the lyrics, singing and playing, and producing. The first had gone gold, and the second platinum.

Jesse Slade had also been the only rock musician in history to have six singles in a row reach number one on the charts. He'd won two Grammy Awards. And on top of that, he'd been gorgeous—with long dark brown hair, coal black eyes, and a sad, haunting smile that drove his fans wild.

"He was talented, Bess—I'll give you that," George was saying now.

"But I didn't like him because he was *talented!*" Bess protested. "And not because he was so cute, either. It was just— Well, there was something about him," she finished helplessly.

Nancy knew what Bess was trying to say. His talent and his looks weren't all that had made Jesse Slade so popular. He'd had a warm and intimate quality that made his songs seem as if they were a private conversation between each fan and himself. Jesse also made each fan feel as if he needed him or her.

Then, at the height of his popularity, Jesse Slade had vanished—without a trace.

No one knew *how* it had happened. Jesse and his band had been the main attraction at a huge outdoor concert on a beach in California. Jesse had been onstage for about forty minutes when he'd announced that he was going to take a short break.

He'd never been seen again.

The rest of the band was onstage when he'd disappeared. None of them had seen him vanish. Neither had anyone on the crew. And neither had any of the thousands of fans who'd been watching the concert. It seemed impossible—but he'd vanished and never come back.

But he'd never been forgotten—not by his millions of loyal fans, and not by the music industry. Both of his albums were still in the Top 100, and not a day went by that he wasn't mentioned in the music press. He might have disappeared, but the mystery of his disappearance had kept his career alive.

"It's even too much of a mystery for me," Nancy mused aloud. "I was just thinking about Jesse," she said in answer to George's quizzical look.

The show the girls were going to watch that night would kick off a week-long celebration of Jesse Slade on TV Rock, a cable music-video station whose nickname was TVR. "Who's hosting the segment tonight, Bess?" Nancy asked, her thoughts returning to the present.

"Dan Kennedy," answered her friend. "He's in charge of the whole week." Dan Kennedy was one of TVR's most popular veejays. "Tomorrow TVR's going to be interviewing the rest of the guys in Jesse's band, and the day after they'll go out to Jesse's hometown to talk to people who knew him when he was growing up. And they're going to play one of Jesse's songs every hour on the hour, and—"

"And they're going to have a seance to try to find Jesse, aren't they?" George put in.

"George!" Bess protested. "How can you joke like that?"

"Well, how can you make such a fuss about a guy you've never met and never will get the chance to meet?" George countered. "I mean, I know he was incredible, and I've heard of long-distance love, but don't you think this is a little *too* long-distance? Like so long-distance it's non-existent?"

"Oh, you're just—Wait, it's starting!" Bess said excitedly. She plunked herself down in front of the TV. "George, hand me that brush. I have to look my best."

"Right, Bess," George grumbled, but she gave her the brush anyway.

The TVR logo flashed on the screen. "TV *Rock!*" an echoing voice boomed. "Where the party never stops-ops-ops-ops-ops—"

5

"Oh, come on, get going!" said Bess. "We *know* it's TV Rock!"

Then Dan Kennedy strolled in front of the camera and sat down. "Hi, teen angels," he said with a grin, pushing his curly blond hair out of his eyes. "Like the shirt? A crazed fan just handed it to me on my way in." He pointed down at his T-shirt, which said "Evil Picnickers Unlock Secrets of the Pyramids" in huge black letters dripping with red. "I don't know exactly what it means," Dan Kennedy went on. "Maybe you do. Send your suggestions to me, along with ten dollars. When I have enough money, I'll retire!" he finished brightly. "Then I can devote my time to figuring out what my clothes are trying to tell me.

"Anyway"—Dan Kennedy's face became serious—"tonight marks the beginning of Jesse Slade Week. As most of you know, Jesse took off, or was taken off, or something, three years ago tonight. We're going to be remembering him at TVR this week—not that anyone who ever had anything to do with Jesse could really forget him. Tonight we're bringing you a very special tape of Jesse's last concert. TVR just uncovered it. It was thought to have been lost in a fire but was found mostly intact. We hope you'll be as moved by it as we were."

There was a burst of guitar music, and onto the screen flashed a picture of Jesse Slade bent over

6

his guitar. It cut to a shot of screaming fans leaping out of their seats at a concert, and then to another still of Jesse, vaulting through the air in one of the leaps that had been his onstage trademark.

"Jesse Slade—the man, the musician, and the mystery," came Dan Kennedy's voice-over. "Will we ever know what happened to him?"

"Nope," said George. Bess kicked her ankle.

"On this night three years ago, Jesse Slade played his last concert," Dan continued. "Tonight, we're bringing you that concert again."

The screen went to dark. At first Nancy wasn't sure what was happening. Then she realized that the screen was dark because the stage was dark. She could hear the occasional sounds of an expectant crowd—a catcall, throats clearing, a few bursts of applause. Then a tiny beam of light flashed onto the center of the stage.

A drum began beating—slowly at first, then fast. The beam of light grew larger—larger— larger. Now Nancy could see the huge outdoor stage that had been set up dramatically close to a cliff at the edge of the Pacific Ocean. Behind the stage, a fading sunset was a background for the black water.

Then Jesse Slade walked slowly to center stage —and the crowd went wild.

"Show the fans!" George said. "I love footage of fans."

As if in answer, the camera panned slowly over the crowd: a sweat-drenched boy waving a hand-painted sign that said "Jesse Forever"; a girl screaming hysterically and jumping up and down, tears of emotion streaming down her face; a forest of hands clapping rhythmically in the air as Jesse picked up a guitar and began the notes of his opening song.

For the next half hour the three girls watched the screen in total silence. Jesse stepped forward and held up his hand. Gradually the crowd grew quiet.

"I'm going to do one more," Jesse said, "and then I'm turning the stage over to my band for a while. They're pretty good, too, you know." There was a ripple of laughter from the crowd. "This one's from my first album," Jesse said, picking up his guitar. "I think most of you know it."

And he began to play the first bars of "Good-bye, Sweet Life."

Bess gasped, and a chill ran down Nancy's spine. "I'd forgotten that was the last song he played," Nancy said.

"Me, too," Bess answered. "It's creepy, isn't it?"

"Totally," said George. "It's almost as if he'd planned it or something. I wonder if . . ." Her voice trailed off, and the three girls fell silent again.

"Goodbye, sweet life," Jesse sang.

"You won't be missed . . .

"It's much too late to cry. . . ."

The crowd fell utterly silent for the next few minutes. Then, abruptly, the song ended. "See you in ten!" Jesse shouted jauntily as he strode off the stage to tumultuous applause.

"And that's *it?*" George said. "He doesn't come back?"

"No," Bess said sadly. "Well, I guess I'll get us a soda now. I don't care much about watching his band." Sighing, she pulled herself to her feet and went out to the kitchen.

Nancy picked up a magazine and began idly leafing through it as Jesse's backup band began to play. She wasn't really interested in them, either. She put down the magazine as Bess strolled back into the room carrying a six-pack of diet soda. On the television screen, Jesse's bass player was jamming with his guitarist. "How about switching channels for a little while, Bess?" she said. "This is getting kind of—"

Suddenly she broke off. What was that?

A strange flicker of movement in one corner of the screen had just caught her eye.

"What's the matter?" George asked.

"Something at the back of the stage," Nancy answered. "See, in that corner—there. Wait! What's going on?"

9

The back of the stage was dark and shadowy now. But Nancy was sure she wasn't imagining things.

She'd just seen what looked like it could have been a body. It was hurtling over the cliff beside the stage!

Chapter

Two

"Bess, stop the tape!" Nancy said excitedly. "Did you see that?"

"See what?" Bess asked. "What are you talking about?"

"I think I saw someone fall off the cliff! I have to check it again!"

"That's impossible! Why would something like that happen during a concert? Anyway, I didn't notice anything. Can't it wait?" Bess asked. "I want to watch the end. And I want the *whole* tape, not just part of it."

"Okay," Nancy agreed reluctantly. But she was so eager to check out what she'd seen that the rest of the show dragged for her. At last Dan Kennedy's face appeared on the screen again.

"We'll have more tomorrow night on Jesse," he said. "Same time, same place, same Dan. And now, take a look at the new video by the Same, ours exclusively on TVR—"

George leaned over and snapped off the TV. "Okay, Nan. What did you see?" she asked.

Quickly Nancy rewound the tape to the point where she thought she'd seen the body fall. At first she couldn't find the exact footage. Maybe it *was* just my imagination, she thought. I can't—

No. "There," she said breathlessly, pointing to the side of the screen. "See?"

"I don't know," Bess said. "It's awfully blurry."

For a second it looked as if the "body" teetered precariously at the cliff's edge. Then it plummeted and vanished into darkness.

George drew a long breath. "If it is a body, why didn't TVR notice it before?" she asked.

"I wouldn't have noticed it, either, if I had been really interested in the show," Nancy said. *"Anyone* watching would have missed it, I bet— the rest of the action's so distracting."

"But if it is a body, it's horrible!" Bess said. "What are we going to do about it?"

"What *can* we do?" George asked blankly. "It all happened three years ago, and if no one caught it then—"

"But three years ago—" Bess broke off. "That was Jesse Slade's last concert, and he was never seen after that. What if—"

"No!" George said. "That's impossible, Bess. If Jesse had fallen off a cliff, *someone* would have discovered his body."

"We don't know that for sure," Bess insisted. "Nancy, don't you think it could be Jesse?"

Nancy shook her head. "I think George is right, Bess. There'd have been no way to hide something like that."

"But it all *fits!*" Bess said. "I bet someone murdered him! Nancy, this is your next case, I just know it! You've got to get in touch with TV Rock right away!"

"Whoa!" Nancy said. "I can see it now." She picked up an imaginary phone. "'Hello, Dan Kennedy? I think I know what happened to Jesse Slade.' They'd never take me seriously, Bess. There's just not enough to go on!"

"Okay. Okay," Bess said, tense. "But if they *did* take you seriously—if they asked you to investigate this—would you do it?"

"I guess so," Nancy replied slowly.

"Then it's all taken care of," Bess said resolutely. "You just leave this to me, Nan."

Nancy couldn't help smiling a little. "Uh, Bess? How exactly are you going to take care of this?"

"Oh, TVR will take me seriously. You'll see,"

13

Bess answered. "Now, I think the best thing for you and George to do is go home and start packing."

"Bess, I have to hand it to you," Nancy said two days later. "You're very persuasive."

"I'll say," George chimed in. "If anyone had told me I'd be in Los Angeles today, I'd—well, it's hard to believe, anyway."

Twenty-four hours earlier Nancy had gotten a phone call. At first she'd thought it was a joke— that the guy at the other end was some friend of Bess's who'd been asked to play a joke on her. But soon she realized that the caller really was Dan Kennedy. And he really had been calling to find out whether she'd take on this case.

"I have to admit I'm intrigued by the whole thing, Mr. Kennedy," Nancy had said, "but I'm not totally sure there *is* a case to take on."

"Call me Dan," he'd answered. "You may be right, Nancy. But I agree with your friend Bess. Jesse Slade disappears at the same concert where a body mysteriously falls off a cliff—well, it's too much of a coincidence to be a coincidence. And I'm willing to fly you and your friends out here—and put you up at TVR's expense—if you'll agree to take a look around. I hear you're quite a detective. Bess told me about your work with Bent Fender, and I'm impressed."

Bent Fender was a rock group whose lead

singer, Barton Novak, had disappeared just min‍utes before a concert at Radio City Music Hall. The case had been one of Nancy's most challeng‍ing, but she had had more to go on then.

"All right, Dan. I'll give it a try," Nancy said. "But don't you have to get some kind of okay on this?"

"I'll get it okayed later. For now, I'll just put it on my expense account—and if there's a prob‍lem, I'll deal with it."

"Well, that's generous of you," Nancy said. "I'll come out with my friends, but I can't make any promises. In fact, I hardly know where to start!"

"Well, let me think about that. I'll try to come up with a few leads by the time you get here," said Dan. "And listen, Nancy—thanks."

That had been a day ago. Nancy had booked a flight for Los Angeles right after talking to Dan. She, Bess, and George had gotten on the plane that morning. They'd arrived just after lunch and rented a car at the L.A. airport. Now they were inching through a four-lane traffic jam toward the TVR studio.

"This is an incredible car," Nancy said. "I've never rented one with a cellular phone *and* super-Sensurround stereo! All this and traffic jams, too? I guess we really *are* in California!"

"If only I'd started my diet when I was sup‍posed to," Bess said wistfully. "I mean, here we're going to be hanging out with rock stars—and I'm five stupid pounds overweight as usual. My one big chance, and I blew it!"

"Bess, you look fine," George said. "How many times have we been over this before?"

"Besides, I bet there aren't going to be a lot of rock stars hanging around TVR," Nancy put in, glancing into the sideview mirror as she carefully changed lanes. "Videos of stars, yes. Stars, no."

For a second Bess looked crestfallen. Then she brightened. "But the TVR veejays are almost like rock stars themselves. I can't wait to meet Dan Kennedy!"

"Whoops!" was all Nancy answered. Honking wildly, a flame-colored Jaguar had abruptly cut in front of the girls' rental car. "This traffic's going to take some getting used to! Let's hope it's not like this all the time."

An hour later Nancy pulled up in front of the three-story limestone building whose address Dan had given her. "Here we are," she said, climbing out and audibly sighing. "Boy, if that's how crowded it gets on the freeways, what's it like to drive on regular roads around here? Well, I guess we'll find out."

She pushed the glass door open into a lobby that was nothing like any other lobby she'd ever seen. It was painted hot pink, and filled with giant plastic palms. In back of the receptionist's desk was a huge screen showing a constant stream of rock videos without the sound. And next to her desk was parked a gleaming silver Porsche with a sign on it that said "Drive Me."

Even the receptionist looked perfectly suited to this place. No older than Nancy, she was wearing a hot pink rubberized dress, lime green stockings printed with tiny neon yellow polka dots, and electric blue high-top leather sneakers. On the black steel desk next to her typewriter was a tiny forest of palm trees just like the ones looming above her. She looked up expectantly as Nancy and her friends approached.

"What's the story with that car?" George asked before Nancy could say a word.

The receptionist smiled. "It belonged to the lead singer of the Slickboys. He gave it to us as a thank-you present when one of their videos went to number one. We didn't know what to do with it, so we just left it out here. Anyway, can I help you?"

"I'm Nancy Drew, and these are my friends Bess Marvin and George Fayne," Nancy told her. "We have an appointment to see Dan Kennedy."

"Have a seat," the receptionist said, gesturing toward a waiting area a few feet away. "I'll give him a call."

She picked up the phone and punched a few numbers. "They're here, Dan," she said. "Oh. Oh, really? Well, okay. I'll send her down."

She hung up and turned back to Nancy. "Dan says you're to see our president, Mr. Thomas, right away," she said. "Your friends can wait here. Dan will be along in a minute to pick them up, and when you're done with Mr. Thomas you can come and meet them."

Uh-oh, Nancy thought. Why do I suddenly feel as if I'm being sent to see the principal? Aloud, though, she just asked, "Which way is Mr. Thomas's office?"

"It's down at the end of the hall. The office with the double doors," said the receptionist.

"See you in a little while," Nancy said, and headed down the hall.

The secretary's desk in front of the office was empty. I guess I'll have to announce myself, Nancy thought.

"Mr. Thomas?" she asked softly, peeking inside the double doors at the man speaking on the phone.

He didn't seem to notice her at first. "Okay. Book them for Friday. I don't care how, and I don't care what it costs—I just want it done!" he said into the receiver. "Now I have to go." Without saying goodbye, he hung up and turned to Nancy. "Yes, I'm Winslow Thomas," he said, "and you must be Nancy Drew." He jumped to his feet to shake her hand. "Please, have a seat."

Except for a huge, bushy ginger-colored beard, Winslow Thomas was the most correct-looking man Nancy had ever seen. He was wearing a navy pinstriped suit, a white shirt, and a navy checked tie. His wingtip oxfords had the burnished shine that could only have come from a professional polishing, and his short, wavy hair looked as though it had been trimmed five minutes ago.

What's he doing at a place like TV Rock? Nancy wondered as she sat down. He should be the head of a bank!

Before she could speculate further, Winslow Thomas cleared his throat. "I'll come right to the point, Nancy," he said. "Dan Kennedy told me this morning that you were coming to investigate the Jesse Slade disappearance." He had a slight southern accent, and his diction was so perfect that it almost sounded affected. "I have to say that I don't think it's a great idea," he continued. "And, frankly, I'm a little irritated at Dan for giving you the go-ahead without checking with me first. If he had, he'd have found out that I think a thing like this is definitely not in TVR's best interests."

"Why not?" Nancy asked, startled.

"A couple of reasons." Winslow Thomas leaned back in his chair. "First of all, the police have officially declared the case closed. It makes us look foolish to open it again with no more substantial evidence than a few seconds of film. Jesse Slade going over a *cliff*? How farfetched can you get?"

"I'll be honest with you, Mr. Thomas," Nancy said. "At first I thought it was a little farfetched myself. But don't you think we should explore any possibility if it could lead us to the right answer?"

"Not in this case," Winslow Thomas said. "I'll be honest with you, Nancy. The police don't think anything violent happened to Jesse. They suspect that he had reasons for dropping out of sight—reasons that wouldn't look too good if they became known. I'm afraid I agree with them. From the rumors I've heard—and I hear quite a lot in this business—Jesse Slade wasn't as perfect as his fans believed. But, what's the point of trashing his image now? What's the point of bringing the past to life if all it does is disappoint people?"

"I see your point," Nancy said slowly, "but I don't think that's a good reason for abandoning this case. What if those rumors you've heard *aren't* true? What if there *was* some kind of violence involved? I think it's more important to find out what really happened."

Winslow Thomas paused for a second. "Okay, I'll tell you what," he said briskly. "If you agree to work undercover in the record business—and to work as fast as you can—I'll agree to bankroll you for a reasonable amount of time. But I don't want any publicity. If the answer to this mystery turns out to be unpleasant, I don't want TVR getting a tainted reputation. We're a music station, not a muckraking business. And I don't want you getting my staff all fired up about this. They have jobs to do—and they don't include playing amateur detective."

Was that a dig? Nancy wasn't sure. "You

mentioned my going undercover," she said. "Do you have any suggestions what cover I could use so I could ask lots of questions."

"We use a lot of guest veejays at TVR. A contest-winner who was supposed to be our next guest veejay had to back out at the last minute. Maybe I could tell people that you're here to fill that slot. You could go undercover right here at the station. You'd have access to just about anyone you'd need to talk to."

"That sounds great," Nancy said.

"As long as you really pull your weight," Winslow Thomas added warningly. "As I said, I don't want my staff suspecting anything."

"Don't worry, Mr. Thomas," Nancy said. "I'll work hard. I promise."

"That's settled, then," said Winslow Thomas. "You can start tomorrow. I'll have my secretary call Dan, and he can start showing you the ropes. I've already told him not to let anyone know who you are, by the way. You can go up to his office now. It's one flight up—Room Two Twenty-four."

"Well, I will say one thing, Dan," Nancy said dryly a few minutes later. "Your boss is very efficient. Obviously he had decided to let me work here, but he made me convince him to reopen the case. Even with all of that, he had me in and out of there in five minutes flat."

"You don't have to tell *me* what he's like," Dan

said, wincing a little. "We've had our share of run-ins. I'm not too efficient. I'm kind of relaxed, myself."

"Yes, we'd noticed that," George said with a smile.

Nancy had arrived at Dan's office—a tiny cubbyhole of a place filled with wind-up toys, heaps of cassette tapes, and leftover pizza boxes —to find Bess and George chatting with him as if he were an old friend. She could see why. Dan was as easygoing and relaxed as Winslow Thomas had been brisk and formal. He had a mop of curly blond hair and laughing blue eyes, and he was dressed in black jeans, black running shoes, and a Bent Fender T-shirt—"put on in your honor," he'd told her. He was just as funny in person as he was on the air.

"I've got to do a taping before the end of the afternoon," Dan said, "so maybe I'll show you around tomorrow. But are there any questions you have now? I feel kind of responsible for you, since I brought you all the way out here."

"Well, I'd like to take a look at the site of the concert," Nancy said. "And I want to talk to someone on the crew that taped Jesse's last performance."

"Well, you're in luck. I've got a friend who worked on that tape," Dan said. "I'll give you her number."

"Great!" Nancy said. "And maybe you can help me make a list of the people I should talk to.

People who worked with Jesse, I mean. His manager, for instance. I don't even know who that was—"

"Tommy Road." Dan's voice was suddenly clipped and urgent. "Funny you should mention him. You know, since Bess's call I've been thinking a lot about Tommy Road. Did you know he vanished at the same time Jesse did?"

"That's strange," Nancy said.

"*Very* strange." Dan leaned closer. "I'd look into Tommy Road's disappearance closely if I were you," he said in a low voice. "If you want my opinion, Tommy murdered Jesse and hid the body before he disappeared!"

Chapter

Three

YOU SEE, NANCY? I *told* you Jesse Slade was murdered!" Bess said triumphantly.

"Wait a minute," Nancy said. She turned to Dan. "That's quite an accusation, Dan. Where did it come from?"

"Shhh! Don't talk too loudly," Dan murmured. "After my conversation with Mr. Thomas this morning, I don't want him to think I'm taking time away from my job to work on this. Anyway, I don't have any hard evidence or even evidence of any kind.

"But I know that there were bad feelings between Jesse and Tommy Road before they disappeared," he continued. "I was a radio dee-

jay then, and I interviewed Jesse a couple of
times. I asked him something about Tommy
once, and suddenly Jesse got really angry. I guess
that's why I can still remember his exact words.
He said, 'Tommy's done nothing to help me—in
fact, it's the opposite. Off the record, I'm looking
for another manager.' I asked him what he
meant, but he wouldn't tell me anything more.
Said it was nothing he could prove, and he'd
appreciate my forgetting what he said. I did—
until now."

"And Tommy Road vanished at the same time
Jesse did?" George said slowly, thinking out
loud. "I wonder why I never heard about it."

"It got some coverage, but Jesse was such a big
star, Tommy's disappearance got buried."

"What was Tommy Road like?" Nancy asked.

"Kind of obnoxious," Dan answered. "I met
him at a couple of parties. He was British, and he
was always going on about how weak the American music scene was compared to that in En-
gland. I always wanted to ask him how he could
complain when he was making so much money
off an American like Jesse."

"What did he look like?" asked George.

"Extremely weird," Dan replied. "He shaved
his head way before anyone else did, and he had
tattoos on his face."

"Ugh! That sounds a little *too* weird." Bess
shuddered.

"Yeah," Dan continued. "Two lizards, one on

each cheek. And he wore a long cape all the time." Dan shot a quick glance at his watch. "Look, I've got to go back to work. You'll be here tomorrow, won't you?"

"I sure will," Nancy answered. "I start work for you guys tomorrow!"

"Well, we can talk more then," Dan said. "Oh! Before I forget—that friend I was telling you about, the one who worked on the concert tape, works near here. She's over on Hollywood Boulevard." He picked up his phone book and handed it to Nancy. "Her name's Cari Levine. Here's her number."

Nancy jotted it down. "Can I use your phone to call her?" she asked.

"Be my guest. Okay, I'm out of here. See you tomorrow," Dan said and vanished out the door.

Nancy picked up the phone and began dialing the number Dan had given her. Bess sighed. "What a great guy."

"Really," George agreed. "Nan, can't you figure out some way to get us a job here, too?"

"Oh, I'll be keeping you busy enough. Hello, is this Cari Levine? My name is Nancy Drew. Dan Kennedy gave me your name. I'm doing some research on Jesse Slade." Nancy couldn't mention the fact that she was a private investigator. She didn't want to blow her cover. "I know this is short notice," she went on, "but I was wondering if you could spare a moment to talk to me and my friends about the night of his last concert."

"No problem," Cari said warmly. "Come right over."

"Hey! There's Melrose Avenue," Bess said as they drove toward Cari's office. "There are supposed to be incredible shops all along there. You know, I've been *needing* a little bit of L.A. to take back home with me. Like that stuff there." She pointed at a store window filled with peach-colored leather clothes being worn by mannequins turned upside-down. "Nancy, don't you think we could—"

"Not now," Nancy said firmly. "You'll get a chance to shop, I promise. But not now."

Cari Levine's office, which was on the ninth floor of a black glass skyscraper, was even messier than Dan's. Cans of film were everywhere, and snipped-off bits of tape littered the floor. The posters taped to the walls had all come unstuck on at least one corner.

Cari herself looked bright and energetic. She was wearing a scarlet jumpsuit with matching ankle boots, and from elbow to wrist her arms were lined with a mass of jangling silver bracelets.

"Sorry about the mess," Cari said. "I keep meaning to clean it up, but somehow every day goes by without my touching a thing. So, enough of my apologies. What can I do for you?"

Nancy explained. "We were wondering if

you'd noticed anything out of the ordinary that night," she said, finishing up.

"I was just a lowly assistant back then," Cari said. "I never actually talked to Jesse, but even I couldn't help notice that he was kind of edgy. He kept yelling at people while we were setting up—and that was the kind of thing that never happened with Jesse. Normally he went out of his way to be nice to camera crews and roadies and people like that."

"Did he say anything that seemed strange to you?" Nancy pressed.

"Well, it *was* three years ago. . . ." Cari thought for a minute. "And the main thing we were all paying attention to was the weather."

"The weather?" George repeated.

"Yes. We were all afraid it was going to rain. The sky looked incredibly dark and threatening, and you could hear thunder in the distance. As a matter of fact, there *was* a big storm right after the concert ended. Perfect timing! If the concert had been the next day, the whole stage would have had to have been rebuilt—the rain made half the cliff collapse."

Nancy looked up, suddenly alert. "Does that happen often?" she asked.

"Well, we do have a big problem with the coast eroding out here," Cari answered. "I'm sure you've heard about all the big beach houses on Malibu that have wound up in the ocean because the shoreline erodes so badly."

28

Nancy didn't answer for a second. "The timing . . ." she finally said. Bess, George, and Cari all stared at her, but Nancy didn't notice. "It's another case of the timing being too good," she said slowly. "Jesse disappears . . . the cliff he was performing on crumbles . . . and a body that may have fallen off the cliff is never found."

"You're not saying someone *made* the cliff collapse, are you?" George asked. "Nancy, that was obviously just—just nature! It can't have anything to do with Jesse's disappearance!"

"Oh, I'm not saying anyone engineered the collapse," Nancy said quickly. "All I mean is that the body might have been buried under the cliff when it collapsed. That might account for no one's discovering it!"

Nancy jumped to her feet. "Well, I wanted to see the site of the concert anyway," she said. "And there's no time like the present. Let's head out to the beach and take a look. It's not much of a lead, but it might tell us something. Can you give me directions to the site, Cari?"

"Sure," Cari said. "It's about an hour north of here. Now, if I can just find a map in all this mess . . . Forget it; I'll just tag along and show you."

"I can't believe how beautiful this is," Bess said half an hour later. "It looks like something from a movie!"

"From many movies," Cari answered. "This shot must be in hundreds of them."

The four girls were standing at the edge of a cliff that jutted out into the churning, white-capped ocean. Below them waves pounded relentlessly against glistening black rocks, and the air was filled with the cry of sea gulls.

"Where are the surfers?" Bess asked. She sounded disappointed. "This place is totally deserted."

"Well, look at the water!" George said. "No one could surf or swim here. It's much too wild, and those rocks would be horrible to crash into." Suddenly she shivered. "I feel sorry for Jesse if he did fall off this cliff. I don't see any way he could have survived."

"You're right," Nancy said. "It would have been almost impossible to investigate, too, especially once the cliff had collapsed.

"Let's see. The band must have been over there." Nancy gestured to a point about thirty feet away. "Right?" Cari nodded.

"And the taping crew was right where we're standing now," Cari added. "That means that the body I saw falling had to have been standing over there."

There was a spot at the edge of the cliff that overhung a huge boulder. Bess eyed it nervously.

"You're not planning to investigate *that*, I hope," she said. "Because if you are, I have to tell you I'd rather be shopping."

"Well, it would be nice to get a closer look," Nancy said. "I wonder what's the best way to get down to the beach."

Cari shrugged. "That, I don't know."

Nancy and Cari walked over to the spot and stared down at the shore.

"It's kind of windy, you two," Bess said fretfully. "Get back a little, will you?"

Cari inched back one foot, but Nancy kept looking down. "I guess I was expecting to *see* a collapsed cliff," she mused. "But, of course, that doesn't make any sense. Three years of tides moving in and out would smooth over the spot, wouldn't they? So there'd be no trace of a body now or of the rubble."

Bess's voice was edgy. "Nancy, Cari, you *know* I hate heights! Let's get out of here and go back and check into the hotel. I'm starving!"

"In one second," Nancy promised. "I'm just trying to fix this scene in my—"

Then she gasped. Under her heels, the cliff was starting to crumble, and the momentum shot her forward.

Instinctively Nancy threw herself back. Her arms flailed the air wildly—helplessly.

Cari made a lunge for her, but came up with nothing but a handful of air.

Nancy's frantic backpedaling only made things worse. Before she could draw a breath to scream, she was sliding down the rocky face to the treacherous boulders below.

31

Chapter

Four

NANCY SLID with her arms stretched above her head, grasping for any handhold. She held her breath, waiting for the terrible moment when she'd smash onto the rocks below.

Then a third of the way down, her shirt shredded and her back skinned, Nancy sped past a small bush rooted precariously in the rock. She opened her hand and clawed at it. Her fall was stopped, but the impact was terrible. Nancy hung, dangling by one arm, her shoulder wrenched and aching.

But she was alive!

She eased her toes down onto a narrow outcropping of rock—just a yard wide—jutting out from the cliff. Below her, the sea licked at the rocks as hungrily as ever.

Nancy lay there trembling. Every inch of her body was throbbing with pain, but she knew nothing was broken. Her shoulder was not dislocated. She ran a hand across her eyes and glanced back up at the cliff top. The others were staring down at her, ashen faced.

"H-hi," Nancy stuttered.

There were tears in Bess's eyes. She opened her mouth to return Nancy's greeting, but no sound came out.

"Don't move," George called. "I'll be right down to help you."

"No, I'm okay!" Nancy called back. "Just a little sore. And embarrassed," she added. "I can climb up myself."

Now that she looked, she noticed that the cliff was *covered* with scraggly bushes. Nancy slid along to the end of the ledge and pulled gingerly on the nearest one. It didn't move. She gave it a harder tug. The bush certainly seemed well rooted.

"I can use these bushes to pull myself up," she called up to the girls. "But keep an eye on me."

"We will," Bess said fervently as Nancy edged herself off the ledge and began her ascent.

"No, Ned, I'm okay. Really!" Nancy insisted. "A little bit scraped up, that's all." She felt the pain shoot down her arm when she eased her shoulder back and tried not to groan audibly. "It's sweet of you to want to fly out here, but I'm just not going to let you. Not with that big paper to finish . . ."

It was nine at night, and Nancy had just put in a good-night call to Ned at college. She still couldn't believe her good luck. She'd made it back up the cliff with very little trouble. Her knees and elbows were rubbed raw from the climb—but she would be okay soon.

"The fall did tell me something," she said to Ned. "It's entirely possible that whoever fell in that tape slid down just the way I did—because of the cliff's collapsing."

"So there might not have been any kind of 'foul play' involved?" Ned asked.

"Exactly. But I don't know what it all proves. It's just something to file away."

"Well, keep me filed away somewhere, too," Ned said. "I hate having you so far away."

"Me, too." Nancy sighed. "I'd better hang up. I've got a lot going on tomorrow—first day on the job, you know. I love you."

"I love you, too, Nancy. Call me again as soon as you can."

"Nancy, hi! You're right on time!"

Nancy turned to see Dan Kennedy striding toward her. "I'm starting to get the hang of driving around here," she said. "You just leave an hour earlier than you think you need to."

"That's about it," Dan said. "What have you done with Bess and George?"

Nancy hid a smile. Her friends would be delighted to hear that he'd asked about them. "They're working," she said. "I gave them their assignments last night. Before we left for L.A., I called Jesse's estate to find out who his accountants were. It's a firm called Lawrence Associates, and Bess is over there now trying to get permission to go through Jesse's financial records. George is at the library looking at old newspaper clippings of that last concert. Something might turn up—you never know."

"Well, tell them hi for me. Now, I'll take you around and introduce you to the people you'll be working with this week." Dan lowered his voice. "I've told them you're a guest veejay, even the receptionist."

Speaking normally again, he took Nancy by the shoulders and piloted her down the hall. "Let's go find out what a rock TV station looks like," he said.

"Here's the control room," he said, stopping beside one door. "There are three directors inside—the director, the associate director, and the technical director. The technical director's responsible for making sure the right tape's put on when it's time to show a video." Nancy pulled the door open a crack and peered in to see a man and two women sitting at a paneled board covered with what looked like millions of buttons.

On the wall in front of them were four television screens, each showing the set from a different angle. She eased the door closed again.

"And here's the sound room," Dan continued, indicating a room with a sliding glass door adjacent to the control room. "It's just what it sounds like—the technician here monitors the show's decibel level."

Dan stuck his head into the sound room and tapped the shoulder of a man wearing headphones. "Wake up, Ken! This is Nancy Drew," he said after the technician had turned around. "She's our new guest veejay. She'll be—"

"I have a lot of work to do," Ken said flatly, interrupting. "I'll talk to you later." And he turned his back on them.

For a second Dan looked bewildered. "Well, *he's* sure got something on his mind," he said. "Maybe one of the higher-ups has been giving him trouble."

They peeked into the makeup room, the editing room, and the preview room—a soundproof chamber where tapes could be played at all different sound levels to make sure the sound was undistorted. A bright red and white electric guitar was propped up against one wall of the sound room. "What's that guitar for?" Nancy asked.

"Oh, that! We had a demo band practicing in here a couple of days ago, and—if you can believe it—they forgot that. I don't think they're going to get far in this business."

Dan introduced Nancy to several more people. She couldn't understand it, but no one she met was very friendly—and a couple of people were even downright rude. As she and Dan continued on, Dan looked more and more confused.

"They don't know who you really are, do they?" he muttered.

"I don't see how they could!" Nancy whispered back. "And even if they did, why would they be *angry* at me?"

"Beats me," said Dan. "But something's going on, that's for sure. Here's the studio. They're taping now, so we'll just slip in the back door. Be very quiet. This is where it all happens."

The studio was an enormous room three stories high—the height of the whole building. The first thing Nancy noticed was that it was freezing in there. "It's so hot under all those lights that the rest of the room has to be kept cold so the veejays won't get too sweaty," Dan whispered.

Nancy looked up at the ceiling. It was hung with massive lights, each burning down onto the set.

"Why do they need three cameras?" she whispered to Dan, staring at the set.

"One's for the center, one's for closeups, and one's for the guest chair," he answered.

The center chair was where the veejay sat. One

was sitting there then in front of a large screen that was pulsing with color and weird shapes.

"What does he do when the video's on?" Nancy asked.

"Anything he wants—for as long as the video lasts. They run the tape in from the control room. Well, I've got just one more person to introduce you to, and that's Renee Stanley. I think she's in the dressing room. She's the veejay who'll be your boss this week."

"I've seen her on TV. She's great," said Nancy as they headed down the hall again. "But I thought my boss was going to be you."

"I wish I could be." Dan sounded genuinely regretful. "But all this Jesse Slade–week stuff's going to keep me too busy. I'll do everything I can to help you, though."

"Okay," Nancy said. She was trying to fight down the rush of nervousness that was rising in her stomach. I know this is just an undercover job, she thought. But if everyone's got a grudge against me, I'm going to need an ally. Maybe Renee will—

But one look at Renee Stanley and Nancy knew *she* wasn't going to be on her side.

The dressing room door was open. Three of the walls were lined with signed photos of rock stars, and the fourth was hung ceiling to floor with one huge mirror. Renee was sitting and brushing her hair, staring fixedly at her reflection when they walked into her office. She didn't stop brushing

—didn't even turn around—as Dan introduced Nancy. Then, very deliberately, she put her brush down and swiveled her chair around to face Nancy.

She was even prettier in person than on TV. She was wearing zebra-print tights and a low-cut sleeveless black T-shirt with a loose-fitting leather belt riding down on her hips. Tousled blond ringlets framed her heart-shaped face. Her eyes were a startlingly deep blue—almost violet— with lashes so long they cast shadows on her cheeks.

But there was nothing pretty about her expression, or about the silence that hung in the air as she stared first at Nancy and then at Dan.

Dan cleared his throat nervously. "I don't know whether you have time to talk to Nancy before you go on—" he began.

"Not really," Renee interrupted. "But I guess I don't have much of a choice, do I?" She glanced briefly at Nancy and picked up a hand mirror. "Well, you might as well sit down, Nancy," she said in a bored monotone. "Got a pad? I want you to take notes."

"Nancy, you look awful!" George said anxiously as Nancy walked slowly across the lobby of TVR. "I didn't find out much at the library—but I guess that had better wait. How was your day?"

Nancy tried to smile. "Not the greatest. I thought four-thirty would never come. If this is the glamorous world of music television, you can have it." Wearily she ran a hand across her face. "Where's the car?"

George had dropped Nancy off that morning. Since Bess had been headed in a different direction, she took a taxi. "It's over there," George said, pointing across the street. "Do you want to go back to the hotel? You look as though you could use a rest."

"Not yet," answered Nancy. "We're going to see someone. I did get one lead today. Do you have the keys, George? I'd like to drive. Okay?"

"I don't know what I've done, but everyone at TVR is mad at me," she said as she pulled the car onto the freeway and headed toward the suburbs. "They must have been told something really horrible about me. But what? And by whom, I keep asking myself.

"Renee Stanley's *really* got it in for me," she continued. "All I did today was clerical stuff— that and errands. Renee treated me like a secretary. She sent me out to get her lunch. She made me type letters for her—thank-you notes for some birthday presents. She made me alphabetize some files. I wouldn't have minded—I mean, it's nice to help out—but she didn't say a civil word to me the whole day!"

"You should tell Mr. Thomas," George said indignantly.

"Oh, I can't do that," said Nancy. "I'm sure it would get out if I did, and then people would be angry at me for tattling. I'll just have to tough it out. But somehow I don't think I'll be learning a lot about the music business or meeting the right people to ask my questions."

"Say, where are we going?" asked George. "You said something about a lead?"

Nancy brightened. "Yes. I did get a chance to talk to Dan in the afternoon—he said to say hi to you, by the way—and he suggested that I talk to Vint Wylie. He was Jesse's bass player, and Dan thinks Vint probably knew Jesse as well as anyone in the business. So I made an appointment with him. He lives in a suburb called North Claibourne—we have two more exits to go."

"What's Vint Wylie doing now?" asked George.

"I don't know. Maybe he's playing in another band," Nancy answered. "Whatever he's doing, I hope he's nicer to me than the people at TVR," she added with a sigh.

They reached the exit and drove for a couple of miles before Nancy reached the right neighborhood. "This is North Claibourne. How gorgeous!" she exclaimed. "Look at all those beautiful gardens!"

They *were* beautiful. Every yard was lushly planted, every lawn an emerald rectangle. Flowering trees were everywhere, and their colors were nothing like those near Nancy's home— flaming reds, corals, and yellows. The houses were no less beautiful. Most of them were one story high, and most looked vaguely Spanish, with red-tiled roofs and stucco walls.

"It all looks sort of tropical," George said. "But so respectable, too. I can hardly believe a bass player would live around here. But I guess he has to live somewhere. Are we almost there, Nan?"

"*Right* there. Right now," answered Nancy as she looked at the address Dan had given her. "Wow! Vint Wylie's certainly done well for himself!"

At the end of a long, winding, flower-edged driveway, behind impressive wrought-iron gates, was a sprawling Tudor mansion—the only two-story house on the block.

The gates were open. "He's expecting us," Nancy said, turning carefully into the driveway and switching off the ignition. "He sounded very nice on the phone—said to come over."

There was no answer when she rang the bell. Nancy stood on tiptoe to peer in through the little lead-paned window in the door. All she could see was a dark, deserted-looking interior. There was no trace of anyone inside.

Gently Nancy tried the door. It was unlocked.

She and George eyed each other questioningly. "Should we go in?" George whispered.

"I don't know," Nancy whispered back. "Wait, why are we whispering?" she said in full voice. "Of course we should go in. He's expecting us. Maybe he's on the phone or something."

But no one was inside the dark, cavernous house with its carpets so thick the girls' steps were completely muffled. And the phone in the hall was off the hook.

Nancy stepped into the gleaming kitchen, which looked big enough to serve an entire restaurant. Through the kitchen window she could see the bright turquoise water of a swimming pool. "He must be out in back," she said, walking resolutely toward the kitchen's french doors.

She stepped outside—and gasped.

Sunlight was dancing on the little ripples in the pool, and a gentle breeze stirred the leaves of the trees overhanging the yard. It was a picture-perfect setting—except for one thing.

A man's body was lying facedown next to the pool!

Chapter

Five

"OH, NO!" NANCY CRIED.

As George looked on, horrified, she raced up to the motionless figure sprawled on the tiles and grabbed his shoulder. "Call an ambulance!" she ordered George. "There's a cordless phone on that table over there!" George dashed over to it.

Then the man stirred a little, groaned, and lifted his head. Now Nancy could see that he was very handsome, with a bronzed, appealingly craggy face. But he looked completely stunned.

His dazed eyes met Nancy's. "Wha—" he began.

"Mr. Wylie?" Nancy asked. He nodded. "I'm

44

Nancy Drew. It's all right. We're getting help," she reassured him. "You just take it easy."

"But I—" Vint Wylie groaned again and rolled over onto his back, raising himself up on his elbows.

Nancy patted his shoulder. "You'd better not move too much—just in case," she said. "Not until the ambulance gets here."

"But I'm okay," Vint Wylie said thickly. George had been dialing, but she stopped and stared at him. He gave an enormous yawn. "Sorry. I was just, uh, meditating."

"Meditating! You *look* as if you were—" George exclaimed. Nancy cut her off quickly. She knew George was about to say "asleep." And she was sure George was right. But there was no point in embarrassing Vint Wylie unnecessarily —he would talk more freely if he didn't feel self-conscious.

"Sorry if we startled you," she said. "We— well, obviously we thought there was something the matter. I guess I jumped to conclusions."

"It's sure lucky I hadn't reached the ambulance company yet," George said, a shade tartly. "It would have been embarrassing to have them get here and find out Mr. Wylie was okay after all."

"Call me Vint, you two. 'Mr. Wylie' sounds too weird. I don't think anyone's ever called me that before." He brushed the dark-brown hair out of his eyes and yawned once. He had meditated himself right into a deep sleep. Suddenly he grinned at Nancy, a slow, infectious grin.

"Great intro!" he said. "Shall we start all over?"

Nancy smiled back. "Sounds good," she replied. "Vint, this is my friend George Fayne. She's helping me on my—uh—research."

Vint gestured toward some teak chairs, and the three of them sat down while Nancy explained why they'd come. "Dan Kennedy said you knew the most about Jesse," she finished. "You two were pretty close?"

"Sort of." Vint bit his lip. "Jesse wasn't—wasn't that easy to get to know, really. He was probably the most private person I've ever known."

"No family?" Nancy asked. "No close friends?"

Vint looked away. He cleared his throat a couple of times, then sighed. "No. He did have a girlfriend," he said slowly. He drummed his fingers nervously on his knee. "I—I don't know about his family, though."

Why does he seem so tense? Nancy wondered. I'm not asking him anything to make him nervous. Aloud, she just said, "Do you know his girlfriend's name? Maybe I should talk to her."

"I—I don't know what her name was," Vint said quickly. "I can find out for you, though."

"That would be great. What about your band's

manager, Tommy Road? Did you know him well?" asked Nancy.

"That creep? I knew much too much about him," said Vint. He put his hands behind his head and stretched his legs out in front of him. In this elegant garden, his faded jeans and cowboy boots seemed out of place. "How much time have you got?" Suddenly he looked much more relaxed.

"Well, Dan Kennedy mentioned something about Jesse's wanting to fire Tommy Road. Had you heard anything about that?" Nancy asked.

"Jesse wanted to *fire* him?" Vint sounded astonished. "I can't believe it! He would never hear a word against him. I mean, *we* all knew what a loser Tommy was, but Jesse always refused to consider switching managers."

He scratched his chin thoughtfully. "Though there was some problem with money. Jesse was always short."

"Short of *money?*" George asked. "How could that happen? I mean, his records sold in the millions."

"I know. But it's true," Vint said. "He used to talk a lot about it. He paid me and everyone else who worked for him on time, but he was always grumbling about how he didn't have enough. That could be what finally came between him and Tommy. But as I said, I didn't know anything was up between them.

"I can tell you one person who might be able to

help you, though," he said, straightening up in his chair. "His name's Martin Rosenay. He lives out in Chelmsford—that's a town about twenty miles east of here. He really gets around in the music business—he's a dealer in rock memorabilia. And I hear he's done pretty well selling stuff related to Jesse. He probably has tons of photos, letters, and junk."

Vint stood up abruptly. "I guess I haven't been much help," he said. "I'm sorry. But I'm sure this guy Rosenay will be better."

It was definitely a dismissal. Nancy and George stood up, too. "Thanks, Vint," Nancy said. "Actually, you've been very helpful." Not *that* helpful, really, she said to herself. "Can I call you if I have any more questions?" she added.

"Sure! Any time!" Vint sounded a little too enthusiastic.

"Oh, there is one thing I forgot to ask," Nancy said. "What are you doing now? For a living, I mean?"

Now Vint looked troubled. "I'm in another band," he said. "You've probably heard of them. The Crisp."

"The Crisp! But they're—"

"Doing incredibly well," Vint finished for her. "It's true. But I'd trade it all in just to be able to play with Jesse again."

And this time Nancy was sure he was telling the truth.

"Well, what did you think?" George asked, when they were safely back in the car again.

"There's something going on," Nancy said, "but I'm not sure what. Did you notice it, too?"

"How could I miss it? When you asked him about Jesse's friends and girlfriend, he just about shriveled up."

"Yes, that's it," Nancy agreed. "But I was afraid that if I pressed him harder, he'd clam up altogether. I'll try again later."

She glanced at her watch. "It's almost suppertime. Let's go back to the hotel and meet Bess and hear how her day went."

The "hotel" where the three girls were staying was actually a group of small bungalows, each with its own kitchen and garage. "Boy, am I exhausted," Nancy said as she parked the car in their garage. "I feel so dirty, too. All I want to do tonight is—"

"Nancy!" Bess was at Nancy's elbow before Nancy was out of the car. "George! You're back! I've been waiting for you guys forever!"

She practically dragged Nancy out. "I've found out something *very interesting* about Jesse Slade," she said breathlessly. "A huge amount of his money is missing—and I'm sure Tommy Road was embezzling it!"

Chapter

Six

NANCY STOPPED on the path leading into the bungalow and stared at Bess. "We were just *talking* to someone who thought Jesse might have been having money problems," she said. "What did you find out?" All of a sudden she didn't feel so tired.

"Well, come in and sit down and I'll tell you," Bess said. "I just made some iced tea."

Her face was pink with excitement—and pride. "Now, are you ready?" she asked. "You're not going to believe I figured this all out on my own!"

Bess took a big swig of iced tea. "Well, I got to Mr. Lawrence's—the accountant's—office," she began. "It's a big, dark, and gloomy-looking place that looks like a men's club or something. I was a little scared, but I acted official and asked a secretary to see a computer printout of the general ledger Jesse's manager had kept—just the way you rehearsed me, Nan. I was told I could read it in this little conference room right next door to Lawrence's office. So I took this huge stack of computer paper and went in there and started looking through all the payments Tommy Road ever made while he was Jesse's manager.

"Most of it I could figure out pretty well," Bess continued, "but there were these huge payments to something called Bailey Promotional. That's where I started to get confused—because there were also huge payments to a public-relations place called Swang and Davis, and both companies were listed in the promotional category in the ledger. And public relations and promotion are pretty much the same thing, aren't they? Besides, the amount being paid to Bailey Promotional was really huge—I mean, hundreds of thousands of dollars. I don't know that much about this kind of thing, but I didn't see how *any* PR place could charge that much!

"*So*. I decided to call them up and just *ask* them about Tommy Road and Jesse. And guess what!" Bess was practically bouncing in her seat. "There was no Bailey Promotional in the directory! Isn't that fantastic?"

"But they could be unlisted," George objected.

"Oh, no. See, this is where I *really* got smart. I called the California Secretary of State's office. They have a list of all the businesses incorporated in the state. So I asked if they had a listing for a corporation called Bailey Promotional. And they did. It didn't have an address—just a post office box number. And it had been incorporated by a guy named S. Thomas *R-H-O-D-E*."

"*Tommy Road!* Bess, that's great!" said Nancy. "He was sending Jesse's money to a corporation he'd set up! But how could the accountant have missed that?"

"Well, I finally worked up the guts to talk to Mr. Lawrence," said Bess. "He said that it wasn't his business to question payments that Jesse's manager had authorized. He just paid them. He also said there are lots of different kinds of promotional expenses. So what do you think?"

"I think you did a wonderful job," Nancy said sincerely, and George nodded her agreement. "I don't see how there's any other way to figure this—Tommy Road must have been embezzling, and Jesse must have found out. At last, a real lead! Now we have a motive—a reason someone would have wanted Jesse out of the way."

Then Nancy's face fell. "Oh. But it's going to have to wait," she said in a disappointed voice. "Renee told me that tomorrow's going to be completely crazy. She said I'd really have to buckle down—as if I haven't already been."

"How'd your day go, anyway?" Bess asked. "I forgot to ask."

"Don't ask," Nancy and George said in unison. Nancy grinned. "At least not until after supper," she said. "Let's go find a good Mexican place. Los Angeles is supposed to have millions of them."

"Perfect," Bess replied. "I was so excited about this embezzling thing that I didn't even notice how hungry I was—if you can believe that."

Without meaning to, Nancy and George spoke in unison again. "I can't," they both said.

"Nancy, why did you ever let me eat so much? I feel like a gorged boa constrictor!" Bess groaned theatrically as they walked back into the bungalow a couple of hours later.

Nancy laughed. "Bess, I refuse all responsibility. No one was forcing you to order that food, you know."

"I know." Bess sighed. "But I've got to blame *somebody.* Do you guys want to see if there's anything good on TV?"

"Not tonight," Nancy said. "I need a good night's sleep. I'm getting up at six tomorrow so I can go in to TVR early. I even arranged for a wake-up call."

"How? By telepathy?" George asked. "I've been with you ever since you left the office, and I haven't seen you go *near* a phone."

"I made the call from TVR," Nancy said, flushing a little. "I wanted to make sure Renee knew I was really trying hard."

Bess—who had heard the whole story of Nancy's day during dinner—leaned over and gave her a hug. "You'll show that Renee," she said comfortingly. "You just wait until tomorrow. She won't know what hit her."

Songbirds were going full-blast outside as the sun streamed in across Nancy's bed and landed directly in her face. Groggily she rolled over and looked at her watch. Then she sat bolt upright in bed.

The hotel management was supposed to wake her at six o'clock. Now it was after eight!

"They must have forgotten about me!" she gasped, throwing the covers back and jumping out of bed. "Oh, I'm going to be so late!"

A tousled-looking Bess peered in, rubbing her eyes. "You're still here?" she said, yawning.

"I sure am," Nancy said grimly, "and the second I'm dressed, I'm calling the hotel desk to find out what happened."

She hurried into a pair of acid-washed jeans and an oversize sleeveless orange shirt. Then she picked up the phone and punched the number of the bell desk.

"This is Nancy Drew. I asked to be woken at six," she said angrily when the clerk answered. "Why didn't it happen?"

"But, Ms. Drew, what about your note?" The woman at the other end sounded astonished.

"What note?"

"Well, I just got on duty, but there's a note on the desk canceling your wake-up call. It's signed with your name. I—I guess the clerk just assumed you had dropped it off. I mean, why wouldn't he?" The clerk sounded completely at sea. "Ms. Drew," she said, "there's obviously been some kind of mix-up. I'm so sorry—I don't know what to say."

"Oh, don't worry," Nancy heard herself answering. "It's not your fault, and anyway, it doesn't matter too much."

And that's really true, she told herself. I have to remember that my job at TVR isn't a real job. But *someone* left that note. Someone's trying to make me look bad at TVR. And I have a very good idea who it is. But I'm not going to give her the satisfaction of thinking she's getting to me.

"Where have you been, Nancy?" Renee asked an hour later. "I thought I told you this was going to be a big day."

Renee sounded offhand, but there was an undercurrent of anger in her voice. Nancy did her best to ignore it. She'd decided on her way over that the most professional way to handle this would be to act as though it had never happened. Renee had probably sent that note—

at least, Nancy couldn't think of anyone else at TVR who would have done such a thing—but on the off-chance that she hadn't, it would definitely be wiser not to confront her.

"I'm very sorry, Renee" was all Nancy said. "What would you like me to do first?"

"Well, I know you don't have any experience working with entertainers," Renee said, "but you're about to get some. A stand-up comic named Bonzo Bob is coming in today. He's been doing the comedy clubs recently, and I'd like you to talk to him to see if you think there's any way you can use him on your show. See what you think, anyway."

"Oh, that sounds like fun!" Nancy said, trying to hide her sarcasm. She could hardly believe her luck. She was supposed to be talking to people in the music business about Jesse, and she had to interview a *comic.*

It didn't take long for Nancy to realize that Bonzo Bob was not going to be on TVR. Nancy couldn't remember ever seeing anyone who made her feel less like laughing. And she'd never seen anyone with so little talent act so temperamental.

Bonzo Bob came bouncing into the little office where Renee had set Nancy up and shouted, "All right! Let's party! I'm a party dude!"

Oh, no, Nancy thought. What is he *wearing?*

Yellow-checked bicycle shorts, wingtip shoes

with gartered black socks, a red sleeveless tank top, and a white beret with a graduation-cap tassel were what Bonzo Bob obviously thought would make people remember him. But he doesn't look funny, Nancy thought—just dumb. Well, maybe he was nicer than he looked.

"I'm Nancy Drew," Nancy said, smiling. "I'm the guest veejay for this week. It's great to meet you, Bonzo—uh, I mean Bob."

For a long minute Bonzo Bob stared goggle-eyed at her. Then he opened his mouth and bellowed, *"Whaaaaat?* So TVR doesn't think I'm good enough for a *real* staff person to interview me, is that right? They think it's okay to send a lousy *guest?* Well, I've got news for you, Miss so-called veejay. Bonzo Bob is worth a lot more than that! Do you know how many people come to see my act at Attention Talent? A lot more than come to see *you!"*

Stay poised, Nancy told herself. You never have to see him again. "Please, won't you sit down?" she asked in as composed a voice as she could manage. "I promise to be as—as 'real' as I can."

"Sure you do," he answered bitterly. Nancy still couldn't tell if he was genuinely angry or if he thought he was being funny. "I believe that like I believe politicians tell the truth. And speaking of politics . . ."

It was all downhill from there. By lunchtime

Nancy's ears hurt from being screamed at, and she could count on one finger the number of jokes that had made her even smile. Bonzo Bob had spent the time alternating between insulting her lowly status at TVR and spewing out the worst humor she had ever heard. When he finally stormed out—again, without making it clear whether or not he was kidding—Nancy felt limp with relief.

"Well, I guess he's not right for us," Renee said briefly when Nancy described her morning's work. "Look, whip down to the commissary and get some lunch to go. I've got another job for you."

Not a word of thanks for all her wasted effort! Nancy was fuming as she walked down the hall toward the commissary.

When she came back with her turkey sandwich, she encountered Renee bent over a street guide. "See this intersection?" she said, pointing to a map. "There's a great bargain basement there called Kendall's. All the kids in the Valley use it—and today they're having a massive sale. I want you to head over there and find out what the scene's like. Take notes, buy a few things if they look interesting—TVR will reimburse you. We're thinking of doing a fashion segment."

Nancy tried to remain cheerful, but it was hard. All this running around wasn't answering any of her questions. It looked as though being undercover was going to be more of a hindrance than a help.

"The scene" at Kendall's turned out to be a huge store, all on one level, filled with long tables. All of them were heaped with jumbled piles of ultrafashionable clothes. The aisles were jammed with girls who were snatching clothes off the tables and trying them on wherever they happened to be.

Nancy took a deep breath and waded in. There was a table of tops in front of her. Curious, she reached out to pick up a leopard-print vest with skull-and-crossbones buttons, but just as she did, a lightning-quick hand snaked in from behind her and grabbed the vest. "I saw it first!" a girl squealed.

Too bad Bess isn't here, Nancy thought. *She'd* actually enjoy this madhouse!

It was almost four o'clock when Nancy finally got back to TVR. Tired but satisfied, she walked up to Renee's cubicle. In her hand was a shopping bag stuffed with clothes. She'd had to wait in line forty-five minutes to pay for them, but it was worth it. The clothes were some of the weirdest she'd ever seen, and she had decided that Kendall's would be a great place to feature on TVR.

Renee was in her office, bent over a pile of

fan mail. "Well, it's really a madhouse there, but I think you could get some—" Nancy started.

She never finished. "Where on earth have you been?" Renee shrieked. "You go on the air in five minutes!"

Chapter

Seven

Nancy dropped the bag of clothes to the floor. "What do you mean?" she said.

Renee was already propelling her down the hall in the direction of the studio. "I told you you'd be doing a live guest-veejay appearance at four!" she cried. "You're interviewing Carla Tarleton!"

"Carla Tarleton?"

"Yes. She's the lead singer for the Temple of Doom."

Nancy's heart sank. The Temple of Doom was a heavy-metal group whom she'd only seen on TVR once or twice. Nancy felt as if she were trapped in a nightmare. "I'm sorry, Renee, but you didn't mention anything about this!" Nancy panted as they raced along.

"I most certainly did tell you about it," Renee snapped. "Yesterday, just before you left. I remember it clearly."

Quickly Nancy reviewed the events of the day before. She was absolutely sure Renee hadn't said anything. This had to be another way she was trying to sabotage Nancy's work at TVR.

But I'm not going to give her that chance, Nancy vowed. I'll make good on this if it kills me!

"Well, there must have been some mix-up," she said in as calm a voice as she could manage. "Just fill me in on what I need to do, and I'll try the best I can not to mess up."

"It's too late to fill you in," Renee scolded her. "Just keep looking at the camera. Someone will cue you when they're about to switch over to a video. Here we are. No time to make you up— they'll have to do it during the first commercial."

They were at the studio door now. Renee pushed it open.

"Where was she?" someone hissed as Nancy and Renee rushed toward the set. "I'll explain later," Renee shot back over her shoulder. "Is Carla here?"

"Yes. I'm her agent," a dark-haired young woman answered. "We wanted some time for Carla to talk to the veejay first. It's really not fair to make a star go on without any warm-up, you know!"

To Nancy's intense relief, Renee didn't blame her for being late. All her energy seemed concentrated on making sure Nancy got on the air. "Sorry. A mix-up," Renee told the agent. "Can't do anything about it now. Okay, Nancy. Here's your chair."

She pushed Nancy into the anchor's seat in front of the camera. "Good luck."

Nancy's heart was pounding, and her hands were clammy. Face the camera, she told herself. And smile!

She looked up and stared into the camera. It was like staring into space. All she could see was the camera—everything else was black. Above her, the floodlights were beating down, but Nancy wasn't even conscious of how hot it was. Every nerve was concentrated on making this work.

A technician to the side of the camera waved to get Nancy's attention. He held up ten fingers—ten seconds to go. Nine. Eight. Seven. Six. Nancy felt as if she had a metal band being pulled tight across her chest. Five. Four. Three. I can't do this! she thought wildly. Two. One. She was on.

Nancy smiled into the blackness and was startled by the sound of her own voice. "Hello. I'm Nancy Drew, your guest veejay," she began, "and I'm brand-new at this. You have to bear with me for a little while because I'm so nervous I can hardly breathe, much less speak." There was a stifled laugh off-camera.

Now Carla Tarleton was slipping into the seat next to Nancy's. Nancy could hear her breathing fast and knew Carla was nervous, too. That realization made Nancy feel much calmer.

"Today we're going to be talking to Carla Tarleton, the drummer for the Temple of Doom," she said. "I mean, the *lead singer* for the Temple of Doom. Sorry, Carla!"

She turned to look at Carla, and for the first time noticed what her guest was wearing—a white leather T-shirt, a turquoise leather miniskirt with metal studs, and thigh-high boots entirely covered with yellow feathers. "Wow!" Nancy said involuntarily. "What incredible boots! Where did you get them?"

For an awful moment Carla just stared, openmouthed, at Nancy. Then she broke into easy laughter. "To tell you the truth, I wasn't ready for that question," she said. "Uh—Big Bird made them for me. No, actually, I made them myself. I bought the feathers at a warehouse and glued them on one at a time."

"But that must have taken forever!" Nancy exclaimed.

"Just about, but it was a perfect thing to do on the road. Gave me something to occupy myself on the bus. Some people do needlepoint, I glue feathers on boots. There's not much difference, really."

"I guess you're right," Nancy said. "But listen, Carla. You said you hadn't been expecting that question. What *were* you expecting, if you don't mind telling us?"

"Oh, something boring about what it's like being the only girl in the band. That's what people usually ask me."

"Well, we'll skip that, then," Nancy said. "What about—Oops! Wait, folks. One of the studio guys is giving me some kind of hand signal. I think—yes—you're about to see Temple of Doom's new video. Let's take a look."

"Okay, three minutes until you're back on, Nancy," said a cameraman. Everyone in the studio began talking at once.

The makeup woman rushed up to Nancy and began powdering her face. "Too bad we didn't get a chance to do this before," she said, "but I don't think anyone will notice. You're doing great."

Nancy was shaking all over. *Great?* she exclaimed. "All I did was goof up!" She turned to Carla. "I called you a drummer! I can't believe it!"

"Hey, it's okay," Carla said. "I'm having a good time. They'll see me sing on the video, anyway."

The makeup woman had finished, and now it was the hairdresser's turn. "Not much to do here," she said to Nancy. "We'll just mousse you up a tiny bit."

The cameraman was looking over the hairdresser's shoulder. "You're doing fine," he said reassuringly. "Very relaxed. Just make sure you don't turn away from the camera. Pretend it's a friend you're talking to."

"Carla, don't forget to mention the name of the new *album!"* came the frantic voice of Carla's agent.

"I will," said Carla calmly, *"if* it comes up. I don't have to talk about music *all* the time. If Nancy wants to talk about something else, that's fine with me."

"Okay, folks, back in places" came a technician's voice. "Nancy, keep up the good work."

The next twenty-two minutes passed in a blur. Nancy couldn't decide whether she was totally relaxed or more nervous than she'd ever been in her life. Whichever it was, she knew there was no point in trying to pretend she was totally comfortable in front of a camera—so she didn't try. And between commercials and switches to music videos, she managed to feel as though she were having a real conversation with Carla. They talked about everything, from what their high schools had been like to their favorite brands of ice cream.

When the show was over, everyone in the studio broke into applause—even Carla's agent.

All the lights came on, and Nancy looked out at the many faces that had been hidden by the dark. "Is that all?" she asked. "I don't get another chance?"

"You don't need one," the director said, walking up to her chair. "You came across completely naturally, and that's the most important thing."

"I hope Renee agrees with you," Nancy said, surprised and embarrassed when she started to yawn.

"It's perfectly natural," an assistant said. "It's the tension draining away."

Nancy smiled gratefully and peered around the studio. "Where is Renee? She was pretty upset with me just before the taping. I'd have thought she'd stick around to see how I did."

"She's probably tense because of the concert. In fact, she's probably *at* the stadium by now," a cameraman said.

"What concert?"

"The Crisp. They're at Featherstone Stadium tonight. I bet Renee left early to go with Vint."

"Vint Wylie?" Nancy asked. "She knows him?"

"Knows him! They've been going together for almost three years—ever since Jesse Slade disappeared."

"But I talked to—" Nancy stopped. She was supposed to be undercover and couldn't go around telling people she'd been talking to Vint Wylie!

The cameraman didn't notice Nancy's hesitation. "Renee doesn't mention it much around here," he said. "There's the thing about Jesse Slade."

67

"What thing about Jesse?"

"Well, you know that she was Jesse's girl before she started going out with Vint, right?"

"She *was?*" Nancy asked incredulously.

"Oh, yeah. They were quite an item. It didn't look too good when she started seeing Vint so soon after Jesse disappeared."

Suddenly he stopped. "Hey, what am I doing? I shouldn't be saying all this!"

"It's all right," Nancy assured him. "I won't tell anyone that you told me."

He seemed to perk up. "Okay," he said. "Anyway, I'm not telling you anything you wouldn't have found out sooner or later. Well, I've got to take off. Nice talking to you!"

Nice talking to *you*, Nancy thought. You've certainly added an interesting new angle to this case. And you've given me some pretty prime suspects, too.

No wonder Vint Wylie had lied about not knowing who Jesse Slade's girlfriend was. What if he and Renee had actually started seeing each other *before* Jesse died? Had they murdered Jesse?

Wait a minute, Nancy said to herself. Where's the motive? Could Renee and Vint be tied in to Tommy Road? Or did they have another reason to want Jesse dead?

Lost in thought, she walked slowly through the halls back to Renee's cubicle. She reached down

to pull her purse out from under Renee's desk—
and that's when she saw the note.

Please send Nancy Drew to my office
immediately.

Winslow Thomas

Instantly Nancy's heart began to pound. Had
Winslow seen her interview with Carla? Was he
angry?

When Nancy reached his office and saw his
grave face, she did not have her fears allayed.

"Sit down, Nancy," he said crisply. "I want to
talk to you. Hang on a second. I want Dan in
here, too."

Oh, no, Nancy thought.

Winslow picked up the phone. "Call Kennedy and get him in here," he ordered his
secretary. Then he hung up and turned to Nancy.

"You did a jolly good job interviewing Carla,"
Winslow said unexpectedly. Then he added,
"Considering your lack of preparation. You *were*
poised, but I think you'll agree that the whole
interview wasn't very, well, professional. I mean,
you certainly hadn't done your homework, had
you?"

What was Nancy supposed to say? She'd had
no time to do any "homework"—but she didn't
want to tell tales on Renee. Before she could
decide on an answer, Winslow spoke again.

"I also heard you were late this morning." He picked up a marble paperweight and began turning it in his hands, staring at it intently, unwilling to meet her eyes.

Finally he looked up. "What kind of progress are you making on your case?"

"Well, I—I have some leads, but—" Nancy knew she sounded as though she was floundering.

"But nothing definite," Winslow interrupted. "I thought that was what you'd say. Look, under the circumstances I can't justify having you here as a guest veejay any longer. I hate to say it, but I'm going to have to ask you to give up this case."

Chapter

Eight

BUT, MR. THOMAS, I've only been working for two days!" Nancy protested. "It always takes me a few days to start unraveling a case!"

"Be that as it may," Mr. Thomas said, "it's—well, disruptive having you here. Some members of my staff have started asking questions already. It hasn't escaped their attention that you came on as a guest veejay without coming through any of the normal channels. I can't fend off their questions much longer."

"But I—I don't understand why it would be bad if people knew who I was," Nancy said. "I'd think it would be good for TVR to get the credit for solving this mystery!"

"Not if the solution's unpleasant," Mr. Thomas countered swiftly. "And I'm afraid it will be."

"You wanted to see me, Mr. Thomas?" Dan Kennedy was poking his head into the room.

"Yes. Sit down. I've just been telling Nancy that I'd like her to stop investigating this matter with any help from us. I think it's doing the station a disservice. I wanted you to know, Dan," Winslow added wryly, "since you brought Nancy and her friends here in the first place."

Dan looked worried. Nancy couldn't blame him. Winslow wouldn't fire Dan because of her, would he?

She couldn't let that happen. She had to *prove* that Dan had been right in asking her to solve the mystery of Jesse's disappearance.

Nancy gathered up all her resolve. "Mr. Thomas," she said, "do you think you could give me another twenty-four hours here? If I don't have the case solved by then, I promise I'll forget it."

"I—I think that's a good idea," said Dan hesitantly. "I have complete confidence in Nancy, Mr. Thomas. She's been so busy since she got here that she really hasn't had any time to do much investigating."

Mr. Thomas met both of their eyes with his steely ones. Then quickly he stood, nodded his head, and said, "All right, Nancy. You've got your twenty-four hours. Use it well."

"Thank you," Nancy said with heartfelt relief. "Thank you very much. I do have an important lead I can follow up tomorrow morning." Last night she'd asked George to call Martin Rosenay, the dealer in Slade memorabilia, to set up an appointment with him for the next morning.

"I guess you'll be late tomorrow?" Mr. Thomas asked with a sly smile.

"I guess I will be," said Nancy, unconsciously holding her breath.

"Go ahead," said Mr. Thomas. "You can leave a note on Renee's desk and tell her I said it would be all right."

"I will. And thanks again, Mr. Thomas."

George and Bess were watching the evening news when Nancy walked into the bungalow and threw herself onto the couch. "I'm never moving again," she groaned.

"Can I get you a soda? Did you have another bad day?" George asked sympathetically.

Nancy sighed. "Yes, please, to the first question. Yes and no, to the second. It was interesting, at least." Quickly she filled George and Bess in on what had happened.

"At least you got to veejay. Do you have a tape?" Bess asked.

"Yes, they gave me one," Nancy said. "But I don't much feel like looking at it right now."

"I can't believe you didn't tell Mr. Thomas it was Renee's fault you weren't prepared!" Bess said. "Why are *you* taking all the blame for this?"

"Believe me, I *wanted* to tell him," Nancy said.

73

"But it just wouldn't be a good idea—especially now that she's a suspect. I don't want *her* to suspect that I suspect her, if you see what I mean. The nicer and more uncomplaining I am, the more relaxed she'll be around me."

"Well, you're just too much of a saint," Bess said. "But I suppose you're right."

"Did you two find out anything?" Nancy asked.

"Not that much," George said, "except that spending all day reading microfilm in a newspaper archive makes your eyes go crazy. I think I know every detail of the police investigation into Jesse's disappearance—"

"And I know every review of every song he ever released—" Bess put in.

"But nothing that looked like a clue," George finished.

Just then the phone rang. Nancy picked it up. "Hi, Nancy!" It was Dan Kennedy. "I just wanted to cheer you up."

"Well, I'm not feeling too great," Nancy admitted.

"Anything I can do to make you feel better? Are you free tomorrow morning after your appointment? Somebody canceled on me, and I've got a couple of hours open all of a sudden. I'd love an update on the case."

"Oh, Dan, I'm sorry. I'm going to be busy *all* morning," Nancy said regretfully. Then, from the corner of her eye, she saw Bess jumping up and down and pointing excitedly at herself and George. "But Bess and George are free," Nancy said. "Can they stand in for me?"

"Sure!" Dan said. "I'll take them to Fumetti's for breakfast. It's the latest hot spot. You know— mineral water and famous people."

"Sounds perfect," Nancy said with a laugh. "Should they meet you at TVR?"

"Sure. We'll go in my Lamborghini. It's my one luxury. I got it last year when my career took off. If it's worth doing, it's worth doing right— right?"

"Right. Thanks, Dan."

Nancy hung up and turned to her friends, smiling for the first time in hours. "We aim to please," she said.

The next morning Nancy dropped Bess and George off at the studio and stopped for a minute to admire Dan's car before heading to her appointment. She had just taken the exit for Chelmsford when her car phone suddenly began to ring. Astonished, she picked it up.

"Nancy? This is Lily, the receptionist at TVR. I'm sorry to bother you, but someone's just dropped off a package for you. There's a note on it that says it's urgent that you receive it immediately."

"A package? Who left it?"

"I don't know. I was away from my desk for a few minutes, and when I came back it was sitting here."

"Well, I'm on my way to an appointment that I really have to keep," Nancy said. "Could you possibly open it and tell me what it is?"

"Uh, gee, Nancy, I don't think I should," Lily answered uncertainly. "There's a sticker on it that says 'Private and Confidential.'"

"I see. Well, I guess I'd better come back, then," Nancy said. "Thanks, Lily."

Shaking her head in frustration, she turned and headed toward the freeway entrance that would take her back to the center of town.

She arrived at TVR, half an hour later, to find Lily looking terribly embarrassed.

"Nancy, you're not going to believe this," she said, "but I can't find the package. I was just on my way down to see if someone had taken it to Renee for you."

"I'll do that," Nancy said.

But there was no sign of the package in Renee's cubicle. And there was no sign of her package in the mailroom. Nancy checked on the off chance that it had been taken there by mistake. There was no sign of the package anywhere.

"I—I just don't know what happened," Lily said, faltering. "I went to the copy machine for a second to make some copies for Mr. Thomas, and when I came back, the package was gone! Do you think it was something important?"

"I hope not," Nancy said. She felt like screaming. A whole hour wasted, when she had so little time left! "Well, don't worry, Lily. It's not your fault." And she headed back out to her car.

Well, I've got to make the trip all over again, she thought to herself as she sat down in the driver's seat and switched on a classic-rock station. Then she headed out into the traffic.

She was just pulling into Martin Rosenay's long, gravel driveway when the radio suddenly stopped working—and the sound began.

A horrible, screeching, unbearably loud blast. A blast in full Sensurround blaring out through the car speakers, filling the car. And it grew even louder—and then unbelievably louder still.

Nancy had never felt a pain like the one assaulting her eardrums then. Black and red spots were dancing in front of her eyes, and her arms were shaking uncontrollably on the steering wheel. She fought desperately to keep the car under control, but the ear-shattering screech was finally too much for her. She doubled over in helpless agony—the steering wheel forgotten, her foot pressing down on the gas pedal.

The car swerved off the driveway, tossing up plumes of gravel before it crashed into the front of Martin Rosenay's house!

Chapter

Nine

WITH A BONE-JARRING CRASH, the car came to a stop. But with the impact, the terrible sound stopped abruptly. White-faced and trembling, Nancy crawled out of the car and collapsed on her knees on the ground.

"Are you crazy? What do you think you're doing? You idiot—you should be locked up!"

Shakily Nancy stared up at the person who was yelling so furiously from the doorway. She saw a plump little man whose face was red with rage and whose whole body was quivering as he glared down at her.

"Mr.—Mr. Rosenay?" she whispered.

"That's right. And who are you?"

"I'm Nancy Drew." Nancy took a deep breath and pushed herself to her feet. But her legs were too weak to support her. She sagged against the hood of her car.

"I-I'm sorry," she said with tremendous effort. "There was something wrong with the—the speakers. It hurt so much that I—"

Now Martin Rosenay's manner changed completely. He jounced down the front steps and rushed up to her.

"That sound was coming from inside your car?" he asked in horror. "I was way in the back of the house, and even there it shattered my eardrums!"

"I think it did shatter mine," Nancy said. Her whole head was throbbing, and Rosenay's voice seemed to be coming from far off, under water.

"Well, it's no wonder you lost control of your car," he said contritely. "I apologize for yelling at you."

"My car! How badly is it damaged? And what about your *house?*"

Her pain pushed aside, Nancy rushed to the front of the car. She couldn't see the front bumper at all. It was buried in the bushes that lined the front of Rosenay's one-story ranch house.

"I'd better check this," Nancy said with a sinking feeling in her stomach. She climbed into the car and held her breath while turning the key. Would it start? The engine turned over once and died. Once again and this time it caught. Nancy backed it up a few feet. Then she got out to assess the damage.

"Only a couple of scratches! Thank heaven for rubber bumpers!" Nancy said.

Then she remembered: the house. What had the collision done to *it?*

Hastily, she stepped forward and pulled back the bushes in front of the house.

Nancy could hardly believe her eyes. There were a few scratches in the siding, but that was all.

"Well, it looks like minimal damage," she said after a second. "I must not have been going that fast—even though I felt like I was flying." I've got to find out how that radio was rigged, she thought to herself. Whoever did it really wanted me out of the way!

"Let's forget about it for the time being, then," Rosenay said. "A little paint will cover it all. Come on in!"

He led her up the front steps and through the door. "Welcome to Rosenay's Rock Memorabilia," he said.

Nancy could hardly believe her eyes. Every available surface—tables, chairs, sofas, and the floor—was covered with mementoes and souvenirs. There were heaps of old 45s and autographed pictures. There were buttons and T-shirts and hats and stickers and posters and fluorescent paintings on velvet and even models of Elvis Presley's tomb.

"Where do you *sit?*" Nancy asked.

Rosenay laughed. "I try not to," he answered. "You're interested in Jesse Slade stuff, I understand."

"That's right. I'm investigating his disappearance, and I just wondered whether there might possibly be any clues here."

"I don't know if there are or not, but come into the kitchen. All my Jesse things are on the kitchen table."

The kitchen was just as cluttered as the living room. "I guess you try not to eat, either?" Nancy said.

"Take-out. All I eat is take-out. Here's the Slade stuff," said Rosenay, gesturing toward the kitchen table. "Have a seat—wait, let me move this stuff." He shifted a pile of magazines from the chair to the floor.

There was a surprising amount of memorabilia, considering that Jesse Slade had been famous for such a short time before he'd disappeared. "I wouldn't have expected so much," Nancy said thoughtfully as she sat down and began leafing through a pile of photos and articles.

Rosenay looked a little uncomfortable. "I've got a great supplier," he answered. "He's in touch with all the Jesse Slade fan clubs—there were about sixty, you know."

"How much of it do you sell?" asked Nancy.

"To be frank, not a whole lot—not yet," answered Rosenay. "I get a few letters a week or so, but mostly I think of this particular collection as an investment."

"Did you know Jesse at all?" Nancy asked.

"Pretty well. No, that's an exaggeration, I guess. Let's say I know people who knew him pretty well. Your friend said you were an investigator. Do you have any ideas about what happened to Jesse?"

"I've got a few. I'm not ruling anything out," Nancy said carefully. *"You* don't have any ideas about what happened to him, do you?"

"Oh, I have ideas. Everyone has ideas," said Rosenay. His chubby face suddenly became veiled. "I don't want to point the finger at anyone, but if I were you I'd ask Renee Stanley and Vint Wylie to explain a few things. Like why they were seeing each other on the sly before Jesse disappeared, and why neither of them seemed very upset once he was gone. It just doesn't seem quite right to me, that's all."

"Do you really think they plotted together to make him disappear?" Nancy asked.

"Off the record? Yes, I think that's exactly what happened," answered Rosenay.

"But is that a real motive?" Nancy put down the stack of photos she was holding. She'd been worrying about the motive ever since she'd first begun to suspect Renee. "I mean, if they wanted to go out together, all Renee had to do was break up with Jesse. It might have been a little awkward —but not nearly as awkward as risking a murder charge!"

"Look, *I'm* not the investigator," Rosenay replied. "All I know is, I watched a local-TV news interview with Renee just after Jesse had disappeared. She didn't mention Vint—even though everybody in the business knew about him. And she kept referring to Jesse in the past tense. Now, why would she do that unless she knew he was dead?"

"Good point," Nancy said. She bent her head to a stack of photos. "I'd better start looking through this stuff. I'm sure you don't have all day."

"Make yourself comfortable," Rosenay said. "I'll be out back putting in my tomato plants."

For the next half hour Nancy sifted through the piles in front of her. There were lots of letters from Jesse to his fans—probably collected from the fan clubs, she thought—and dozens of pictures and fan magazines featuring him. But no clues leapt out at her.

At last she stood up and walked out back. "Mr. Rosenay?" she said. "I think I'm done."

He put down his trowel and stood up, brushing the dirt off his hands. "Find anything?"

"Not really," Nancy said. "But if it's all right, I'd love to borrow a picture of Jesse to take with me. I'll bring it back, of course."

"No need for that," said Rosenay. "I'll donate it to the cause. I hope you find out what happened to him."

"That's very nice of you," said Nancy. "Is it okay to take this one?"

It was a photo of Jesse Slade standing in front of his car. He was laughing at something off-camera, and he looked totally relaxed.

"He looks so happy here," Nancy said. "I guess that's why this is my favorite of all the ones you have."

"He does, doesn't he?" For a second the two of them stared at the picture in silence. "You're welcome to it," Rosenay said. "And give me a call if there's anything more I can help you with."

"I sure will. Thanks, Mr. Rosenay," said Nancy sincerely.

He walked with her to the front of the house and watched as she got into her car. "Careful, now," he said anxiously.

"Don't worry," Nancy replied. "Your house is safe from me!"

Feeling more cheerful than she had when she'd set out that morning, she headed back to TVR. This time, she kept the radio turned off.

Bess and George were waiting for her in Dan's office when she got back. "We were hoping you'd get here soon. Oh, Nancy! We had the greatest time!" Bess exclaimed when she saw her. "The restaurant was so good—and there were all *kinds* of stars having 'power breakfasts'—and Dan's the coolest guy in the world! Thanks so much for taking this case! Did you find out anything at that guy's house?"

"Well, nothing too specific," Nancy answered, "but he did give me a few ideas—and this picture." She took the picture out of its envelope and held it out to her friends.

"Nice," George commented. "Hey, that's a different color, but it's just like Dan's car."

Nancy went to George's side and stared at the picture again. Then she snatched it out of her friend's hands.

"Rosenay knows where Jesse is!" she gasped. "This picture proves it!"

Chapter

Ten

"YOU'RE RIGHT, GEORGE—it *is* just like Dan's car!" Nancy said angrily. "Dan bought his a year ago! Jesse's car is a Lamborghini, too, so this has to be *last year's model!*"

"Last year's model? But that means . . ." Bess began.

"Right, Bess," said Nancy. "It means Jesse was around last year. And *that* means he's probably still around now! Jesse could even be the 'friend' Martin Rosenay talked about—that would make sense. And Rosenay may be keeping his whereabouts a secret so that he can corner the market in Jesse Slade memorabilia. To think that I trusted him! And Jesse—why is he hiding out?"

"Are you *sure* about all this?" asked Bess.

"As sure as I can be without Jesse standing here. I can try to trace the license plate—too bad Jesse's standing in front of the second half of it. I'm sure that car is no more than a year old."

"Well, what are you going to do?" asked George calmly.

"I'm going right back there and tell Rosenay— No, wait. I can't do that." Nancy stopped pacing. "I've got to stay here. If I have only until tonight before I have to leave TVR, I'd better not waste any time. I'll go down and see if Renee's in and if she can use me for anything."

"What about us?" asked Bess.

"Let's see . . . I can't think of anything right now, guys. I guess you'd better take the afternoon off and go shopping."

But Bess was frowning. "Ordinarily you know I'd take you up on that like a shot, Nan. But don't you think you could use us for something around here? If it's your last day and all—"

Nancy felt very touched. Even if she never managed to solve this case, it was great to have such good friends. "That's nice of you, Bess," she said. "I really can't come up with anything at the moment, but why don't you two come down to Renee's office with me? I could use some moral support when I talk to her."

"Fine," George said. "And if she has any filing or something to do, *we'll* do it."

When the three friends got to Renee's office,

87

she wasn't there. "She's in the conference room down the hall," a man said as he walked by and saw them. "I just saw her in there."

Renee didn't notice them walk in. She was too busy watching a tape of some concert—and when Nancy looked more closely, she saw Vint Wylie on the screen. It must be the concert from the night before.

"Hi, Renee," Nancy said, plunking herself down next to the veejay. "What are you watching?"

"Oh! You startled me!" Renee whirled around with an irritable scowl.

"It's just a tape of the Crisp concert from last night," she told Nancy. "I was watching it to see—uh, to see whether we could use any of it."

"And to see Vint, right?" Nancy asked. Behind them, Bess and George silently sat down. "You two *are* going out, aren't you?"

"That's none of your business," Renee snapped.

"Well, I guess I should level with you. I'm a private investigator," Nancy said, and Renee's jaw dropped. "I didn't really come to TVR as a guest veejay. I'm looking into Jesse's disappearance." I don't have to mince words, she told herself. There's no reason why I need to stay on Renee's good side anymore. "I was surprised to find out that you and Vint are going out."

"Do you know Vint?" Renee asked cautiously.

"I talked to him yesterday," Nancy said.

"You *talked* to Vint?" Renee whispered.

"Uh-huh. But he didn't mention that the two of you had been together for three years. Didn't he mention that I'd come by?" Nancy continued.

Renee shook her head.

"I wonder why not," Nancy said thoughtfully.

"He—he probably didn't want to worry me."

"*Worry* you? About what?" Nancy asked.

"Well, he knows I get pretty upset whenever—whenever anybody asks about Jesse. I— He wouldn't have wanted me to know that someone was stirring the whole thing up again." Renee drew in a shaky breath.

"And is there any reason you didn't mention that you and Vint had been seeing each other?" Nancy continued implacably. "It's not a secret, is it?"

"N-no," Renee stammered. "But we never—" She cleared her throat. "I— Well, it's just a little bit awkward. That's really the only reason I try to downplay it. You know, a veejay and a musician going out . . . people might get the idea there were possibilities for—well, conflict of interest."

"I can see how they might," Nancy said. "I haven't had time to check Jesse's will yet, Renee. Is there anything in it I should know about?"

Renee was scowling now. "What is this—a firing squad? Oh, all right," she muttered after a second. "Yes. He left me some money."

There was a little pause. "Oh, I know what you're thinking, Nancy!" Renee burst out. "But Vint and I don't know what happened to Jesse. We really don't! You have to believe me!"

"Why?" was all Nancy said.

"Because—because—why would we do something like that?" Renee was twisting her hands together so hard that her knuckles were white. "It's true that we didn't tell Jesse we'd started going out—but that doesn't mean we'd kill him! And he wasn't going to leave me *that* much!"

"I didn't mention killing him!" Nancy said sharply. "Do you think he *was* killed?"

"Why, of course I do. I mean, what else could have happened? How could he still be alive?" Renee's eyes were enormous in her white face. She leaned forward and grabbed Nancy's wrist painfully hard. *"He isn't alive, is he?"* she almost shrieked.

"I'm not sure, Renee." Gently Nancy pulled Renee's clawing hand off her wrist. "But I never rule out anything."

"Oh, no," Renee said breathily. "It can't be!" She stood up on shaky legs. "I-I'm on in fifteen minutes," she said. "I don't want to be late." And she walked slowly from the room.

"If Jesse is alive, what's Renee worried about?" Nancy asked out loud. Unless—unless she thought she'd killed him herself—

Nancy gave herself a mental shake. "I'm wasting time sitting here speculating about all this," she said. "I bet Renee knows more than she's saying." She leaned forward to switch off the tape in the VCR, and then paused. "I can't resist watching Vint for a second," she said.

The Crisp was the kind of group that was really proud of being down-to-earth and unflashy. They never wore anything fancier than T-shirts and jeans, they never used any lighting effects fancier than a strobe, and they always sang songs about ordinary working-class people. Nancy didn't follow them much—she actually thought they were a little boring—but they'd been topping the charts for six months now. Vint certainly knew how to pick people to play with!

There he was in back, brandishing a two-necked white bass guitar and looking much more wide-awake than when Nancy had talked to him in person. He appeared to be unconscious of the camera—except that he had an uncanny knack for always facing it. Even when the concert ended and the band took a bow, Vint angled his body slightly toward the camera instead of the crowd. Very subtle scene stealing.

The audience screamed in disappointment when it finally became clear that the band wasn't going to do another encore. Once again Nancy leaned forward to turn off the tape—and once again she stopped. The tape had just cut to what was obviously a huge post-concert party at Vint's house.

"Hey!" said George. "Let's watch this for a second, too! Bess never got a chance to see what Vint's house was like."

As she watched, Nancy saw that all the trees on Vint's property had been covered with tiny hot-pink lights, and the swimming pool was ringed with potted tropical trees of all kinds. There was Renee on Vint's arm. He was wearing jeans, but she was in a skin-tight strapless leather mini dress.

The camera focused in on a waiter's tray next. It was full of tiny hollowed-out potatoes filled with caviar. As Nancy watched, a woman's hand with fluorescent green nails reached in and picked one up.

Then the scene shifted to Vint's front yard, where what looked like an entire precinct of private security guards was directing traffic and keeping out gate crashers. Behind a barricade was a crowd of people trying to get a glimpse of the party, and behind them was a mess of cars trying to get through.

Poor guys, Nancy thought. It must be really maddening to get stuck in the middle of party traffic.

But wait! What car was that?

The car Nancy noticed was nosing slowly up to

the edge of the crowd. It was impossible to see the driver, but the first half of the license-plate number looked awfully familiar. And the car itself was a white Lamborghini—last year's model.

"That must be Jesse!" Nancy gasped.

Chapter

Eleven

THAT PARTY was last night!" said Nancy. "If Jesse was there, then that means he can't be that far away! We've got to find him!"

"Where are you going? What about Renee?" asked Bess as Nancy jumped to her feet.

"We'll worry about her later," said Nancy. "There's one person who I'm *sure* knows where Jesse is—and that's Martin Rosenay. Let's get out to his house right away!"

Nancy was almost out the door when she suddenly remembered something else. "Let's get all of Jesse's license-plate number from the tape," she said. "If Rosenay won't talk, we might still be able to track Jesse down. At least I hope so. We *can't* let him get away when we're this close to him!"

The three girls dashed out of the studio and into their car. Miraculously, the traffic wasn't too bad and they reached Chelmsford quickly to find a car in Martin Rosenay's driveway. With a screech of brakes Nancy stopped behind it and jumped out. "Come on," she said over her shoulder to Bess and George. "Let's get this over with."

The three girls stalked up the front path, and Nancy rapped loudly on the door. In a second Martin Rosenay appeared, wiping his mouth with a napkin. He was carrying a huge bowl of chocolate ice cream.

"Nancy!" he exclaimed. "And?" he asked, looking at Bess and George.

"These are my friends, George Fayne and Bess Marvin," Nancy said, making the introductions fast.

"Come in, come in! Wait, let me put this down somewhere. Let's see. Where?" Rosenay asked himself, looking for any place that wasn't piled high with memorabilia. "Don't want it to spill on anything—the fans would *not* go for that." He chuckled. "I can just see telling them the picture they wanted was—"

"It's the picture we're here about, Mr. Rosenay," Nancy interrupted. "The one of Jesse that you gave me."

He looked startled. "What about it? I said you could keep it, didn't I?"

"Yes, you did," Nancy replied. "But I'm surprised. Are you sure you wanted me to have such a recent picture of Jesse?"

"A what? What do you mean?" Suddenly Rosenay didn't look quite so cheerful.

"I mean that can't be an old picture. I mean that picture was taken only last year. I mean that Jesse Slade is still very much alive and living very near here."

Rosenay just stared at her.

"Let me refresh your memory," Nancy said.

She reached into her bag and pulled out the picture. "Whoever shot this must not have known anything about cars," she said, pointing to the Lamborghini in the picture. "This model is not three years old! You've been running a pretty good scam, Mr. Rosenay—but now it's time to stop."

"Let me see that picture," Mr. Rosenay said in a ghost of his usual voice. Slowly he reached out and took it from Nancy's hand. He stared at it for a second, then collapsed onto a pile of letters in a nearby chair.

"You could be right," he whispered. "Maybe he *is* still alive." Still staring at the picture, he absentmindedly took a spoonful of ice cream. "But who would have guessed?"

"You mean *you* didn't know?" Bess burst out.

Rosenay shook his head. "I didn't. I didn't think he was still alive. I thought some of my pictures might possibly be fakes—but I thought they'd been made with a Jesse Slade look-alike. Not the real Jesse!

"I know—I know what you're going to say," he said when he saw Nancy's expression. "I shouldn't have sold them if I thought they weren't genuine.

"But look at it from my point of view," he went on. "Jesse memorabilia may get really big one day. And when I suddenly started hearing from a supplier who could give me all kinds of stuff, including great pictures, I couldn't resist. Sometimes I did wonder if the pictures were fakes, but I didn't *know* for sure. Was I supposed to rock the boat?"

"Yes," George said bluntly.

Rosenay gave her a sad smile and a shrug. "Maybe," he said, "but you don't know what it's like trying to earn a living in this business. Also, I didn't want my supplier getting in trouble. I was thinking about protecting him—if you can believe it."

Nancy could almost believe it, but not quite. She'd liked Rosenay when she first met him, but now she wasn't sure how she felt. But one thing was certain—he was definitely out for himself.

"I'd like to believe you, Mr. Rosenay," she

said, "and I would like your help now. You can't protect your supplier any longer—not if he knows the truth about Jesse. It's our duty to inform the world if Jesse's still alive."

Nancy didn't mention the fact that she thought Jesse himself was probably the "supplier." That wasn't information she wanted him to have. "You can understand that, can't you?"

"Sure," he said after a minute. He stood up decisively. "Let me get this stupid ice cream out of my hands"—he took one more bite—"and I'll go and find the shipment that that picture came in. I haven't cataloged it yet."

"This is an incredible place," Bess whispered when Rosenay had left. "How can he give up his living room like this?"

"It's not just his living room; it's the whole house," Nancy whispered back. "The Jesse Slade things are in the kitchen. I hope he can *find* the shipment he's looking for."

From the sounds coming from the kitchen, Nancy decided Rosenay was having trouble. There were several thuds as though he'd dropped some boxes, an "ouch!" and then the unmistakable noise of a pile of papers slithering to the ground.

At last Rosenay reappeared, clutching a large manila envelope. "I think these are the ones," he said. "Let's hope so. I kind of tore the place up looking for them."

Eagerly Nancy took the envelope. It was

postmarked Los Gatos, California. "No address, I suppose," she said to Rosenay.

"No. Just a post office box—box forty-six. But Los Gatos is tiny—it shouldn't be hard to track someone down there."

"I hope you're right," Nancy said, taking a stack of photos out of the envelope and dividing them among the three of them. "Just look through these for a sec," she said.

"What are we looking for?" George wanted to know.

"I'm not sure. Background details, I guess. Anything that might tell us where the pictures were taken."

It was eerie seeing so many pictures of Jesse Slade and knowing that he must be alive after all. *I wonder who knows about him besides us?* Nancy thought. *Can it be possible that we're the only ones?* She shivered suddenly.

Bess must have been thinking along the same lines. She looked up from her stack of pictures and said, "I should think it would be lonely, having no one know you're *you.*"

"Maybe so," Nancy said. "Have you guys noticed anything? Because I haven't."

"I haven't, either," said Bess, and George shook her head.

"Then we'll just have to go out to Los Gatos and see what we can find," Nancy said. "And we'd better get going. The afternoon's going to be gone before we know it."

"And we haven't had lunch yet. . . ." Bess said plaintively.

"After that giant breakfast?" George asked, amazed that Bess was hungry already.

"We'll pick up something on the way," Nancy answered to keep peace. "Mr. Rosenay, thanks."

"No problem," he said a little sheepishly. "I hope you find him."

"What a gorgeous town Los Gatos is," Bess said gloomily half an hour later. "Really, Nancy, you do take us to the glamor spots!"

"Welcome to Los Gatos—Pop. 182," said the fly-specked sign just outside town. It was hard to believe such a dusty little place could be just an hour outside of Los Angeles. Los Gatos looked more like a ghost town in an old western movie than anything else—hot, dirty, and empty. There was even an old dog sleeping lazily in the middle of the road in front of the post office.

Carefully Nancy steered her car around him. "We might as well ask someone at the post office whether they can help us," she said, "since the gas station is closed."

A woman reading a magazine behind the counter looked up in mild surprise as the girls trooped in.

"Afternoon, ladies," she said. "May I help you with something?"

"Well, it's a little complicated," said Nancy.

"We're looking for the address of one of your boxholders. The box number is forty-six."

"Let's see." The woman put down her magazine, heaved herself to her feet, and ran her finger down a list of names on the wall. "Mr. Joplin, that is," she said. "Out on Horse Pasture Road. Take a right at the stop sign out front and drive for about a quarter of a mile. You'll see Horse Pasture on your left. It's a dirt road, and his house is the only one on it. You can't miss it."

"Thank you so much," said Nancy. "We really appreciate it."

"We're lucky this is such a small town," she said to George and Bess once they were safely back in the car. "In a bigger place I don't think she'd have given us the address like that."

"Well, we don't exactly look like dangerous criminal types," said George. "She probably knew she could trust us. Look, there's the turn. We're here at last!"

The modest gray house at the end of the road seemed to huddle forlornly in the shade of the steep hill behind it. Shades had been drawn across most of the windows, and the lawn had gone to seed.

Nancy's heart was pounding as she switched off the ignition and heard the refrain of a wailing guitar float out an open window. The three girls slid out of the car. Nancy couldn't place the melody. I know I've heard it recently, she said to herself. But when?

Then she remembered. It had been the night they'd been watching television at Bess's. It seemed so long ago now! The song was "Goodbye, Sweet Life," and it was turned up to top volume on the stereo.

The melody broke off in the middle, then started up again. It wasn't a record. *Someone inside was actually playing the song.*

Nancy pressed the front doorbell, and the music stopped in the middle of a measure. She heard footsteps move toward them.

The man who answered the door looked thin, and his jeans and grubby T-shirt were threadbare. He looked as if he hadn't shaved for a couple of days. But all three girls recognized him right away.

"You're—you're—" Nancy had trouble getting the words out.

"Yeah," said the man with the crooked grin. "I'm Jesse Slade."

Chapter

Twelve

"SO SOMEONE FOUND ME at last," said Jesse Slade. "I knew it had to happen sometime."

The face that had smiled out from millions of record covers was now staring suspiciously at the three girls. "Can I do something for you, now that you're here?"

Nancy found her voice. "I'm a private investigator. Could we possibly talk to you for a few minutes?"

"Depends," said Jesse. "What are you planning to do with whatever I tell you?"

"I—I don't know yet," said Nancy. "I haven't thought about that, actually. I guess it depends on *what* you tell us."

Slade shrugged. "That's honest, anyway. Come on in."

He led them into what Nancy guessed would have been called the living room if it had had any real furniture. There were two tattered armchairs, a television, an electric piano, a stereo and compact-disk player, and an amplifier.

"It's a little primitive in here," Slade apologized. "I hope you don't mind. Let's see—two of you can have the chairs, one can have the piano bench, and I'll take the floor."

Nancy took the piano bench. From there she could see most of the other rooms in the house. All of them were furnished, or not furnished, like the living room. The walls were bare, the floors were bare. There were no homey touches—it all looked as though Jesse Slade had just moved in.

"How long have you lived here?" she asked.

"Going on three years," Jesse answered. "Ever since—ever since I disappeared." He looked around as if seeing the place with an outsider's eyes. "It still needs fixing up, I guess. I just can't seem to get around to it.

"Well!" he continued. "What brings the three of you to my doorstep?"

"My name's Nancy Drew," Nancy said, "and I'm a private investigator. These are my friends Bess Marvin and George Fayne." Jesse nodded at them. Bess just stared, open-mouthed and wide-eyed. George did return his nod.

"We were watching a TVR special—you know

what TVR is, right?" He nodded again. "A TVR special about your last concert, and I noticed some movement, what looked like a body falling off a cliff just beside and behind the stage. We began wondering if maybe you had fallen off that cliff."

"So someone finally noticed that," Jesse said grimly. "It sure took long enough. I decided that maybe the cameras hadn't caught the actions."

"It was on the tape, but a good tape wasn't found until very recently," Nancy told him. "And it was just by accident that I saw the fall. It was very dark, and I only saw it because of the movement. Anyway, Bess called TVR, and they agreed to let me use the station as a base of operations while we looked for you. And—here we are.

"We thought you could have been hurt," she went on. "That's why we decided to investigate in the first place. If someone had hurt you—or even killed you—and there was some way to catch that person . . ."

"But I'm that person," Jesse said softly.

The three girls stared at him, not understanding.

"I *was* involved in that accident on the cliff." he said. "But I wasn't the one who fell."

Nancy's mouth was dry.

"*I* knocked *him* off. My manager, Tommy Road. We were yelling at each other. I took a step toward him—I guess I must have looked pretty scary—and he stepped backward. The cliff crumbled under him, and he went down." Jesse didn't speak for a long minute. "Did he die, do you know?"

His eyes were fixed on Nancy's with painful intensity. "I don't know," Nancy said. "No one knows. He never turned up after that night—he disappeared just like you."

Slowly Jesse let out his breath. "So I'll never know if I'm responsible for his death or not."

"Jesse," Nancy said gently, "maybe you'd better start at the beginning."

"Okay," he said after drawing in a ragged breath. "You probably know that my career was going pretty well before that concert."

That broke the tension in the room, somehow. All four of them laughed. *"Pretty* well," George said.

"Yeah. Well, I guess that is an understatement. And a whole lot of the credit has to go to Tommy Road. He took a chance on me when no one else would. He practically never slept, trying to get someone in the industry to listen to me—and when Clio Records finally signed me, he got me just about the best deal in recording history."

He stood up and stared out the window at the drab view outside. "But after a while I began to suspect that Tommy wasn't being exactly straight with me. It's partly my fault, I know. I mean, I *let* him take control of my money, just the way he took control of my career. I didn't want to be bothered with financial details. I hate numbers and making boring phone calls to accountants and things like that. And he was great at it.

"But every now and then I'd wonder where the money was all going. He said he was investing it for me." Jesse gave a short laugh. "Funny way of investing it—funneling it into his own account."

"I found out about that, too," Bess put in timidly. "I checked your general ledger at Lawrence Associates."

"Yeah, that's what I finally did, too. And I figured it all out the day before that last concert. I was furious, as you can imagine. My own manager—the guy who'd been like my best friend for *years*—embezzling from me practically since day one!

"I didn't have a chance to talk to him about it until the night of the concert," Jesse went on. "That gave me a lot of time to decide what to say. When I took my break, I found Tommy and said that I was never going to perform again unless he returned every dollar. I figured that would scare him. You know—that he wouldn't want to lose his biggest client.

"But it turned out he'd been waiting for this," Jesse said savagely. "Tommy told *me* he didn't want to be my manager any longer! He said he was going to leave the country—*with* all my money—and that I'd never see a cent of what he'd taken. On top of that, he started insulting me for not having noticed what was going on before then. . . ."

Jesse's voice faltered. "So I took a step toward him. I don't know if I meant to punch him or what. He—he went down without a sound, just like something in a nightmare. I was terrified to look down over the edge. I was afraid of what I might see. It must have only been a couple of seconds, but it seemed like hours before I looked down." He closed his eyes as if the memory was too painful for him to stand. "Then I looked. There was his body lying down there, all crumpled up on the rocks."

Bess winced.

"I looked around the stage," Jesse continued. *"No one had noticed a thing!* My backup band was still playing, and all the technicians were running around setting up for the finale. If I'd wanted to, I could just have gone back and rejoined the band, and maybe no one would ever have found out what had happened. But I couldn't do it. Even though he'd been cheating me, I couldn't leave him down there."

"So you climbed down after him?" Nancy said.

"Right. Boy, I had plenty of time to think about how he must have felt going down! It was pitch dark, and the wind was whipping around, and pieces of the cliff kept crumbling under my feet. . . ."

"But when I got down to the bottom—down to where the rocks were—the body was gone. A wave must have come in and carried it out."

Jesse sighed. "So there I was. And right then I decided to take off for Mexico. No way could I go back up there without people realizing something had happened—and I couldn't stand the thought of facing a murder charge. I had about two hundred dollars in my pocket. I walked down the beach for about an hour, then climbed up another part of the cliff, found a road, and started hitchhiking. I crossed the border into Mexico the next day."

"No one recognized you?" George asked.

"Nope. You know, people don't usually recognize famous people unless they're expecting to see them. They usually just think, 'Gee, that sure looks like so-and-so.' Once in a while someone would say how much I looked like Jesse Slade"—he smiled—"and I'd just tell them I'd heard that before."

"But how have you been living since then?" Nancy asked.

"In Mexico things were pretty hand-to-mouth for a few months, until I got a job as a waiter. I scraped up enough money to buy a guitar, and when I could afford to come back here I started giving lessons. But I don't do that too much. Mostly I do odd jobs. I'm a caretaker for the big house back up the road. The owner's great. He lets me use the pickup parked outside."

Nancy happened to glance over at Bess, who looked as if she were wilting in her chair. Nancy was sure she was crushed that her idol had sunk so low. But to Nancy, it didn't sound as if Jesse was unhappy about the direction his life had taken.

"You don't seem to mind your obscurity and poverty too much," she commented.

Jesse thought about it for a second. "Nope. I guess I don't," he said thoughtfully. "It's a relief not having everyone look up to me—and not feeling as if I'm responsible for making a million fans happy. Having all those girls in love with me got kind of—kind of exhausting." Bess looked up, a little startled.

"Well, I've managed to fool everyone till now," Jesse said. "How did you finally find me?"

Nancy explained about Martin Rosenay, and Jesse grimaced. "Of course. Of *course,*" he said. "I should have known that car would get me in trouble. It belongs to the guy whose house I take care of."

"Who took the pictures, by the way?" George asked.

"I did. I gave some guitar lessons in exchange for a secondhand Nikon. I cleaned myself up, set the timer, and started posing. Selling the pictures was an easy way to get cash."

"I wonder what did happen to Tommy Road," Nancy said thoughtfully. "Is it possible that he's still alive? It seems hard to believe that his body was never found. The police combed that whole site so carefully. What if he survived the fall? What if he slid down the cliff instead of falling?"

"I guess he could have gone underground like me," Jesse said. "And he was such a crook that he's probably managed to do a lot better for himself than I have," he added bitterly.

Silence fell. Suddenly the little house seemed as remote and forgotten as Jesse Slade himself.

"What are you going to do now that you've found me?" he suddenly asked.

Nancy stared at him. "I don't know. I just don't know," she said. "I don't blame you for what happened, and you're not a murderer. What do you *want* me to do? I'm sure that if you came forward with your story, people would believe you. The general ledger will bear you out—"

"No. I don't want to come forward," Jesse said in a strained voice. "I don't want to live in that fishbowl again. I'm all right where I am, and I'm not bothering anyone. Please, Nancy," he begged, "can't you leave this alone? Can't you forget you ever saw me, and not tell anyone where I am?"

Nancy looked from him to Bess and George. Almost imperceptibly they nodded.

"All right, Jesse," Nancy said. "We'll go back to L.A. And we won't tell anyone about you, except the people at TVR. I think I can promise that they'll keep it confidential, and I really owe it to them."

"Thank you," Jesse said. "Thank you more than I can say."

"You're welcome," Nancy said, getting to her feet. "I guess we'll be on our—"

Just then they heard a car door slamming, quickly followed by footsteps coming up the walk. Then there was a frantic knock at the front door.

Everyone froze. "You expecting anyone else?" Jesse muttered.

The knock sounded again, even louder this time. Jesse strode forward and opened the door.

A blinding burst of light exploded in his face!

Chapter

Thirteen

JESSE STAGGERED BACKWARD, his hands covering his face. Another strobe light went off, and another and another, as if someone had hurled a bunch of silent firecrackers into the house.

Now the three girls could see the reporter framed in the doorway, a cameraman at his back. He jammed a microphone into Jesse's face. "You're Jesse Slade, aren't you?" he asked. "I'm from Channel Six. What a story this will make! Hey, who are the girls?"

"Get out of here!" Jesse shouted, hurling himself against the door. Quickly he slipped the bolt shut. Then he leaned against the door, breathing hard.

"You didn't tell anyone you were coming here, did you?" he asked Nancy.

"No, except for—except for Martin Rosenay," Nancy said. All of a sudden she knew exactly what had happened.

So did Jesse. "Rosenay! Of course! He must have finally figured out that I was the supplier. He'd do anything to sell that junk of his. He must have called all the press in town, that little—" He stopped. "Well, there's certainly no reason for you to keep quiet *now*."

"I guess not," Nancy agreed quietly. "I'm so sorry, Jesse. I hope you know I didn't expect things to turn out this way."

"Oh, I know," said Jesse. More cheerfully, he added, "It could never have lasted, anyway. I always told myself that. And maybe I can fend them off for a while, at least long enough for me to track down a lawyer."

"Good idea," said Nancy. "And speaking of tracking down people—I'd better call Mr. Thomas at TVR and let him know what's happened."

"Why?" Jesse inquired. "He's sure to find out soon enough, the way things are going!"

"Yes, but it wouldn't be fair to let this kind of news catch him unprepared," said Nancy. "He'll have every reason to be angry at me if the regular networks scoop him. I'm not saying he'll send reporters out here," she added hastily when she saw Jesse's face, "but he should know."

But Mr. Thomas's personal line was busy. It was busy a couple of minutes later when Nancy tried again, and a couple of minutes after that. At last she gave up.

"We'll just drive back and tell him in person," she said. "Is there a back door?"

"In the kitchen." Jesse led the way, but just before Nancy opened the door he put out a hand to stop her. "Do you three think you can come back later?" he asked almost shyly. "It would be nice to have some supporting troops around. I have a feeling this is all going to get pretty heavy."

"Sure," Nancy said immediately. "It's really the least we can do. Okay, Bess and George, when I open the door, run for the car. And don't answer any questions."

They were almost to the car when the reporter at the front door saw them. "Girls! Girls!" he shouted, racing toward them. "What were you doing in there? Where's he been all this time?"

"No comment," Nancy said firmly as they clambered into their seats. Frantically the reporter beckoned to the cameraman to come and join him in front of the car. "You'd better get out of the way when I start this thing," Nancy muttered under her breath.

To her relief, the reporter and cameraman scuttled out of the way once the engine turned over.

"Okay, we're off," Nancy said.

"You solved the case, Nan," Bess said. But she didn't sound too enthusiastic about it.

"Yes," Nancy agreed wearily. "And I'm not sure that's a good thing at all."

"And he's been living there all this time?" Winslow Thomas asked in amazement.

"That's right," said Nancy. "Giving guitar lessons and being a caretaker."

"Well, blow me down," said Mr. Thomas, and he really did sound as though someone *had* blown him down. He sat at his desk a moment, considering—and then stood up and shook Nancy's hand vigorously.

"Very impressive work, Nancy," he said. "As you know, I had my doubts, but you're obviously very good at what you do. Congratulations."

"Thank you," Nancy began. "I'm happy to have cleared up *one* aspect of this case, anyway. But Mr. Thomas, do you think you could possibly downplay this story for a few days? I know it's big news for a station like yours, but Jesse seems—well, he seems a little out of it. I think it would be unkind to make him talk now."

"I think you're right," said Mr. Thomas. "Let's be as kind as possible to the poor blighter." Where does he get these odd expressions? Nancy wondered irrelevantly. "I tell you what," Mr. Thomas went on. "I've got an appointment now, but before I go I'll have my secretary call a meeting of all the TVR executives so that we can decide how to handle this story. First of all, we'll schedule a press conference. When Jesse's feeling more on top of things—"

"Jesse who?"

It was Renee. She and Vint Wylie were standing in the office doorway—and both of them looked as though they'd seen a ghost.

"What are you doing here, Renee?" Mr. Thomas snapped. "I thought you weren't on today."

"I'm not," Renee said in a strangled voice. "Vint and I just stopped in to pick up something I'd forgotten. Mr. Thomas, wh-who are you talking about?"

"Well, I have to confess I wasn't going to tell the staff yet," said Mr. Thomas, "but it seems Jesse Slade has come back to life."

"Oh, no!" Renee put her hand to her throat. "I—I can't breathe!" she cried. "This is terrible!"

And she burst into tears. "I can't handle this!" she cried, and raced out of the office.

"Renee! Wait!" Vint called, rushing after her.

Mr. Thomas shook his head. "These temperamental stars!" he said with a chuckle. "Well, I'm off." He gave them a cheery wave as he disappeared down the hall.

"I wonder if Dan's around," Bess said hopefully. "He should hear about this, don't you think?"

"I definitely think so," Nancy said. "Let's go to his office and see."

Dan *was* in, and he was as amazed by their story as Mr. Thomas had been.

"The poor, poor guy," he said, shaking his head. "When you think of what he's been through—he's got to feel totally shell shocked. Look, Nancy, do me a favor. If he wants somewhere to stay until all the publicity dies down, will you give him my address?" He was scribbling it down as he spoke. "I won't call him and bother him, but tell him he can call me or come by any time he wants."

"That's great, Dan," Nancy said warmly. "I wouldn't be surprised if he takes you up on it. We're heading back there now, and I'll tell him first thing."

"What time is it?" George asked as they passed the sign for Los Gatos. "I feel as if we've been doing nothing but drive for about ten hours."

"It's six," Nancy replied. "We'll just check in with Jesse, and then we can go back to the hotel and call it a day."

"And get some supper," Bess interjected.

"And get some supper," said Nancy. "Oh, no. What's going *on?*"

She'd just turned onto the dirt road leading to Jesse's house. "I bet every camera crew in Los Angeles is here," Nancy said hopelessly.

It certainly looked that way. The little dirt road was crawling with people. Cars and camera trucks were parked all around the house. Reporters were thronging the front yard—and the hill in back was packed with spectators. The little house, all of its lights out, looked as though it was under siege.

"Oh, why can't they leave him alone!" Bess cried. "We don't have a chance of getting in to see him!"

"I'm afraid you're right, but we have to give it a try," Nancy said.

Just as the girls got out of the car, a roar went up from the crowd. Nancy turned quickly.

A light had just been turned on in Jesse's living room. Now the front door was opening a crack—and then all the way. And now Jesse was walking out onto the front step.

He stood there for a second, silent, making no attempt to shield his eyes from the glare of the flashes. "All right! All right! I'll tell you everything you want to know!" he shouted at the crowd.

At that exact moment a gunshot rang out—and Jesse Slade crumpled to the porch.

Chapter

Fourteen

ANOTHER SHOT ripped through the silence—
and then there was instant noise and pandemo-
nium.

"We've got to help Jesse!" Nancy shouted to
Bess and George. But the screaming, panicky
mob that was now rushing away from the house
knocked her down before she could take a step.
Dizzily she struggled to her feet and forced
herself upright into the sea of elbows and knees.
At last she pushed her way to Jesse's front steps,
Bess and George right behind her.

Jesse was hunched over, covered with blood.
When he lifted his head, the skin on his face was
pulled tight with pain.

"Just—just my arm," he gasped. "Lucky. But get me inside."

Nancy was already moving. She, George, and Bess dragged him into the house and slammed the door. Just then a third shot rang out.

"Keep down, everybody!" Nancy ordered as she bolted the door. "Call the police, George— and tell them to bring an ambulance!"

She threw herself to the ground, slithered across the floor on her stomach, and lifted her head to peek cautiously out the window. On the road dozens of shrieking people were rushing to get into their cars. Nancy shuddered. Not all of them were driving away, but most of them were staying put, secure in their cars.

"Let's get you cleaned up, Jesse," she said briskly, turning away from the window. Quickly she tore his shirt open at the shoulder. Then she sighed with relief.

"You were right. It's only your arm," she said. "I can't get the bullet out, though—it's too deep. It must hurt incredibly."

"Burns," said Jesse through clenched teeth. "Who do you think is after me?"

"You'd know that better than I would," Nancy said as she hastily tied a strip of shirt around the wound. But Jesse just shook his head. She could tell that the effort of talking was too much for him.

"Nancy," said Bess in a trembling voice, "do

you realize we're trapped in here with a killer outside waiting for us?"

"Don't worry, Bess," said Nancy as calmly as she could. "The police should be here any minute."

"But what if he's right outside the door?"

"The door's locked. We've done everything we can. They'll be here before you know it," Nancy assured her friend. She only hoped it was true.

Jesse moaned. His lips were gray now, and his eyes kept rolling back in his head. Nancy checked his pulse. She could hardly feel it—and the bandage she'd put around his arm was already drenched in blood.

"They've got to get here soon," she repeated. "We've done everything we can."

But ten minutes crawled by before Nancy and her friends heard the welcome sound of the police siren.

"They're here!" Bess was almost sobbing with relief as she ran to the front door and yanked it open.

In just seconds the house was swarming with people. The reporters piled out of their cars and were furiously snapping pictures again. Two paramedics bundled Jesse onto a stretcher. They were pushing through the crowd to carry him out the door when Jesse whispered hoarsely, "Nancy," and stopped their progress.

"Here I am," she said, moving over to stand next to the stretcher.

"Where are you staying, in case I need to get in touch with you?" he asked, and Nancy told him the name of their hotel. "A friend of mine at TVR has a place where you can stay when you get out of the hospital," she added, "so you won't need to come back here if you don't want to."

He smiled. "I—don't," he whispered. His head was lolling sleepily to the side now.

"We'd better take him in, miss," said one of the paramedics. "You can call to see how he is later."

Jesse gripped Nancy's hand for a second, and then the paramedics carried him away.

Nancy felt tears stinging her eyes as she watched them load the stretcher onto the ambulance. What have I done to that poor guy? she thought. If I'd never come looking for him, this might never have happened! If only—

"Miss?" A police officer was standing at her elbow. "I'm Officer McIntyre. I wonder if I could get a statement from you."

When she'd told him everything, he shook his head. "Not much to go on in the way of suspects," he said.

"I do know of two possible suspects, though," Nancy said and told him about Renee and Vint.

"That's something, anyway," Officer McIntyre said. "I'll have someone track them down. But what about this Tommy Road? Do you really think he could still be alive?"

"I don't know. I just don't know," said Nancy.

Something flitted across her mind just then, but she didn't have time to identify it before it was gone. "That cliff was so steep I don't see how anyone could survive a fall from it. But I can't believe a body could disappear without a trace, either."

"Stranger things have happened," said the officer. He turned to a younger officer who'd just come in. "Yes, Rogers? What is it?"

"This, sir." The younger man held out his hand. "It's a spent rifle cartridge. We found it way up on the hill behind the house. No other signs of the gunman, though."

Or gunwoman, Nancy said to herself.

"Probably long gone," said Officer McIntyre. "But we'll post two guards here overnight, just to make sure." He turned to Nancy. "I'd like your number, in case I need to ask you anything more. Other than that, you and your friends are free to go."

In silence the three girls drove back through the dark to the hotel. Silent still, they parked the car in the garage, went into the bungalow, and sat down facing one another.

At last Nancy spoke. "We never got any supper," she said. "Anyone hungry?"

"I'm not, that's for sure," Bess said in a small voice. Then she burst into tears.

"I feel so terrible for Jesse!" she wept. "He's been through so much. And he's—he's not even like a real person any more. There's nobody inside. He's just a—a robot!"

"I feel bad, too," said George. "It was horrible to see someone who'd once been such a star living like *that*. I wish we'd never come here in the first place."

When Nancy spoke, it was as much to reassure herself as her friends. "Anybody would get a little strange living alone for so long—especially with that cliff scene in his past," she said. "He'll become himself again now that he's out in the real world again. He won't be able to help it. Someone that talented can't hide from things forever."

"As long as whoever's after him doesn't *get* him," George said darkly.

Nancy shivered. "That's the thing I do feel awful about," she said. "If we hadn't found him, the person with the rifle wouldn't have, either."

Then she squared her jaw and sat up straighter. "We'll have to catch that person, that's all," she said. "We started this, and we're going to finish it. But we need a good night's sleep first. I'd better call Ned. He'll be wondering what's happened to me."

"Hello?" came Ned's groggy voice after she'd dialed his number. She was using the phone next to her bed.

"Oh, Ned, I'm so sorry!" said Nancy, aghast. "I forgot about the time difference. I'll call you back tomorrow—"

"No, you won't. Talk to me now," said Ned. "I'm getting more awake every second. How's the case going?"

"Oh, Ned . . ." Nancy poured it all out to him, and when she was done she was almost in tears herself.

"This just isn't the way cases are supposed to go," she said in a wobbly voice. "I'm supposed to come in and solve them, and then everyone is happier and I can go home. But this time it seems as though I've only made things worse!"

"Not true," Ned said emphatically. "You've helped that guy, whether it seems like it now or not. And you'll catch whoever shot him—you always do, you know. I'm not even going to tell you to be careful this time. You just go out and *get* that gunman. But be careful," he added at the last minute.

Nancy giggled. "I love you, Ned. I feel a lot better now. I'm really glad I called—even if I did deprive you of your beauty sleep."

"Hey, I'm already gorgeous enough," Ned said lightly. "Now you go and get some beauty sleep yourself—not that you need it, either. And give me a call when you get a chance. I love you."

The phone woke her early the next morning.

"Nancy?" It was a man's voice, hoarse and hesitant, and for a second Nancy was too sleepy to recognize it.

"It's Jesse. I'm sorry to call you, but I didn't have anyone else to call."

"Hi, Jesse," Nancy said, struggling to sound alert. "How's your arm doing?"

His answer startled her. "The arm doesn't matter. Nancy, I'm in trouble. Really big trouble."

Nancy was wide-awake now. "What's the matter?" she asked.

"The matter is that there are two policemen standing at the foot of my bed right now. And they're here to arrest me!"

Chapter

Fifteen

Yes, I THINK we've finally got the proof we need," the police officer told Nancy. "It will be nice to see this case closed. I'm sorry for Slade, though. It doesn't look good for him."

Jesse had been so frightened by the sight of the police at the foot of his bed that he'd panicked. He hadn't been under arrest at all—the police had just wanted to ask him a few questions. But the direction the questions had led was all too clear to Nancy.

"Where's your evidence?" Nancy asked, controlling her anger.

When she'd finished talking to Jesse Nancy had woken George. Bess had been so sleepy that

Nancy had had to give up trying to rouse her. She'd left a note before she and George hurried into clothes and rushed off to the police station to see what was going on. Now they were talking to one of the men who'd questioned Jesse—Officer Squires, a tall, gangly man with an infuriatingly patronizing expression.

"We've got some very convincing evidence," he said. Nancy half expected him to add, "Young ladies." "Last night someone delivered us an anonymous package. I'm the one who opened it." For some reason he seemed quite proud of himself. "Inside there was a bloodstained T-shirt— and a note. Here's the note, if you'd like to see it. Careful not to touch it, though."

Nancy and George stared at the note. It had been scribbled in pencil on a torn sheet of notebook paper.

This shirt once belonged to Tommy Road, who was viciously murdered by Jesse Slade. I saw it happen and found the body. Slade's been hiding out all this time—but he can't get away from justice.

It was signed, "A Friend of the Law."

"But this is ridiculous!" Nancy protested. "There's no way to prove that the shirt is Tommy's—or that whoever wrote this note witnessed anything at all!"

"There's no way to prove it," agreed Officer

Squires. "But you may be interested in knowing that we did a lab check on the T-shirt. The blood type is the same as Tommy Road's. And the bloodstains are the right age."

He stared smugly at her, and for a second Nancy could think of nothing to say.

I know Tommy Road's not dead, she said to herself. I'm just sure of it. I've got to keep Jesse from going to trial for murder! But how do you explain a hunch to a police officer?

At last she found her voice. "As you say, that's interesting," she said. "But it can't be true—for a very simple reason. I know that Tommy Road is still alive." From the corner of her eye she could see George turning to stare at her, but she kept her gaze on Officer Squires.

"And just *how* do you know that?" he asked.

"I'm working on the evidence right now," Nancy replied. I'll find some, anyway, she thought. "And I'm sure that TV Rock will back me up. I'm heading right over to the station to bring one of their camera crews here."

To her secret satisfaction, Officer Squires was starting to look worried. "And now," Nancy asked, "where's Jesse? We'd like to talk to him."

"He's out of the hospital," the officer answered a little sullenly. "You can see him any time. He's waiting for you in there." He pointed to a door at the end of the room and turned his back on them. "I've got a lot of work to do," he muttered. "What a way to spend a Sunday morning."

Jesse was sitting on a bench, his head against the wall. He stood up when he saw them—and then winced. "I've got to remember to move more slowly," he said.

Under his shirt, his shoulder was bulging with bandages. "How's your arm?" George asked solicitously.

"Much better." He started to smile, but the smile faded instantly. "It'll have plenty of time to heal in jail, too."

"Don't talk that way!" Nancy said. "You're not under arrest. And we're going to beat this thing!"

"I'm glad to hear you say that, Nancy," George said, "and I can't wait to hear how. But let's talk about it outside. I don't want to turn around and find Officer Squires looming over me."

There was a little coffee shop next to the police station. Over coffee and doughnuts Nancy told George and Jesse about her hunch. Both of them looked at her doubtfully when she'd finished.

"It would be great if it were true," Jesse said, "but why are you so sure? Just because there's no body doesn't mean there wasn't a body once, if you know what I mean. Believe me, I'm not eager to face a murder rap, but I don't trust hunches."

"Nancy's hunches are *always* right," George said loyally. "And not because she's psychic or anything. She only gets hunches when she's noticed some little detail subconsciously. It's as if something trips her memory. That's why I'm sure she's right now. But how you're going to explain this to the police and Mr. Thomas, I just don't know."

"It's the shirt," Nancy said.

"Excuse me?" Jesse asked.

Nancy was frowning thoughtfully. "When you think about it, that bloody shirt doesn't make any sense," she said. "Let's just say it's true that there's a witness to the fight who doesn't want to get involved. Let's take it even further and say that the witness did hang onto the shirt all this time, hoping that when Jesse did turn up, he or she would be able to incriminate him. Okay, it's possible—barely.

"But it was a T-shirt! Can you imagine anyone who'd watch the fight, wade into the water to retrieve a body, take a bloody T-shirt off a *corpse,* and then decide just to leave the body in the water? It's not believable. It just doesn't make any sense! I don't think there was ever a dead body. I think Tommy Road survived the fall, kept his shirt, and only came forward now that Jesse's back."

"You know, you're right! That's just Tommy's style," said Jesse. He gave a giddy laugh. "I guess I'm not a murderer after all! Boy, I feel as though you've lifted a ten-ton weight off my head!"

"But we've still got to convince everyone else," Nancy said. She set her coffee cup down with a click. "Let's get over to TVR now. I'm going to call Mr. Thomas and ask him to meet us there."

"He's on his way," she said, returning from the pay phone. "He wasn't tremendously happy to be woken up this early on Sunday, but I told him it couldn't wait."

The TVR building was all but deserted. A sleepy-looking receptionist in the lobby winced when she saw them rushing in. "You look *much* too wide-awake," she said with a yawn. "Go on into Mr. Thomas's office. He's expecting you."

He was sitting behind his desk when they walked in, his fingers drumming the desktop impatiently. "This had better be good," he began —and then he saw Jesse.

His eyes widened. "Jesse Slade!" he exclaimed. "I thought you'd been arr—I mean, taken to hospital!"

Nancy was sure Mr. Thomas had been about to say "arrested." Now, how did he know that? she wondered. Did he find out about it on TV? But what news station could have gotten the story so quickly? Jesse had only been with the police for half an hour.

And why had he said "taken to hospital" instead of "taken to *the* hospital"?

The ghost of a suspicion was beginning to float around Nancy's brain. Could Winslow Thomas be British? Tommy Road had been British, too. . . .

Before she could think about it further, Mr.

Thomas jumped up with his hand extended. "I'm so pleased to make your acquaintance," he said rapidly. "On behalf of TVR, I'd like to welcome you back to the world."

"Nice to meet you," Jesse said. He was looking a little perplexed, Nancy thought. "We—we haven't met before, have we?"

"I wish we had," Winslow said regretfully. "But TVR hadn't really taken off when you—uh —vanished. I hope we'll have the pleasure of working together often from now on."

He turned to Nancy. "Was this why you had me come—to meet Jesse?"

"Not exactly," said Nancy. She took a deep breath. "Mr. Thomas, I've gone ahead and stuck my neck out on something. I hope you won't mind." And she described what had just taken place at the police station.

"You *what?*" Mr. Thomas asked, reddening angrily. "How could you involve this station in something so farfetched? That seems a little nervy to me, Nancy."

"I really had no choice." Nancy met his gaze steadily. "You see, I know I'm right."

Winslow Thomas's face was contorted with rage now. "I've never heard of such a thing! You wheedled your way in here, and now you're going to make a laughingstock of us! I should call the police and have you thrown out of here!"

What was happening to his accent? All of a

sudden it was British! Nancy looked at her friends and saw that they were as puzzled as she.

The hint that had been nagging her began to surface. Suddenly she realized it had to be true.

"Go on, get out!" he was shouting.

"You are Tommy Road!" Nancy whispered.

Mr. Thomas froze. "What—what are you saying?" he sputtered. *"You* really are crazy!"

"No, she's right!" Jesse gasped. "I *knew* I'd seen you before!"

"It's all starting to make sense now," Nancy said. "Your voice. The British phrases that kept popping out. Your weird-looking beard. And there was plenty of time for you to get over to Jesse's house last night, once I'd told you everything. You were the one who shot him. You must have been hanging around and watching to see what happened. You gave that shirt to the police. That's why you thought Jesse had been arrested!"

Mr. Thomas—Tommy Road—hesitated for a second. Then he gave her an ironic bow. "I must congratulate you," he said, his eyes full of hate. "I'm only surprised our friend Mr. Slade didn't recognize me sooner."

He wheeled around to turn his full fury on Jesse. "You tried to kill me," he spat out.

Jesse's face was white with shock. "I—I didn't! You know I didn't mean for you to fall off that cliff! It was an accident!"

"It may have been an accident," Tommy Road

said in a steely voice, "but you'll pay for it. When I'm done with you, you'll wish *you'd* been the one who'd slid off that cliff."

"You didn't even really manage to hurt me," he sneered. "I sprained my ankle, but that was about it. I watched you come down the cliff. I could tell it was too dark for you to see me. I swore I'd kill you when you reached the bottom. But when you took off down the beach, I thought —wait, this is my big chance!

"I assumed you'd report that I'd died. I hoped you'd be found guilty of my death. Whichever one happened, I knew no one would be trying to arrest Tommy Road for embezzlement. You can't arrest a dead man! It was my big chance to get away with the money and start a new life. I wouldn't even have to leave the country.

"Of course I saved my bloody shirt just in case it might come in handy someday," he continued. "And earlier that week—when I found out you'd been snooping around the accounts—I'd taken the precaution of switching the money in my account to a numbered Swiss account. No names necessary. All I had to do was grow a beard, wait until my hair grew in—and start life over. First I invested in record production. Then in music videos. And then I got my own music channel." He chuckled suddenly. "Of course I don't let any of the bands I used to handle perform on TVR."

Now he turned to Nancy. "You've obviously done a lot of thinking, Ms. Drew. It's a pity that you're so clever, because I'm not about to let *anyone* interfere with my plans. Not an amateur detective. Not a has-been rock star. Not *anyone!*"

And before anyone could stop him, he bolted from the room.

"We've got to catch him!" Nancy shouted.

The three of them dashed out of the office. Tommy Road was just disappearing into one of the preview rooms at the end of the hall. They pursued him to the door.

"It was this room," Nancy called, and they ran into it so fast that they piled up at the entrance.

The little room was pitch-dark. "Wait!" Nancy said. "He's not—"

There was a click—the sound of the door being locked.

Nancy whirled around to test the door they'd just come through. "He just locked it," she said.

Frantically Jesse rattled the knob of the door at the other end of the room. It was locked, too.

Then a light came on in the production booth on the other side of the glass wall. Tommy Road was sitting at the controls.

"Now that we're all gathered together, I've got a little number for your listening pleasure," he cooed into the microphone. "It's the first play of a song that I know will go gold. I know you're going to love it."

He smiled—and hit a switch in front of him.

A screeching blast filled the preview room. It was the same noise—the same unbearably loud noise—that Nancy had heard in her car. But now it was magnified a hundred times.

Nancy clapped her hands over her ears, but it was no use. Nothing could protect them against that deadly shriek.

Jesse collapsed to the floor, writhing. George looked as if she was screaming, but the evil blast was drowning out her voice.

So he's the one who rigged the car stereo, Nancy thought dazedly. It was all she could do to hold on to that thought. George had fallen to the floor, and Nancy knew she also was about to collapse.

The sound was killing them!

Chapter

Sixteen

AS SHE FELL to her knees, Nancy could see Tommy Road laughing maniacally. She reached her hand pleadingly out to him, but all he did was wag a teasing finger at her. He'd gone mad. He picked his suit jacket up off the chair next to him and strolled leisurely out of the control booth.

He's leaving us to die! Nancy thought desperately.

The preview room was soundproof. If there was anyone in the building, he or she couldn't hear the sound that was slowly draining the life out of Nancy and her friends. Nancy hurt so badly she couldn't move a muscle.

But she knew she had to try.

The electric guitar, Nancy ordered herself. Someone had left it there—she couldn't remember who. It was still leaning against the wall across the room.

With torturous slowness Nancy set out to crawl across the floor toward it. She felt like a diver whose last bit of air was gone, but she made herself move until she'd reached the wall.

Pick up the guitar, she ordered herself. She reached forward—but her hand wouldn't close.

Pick it up! she screamed at herself. And this time she did. Staggering, she dragged the guitar over to the sound booth and hoisted it into the air. With all the force she had, she hurled it at the glass separating them from the sound booth. Then she grabbed the window ledge and pulled herself up into the booth.

Her brain was screaming instructions at her. What switch? *What switch?* It had to be that one—the red one right in front of her. Feebly Nancy reached forward and flipped it.

The sound stopped, and a miraculous silence filled the room.

Nancy let out a long, shaky breath and collapsed into a chair. All she wanted to do was let the quiet soak into her.

On the floor in the preview room, George and Jesse were slowly uncurling and sitting up. To Nancy, both of them looked as though they were just coming out of a long, wrenching nightmare.

"Thanks, Nancy," Jesse said. He cleared his

throat. "Sorry I couldn't be more helpful. I really think that if that sound had gone on for one minute longer, I'd be dead now."

"I know I would have been," said George, and quickly shuddered. "I can't believe you've had to go through this twice, Nancy." She looked around. "I suppose it's no good hoping that Tommy Road is still around."

"No. He left a few minutes ago," Nancy said. "I'm sure he didn't hang around, either. He's probably off to plan some alibi."

"Do you mean he's going to get away with this?" George asked in horror.

"No, he's not," Nancy answered firmly. "What we need to do is think up a way to trap him. And I think I've got a perfect idea. Tommy Road has never seen Bess, has he? Well, then . . ."

Winslow Thomas's press conference at the Wilshire Hotel was attended by everyone who *was* anyone. The dozens of reporters packed into the room listened attentively as he described his feelings about Jesse Slade's return.

"To put it simply, I couldn't be more delighted," he said, "both for the music world and for TVR. This is a bloke with a tremendous talent who hasn't even begun to tap his potential in music videos. We're going to do great things together."

"Do you know Slade personally?" one reporter asked.

The flicker of a frown passed across Mr. Thomas's face and quickly vanished. "Of course I do," he said sincerely. "He's a fabulous, fabulous person. It wouldn't be putting it too strongly to say I love him."

"What about his legal problems, Mr. Thomas?" another reporter asked. "Will he be charged in Tommy Road's disappearance?"

"As far as I'm concerned, that problem doesn't exist," Mr. Thomas said graciously. "Of course we'll do all we can to help him if he *needs* help, but we're not interested in dragging up the past here. It's much more important to—"

"He's dead! Jesse's dead!" came a heartbroken wail from the doorway.

There was a gasp of shock. Everyone turned to see Bess standing by the door. Her face was contorted with grief and terror, and she was shaking from head to foot.

"They're all dead," she sobbed. "I—I went over to TVR, and they were all lying dead in one little room! Oh, Jesse!" And she burst into fresh tears.

It was Winslow Thomas's finest hour. As he listened to Bess, he actually grew white. Horror seemed to shrink him in his clothes. He groped blindly behind him for a chair and sank into it.

"What—what happened?" he asked hoarsely. "What do you mean, he's dead? How can that be?"

Bess wiped her eyes. All the cameras in the room were focused on her now.

"I—I went to TVR to pick up two friends," she choked out. "I couldn't find them anywhere, so I started looking up and down the hall. And in one of the rooms at the end, I—oh, it was too horrible!" She buried her face in her hands for a minute while the cameras clicked avidly. "I saw my friends and Jesse just lying there in a pool of broken glass!"

"Mr. Thomas" was clearly stricken. He rose tremblingly to his feet.

"Because of the tragic circumstances," he almost whispered, "I'd like to end this press conference immediately."

There was a murmur of sympathy through the room. Mr. Thomas tried to walk toward the door, but shock had made his legs too weak. Two men sprang to his aid, and—leaning heavily on their shoulders, the very image of a broken man—he staggered toward the door.

"Hi, Tommy," said Nancy breezily as she, George, and Jesse walked in right in front of him.

"Jesse!" It was a strangled scream—and Nancy knew that this time Tommy's horror was real.

"You're not here. You're not," he babbled. "None of you. No one could survive a noise like that—I made sure of it. You're dead. You've got to be dead."

"Why, Tommy," Jesse protested in a syrupy

voice, "don't you know that it would take more than a little rock 'n' roll to kill *me*? What do you take me for?"

Tommy Road just stared at him, transfixed. Then, for the first time, he realized that all the cameras in the room were still rolling. Screaming, he turned to run.

But he wasn't quick enough. Nancy tackled him like a ton of bricks—and the reporters were there to catch every detail.

Chapter

Seventeen

So Tommy Road has confessed to everything?"
Dan Kennedy asked.

It was the day after the press conference.
Nancy, Bess, and George were entertaining a few
visitors in their bungalow. Renee Stanley and
Vint Wylie were sitting next to each other on the
sofa. Dan Kennedy was lounging comfortably on
the floor. And Jesse Slade was sitting in an easy
chair that supported his bandaged arm.

Even with the bandages, Jesse already looked
like a different person. It wasn't only that he'd
shaved and bought himself some new clothes. "If
I'm going to pick up where I left off, I need to
dress the part," he'd told Nancy. And Bess had

had a wonderful time helping him shop. It was more a change in his expression. He no longer seemed beaten, lost, and withdrawn. Now he looked calm, relaxed, and confident. As George had teasingly told him, his star quality was back.

"Yes," Nancy told Dan. "He confessed to everything. Including spreading rumors at TVR that I was a spy from a rival video station."

"I sure fell for that one," said Renee, wincing. "He came in the night before I met you, Nancy, and told me that he'd hired you as a guest veejay because he thought that would be the best way to keep you from finding anything out. In fact, he *ordered* me to keep you from finding out anything. He told me it was fine to give you a hard time on the job—and he also told me to keep him posted on your schedule. It wasn't my fault that you're so quick on your feet." She smiled at Nancy, and Nancy smiled back.

"I'd kept wondering why Mr. Thomas insisted on making me go undercover and made me promise not to tell anyone," Nancy said. "Now I know that it was because he didn't want anyone to notice that his story and mine were so different. And now I know why everyone seemed so unfriendly that first day!"

"Did he plant that phony package for you, too?" asked Bess.

"Yes. Mr. Thomas—I mean Tommy—

managed to drop it off without the receptionist seeing, and then picked it up when she was off making the copies he'd asked her to do. While I was trying to track it down, he wired my car stereo."

Bess shivered. "I can't believe how lucky you were, Nan. What if you'd been driving on the freeway when that noise started up? You could have been killed!"

"Believe me, I thought of that," Nancy said dryly. "So could a lot of other people—but Tommy didn't care about that. He's *really* charming."

"What happens to him now?" George asked.

"Well, he'll be charged with embezzlement, of course," Nancy said, "*and* attempted murder. You know, he's claiming there's no evidence linking him to that little scene in the preview room. He's so convincing that I'd almost believe him myself. It's lucky he spilled the beans in front of a roomful of reporters."

"What about TVR?" Bess asked, and Dan smiled.

"I got the news about that this morning," he said. "Winslow's—I mean Tommy's—second-in-command will take over. She's really great. And I've been promoted, too—to head veejay."

"Congratulations!" Renee said, and she sounded as though she meant it. "That's great. It will be fun to work for you."

She cleared her throat nervously. "Nancy, you

know I owe you an apology—but at least I behaved badly to you because I thought you were out to sabotage the station. But there's another person here who deserves an apology, too. Jesse—I don't know what to say."

"I don't, either," said Vint. "We're just really sorry, Jesse. We didn't mean to hurt you."

"That's why I freaked out so much when I heard that you were still alive," Renee said. "I couldn't stand thinking that you'd find out I'd started seeing Vint. It seemed like one of those horribly sad movies where the hero goes to war or something, and when he gets back his girlfriend has married someone else . . ." She took out a tissue and blew her nose.

"Don't think about it," Jesse said. "It's all past tense now. You're two of my favorite people, and I'm glad you're together. Besides, my life-style for the past few years hasn't exactly been the kind of thing I'd want to make a girl share.

"Anyway, now that I'm going back into the rock-star biz I'll have lots of money again. And I'll be able to date all kinds of incredible girls," he added teasingly—then dodged as Renee hurled a throw pillow at his head.

"What are you planning to do, Nancy?" Renee asked.

"Oh, we're heading home," Nancy told her.

"You know, you don't *have* to leave right away," said Dan. "I found out something interesting just before I came over here. It seems that guest-veejay interview you did was a big hit. We've been getting a lot of calls about it— everyone wants to see you on TVR again. Any chance you'd consider taking a job with us?"

"You're kidding!" Nancy gasped. "Me, a veejay? That's great! I mean, it's a great compliment. But, Dan, I'm a detective. I *like* being a detective. I like my life in River Heights. Thanks, though."

"Well, couldn't the three of you stay a little longer just for a vacation?" Dan asked. "As head veejay, I have an even bigger expense account now. I'd be more than happy to put you up at the hotel a little longer. And I could make some time to show you the sights, too."

Nancy looked at Bess and George. They all shook their heads.

"It's a tempting offer. Maybe we could take you up on it in a couple of months. But I want to go home for now," George said. "All I seem to do is sit in cars here."

"I'd love to come back here someday, but I want to go home, too," said Bess. "But I'll watch you every day, Dan. And Jesse, I expect you to write at *least* one song about all this."

He smiled at her. "It'll be dedicated to you, Bess," he said, and Bess giggled happily.

"I have to go home, too," said Nancy. "I miss Ned too much—and besides, there are sure to be other cases waiting for me back in River Heights."

"But they won't be as *glamorous* as this one was, will they?" Renee teased her.

"I hope not!" Nancy said fervently. "I've had enough of the glamorous music world to last me a lifetime. From now on, I'm sticking to plain, ordinary, uncomplicated everyday life."

But no one in the room believed her for a second.